THE DEATHLESS DARK

KEVIN KEELE

THE DEATHLESS DARK

This book is a work of fiction. Names, characters, places, and incidents are products of the author's imagination, and any resemblance to actual events, places, or persons is entirely coincidental.

Cover, map, and interior illustrations by Kevin Keele.

1st edition 2025

ISBN: 979-8-9934533-0-9

For Dad.

THREYA

UTHIR

Meareth Sound

Krafoa

Fullirin

Oberon

Pyressa

Threya River

Viburnam

Istle

Oatem

Wolgen Fort

Isella River

Igella Lake

Enderell

Erwa

Imiggan

Crenel Rock

Rivertree

Avender Lake

The Western Plains

The Gray

Epiraff

Ellysum River

Rave River

Lake Fork

Kodara

Orden River

Bellawych

Ankr Pass

MEARETH

Tannis Field

The Southern Plains

Mellir River

DEMERRA

N
S
E
W

Barrimus Bay

Dyrwood

Lyra

Brockett Island

Rawk

Port Arth

Ochre Bay

Drift

Lopra's Gap

nâra

Wolf
Lake

Briar

Table
Rock

Mountains

Red Chapel

Sentrial

Lurie Beach

ORYX

Lockwood

Idryll River

Castle Mountains

Silver Hills

Coyote

Coyote

Castle River

Creek

Durado River

Market

Durado Canyon

Rockmond

Carrion River

Andira

The Eastern Waste

Osgerath

Outpost

Dune Basin

TAGGEROTH

The prophecy of the Illumed Blade from the
Lyprakarum, a book of ancient scripture
(Arra Translation - Book of Grath, twenty-second chapter, verses
fourteen and fifteen):

The Elder Demons: Molg, Vulsipher, Tigyra, Ghuram, and Deiya—all immortal and all most favored of Okgram. By no weapon of man's make may they be slain. Only the Illumed Blade, gifted to men by the gods on High Heilaroth, may sever their connection to the further realms from which they draw blood and breath.

Yet none may wield the Illumed, save one born within the mother's water, while Okgram's eye is blinded, within the Hunter's Year. All else, by a blow both mighty and holy, shall be struck down.

PROLOGUE

THE WATERWOLF

Threya, Port Arth, the year 624
One year after the end of the war

The Waterwolf launched upon tranquil waters, under a clear sky. It was the third day of the week—the most favored of all launching days. A leaping pod of dolphins raced the ship out to open waters where steady winds filled the sails day and night, driving cargo and crew ceaselessly towards their destination.

These heralds promised good fortune and raised the spirits of everyone aboard. Everyone save Ashal Vate, the man who had hired the Waterwolf for this venture. There was no omen bright enough to chase away the gloom of his thoughts, and even if there were, he placed precious little value on such things. He was no sailor.

The ship's captain limped towards Ashal, every other step accentuated by the thump of his cane. As with most men who lived upon the sea, he bore more than his share of years upon his squinted face. The red contours somehow split into more creases when he adopted a wide grin.

"Well Ash," Captain Ravvik said, "were I a less cautious man, I'd say the gods have given their blessing to this voyage of yours. But I ain't, so I won't." He barked a laugh.

Now that their port of call was in sight, many others on the crew had expressed similar sentiments. Some of them cited the boons of gods Ashal had never heard of. It seemed to him that every deity that dwelt in the realms above and below the mortal Midlands was eager for his success. A success he had no confidence in. After a dry swallow, Ashal managed a nod.

"What's got your gob?" Ravvik asked.

"Nothing...it was an excellent voyage," said Ashal, looking out at Port Arth. Ashal was pleased to see the lovely city had weathered the war without too much damage. At least to the buildings. The readied warships in the harbor with catapults trained on the Waterwolf spoke to internal wounds.

"You think the Threyans will try to sink us?" Ravvik asked.

"I would if I were them," Ashal muttered. "But you needn't worry about your vessel. I sent letters ahead to both the mayor and harbor master and received answers from both before we left. They assured me we'd at least be safe to drop anchor."

"Where they'll search us stem to stern," Ravvik guessed.

"And if they find anything they don't like, *then* they'll sink us." Ashal sighed. He'd once enjoyed pleasant business in Port Arth with both the mayor and harbor master. Now, he was nervous to see them again. War, by its twisted nature, made enemies of old friends.

Ravvik leaned in close enough that even the healthy harbor breeze couldn't carry the man's rank odor away fast enough, especially when he breathed in Ashal's face. "I'm a man what likes to keep his business twixt his ears and away from his tongue, so I won't blame you for not telling me, but...why exactly you doing this?"

"It's hoped this venture might...repair relationships between our two nations," Ashal said, a carefully constructed lie.

"Well, if they let you keep your head, I suppose it might." Ravvik clapped him roughly on the back before shambling away, barking orders at his men.

The men complied, and the Waterwolf eased to a stop—as much as a boat at sea *could* stop. Ashal stumbled to the rocking bow and watched a contingent of Threyans in a longboat, rowing to meet them.

As they drew nearer, Ashal raised a hand in welcome to Harbor Master Kentel. The gesture was not returned.

Ashal looked about. Was there anything they could do to look less threatening? He wished he'd charted the Blue Barrel instead. Its figurehead was a smiling, bare-breasted mermaid. The Waterwolf's, in contrast, was a snarling wolf, frozen mid-pounce. It was aimed directly at the approaching Threyans.

"Remember your orders," Ravvik growled to everyone on deck. "Calm as kittens."

Ashal had known a number of kittens in his life, and none of them were particularly calm. This was all going wrong. Why hadn't he fled his country after this mad plan had been presented to him? He'd been tempted to but was certain he'd be less adept at hiding than the Uthiri Empire was at finding.

The Threyans climbed aboard, and Ashal forced a smile. Each member of the Waterwolf's crew remained at their stations, hands raised. Kentel approached Ashal and the captain, greeting them. He spoke enough of the Uthiri language to be haltingly conversant, but Ashal still sensed an added stiffness beneath the words.

Ashal and Ravvik bowed in response.

A stern-looking, uniformed man shouted orders to the soldiers, and all but three spread out across the ship.

Kentel watched them a moment before addressing Ashal. "Weapons on board?" he asked.

"Only a few and locked away in a box below," Ashal answered. "I alone have the key. We plan to arm a few men to protect ourselves as we travel through your lovely country."

"Then you will do so with a greater number of Threyan soldiers as well."

"As you wish," Ashal said. Soldiers meant to guard his guards. He'd expected nothing less and was already dreading the days of tension ahead.

"What else do you plan to bring ashore?"

"Only building tools and supplies; we've a cart and mules to transport it all."

"How long do you and your team plan on staying?"

"As long as it takes to rebuild the cathedral in Red Chapel."

Kentel leaned in close, dropping his voice and neutral tone, asking Ashal the same question everyone had been asking him for weeks, "Ashal, why are you doing this? It has been a great..." he concentrated, trying to find the right word, "*struggle* to arrange. A few more years of peace between us—our countries—would have made things much easier...for we...two...both of us." He punched his palm with his fist. Ashal knew he was frustrated with the language, but his guards did not. Their hands were upon their weapons in an instant. Kentel raised a hand and said something to them in Threyan. Their fingers eased off their sword hilts, and Kentel's gaze returned to Ashal.

Clearing his throat, Ashal said, "I represent certain Uthiri business interests that are eager to heal the rift caused by the war."

"As you explained in the letter, but what of your..." Kentel winced, "demon king? Is he—it—involved?"

"No," Ashal answered, and the response tasted so sour upon his tongue he worried it would show in his expression. In the following tension, Kentel fixed Ashal with a thoughtful gaze, and Ashal miserably recalled, yet again, how he had come to be here.

A late-night summons to the Uthir Royal Palace. Being escorted through the castle's progressively deeper and more secret chambers. A private meeting with the Demon's chief sorcerer, a woman, and her request of him, made on behalf of the Demon Lord. Considering

4

all this afterwards, when his wits had returned, he decided the De-mon-god must be a ruse crafted by whatever faction had secretly tak-en control of the government. A faction made up of his fellow mortals. That notion had made him feel better—at first. Then he realized that working at the behest of a dark group of conspirators was little better than doing so for an immortal monster. At least, not to him, the man whose life was on the line.

"Does that...*thing* object to you doing business with us?" Kentel asked.

"I don't get the sense it understands or cares about business mat-ters. My country is a strange one, friend. Half of it—those like my-self—long to join the rest of the more enlightened world, while the other half consults wizards, reads bones, and divines the future from bird entrails."

"Such traditions, absurd as they are, can still hurt a great many people."

"Of course, I'm sorry."

Kentel's voice dropped to a whisper again. "Is it true? Has an Elder Demon returned from the old world? Reports from the last battle of the war are...extraordinary—if that is the right word. Unlike anything the Midlands has seen in ages. But the survivor accounts are also wild-ly inconsistent. Especially about the Demon. Is it real?"

"Believe me, I wish I knew," Ashal said, and it felt good to tell the truth.

The soldiers returned, reporting their findings to the harbor mas-ter and the stern-faced man. Despite the lack of threat in their appear-ance or voice, Ashal was on edge as the conversation continued.

"I'll be hanged if I let this ship dock," Kentel said. "Transport your-self and your supplies via longboat. I would not make this exception for just anyone, Ashal. Please do not make me regret it."

At first, Ashal smiled in relief. Then the trust in Kentel's words struck him, and he suddenly wanted to put stones in his pockets and jump in the harbor. "I won't." He had to push the words past the weight that had settled on his chest.

5

Under the Threyan's observations, Ashal and his men went to work. His team of guards and builders, along with all their supplies, filled two longboats.

As they were rowing to shore, a young man in the seat next to him watched him closely. His eyes were full and anxious.

"Are you alright?" Ashal asked.

"The Demon-god," the man said, leaning in closer. "Vulsipher—you said you didn't know if it was real."

"You were at the great battle?" Ashal guessed. "The last one of the war?"

The young man nodded. "It exists, sir. As real as you or me. I saw it with my own two eyes." He shivered. "Just like in the old stories. An Elder Demon. I'll never forget it, much as I'd like to."

In the face of this man's haunted expression, Ashal felt his reasoning about the Demon-god's existence coming loose. Perhaps it was real.

And he was secretly working for it.

PART 1

CHAPTER 1

PROVIDENCE

Uthir Border, 623—three months before the end of the war

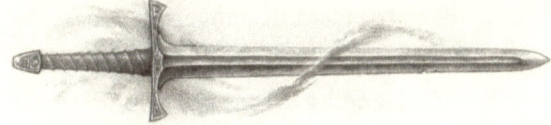

Overhead, a sparrow fluttered out of the thick boughs of a ponderosa pine, and the man beside Daverell nearly jumped out of his boots. He'd done the same moments ago when a squirrel sprinted through the underbrush. And earlier, when they'd disturbed a grasshopper and it leaped away, clapping its wings. The man's horse whinnied in annoyance, and Daverell Kain pulled his own mount to a halt.

"Norris, was it?" Daverell asked. He'd grown weary of remembering the names of new recruits.

"Norill, sir—Captain," the young man stammered.

"This your first time over the border?"

"You mean...we're already in Uthir?"

"Have been for five minutes," Daverell answered and, observing the change this news brought to the young man's expression, said more, "the enemy ain't crouched behind every tree, despite what the stories say."

"What about the other things they say? The...unnatural things the Uthiri do to their victims?"

"To those tales, I'm afraid, there is more than a little truth. But this is war; they won't have time to do anything more than kill you."

"I don't want them to do that either."

Daverell smiled. "We'll do what we can to avoid it then."

"I thought our orders were to only go as far as the border," Norill protested.

"True enough, but in the event we found a trace of our men, we were to follow."

"And we did?"

"Whose trail you think we've been tracking?" Daverell asked. Though, in truth, he was the one who should be embarrassed. The whole reason they paired sapling soldiers with old oaks like him was so the younger men might learn a thing or two. Yet, until this moment, Daverell had stayed quiet as a midnight tomb. His mind was elsewhere. Something not only discourteous but dangerous when in enemy territory.

"Where are you from?" Daverell leaned towards the young man, hands resting on his saddle horn.

"Briar," Norill answered.

Daverell paused, thinking. "Frontier town? East of the Grays?"

"Yes, sir."

Another frontier man, Daverell thought. *Just like the one from the campfire two nights ago.* Tamiron had been his name, from Lockwood. It was his tale that had kept Daverell so distracted. Not even a tale, really, just an errant remark. One of the little things soldiers shared with each other around evening fires. It had meant nothing to anyone

10

else. A simple peculiarity about Tamiron's family. A family that would, within days, receive the tragic news Daverell himself had learned when he'd attempted to find the man again only yesterday.

"What did you do before the Crown decided you were a soldier instead?" Daverell pulled a flask from his pocket and stole a swig of whiskey.

"I cut stone," Norill said.

Daverell nodded. The Crown was conscripting more tradesmen and farmers in a desperate effort to save the failing war effort. "Well, Norill." Dav pointed at a bush ahead of them. "You see those freshly broken branches?"

"You think that's from the scouting party?"

"I do," Daverell said, urging his horse into motion. "You keep your eyes open, and you'll see more. Along with trampled grass and the like."

Norill concentrated on finding and following the trail. At some point, he began nervously talking again, but Daverell only half listened. Eventually, he held up his hand to stop the young man from running both his mount and mouth.

"You hear that?" Daverell spoke softly.

"Hear what?"

Daverell didn't answer. His eyes weren't what they once were, but his ears worked just fine. In the absence of hoofbeats, the distant sound of a man's frightened screaming was clear.

"Do you think that's the missing squad?" Norill asked.

"One of them," Daverell answered. "He's yelling in our language, not theirs." The captain turned Druid off the path marked by their quarry's passage.

"What are we doing?" Norill followed closely behind.

"If it's a trap, that's the direction they'll be expecting us to come from."

"A trap," Norill repeated. "Should we turn around? We found the last of the scouting party. If the rest of them are dead, then..."

Daverell fixed Norill with a steady stare. "What if that was you hollering?"

Norill paused, listening. Seconds later he dropped his head and nodded.

"Once our man is visible through the trees, we'll dismount and prowl in a circle around him, looking for archers."

"But what if—"

"You can do this," Daverell said. "Those Uthiri are masters with a bow, but with a sword? They'll lose to a Threyan near every time. Keep the fight close and it's yours."

Norill swallowed, his eyes wide, breath shallow. "Yes, sir."

They followed the man's echoing cries until Daverell spotted him through the trees. He'd been tied to the trunk of a dead maple. Naked and beaten. Probably thinking he'd been left for dead with no idea he was a part of an Uthiri scheme. Daverell dismounted and motioned for Norill to do the same. They both bent below the level of the bushes, stealing away.

Daverell was only just out of sight of Norill when he came across an Uthiri archer. This man waited in a tree, facing the direction of the scouting party's leftover trail. Daverell eased a throwing knife from his belt. The man, retrieving something from a breast pocket, started when his gaze fell on Daverell. With a grunted curse, Daverell rolled behind a tree. An arrow split the air just behind him, and the enemy had another arrow, nocked and ready to draw, when Daverell darted out of his cover and flung his knife. It struck the man in the ribs, shocking him well enough to send his next shot wide as he fell from his perch. The archer made an awful commotion on his way to the forest floor, landing in a rain of broken branches. Before he could recover, Daverell sprinted to him, wrenching his blade from the man's chest and replanting it in his neck. The Uthiri's cries cut off in a crimson gurgle. Daverell retreated to cover again, watching for any enemies drawn by the commotion.

None came. He moved on.

Minutes later, his path intersected with Norill's. The man was trembling.

"Captain," he whispered. "I...I saw one. Killed him, just like you said. I don't think he even knew I was there until my dagger found his throat."

"You did better than me, then," Daverell said. "Mine made quite the ruckus falling out of a tree. Since no one came running, I reckon the main force that took out our search party has moved on and we're dealing with a smaller group left behind. Maybe even just the two archers, but I wouldn't breathe easy just yet. Those devils are a crafty lot. Let's tighten the circle on our way back to the horses."

"It's hard to concentrate with our man carrying on as he is."

"We'll help him soon as we can. In the meantime, he's giving us good cover. That racket makes it much harder for anyone to hear us, don't you think?"

"Yes, sir," Norill agreed.

The two separated again. Daverell wondered if he should have told Norill the man's pleas also provided a mask for any Uthiri creeping up on *them*. In the end it made no difference: they met back where they started without incident.

"Alright, I'm going to set our man free," Daverell said. "If there's any Uthiri lying in wait close up, they'll attack when they see what I'm doing. You stay here. I'll send him running for you while I deal with anyone needs dealing with. Wait for him but not for me. If he reaches you safely, you both tear out of here fast as jackrabbits. You'll have to share your mount—don't you dare take my horse."

"What if it gets spooked and runs away?" Norill asked, looking at the snow-white charger. "You'll be stranded."

"Not Druid." Daverell patted the fine animal on the neck.

"I'll come back if you don't follow," Norill said.

"Don't bother. I'll be dead."

Norill managed a smile. "Ain't nothing can kill you, Captain."

"If only that were true," Daverell said before crouching and setting off. He stuck to the path that offered the best cover, then circled to the prisoner's back as he drew nearer and closed the remaining distance at a run. He immediately set to cutting the man's bonds.

"Who...who's there?" the man stammered.

"Keep calling for help, you fool," Daverell hissed.

"It...it can't be," the man croaked, ignoring Daverell's orders. "Captain Kain? Oh, thank the Goddess above and praise her name forever. I'm sorry sir, I'm the only one left. Those monsters...they took us by surprise...they...they..." Under a fresh wave of heavy sobbing, and without the ropes to prop him up, he fell forward, barely catching himself on hands and knees.

Daverell grabbed the blubbering man by his shoulders and shook him. "Listen to me," he spoke directly into his ear. "Run through them two dead aspens on your right and don't you stop. I've a man waiting with a horse. He'll take y—"

An Uthiri soldier burst through the brush, his sword over his head. Daverell leaped to his feet and parried the heavy blow, pushing the assailant back.

"Go! Now!" Daverell shouted to the freed prisoner.

Thankfully, the naked man struggled to his feet and began limping in the direction Daverell had indicated as the enemy came at Daverell again.

He dodged another wide swing from the serrated blade and took advantage of the opening, sinking his own sword deep in the man's torso. Daverell's target groaned, clutching at the wound as he toppled.

Before the enemy's body had even struck the ground, another soldier attacked. This man was much larger and wore blackened steel covered in twisted spikes. Uthiri sometimes dressed themselves up like monsters when they did battle. It was often hard to believe there was an average man under all the fearsome trappings. While it could make them intimidating, it generally made them slower too. This warrior relied on heavy attacks, like his fallen comrade, but did so without exposing his vulnerable areas near as much. Daverell sidestepped an incoming thrust but wasn't expecting the man to follow it up with a swing from his plated fist. It caught Daverell in the shoulder, one of the few places on his leather duster that *was* armored. The prongs on the man's gauntlet glanced off the Threyan steel, but the full force of

14

the blow sent Daverell flailing. His fumbling hands found a branch that kept him upright. He pulled it back as he scrambled away, then let it go as his combatant closed in. The branch struck, surprising and blinding the attacking man just long enough for Daverell to swing his blade, fast as lightning, through the narrow gap between the breastplate and helmet.

The Uthiri went slack, tumbling to the ground and coming to a twitching rest next to his fellow soldier who was still moaning in pain. The first man's injury was just as deadly as the second's but would take hours to kill. Miserable hours. Daverell spared him the time and anguish with a stab to the heart.

In the stillness that followed, Daverell caught his breath. He removed his hat and wiped the sweat from his brow before stealing another swig from the flask in his coat pocket. Peering in the direction of the horses, Druid—and only Druid—stared back at him. Norill and the survivor had gotten away. Daverell whistled for his horse before stepping into the small grove the Uthiri had sprung from. What he saw there made his blood run cold. He hardly heard his horse's sturdy hoofbeats at his back.

Eight men, the rest of the scouting party, all dead. The Uthiri had done a thorough job. The bodies at his feet had been butchered. Daverell hadn't detected an odor before entering the small grove, but now he squinted against the fetid air filled with clouds of flies. The insects had claimed the space so completely he felt like an intruder. The appearance of the corpses, motionless and pale gray, made the dark crawling creatures stand out all the more. Daverell watched a fly land on one man's glassy eye, a beetle scurry out of his mouth.

His gaze stopped roaming when it met the remains at the far edge of the grove. His insides twisted, and the air left his lungs. Cautiously, Daverell edged forward.

At first, the body appeared to be a random, bloody muddle of limbs and organs within a ring of river-smoothed stones. Now that he was closer, however, it was clear this poor soul had been expertly dismembered and dissected. The pieces placed in a grotesque, almost artful arrangement. The head sat on top of the pile, facing Daverell. It had been robbed of its eyes, nose, lips, and teeth—all of which had been positioned elsewhere in the display. Strangely, the bugs, so interested in the gore and viscera elsewhere, ignored this...*thing*...completely. He couldn't blame them. It repelled him too, and he was accustomed to the sight of men as meat.

He'd witnessed no shortage of horrific acts perpetrated by the Uthiri against their enemies but had only ever heard rumors of things like this. Slaughter made blasphemous and ritualistic. Uthir was an old land of demon-worship and dark magic. This was one reason the Threyans so distrusted them. Those same fears rose in Daverell as he stared at the scene. It held him, motionless, wary of getting much closer lest the evil of the act mark him somehow.

He took a step backward but paused before taking another. Was there something he could do for the fallen soldier? For all of them? Some dignity he might grant their remains? No, he had lingered long enough. Daverell had gained answers, saved one of the missing men, and cut short the days of a few Uthiri. Young Norill would feel appropriately heroic for what they'd done. It was more than he'd dared hope for when setting out.

In turning to leave, something else caught his attention. Lying, like a puddle of milk, behind some trees to his left was another bloody body. Not a man, but a horse as white as his own. In fact, the similarity was so uncanny, Daverell found himself glancing back at Druid to be sure they weren't one and the same.

Druid was no common stallion. He was a purebred Demerran charger, and a rare white one. A gift from General Entwest himself. Daverell had scarcely seen his equal, yet here one was. A magnificent creature, freshly killed. The scouting party had been on foot. Where had this steed come from? Could they have met someone along the way? A random traveler? Had this belonged to one of the Uthiri? Why was it here? The answer to this last question, at least, emerged as if it were the sun breaking through clouds: Providence.

In a flash, he saw his life in a way he never had before: as something that made sense. Daverell nearly dropped to his knees under the sudden weight of it. Every wayward direction and fitful wandering from his angry youth up until the night at the fire and to this very moment came into perfect focus. Purpose, real and exquisite purpose, clarified with every beat from the drum in his chest until it filled him completely.

He had to act quickly.

Norill might come looking for him. Even if he did not, someone would when Captain Daverell Kain did not return.

Shifting the dead horse was almost beyond him. The thing was heavy as an anvil, but he eventually managed to trade its saddle with his own. He rifled through his bags, gathering everything the Uthiri would have taken had they captured him, while leaving a few worthless but identifiable things behind. The local Uthiri knew he was a significant Threyan military figure. They would have dragged him away as a trophy. His body not being among the others wouldn't even raise suspicions.

Lastly, he pulled the priceless Lagrim dagger out of his saddlebags. It had been at the bottom where he was less likely to come across it. For a time, he'd kept it at the top, hoping it would be stolen. It hadn't, the cursed thing. He'd have to take it with him. It would be the last thing any plunderer would leave behind. As he packed it away, he remembered the words that were spoken when it had been presented to him. *The perfect soldier,* they'd called him. Well, what would they say if they saw him now?

Deserter.

No, he thought. *I'm not deserting. I'm still a soldier. Only following the command of a higher power. I'm still fighting to end the war, just in a different way...perhaps in the only way it might actually be won.*

When he was finished staging the scene, Daverell stood back and took it in. It was perfect. Anyone returning here would think he'd been slain.

Daverell Kain was a dead man.

He climbed into the inferior saddle now on Druid's back and raised his legs to kick the horse into movement when a new thought wriggled its way into his mind.

What if this is not providence? Not of the Goddess?

He was in Uthir, after all. A land where dark forces and trickster demons watched from the trees and infected the very soil. Cruel devils were said to play with the hearts of men here. Could anything good come out of this place? Or that awful grove of death? Could the Goddess or her work be found in such a place?

Yes, he told himself, riding Druid away. *Yes, She could.* Faith had become a stranger to him, but, if he was going to do this, he could not let it remain so.

He turned for one last look at the place and flinched. In the dappled shade of that little thicket, he saw her. The girl that watched him. The child that proved he was either hopelessly damned or hopelessly mad. A shiver rushed through him as he whipped back around. She couldn't stop him, nor remind anyone of his crime against her.

I made sure of that, he thought miserably.

He stole another drink as he rode on. It didn't grant him courage, but it did help him forget those ghosts from his past. He had purpose now. A new mission. Sticking to the empty wilderness and side roads, he would ride hard for Lockwood. He must find Tamiron's family.

Tamiron's son.

CHAPTER 2

THE NIMARA PATH

Pyressa Abbey, 623

Pellary stepped into the room and shut the door behind her. Her fellow novitiate, Maiyen, was still sleeping. Pellary's entrance had not disturbed her. Pellary opened the door again and slammed it. Maiyen slept on. It wasn't until Pellary had prodded her, saying Maiyen's name loudly, that the young woman's breath caught. Groaning, she rolled away.

"What is it?" Maiyen asked. At least that's what Pellary thought she said, she'd spoken directly into her pillow.

"Time to wake up," Pellary pronounced.

Maiyen groaned. "I slept through every morning bell?"

"The clock has only chimed once so far."

There was a pause and the rustle of bedding. When Maiyen spoke again, Pellary could tell her friend was facing her. "Then why are you waking me? I thought you were spending the morning in the library."

"I intended to. But I was stopped by the Iress Matriarch; she was on her way here to speak with us."

"What did you do this time?" Maiyen asked with a sigh.

"Nothing," Pellary answered. "We have an appointment this afternoon."

"Appointment?"

"With the Pathmaster."

"The Pathmaster?" Maiyen repeated. "The Pathmaster!" It came out in a shriek. "Both of us? That's not true; it can't be. You must be joking." She gasped, then went silent a moment. "No, that is much less likely."

"It's true, Maiyen. It's finally happened," Pellary confirmed.

The sound of Maiyen's feet padding across the wooden floor in a frenzy met her ears. Pellary could hear the wide smile in the other girl's voice when she spoke again.

"The Pathmaster. We can finally leave this place. I'll get to see my father again, my brothers. The Iress always said it would happen without warning. Can you believe it, Pell? We must tell everyone. Remember all those farewell dinners we went to? We'll finally get to attend one just for us."

"Actually, Maiyen, we can't tell anyone," Pellary said.

"What? Why not?" Maiyen ceased her pacing.

"I don't know, but the Iress Matriarch made it very clear to me that we're not to inform a soul."

"But that means we won't get a banquet," Maiyen huffed. "This is unfair. I've never heard of such a thing. Did she say why?"

"No. I imagine it has to do with the war." Pellary shrugged. "I haven't heard of any Path Settings since it broke out, but perhaps they've just been done in secret."

"Perhaps…" Maiyen mused. "Those stupid Uthiri. That really sours the sweet of the whole thing." After a pause, she filled the room with shimmering laughter. "*You* were probably happy to hear that we won't be getting a formal celebration," she accused.

"No," Pellary protested. "Not when I knew it would disappoint you."

"Well, I shall try to follow your example then and be happy you get to avoid the social event, even if I'm sorry to miss it." Maiyen found Pellary's hands and gripped them. "Besides, who could be dour in the face of such news. Saints and stars, the Pathmaster! I can scarcely believe it. There's no chance of me falling back asleep now. Wait a moment while I get ready, will you?"

"Of course," Pellary said, walking to her side of the room and settling silently on her bed. Maiyen had reacted just as she'd expected. Pellary was thankful they hadn't connected minds. Her contrasting emotions might have diminished Maiyen's joy.

Pellary lifted her hands to her face and, with gently probing fingers, explored the subtle texture of the blindfold that had been placed over her eyes four years ago. Four of the best years of her life. She'd welcomed the chance to block out the world and much preferred her inner Sight to her physical one. Four years seeing the world almost exclusively through the eyes of others.

Maiyen was ready much faster than usual and, for the first time since they'd shared a room at the abbey, was as eager to go to the library as Pellary. She wanted to study each of the potential Paths they might be called to. Pellary had looked into each of them extensively already but wasn't opposed to fortifying her knowledge a little before her Setting. Her own Path Setting. She took deep, steadying breaths while Maiyen practically skipped her way to their destination.

To read, Embrells had to employ the help of another person. People from the city—typically children—worked in the library, making a doret an hour by simply sitting and staring. They didn't even need to know how to read. That day, Pellary and Maiyen shared the eyes of a nine-year-old boy. Pellary quickly located the volumes they needed before finding a table to study at. They spent over an hour familiarizing themselves with the different Paths they might be set upon.

I know they tell us not to hope for any Path over another, but I think the Ottil Plain sounds lovely, Maiyen projected her thoughts to Pellary's head, so as to not be overheard.

I don't see what difference it makes, Pellary replied through their mental link. *We need to traverse the whole thing blindfolded. I like the sound of Hara Canyon. More animals to connect with, easier to see our way.*

Kiata Road ends at the Red Chapel Abbey, we could visit the cathedral there.

Oh, that would be wonderful, I admit, Pellary agreed.

I think we've covered all of the Paths, haven't we? Maiyen asked.

No, there's one more.

Which one?

Pellary could sense a mental fluttering as Maiyen pondered the options. Pellary answered for her, *Ankr Pass.*

No one actually gets called there, do they?

I remember someone did when we first got here, though I can't find a record of it. It sounds awful. Pellary flipped to a new page in the collection of surveys and maps they were looking at. *Listen to this,* she said before reading. *The area is an anomaly. The Gray Mountains run north to south, cutting Threya in half. The west side is the more populous and verdant of the two, while the more arid frontier is to the east. However, it becomes all but a desert on both sides of the range south of Epiraff, with the exception of Ankr Pass which is essentially a miniature range itself, cutting west to east through the Grays. Any rainclouds that might drop their water on either side are often funneled into the pass where it rains nearly every day. Ankr Pass, however, is far from a green oasis amid the dry surroundings. The whole canyon is swampy, malodorous, and choked with thorns and brambles.*

No, thank you, Maiyen declared. *I remember hearing about it when I was first here. The older novitiates would try to scare us, said anyone called there never returns.*

22

Never returns... Pellary mused.

"What are you reading?"

Pellary recognized that voice. She snapped the book shut in the same moment it was pulled from her grasp.

"Maps and land surveys?" Novitiate Enniver jeered. "Demon girl, I didn't think you could *get* more boring."

A second voice snickered at this.

Pellary could sense Maiyen's burning desire to tell them it was because they were about to meet with the Pathmaster. Instead, she said, "Enniver, don't you have a tablecloth to go straighten or something?"

Enniver and her friend were training to be Arrantines, experts in aesthetics and organization that invited the Light of the Goddess. It was the Iress faction Pellary respected the least.

"And Maiyen, the shadow's shadow," Enniver scoffed. "You think what we do is easy? Believe me, studying is more difficult when you're unable to borrow someone else's brain."

"Sometimes that makes studying much *harder*," Pellary countered, rising. "Imagine if we were to borrow your brain for example."

"Is that an ericle?" Enniver asked.

Pellary started, nearly reaching for the copper demon-warding charm around her neck and tucking it beneath her robes, where she usually wore it.

"It's only sentimental," Maiyen said. "Her grandmother gave it to her."

"And they were out of style even when *she* was young," Enniver laughed. "What's the matter, Pellary? Afraid the demons will get you?"

She said these last words mimicking Pellary's accent. Pellary had tried hard over the years to rid herself of such imperfect pronunciations and had been successful enough to mask where she was from, but not enough to fully replicate the way most people talked here at the abbey.

"What do you want, Enniver?" Pellary sighed.

"Just a table to study at and you're always here, taking up more than your share of space."

23

"There are plenty of other open tables," Pellary said.

"Actually, there isn't, demon girl. You'd know if you could see."

"And if *you* could see, you'd know that we were here first," Pellary growled, fists clenched.

"It's fine, it's fine," Maiyen said calmly, also rising. "We were just leaving anyway."

Hours later, Pellary and Maiyen stood on the landing before the Historian's room that, in turn, held the door to the Pathmaster's sanctum. Pellary sat on a bench outside the door, trying to meditate or do anything that might settle her racing heart. Maiyen wasn't fighting hers. She let it set the pace to her hurried march back and forth.

The Iress Matriarch didn't arrive until after the clock had struck four. They both immediately shared her sight after she'd climbed the stairs. The Iress Matriarch was a fellow Embrell, but she rarely covered her eyes anymore, allowing the Embrell novitiates to use her sight while in her presence.

"Excellent, you're both here," the Matriarch said before knocking on the door.

The Historian answered and wordlessly invited them into the small room. He immediately tapped on the door opposite the one they'd just walked through. The Pathmaster's door.

After a pause, it swung open, revealing only darkness beyond.

"Step forward," the Historian whispered to Maiyen and Pellary, before turning and speaking into the shadows. "Two novitiates stand ready to walk the Nimara Path."

There was a silence in which Pellary sensed a discerning gaze wander over Maiyen and herself. She'd rarely thought of her appearance since adopting the selfless life of an Embrell. Now, however, she was reminded of how small and simple she looked, especially when standing beside her elegant friend.

"Let them enter," answered an ancient voice.

"Go ahead," instructed the Matriarch. "May the Goddess ever guide your steps."

Maiyen and Pellary took deep, simultaneous breaths and watched from the Matriarch's eyes as they were swallowed by the dark room. The door closed behind them. The room was lidocrafted in a way to block their connection to the Matriarch, leaving them in total darkness.

The old man's voice cut through the gloom. "Novitiates Pellary and Maiyen, you stand before the Pathmaster. For what purpose do you come to me?"

"We ask for a Path to walk," they recited in unison, using the words they'd memorized ages ago in preparation for this moment.

"Novitiate Maiyen," the Pathmaster said. "What subject has been your main focus during your time here?"

"Saerisian history. Specifically, the life of the prophet, Jophrat, and the first student, Embrell, founder of the Goddess's Sight," Maiyen answered.

"Very good. I've heard you've also an uncommon skill for reading intent beyond senses and emotions. A rare find in one so young and new to the Sight."

"Thank you, Pathmaster," Maiyen said.

There was a brief pause before the voice continued. "And you, Novitiate Pellary?"

"My studies have focused on the *Lyprakarum*. Also, on Uthiri culture, and...and on the old-world demons they worship." Pellary's words tumbled clumsily out of her mouth.

"An interesting, even dangerous, topic of late. And from a young lady who I'm told is quite willful. It could be said of this pair before me that one has bathed in the Light and the other, Shadow. But both embraced by truth, I hope. Tell me, Novitiate Pellary, do you feel drawn to the Dark?"

Pellary hesitated before whispering, "Yes."

"Facing the Dark is something all who wish to be Iress must do.

Indeed, it is the soul of the Nimara Path. Let your Sister who bathes in the Light guide you."

"I will."

"And Maiyen, those who've studied the Shadow often bear greater respect for its power. Let your Sister, in turn, guide you as well."

"Yes, Pathmaster."

"Do either of you know where the Path Settings come from?" the Pathmaster asked, then answered his own question. "They come directly from the Jophrat Seat. He has informed me this is a unique case. None but our prophet, myself, and the two of you may know the location. Listen to my instructions very carefully; you are to leave here this very night. We've a man preparing to escort you. From now until you depart, none are to know even that you are leaving. You must enter the Path exactly eight days from today. Eight days. And remember this phrase: 'Let faith guide you in the places the Light cannot reach.'"

He cleared his throat before continuing. "It's not widely known, but we've ceased calling novitiates to the Nimara Path during this war. An exception is being made for you two. While the Uthiri have yet to pose much threat to us here in Pyressa, the outlying villages are suffering. Just getting to the Path will be dangerous, not to mention the Path itself. People have died upon the Path; others have failed to complete it or refuse to be set upon it and are banished from the service. If you wish to decline, this is the moment in which to do it. There are no second chances. Knowing all this, do either of you wish to turn away at this point?"

"No," Maiyen replied immediately.

Pellary took longer to respond but eventually gave the same answer as Maiyen. What choice did she have?

"Very well," he said. "After Jophrat, the prophet, escaped as the lone survivor of the destruction at Tardten, he walked what he called the Nimara Path. The Path granted him solitude, challenge, purpose, and an intimate relationship with the Goddess. These things served and taught him in ways that allowed him to serve and teach others. We wish the same for you. However, none know where the true Ni-

26

mara Path is. Thus, you are called to any number of potential Paths, and the requirements of the Path are different for each Iress faction. The physical test for Embrells is to walk the Path by relying only on the inner Sight."

A finger lightly pressed the center of Pellary's forehead and traced a line from there to the tip of her nose. The same was done to Maiyen.

"A seal has been placed upon you. If you remove your blindfolds between now and the end of your Path, it will be known. Once that destination is reached you will be met and escorted to the Andira Abbey for your spiritual test: a task devised by the resident Iress Matriarch. Upon completion of this task, you will be Raised, full Iress within the Church of Saeris. Do you understand what is expected of you?"

"Yes," they both said.

"In Light and Truth, then, you are called to..."

In the slight pause before he spoke the answer, Pellary, by some deep instinct, was suddenly certain of what he was going to say. She could have spoken it with him.

"Ankr Pass."

After dark, there was a discreet knock on their door. It was the Matriarch.

"Come," she said. "We must move quickly."

Pellary and Maiyen followed her, carrying their bags. The life of an Iress novitiate was a simple one. In addition to a copy of *The Song of Saeris* and *Lyprakarum*, Pellary carried only a change of underclothes, along with an outfit more suitable for hiking than the robes she wore now, a few towels she used to wash her face and teeth at night, and the same ratty hairbrush she'd arrived with.

The Matriarch whispered as they walked, "We've enlisted the help of a man called Striker. He's a bit ragged in the wrong places, but he's never failed to deliver anyone to their Nimara Path before. You may borrow his sight, so don't worry about that. He's already been paid. So do not let him at any of this." She handed them a small bag of coins. "Enough to pay for your rooms and meals. He's been told to take you to Bellawych," the Matriarch continued. "You're not to tell a soul, including Striker, where you're going after that. Even I don't know. Understood?"

"Yes, Iress," they said.

She waited a moment longer, letting the silence punctuate her point. Retrieving a large key from her robes, she unlocked the front gate. The lock made a deep, metallic clang when she turned the key and the hinges a mournful groan as one of the double doors swung open. She stopped when it was only just wide enough for them to slip out.

"Striker," she called softly.

"Yes ma'am," a rasp answered.

"The girls are here. Deliver them as quickly and safely as you can."

"Will do, Iress."

"Thank you," she said, turning back to the novitiates. "It was a pleasure having you here with us, girls. May you be ever bathed in Light and embraced by Truth."

"Thank you, Iress," they answered.

And then the Matriarch was gone. The hollow sounds of the door shutting and the lock re-engaging was the last Pellary would ever hear from this place that had been her home for the last four years. The fortunate souls still within its walls would be shocked to learn she, of all people, did not wish to leave. Much of her time had been spent arguing with her teachers and fellow novitiates. However, unlike Maiyen, she had nowhere else in all the mortal Midlands she might call home.

Turning reluctantly away, Pellary cast her awareness out before her. By the Embrell Sight she saw the living things around her appear as points of light. In a crowded room it was like standing amid the stars. Here, she saw only the spark of Maiyen beside her and three glowing dots ahead corresponding to the driver of the stagecoach and the two horses hitched to it. Pellary reached out and mentally grasped

Mr. Striker's light. It suddenly seemed as if she, at least most of her, was in the driver's seat, staring out at the dark city streets.

"Step aboard, ladies," said Striker. "We may get through Istle and into Wolgen Fort by this time tomorrow if you don't hold us up too much."

"Of course," said Maiyen. "Sorry sir, it's just…saints and stars, the city is quite a sight."

"It's a shame you've only my sorry eyes to see it with," the old man said.

"No sir, they're quite suitable," Maiyen insisted politely as she and Pellary ducked inside. Pellary sat first, but before Maiyen had time to settle, the stagecoach pulled away, forcing her backwards into her seat with a nervous laugh.

We're actually on our way; can you believe it Pellary? Maiyen's inner thoughts seemed brighter, and Pellary sensed her friend's excitement had begun to outweigh her trepidation.

Only an hour ago, in their room, Maiyen had been all but sobbing with fear and fury at the thought of their destination. Pellary had reminded her that grim assumptions were made of nearly every place cloaked in mystery, and this seemed to be enough to calm Maiyen's emotions. However, while Pellary believed her own words, she remained pensive. There was no denying the ominous shadow being cast over the journey by the grim reports of Ankr Pass. What might be waiting for them there? It was yet another reason Pellary was loathe to leave.

She watched the twinkling city pass by through Striker's eyes, longing for him to turn around so she could catch one more glimpse of the abbey.

He never did.

CHAPTER 3

THE STRANGER

Near Lockwood

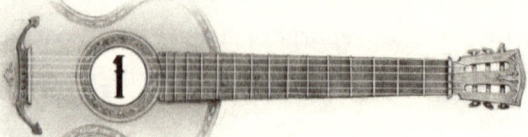

It happened just after sunup. She'd said her morning prayers, and the daily chores were well begun. The golden light was only beginning to throw blue shadows across the sand. Ameryn closed her eyes, feeling the heat on her skin and breathing in the new day. She tried to enjoy it. To make the moment last. In seconds, however, her familiar fears returned, and she opened her eyes again, cursing the fleeting nature of peace.

That's when she saw it. A growing speck on the open horizon. In this harsh place, where any variation might mean doom for her little family's fragile existence, the sight filled her heart with dread.

Romy, her hound dog, began barking at the shape as it drew close enough to identify. There was little in the desert frontier to hide a man approaching, especially a man on horseback, and when he was close enough for Ameryn to see his uniform, her heart leaped. The last time she'd seen her beloved husband, it was the reverse of this scene. A man, her man, in an identical uniform disappearing into the unfeeling distance. But no, as the figure drew closer, she could see that this man was not hers. As high as her heart had risen, it now plummeted, and this emotion was not banished so easily.

Her mind desperately scrambled for any explanation for the stranger's approach other than *that* one. The one that stuck. The one that must be true.

He was here to inform her of her husband's death.

Her heartbeat thundered in her ears and forced the air from her lungs. The voice of her son drifted towards her as if he were far away.

"There's a man approaching," he said.

"I see him, Crowan," she managed, wanting him to be someplace else. "Did you tend to those chickens?"

"Seven eggs!" he declared, lifting the basket in his hands. "But I dropped six of them."

"I'm in no mood for your jests," she groaned. "Get them in the house and clean the ones that need cleaning. I'll see what this stranger is about."

"Do I have to?"

"Now, Crow."

The careful way her son carried the basket away made her ache. Only eleven winters to his name and now without a father. *You don't know that*, she scolded herself, while not allowing any other notion to take its place. She'd always thought it best to expect the worst. Took the sting out of bad news when it came. *But does it really?* she wondered. *Or does it only make an enemy of the future as* The Song of Saeris *says?*

"Hush, Romy," Ameryn said to the still-barking dog. Romy tried to

31

obey, but small, worried yelps still escaped the animal as she followed Ameryn, walking out to meet the stranger.

The man pulled his mount to a halt before her. Ameryn resisted the urge to rake her brunette locks down around her face and hide the scars on her cheeks, souvenirs from an acute case of pox that had afflicted her as a child. He bore scars as well, made even more visible by the way they interrupted his short gray beard, but less so as they got lost among the lines on his face. She'd guess he'd seen four dozen winters at least, about twenty more than herself. His expression was stern but not without kindness, a description that matched his deep voice when he spoke.

"Mrs. Ameryn of Vowery?"

Had her hammering heart not been in her throat, Ameryn would have laughed at the stateliness he attached to her simple name in this wild place. Additionally, her closest neighbors were more than a mile away; who else might he expect to find here? While all this ran through her mind, all she did was nod in answer.

He fixed her with a concerned expression until his gaze moved past her. She didn't need to turn around to know her son had just appeared in the doorway of their simple cabin. The stranger's eyes lingered on the boy a moment before he swung down off the horse and landed with a ringing of the spurs on his boots. He removed his hat and, reluctantly this time, met her eyes again.

"I'm afraid, ma'am, I have some unfortunate news," he began.

"My husband is gone," she said, thinking it might hurt less to voice it herself. It didn't. When he nodded in answer, even though it was what she expected, the news struck like a hammer. "Don't say a word more until I tell the boy," she instructed, surprised at the steadiness of her voice.

Her control broke a little once she was turned away from the stranger. Her son could tell something was wrong.

"Mother?" There was a quaver to his voice.

"Inside."

Crow stepped back, and she shut the door behind them both.

Ameryn rested her back against the planks, shutting her stinging eyes and sending welled tears tumbling down her hot cheeks. Every gasp of air was like claws on her throat, while a branding iron burned her chest.

"What is it? What's going on?" her son asked.

Ameryn slid to a sitting position, exhaling as if she were blowing out a candle, bracing herself for what she was about to do. She had to tell her boy, her sweet boy, who loved his father with all his young and mighty heart. Then she had to watch that heart shatter before her eyes.

"Crowan," she said. "The man outside came here with news about your father."

"He's...he's." Crowan couldn't form the words.

Ameryn forced herself to speak them. "He's gone, Crowan. Passed."

His reaction startled her. Instead of crumbling, she watched as the blood drained from his face and the youthful innocence from his eyes. His gaze shifted from her to the north window, his expression shocked, then hard. Harder than she'd ever seen it. He was silent a long while.

"How?" he asked.

"I...I don't know," she admitted. She'd not asked that question, even to herself, until now. Her mind was flooded with violent images of his cold and bloodied body alone on some battlefield, forgotten by all but the buzzards. She forced the visions away, sure she'd die from the pain.

What did you expect? she chided herself, *Tamiron was no soldier. Did you really think he'd return when the Uthiri were cutting through so many experienced warriors?* But, when he'd left, he was so certain he'd see her again and vowed to return. She'd felt the rightness of his confidence like a promise from the Goddess Saeris Herself.

Once more, it was Crowan who broke her spell of stunned silence. "Does *he* know?" Her son inclined his head in the direction of the stranger outside.

"What's he doing?" Ameryn inquired, scrambling for the window. She peeked over the sill, as if hiding from the man. He'd not moved, was only rubbing the neck of his brilliantly white horse. Romy had protectively parked herself on their doorstep, barking and growling.

"I want to ask him," Crowan said.

"What?"

"I want to ask him how my father died."

"Oh, yes, of course. No. Stay here."

"Why?"

Ameryn didn't answer. She had no answer. It made no sense and part of her knew it, but she needed some space to let her thoughts untie themselves from the knots they had been tangled into. Thankfully, Crowan fell silent. There was a long pause wherein neither of them said anything. Ameryn stared at the floor planks, at a spiral in the wood grain she'd never noticed and wasn't really seeing now. No sensation felt real anymore. Eventually, she moved from small, hiccupping gasps to slow, stable breathing. Whether ten minutes or an hour had passed she didn't know.

"I'm going to ask him," Crowan said. There was hesitation in his voice, as if he was unsure of the reaction he'd elicit with this mild disobedience.

"Go then," was her only answer.

He opened the door but didn't close it all the way. For once this failed to earn him a reprimand. Romy's nervous shuffling and whining followed the boy's diminishing footsteps.

"Mister?" he asked.

"Yes lad?" the man answered.

"How did it happen? How did my father die?"

A silence followed. Ameryn was pretending, even to herself, to not be listening though she was hanging on every sound—afraid to even blink lest she miss anything spoken. She heard the stranger move toward Crowan now, each step accompanied by the groan of leather armor and the chime of spurs. Though her eyes never strayed from the floorboard knot, she could track the movements outside. The stranger was kneeling, looking at her son in his big, brown eyes.

"Your name is Crow, right?"

"Crowan, but people call me Crow."

34

"Crowan, then. Good name, you wear it well." He paused before continuing. "The Uthiri had weakened some of the battlements more than we'd realized. A group of soldiers, your father among them, were stationed as lookouts on a wooden tower; it collapsed, killing most of them."

"He didn't die fighting?" Crow asked.

"He died in the line of duty, doing his part to hold the enemy back. It was a valorous end. Don't let anyone tell you different."

"But...but..."

"I know that's hard to understand, but you should know your father was as brave a man as I've ever seen wear the uniform, and I've seen more than most in my time. At least he'll be missed by good folk. Many meet their end and are forgotten the next day."

Ameryn sensed her son wanted to say more, but either emotion or the lack of words held him from it. The stranger spoke again.

"Your mother, when might she be fit to speak?"

Ameryn, under a sudden rush of anger, found herself on her feet and marching out to them.

"What's got you in such a hurry, sir?" she spouted. "You show up, unannounced, out of the desert bearing tragic news and expect us to... to..."

The stranger also stood. "I meant no disrespect, ma'am. I have more to discuss with you is all. I'm in no hurry; I'll wait 'til nightfall or tomorrow if you wish it."

The level of calm control he wielded in the face of her naked vulnerability outraged her further. "Nothing you say could possibly be worse than the news you've already brought us. Speak the rest of your piece now, then be on your way."

"Well, that's just it. I'd prefer to not be off at all," he said. "Tamiron and I were friends. I promised him that if he were to die in service to the King I'd look after you and the boy for a while, seeing as I have no home or family to return to. I'd like to help out, at least until Crowan here is old enough to handle things."

"And who says we need your help?" Ameryn shocked herself with her severity. In truth, she would desperately need all the help she could get, come harvest time. She'd been lost in a constant state of worry as the year wore on, unsure how she and Crow would handle the workload alone. An extra pair of strong hands in the fall could mean the difference between living and dying in the winter.

"Certainly not me," the man said. "I'm at your mercy, ma'am. Say the word, and I'll ride out of here faster than I came."

"And how did you get away when the war effort is going so poorly they've resorted to drafting farmers?" she asked.

His answer came reluctantly. "I'm getting too old for war, ma'am. As bad as things are, the army's got no need for an old, broken-down soldier. They let me go without a fuss. These days, I get in the way more often than I help."

"So you've decided to get in our way instead?"

Her words drew a sad smile from the man. "Yes."

Ameryn paused, considering. She took him in more critically now. He appeared old but not ancient and, given how well he carried himself, far from feeble. However, she imagined war was, indeed, a young man's game. "What is your name?"

"People just call me Dav."

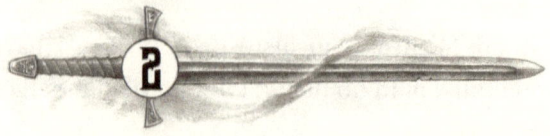

A small, glossy spider clung to the silver tendrils of its fine web. The web itself clung to the corner of the open hatch in the barn's roof. Daverell's gaze moved to something far beyond the spider: the Star of Saeris. It had been a long time since he'd taken much notice of it. Even longer since it had raised his thoughts to the Goddess.

Ever bathed in Light, he thought. *Ever embraced by Truth.* Those words, an old Saerisian adage, had come to mean precious little to him. In this moment, they brought his mind to his dagger. The one he'd hidden under the bedroll. He pushed it further beneath him, praying Mrs. Vowery would never find it. Her tenuous trust in him would snap in an instant.

She had mostly stayed within the cabin all that day while her boy, Crow, had given Daverell instructions on everything to be done. There had not been much time together, really, but it was enough to convince Daverell that the boy was the one. A real-life child of prophecy, like in a story.

How was Daverell going to take the child away? Ameryn was a hard frontier woman. Strong-willed and protective. She'd never let Crow go, and Daverell couldn't wrestle the child across half the country. If he could gain the boy's trust, would the youngster come with him willingly? Leave his mother behind? Daverell couldn't say. He knew for certain, however, that if he took Crow—cooperative or not—Ameryn would curse the name of Daverell Kain for the rest of her days.

But I'd only take him for a short while, Daverell reasoned. *And when Crow returns, it will be as the young man who saved the country—maybe all the Midlands—from destruction. And if that fails to douse her rage...well, even then, I suppose it would be worth it.*

He'd done worse for less. It was a heavy burden the Goddess had placed on his shoulders. Being the man to inform Ameryn of her husband's passing before taking her son away. However, if that was the path the Goddess had set before him, he must walk it. Betraying one good woman for the benefit of all was surely a fair trade in Her eyes.

What if Daverell told Ameryn what he believed about her boy? Was there a chance she'd think he was anything but a madman? It was too early to say.

For now, he could do nothing but wait and watch. But eventually, they'd run out of time. Either his cover would be exposed, or the war would reach them. Until either of those things happened, Daverell would foster as much trust with mother and son as he could. It would make things easier when time came to do what needed doing.

The longer sleep eluded him, the less this conclusion sat well. Was he a common liar, weaving a trap for good people? He suddenly suspected he was more connected to the spider above his head than the star. Daverell reached up and pulled the hatch shut, cutting out the view of both.

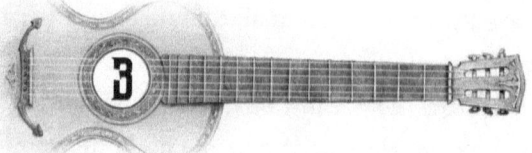

Tamiron is gone.

In the days that followed, these words—this brutal truth—rang so loudly through Ameryn's head, she struggled to do the simplest of tasks.

Tamiron is gone.

Her foundation. Her light in the dark. Her rescuer.

Fifteen years ago, in Pyressa—city of the eternal flame and Threya's capitol—a blaze had broken out during the night of the annual fire festival and burned down half the city. An irony that might have been humorous if not for the hundreds left dead. Ameryn had been performing in a saloon when she first heard the screams and ran home. She'd arrived just in time to watch her home collapse in an explosion of embers. Her mother, father, and sister—the entirety of her family—killed in the inferno.

From that day to this, whenever fear seized her, she could feel the reaching flames, smell the choking smoke, and hear the crackling roar.

Then there were the numb days after the fire. Homeless. Wandering the blackened streets.

That's where Tamiron had found her, pulling her out of a fog of misery. Loving her before she could love him back. When she could, she did. More than enough to marry him and follow him out here. He'd wanted to build something new. A life wholly theirs. Ameryn had wanted to escape the city. On the frontier, the trees and houses were far apart. When they burned, they burned one at a time. Getting out would be easier. Her new family would be safe.

Life, however, is creative in finding ways to steal people away, and war is as merciless a beast as fire. Tragedy was the truth of life. The moments of joy in-between? A cruel lie.

Tamiron is gone.

Reminders were everywhere. She didn't much mind those that brought Tam as he was in his radiant life to mind, but she'd begun taking the long way into town to avoid the Lockwood cemetery. She came across a dead coyote at the far end of her field, its bloated carcass covered in maggots, and was unable to stop herself from imagining Tamiron's body in the same state. Discarded and decaying on some abandoned battlefield.

Her torment ran so deep she feared her heart would cease beating or her lungs refuse the air. How damaged could a soul get before it affected the body that housed it? If dying from grief was possible, she'd perish in an instant if not for the correcting terror of leaving Crowan alone in the world.

Crow had been crying himself to sleep at night but warming to the stranger by day. The boy burdened Dav with foolish questions. Was his sword heavy? Would he let Crow see it sometime? Maybe hold it? How many swords did he own? What was the best type of sword? Ameryn would have swept the boy away from the man, as much for his pestering as for his concerning subject matter, if she weren't so oppressed by her emotions. Besides, Dav only offered short answers and asked a fair share of his own questions as he tried to make himself useful.

A day came when her son laughed again, amused that Dav, a grown man, was ignorant of how to milk a cow. Ameryn was at once annoyed at Crow's exclamations of mirth while also being comforted by them. She wondered in disappointment at his ability to find joyful moments under the shadow of Tamiron's absence but was simultaneously grateful, perhaps even a little envious, that he could.

"I think he's a good man, here to help us," Crowan said one day.

"Maybe so," Ameryn replied. "But your father built our home and planted our garden. Even in his absence he provides for us more than anyone else can—save the Goddess above, of course." As she said it, the truth of the words settled into her bones. Yes, Tamiron was gone, but he had left his mark on this place. The trees he'd planted and the structures he'd built endured. As long as she had a life here, it was a life with him.

This was the first hopeful notion she'd had since learning of Tam's fate, and it led her to another bit of inspiration.

"Why don't we have a little fireside gathering tonight. In honor of your father."

"A funeral?" Crow asked.

"No," she answered a little too forcefully. "Something to keep him... the memory of him alive. I think it would do us all some good to talk. Celebrate the life he led with some food...and maybe song."

Later, under a dimming sky, Dav and Crowan carried armfuls of wood and their supper down to the river pool. Ameryn reached into the small cupboard where she stored her clothes. Tucked away, on the top shelf, her probing fingers closed around the neck of her guitar. Pulling it down, she blew away the dust. Had it been so long?

She plucked at the strings. They were woefully out of tune but not yet too brittle to play. Could she do this? Dav was still a stranger to her. Playing before him would be difficult, but she could manage if she kept it slight and simple. Music had become too personal to share with any but those closest to her. Other musicians seemed able to sing and play without exposing their heart, but Ameryn could not. Baring herself enough to perform in the way she used to made her feel exposed. Weak. Like she had that long-ago night in the face of the blaze. She sighed, mourning that part of her, lost forever. Ameryn slung the instrument over her shoulder and stepped outside to walk down to the river.

The frontier had once appeared desolate to her, even grotesque. A sharp contrast to the deep, saturated forests of her youth. In the thickets, color was abundant and innate. Shapes were intimate and vertical. The painters of the forest were blossoms and beetles, the little things. Out here, the horizon was always laid before her, and the colors, while muted, were richer in variety. On a canvas this big and neutral, the sun and clouds were the painters, and they created a vast and living landscape of forever shifting shadows and hues. It was an untiring marvel. One she enjoyed enjoying.

40

Crowan greeted her with a smile. Dav ladled the meaty meal into three wooden bowls. Ameryn picked at the food, unsure of her appetite. Eating sparingly and automatically.

Dav pulled out a small book and began drawing by the last of the light while Crow looked over his shoulder.

"Wow," the boy said. "Dav, did you draw those?"

"I'm afraid so," Dav responded.

"Can I see more?" Crow asked.

Dav began flipping through the book.

"How did you learn?"

"In the army, between the training and fighting, there's a whole lot of sitting and waiting," Dav said. "Soldiers often acquire some sort of hobby to fill the time. Some of the best jugglers I've ever seen are military men. I took to sketching."

"Mother, have you seen these?" Crow turned to look at her.

Ameryn walked over and studied the sketches with her son.

"My, they're wonderful," she observed. "I half expect the pages to glow."

"Glow? Why would they glow?" Crowan asked.

"It's just an expression," Ameryn answered.

"A reference to lidocrafting," Dav said. "Holy art so lovely it drives away the darkness."

"Enough to glow?" The boy glanced between them both.

"Of course not," Ameryn said.

"Oh yes," Dav replied at the same time.

Ameryn studied Dav, confused, before turning back to her son. "No. Saying so is just a compliment."

"One my scribbles are far from worthy of." Dav closed the book.

Crow threw another log on the fire, sending sparks frolicking upwards.

"Keep it small, Crow," Ameryn advised, backing up from the fire and pulling her instrument into her arms. Closing her eyes, Ameryn tuned the guitar, getting the notes just right. Like slipping back into old boots not worn in a while, the guitar in her arms and strings under her fingers were effortlessly, comfortingly familiar. She went from tuning the strings to plucking out a few familiar melodies, weaving from one to the next and warming up her voice by gently humming along. She kept it light and playful, but it still hurt.

She would endure it tonight. For Tamiron.

"These are some of the songs Tam loved," she said, playing rousing frontier tunes about the freedom found in an open horizon, under a vast carpet of stars. About life in the wilderness, taming the untamable. The itch of vulnerability crept up on her, and she pivoted to something silly—*Captain Crig*—a lively tune about a mischievous dog. Crow and Dav were grinning, slapping their knees and bobbing their heads. Finally, it became too much. She stopped, letting the vibration of the strings slow. The world returned to the crackle of the fire.

Crow clapped and whistled.

"That was..." Dav said breathlessly, "I've rarely heard playing and singing so fine."

"Thank you," Ameryn said with a tired smile. "But after seeing your sketches, I think I'd trade talents if I could."

"That would be a mighty unfair exchange." He shook his head.

"Music is a very momentary thing. It really only exists when it is being played. One hundred years from now someone will look at your drawings and see the very marks you made with your own hand. There's something lasting about it that appeals to me."

"No one will look at my drawings in a hundred years."

"Even if that's true, if I were to write my music down it would really only be instructions for another to recreate it. The music itself cannot be captured in the way your art can."

"So play some more!" Crowan urged.

"It's getting late, son," she said.

"You mean, we have to go back?"

"Well, perhaps not quite yet, but stop feeding the fire."

They watched it, chatting as it burned itself into red shimmering embers.

"Have you ever fought hellspawn?" Crowan suddenly asked Dav.

42

"Crow, don't say that word," Ameryn scolded.

"It's in *The Song*," Crow protested. "Why can the prophet write it, yet I can't say it?"

"Because the prophet didn't have me for a mother," said Ameryn. "There's no reason to say it. Dav hasn't fought any demons. No one has. Hardly anyone believes in them anymore."

"The Uthiri do," Dav said. "This war was started because Uthir, or at least that king of theirs, got it into his head that Threya has hidden and imprisoned their ancient god. One of the great, old-world Elder Demons."

Ameryn blinked in surprise. She'd heard as much in town but had dismissed the notion. She wished Crowan hadn't been listening. The last thing he needed was nightmares about monsters and Uthiri. However, the boy was looking at Dav with wide eyes filled—not with fear—but eager wonder.

"Really?" he asked. "Where are they searching?"

"Everywhere," Dav informed him. "Multiple war parties of different sizes. There's no pattern or plan that anyone can figure."

"So we're not safe here?" Crow asked.

"Of course we are," Ameryn insisted. Dav fixed her with an expression that made it clear he didn't agree with misleading the boy.

"But the war—" the boy started.

"Can't reach us."

"Is that true?" Crow turned to Dav.

Ameryn could see the fight behind the old soldier's eyes.

"Maybe it'll end soon," he finally said.

"How?" Crow asked.

"There's a passage in scripture that talks about someone who might wield the Sword of Light; no army, not even the Uthiri or this demon-god they're searching for, could stand in the face of such a weapon and warrior."

"The prophecy?" the boy whispered.

"From the *Lyprakarum*," Ameryn clarified, "not *The Song of Saeris*—the holier book."

43

"Indeed, but you've heard it?" Dav asked Crow.

"My mother told me."

"Did she?" He glanced in her direction. "Did she tell you the second verse? It says, '...*none may wield the Illumed save one that is born within the mother's water while Okgram's eye is blinded within the Hunter's Year.*' Can you imagine? Someone fitting that description might be out there somewhere right now."

"I think it's time we went to bed," Ameryn said, standing.

CHAPTER 4

ON THE ROAD

South of Pyressa

On the first day of her journey to Bellawych, Maiyen felt as though she were living one of her favorite fairy tales, off on her grand adventure at last.

By the second day, she felt like more of a parcel than a person.

At least she wasn't feeling sick as poor Pellary was. Maiyen's time at sea as a child had fortified her stomach into something wholly undisturbed by the motion of the coach, even while wearing a blindfold.

They spent their first night on the road, like commoners. It was not only the cramped and awkward position within the coach that denied Maiyen a peaceful rest, but unfamiliar bird calls and rogue winds rustling the trees.

Mr. Striker promised them a real room in Wolgen Fort the next night. Maiyen's face fell, however, when he stopped the coach before a cramped and crooked structure. Even worse, he requested not to be seen with them.

"No one will play cards with me if they see us enter together," he said.

"Oh. Certainly, Mr. Striker," Maiyen responded politely.

"Of course, it'd really butter my day if you helped me win a few games," he said with a laugh.

Maiyen sensed he was joking but also knew he'd take her up on it in a hummingbird's heartbeat if she agreed.

"Thank you, Mr. Striker," said Pellary. "I'm sure you don't need our help to cheat at cards."

He laughed as he strolled away from them. She and Pellary waited behind the inn, allowing him to gain his distance. Maiyen longed to be raised to full Iress all the more. Once she'd attained that position, she would never again be made to endure such treatment.

It makes sense, Pellary said, sensing her thoughts. *People in these smaller towns are unused to Embrells; they find us unsettling.*

I suppose, Maiyen replied, strolling into the little yard.

Casting her awareness out, the little lights and vague shapes that represented the consciousnesses of the living things appeared. That alone gave her a sense of the area, but she began collecting glimpses of the environment through the eyes of the creatures themselves. There was a horse tied to a fence, grazing. A cat lounging on a stack of empty crates. There were thousands of insects everywhere; however, while they could be detected, their minds were insufficient to form a bond. There was even a snake in the cool crawlspace under the inn's floor.

This excited Maiyen until she searched its mind and found it was a common garter. As a girl, she'd connected with a serpent on a beach far to the South on one of her father's expeditions. She hadn't intended to bond with the creature's senses. As with most early manifestations of the ability, it had just happened—the novitiates quarters were filled with shocking stories of accidentally connecting with a neighbor, parent, or sibling under private circumstances. Through the snake's eyes, though it had been a black and moonless night, she saw herself as a warm, glowing shape. The experience convinced her that there was more to the Goddess's Light than humans could discern. It had a wide range of alternate qualities, and the answers lay in exploring the senses of animals everywhere. This was just one subject of study she was eager to pursue once she was an Iress.

"Come on," Pellary said. "We've waited long enough."

"Yes," Maiyen agreed, "I'm eager for a real bed tonight."

Once again, her enthusiasm was misplaced. The limp, straw mattress did nothing to mask the hard ropes supporting it. Additionally, she was forced to share the bed with Pellary. And while Maiyen loved her like a true sister, at night she became a buzzing creature made of nothing but elbows and knees.

The days that followed were frightfully dull.

Maiyen wanted to recline and watch the blue sky roll by above the green Threyan countryside. Unfortunately, Mr. Striker had a habit of staring only at the road and backside of the horses, a view that appealed to her considerably less.

At least there was an odd appeal to spending a day in a new area, meeting a few men and women, then moving on. She'd barely sample the flavor of a place and people before they were off on the road again. What she experienced as only a temporary stop along their way was someone's rooted home. Lives, whole and rich, were spent in these villages that swiftly disappeared in the dust kicked up behind them.

When Striker's eyes *did* leave the road, it was to wave at travelers going the opposite direction. Most appeared to be desperate people setting out for destinations they hoped were unlikely to be burned by the Uthiri invaders.

At a few of their stops, she engaged Mr. Striker in conversation, finding him to be a decent fellow at heart. She thought he might have warmed to them as well when he made no repeat request that they enter separately at the Crenel Rock Pub. After entering, however, Maiyen saw only three other individuals in the pitifully small place. A man and his young daughter eating soup and another man, drinking alone in a corner. They took seats and received their own portion of the soup, which turned out to be quite good. Mr. Striker, in high spirits, spoke with them throughout the meal.

"Let me try it one more time," he said, then thought the word *fiddlesticks.*

"Fiddlesticks," Maiyen repeated out loud.

He pounded the table, laughing. "That's amazing, Sister. So you *can* read minds."

"Not really," Maiyen clarified. "Only a clear and complete thought like that. Most of the time people think in fragments far deeper in their brains. Getting to those are tricky; we'd have to connect longer and more often. Much easier to share senses. They're closer to the surface."

"So why the blindfold?" he asked.

"It's the easiest sense to block out and the one we're most dependent on. It forces us to develop our ability."

Goddess above, Maiyen. Why not just enroll him in Iress Eld's class back at the abbey? Pellary thought at her with exasperation.

I'm not giving him anything that's not easily obtained at any decent library, and it's better he get accurate information, Maiyen answered.

"And what sort of thing does the Church have you do with this… ability?" he asked with a wave of his hand.

"Oh, all sorts of things. I'd like to work in an infirmary. At least until I can get a grant for some research."

"Infirmary?" Mr. Striker said. "Ain't that the place for Curials?"

"The healers are always on the lookout for help from an Embrell. Some patients can't communicate the source of their pain. Pellary here has talked about working for the law," Maiyen said.

"The law?" he asked.

Pellary smiled. "We can tell when someone is lying and—if we're close enough—listen in on conversations between people who think they're alone."

Mr. Striker shook his head. "I imagine just having you in the room would be enough to make a man confess. I mean no offense in saying it, Sisters, but regular folk find you all a little..."

"Spooky?" Pellary suggested.

Mr. Striker raised his mug to her and took a drink. He lowered it and watched the man and his daughter leaving the pub. Maiyen saw them too, through Striker's vision. The little girl had scarcely taken her wide eyes off them the whole night. Now, lingering in the doorway, she tentatively stuck her tongue out in their direction. Maiyen faced her and stuck hers out in return. The girl's jaw dropped before she darted out the door.

Maiyen chuckled at the exchange when Mr. Striker posed one more question to her.

"What do you most enjoy about your ability?" he asked.

It was a question Maiyen hadn't anticipated, and it took her a moment of self-reflection to answer honestly. "Every person sees things distinctively. Even beyond one's mental interpretation. Physically, light and color are subtly different to each pair of eyes. It's a very rich way to view the world around us."

Mr. Striker nodded, his mood suddenly a bit melancholy when the lone man from the corner stood and approached them.

"You two from Rivertree Abbey?" the stranger asked.

After a pause, Maiyen answered, "No, we're traveling south from Pyressa."

He bowed his head, solemnly. "Word is the Uthiri struck Rivertree, killed everyone, burned it to the ground. There's an abbey there. I thought maybe you'd escaped."

"You have family in Rivertree?"

He regarded them with a hollow-eyed expression. "My brother and his wife. They have—had...two children."

"I will sing for their souls during my prayers tonight."

"Thank you," he said. The man returned to his seat and took another drink, perhaps attempting to drown his emotions. Judging by the look on his face when he lowered the mug, it wasn't working.

The next morning, the acrid smell of smoke was faint, but unmistakable. Maiyen was nervous until they entered the large and well-defended city of Epiraff.

It was the second largest city she'd ever been in. Pellary had spent time in Oberon, and it was supposed to be as big, if not bigger, than this. Perhaps that was why she was less impressed with this bustling place. Maiyen longed to see more of the city, to spend a week or more exploring. She decided to return after her Raising and do just that.

In the warm, dying light of the day, they exited the stagecoach to the sight of a white, sophisticated building with red-painted batten shutters covered in trellis-supported rosebushes. The sign above the door read *The Star Rose* and had a carved symbol of a star artfully integrated into a rose blossom.

"Mr. Striker," Maiyen said, "this is lovely. Quite preferable to any place we've stayed yet. Thank you."

"Oh, Sister, let me tell you a bit about it first; you'll want to thank me again with extra sugar," Striker said. "The proprietor here, a Mr. Verayum, is a devout believer and generous where it counts—hefty discounts to traveling Sisters, such as yourself. Usually, this inn would be far outside the budget set aside for our travel. The novitiates I've brought here before never want to leave, say it's quite luxurious."

"It sounds like just what we need. Thank you again," Maiyen said.

"As luck would have it," continued Striker, "we're not too far from a lively little place I quite like called The Salted Shoe—they've better food than the name implies. Be ready to depart on the morning after next. You'll find me right here for you, ready to move on."

"I think that warrants a third expression of gratitude, Mr. Striker."

He held up a hand. "I've had my fill, Sister. All I want now is a strong drink and you can't help me with that." He tipped his hat and slapped the horses into motion.

They slept in the next morning and, when they finally did leave the opulent comfort of their soft and separate beds, it was to a meal equally as exceptional as the one they'd enjoyed the night before. As their plates were taken away, Maiyen sighed with deep contentment for what Pellary informed her was the fifteenth time since they'd arrived. Maiyen was mostly sure she was teasing. She wouldn't have actually kept count, would she?

It was a shame when, the next day, the innkeeper informed them that Mr. Striker was awaiting them outside.

Walking onto the lively street felt like an embrace. Nothing felt so good underfoot than well-ordered cobblestones, and the clip-clopping of a horse passing by convinced her that nothing sounded better either. The air was alive with other noises. Maiyen longed to engage in the vibrant conversations, dance to the spirited music, join in the children's games, and buy some exotic silk from the busy markets. Tragically, all she could do for now was breathe it in, which she did before connecting with Striker and noticing a disturbance on the other side of the street. Something was wrong.

"What's going on?" asked a passerby to someone in the gathering.

"The cathedral in Red Chapel has been destroyed," a voice said.

Maiyen gasped, clasping her hand over her mouth.

The man selling newspapers shouted the story in more detail. "Read about it here, folks, only just been pressed. The Uthiri strike a major blow—the Great Cathedral in Red Chapel has fallen."

The man's tone shocked Maiyen. It was as if he were announcing the King's travel plans despite the weeping from several people in the group before him. Maiyen herself was shaking her head in disbelief. Someone behind her was sniffling.

Saints and stars! Can you believe it? Maiyen asked her friend and was shocked to find the sniffles were coming from Pellary. In all their years together, she'd never once seen Pellary cry. *Pellary, are you alright?*

"I'm fine," Pellary answered out loud and in a much steadier voice than Maiyen would have thought her capable of, given her internal state.

"Pell, you can't fool me; I'm in your head."

Pellary ignored her, ducking into the stagecoach. Maiyen followed, and Mr. Striker closed the door but drew back the curtains. "It ain't just the cathedral. Everyone at The Shoe was talking about Uthiri ambushes along the main roads. I think we'll avoid them if we stick to the mountain path. Not many use it anymore. It might mean two nights on the road instead of one, but better to get there alive than not at all."

"Yes, I agree," said Maiyen. After he dropped the curtain and climbed into his seat, Maiyen turned again to Pellary.

What is it? Maiyen probed.

Pellary took a deep breath. *It's just...that place—the Red Chapel Cathedral. I fell in love with it as a child. It was there that I first felt the Light of the Goddess and thought of a deity as something kind and bright. I've always wanted to go back someday. Now...*

I know. Maiyen embraced her as the coach began moving again. *I'm sorry.*

While the main road had been wide and straight, the mountain path wound like a snake through the foothills. Pellary preferred the former, especially since they had left the tall, proud trees of the great forests far behind. Now they clattered between scrub oaks and quaking aspens. The Gray Mountains, closer now, passed seemingly without end on their left. Those peaks had been the only constant companion the landscape had offered on this journey.

They spent the night on the road in a small glade where some long-ago travelers had once built a modest fire pit.

The next day was an uneventful one. Almost ominously so.

"Is he aiming for every rut and bump in the road?" Maiyen complained after the coach rocked, shaking them about.

Pellary's own annoyance was building. They needed to get out of here. It didn't help that they didn't pass a single other traveler and stopped in a grove almost identical to the one at which they'd spent the previous night. Pellary could only be sure they hadn't gone in one large, maddening circle because this place included a clamorous stream flowing through it. The water from the peaks above neutralized the other nighttime sounds enough for Pellary to get much better sleep than the night before.

However, that very noise also served to mask the approach of the Uthiri the next morning.

The attack happened after she'd eaten breakfast and attended to her morning necessaries. The horses were hitched up, she and Maiyen were back in the stagecoach, and Striker was in the very motion of slapping the horses into action when he—and the two young women connected to his mind—were simultaneously struck by a sudden, white-hot pain in their back and chest. Striker glanced down, and they could all see, in the middle of a fountain of blood, a wicked-looking arrow point protruding from the center of his chest.

Through a fog of hurt and horror, Pellary and Maiyen were jolted back to their own senses. Senses that delivered thudding hoof beats to their ears, the only discernible sound over the creek. That was until a voice cut in, shouting to them in Uthiri.

It's an Uthiri soldier, he wants us to exit the coach, Pellary translated.

You speak Uthiri? Maiyen asked, bewildered.

Yes, Pellary answered before taking a steadying breath. *This is it, Maiyen. We're alone out here and must defend ourselves.*

Maiyen wiped the tears from her cheeks. *Yes, you're right.*

Pellary forced her fear behind a wall of determination. She could sense Maiyen trying to do the same, but the panic kept breaking through.

They killed Mr. Striker!

We can't help him now, Pellary responded. *And there's no one here to help us. We can do this. Remember our training.*

The Uthiri soldier impatiently barked at them again. Pellary opened the carriage door. Slowly.

She cast her mind and could detect three of them, all on horseback. She connected with the one in front. He was watching them warily.

One of the Uthiri behind him began reading from a scroll. He spoke in the Threyan language but with a thick accent. "The Uthiri Empire has confirmed the Threyan treachery it long suspected. We are searching for our God, Vulsipher, imprisoned somewhere in your country—"

The one in front interrupted with a shouted order.

He ordered him to stop reading and just kill us, Pellary explained. *You take the one in front, I'll take the archer.*

I don't know if I can!

He's readying an arrow. We must act—now!

Pellary sensed Maiyen take a deep breath and hold it while she fed false, blank sensory information into the mind of the man who had ordered their execution. There was almost nothing more confounding. As if blowing out a candle, all sight, sound, and feeling ceased, and one was plunged into a weightless void of emptiness.

Fooling the mind to believe it was experiencing a different reality required a lot of practice and almost total concentration. It could only be done to one person at a time as it was limited by the Embrell's own portion of the Goddess's Light fueling the connection. It was extremely effective—unless the Embrells were outnumbered. Pellary wished there were only two attackers since it took nearly all Maiyen's effort to keep the leader blind, and she could not engage the other two simultaneously.

Thankfully, while their teachers had called Maiyen adept at mental defense, they'd praised Pellary as exceptional. She could not only cut off all senses but had the rare ability to replace them with false ones, a power that was a closely guarded secret among Embrells.

Connecting to the one holding the bow, Pell made it appear to him that she'd run to the side, behind the man at the head of their trio. That man ducked, granting the archer a clean shot. Only the leader, held under Maiyen's influence, hadn't actually moved at all, and when the bowman let the arrow fly, it plunged directly through the other man's back, killing him the same way—by even the same hand—as Mr.

Striker.

Maiyen released the struck man from the sensory vacuum into a world of agony. At least it was brief. He fell from the horse to swiftly die in the dirt. The third man began screaming in shock that his fellow soldier had fired on the other one. He fell into confused silence when Maiyen blinded him. Pellary continued her connection to the archer.

The bowman now saw a flaming skull gliding around him. He could feel the heat from the fire and hear the otherworldly howl it made as it accosted him. The man cried in panic, tracking the nightmare as best he could with another drawn arrow. When the creature lingered for a moment at his side, he loosed the taut bowstring.

Maiyen released the other Uthiri from the void just as the arrow lodged in his skull, and he was thrown back, dead before his body was lost in the brush.

To the archer, the flaming skull cackled as it settled, amidst a cloud of swirling embers and smoke, atop what the man perceived as Pellary's shoulders. She was now a towering monster of bone and cinder and still growing as the environment lost all light and color. The man shrieked and kicked his black horse into a wild gallop, tearing away from them.

Immediately, Pellary and Maiyen began running in the opposite direction, sharing the sight of critters on the side of the path as they went. Even then, they were moving too slowly.

I think hiding is our best option, Pellary suggested. They left the road and crouched behind some boulders, making no sound beyond their heavy panting.

I don't think he's coming back, Pellary thought once she'd caught her breath.

You probably scared him witless, Maiyen thought back.

I got carried away.

What...what was that thing?

Belayat, a trickster demon, Pellary explained. *Uthiri children are raised on frightening stories of it.*

Why would he try to kill it? Maiyen wondered. *Don't they worship those things?*

The Elder Demons, yes, but not Belayat. That Uthiri was only trying to drive it away.

Instead, he...you...we killed his friends. Maiyen was trembling.

We didn't kill anyone. He did. Pellary tried to appear calm. She didn't know why since Maiyen could easily discern the storm within her.

We're killers, Maiyen thought miserably.

We're not! They would have killed us, Maiyen, Pellary told her. *We had to. We had to.*

Yes. Maiyen nodded. *We were defending ourselves. We were forced to...to...do what we did.*

And they killed Mr. Striker. Shot him in the back without warning, Pellary snarled.

They waited without moving. Every time Pellary connected to Maiyen, she was replaying the bloody encounter in her mind.

It was close to an hour before they crept out of their hiding place.

Looks like we're walking the rest of the way to Bellawych. Poor Mr. Striker, Maiyen lamented, tears in her eyes again. *I pray he died in the Light.*

We have to go back, Pellary thought to her.

No! Pell, they may return at any moment—if they're not there already.

But the stagecoach— Pellary began.

We have to leave it; we'll be too easy for the Uthiri to find if we try to use it. I sensed, when I connected with one, that they're regularly accosting coaches on the road, just like ours.

I agree, it stays. But we must at least release the horses, take the supplies with us.

Maiyen bit her lip, contemplating. *You're right. Let's be quick about it!*

They hurried back. While Pellary unhitched the animals, Maiyen retrieved their food and meager supplies from the coach's seating area.

Is there nothing more we can do for Mr. Striker? Maiyen asked.

We shall sing his soul home to the Goddess at sunset, Pellary thought to her as they returned to the trail. *Make haste, Sister.*

And so they walked. Pellary wished she could make her heart quit beating as if she were physically sprinting. It shocked her that her accelerated pulse was driven less from fear than from exhilaration. Now that they'd gotten away, there was a part of her—beneath her grief for Striker—that found the whole affair quite thrilling. She'd been so furious! She'd wanted to make the men flee in terror, if not pay with their lives. But now, in the silence of the wilderness, fear crept back into her. What if the Uthiri returned? She listened closely with her own ears along with the ears of the creatures around her for any break in the normal ambient sound of the shrubland. She thanked the Goddess for little birds perched in trees that offered the only decent view of their surroundings. The three Uthiri they'd encountered could not have been alone. Might she and Maiyen be under pursuit by greater numbers even now? Perhaps the man who got away would avoid leading more forces back to the area since his fellow soldiers would find the other two men killed by Uthiri arrows. Suspicion about who caused their deaths might well fall on him. Then again, perhaps he'd convince his troops to ambush the two women further down the road. Might more enemy soldiers be waiting around any one of the blind turns of the path?

Pellary, Maiyen asked, *what did they say about...was it...Vulsipher?*

They're looking for it. When the Pathmaster called us, he said the Uthiri were searching for their god.

He did? I don't remember. Why search out here?

No idea.

The name sounds familiar, Maiyen thought.

It's featured prominently in the Lyprakarum.

Of course! Vulsipher, Maiyen thought with a shudder. *Okgram's first Lord of Death.*

A fire demon. The Lord of Long Shadows, Pellary confirmed. *The Uthiri worship it.*

And for something so...foolish, they terrorize and murder innocent people?

Pellary didn't answer, she knew what Maiyen believed about demons and Darkness. They'd argued about it when they'd first begun sharing a room. It had become a subject they simply didn't touch upon. Pellary thought the Uthiri beliefs misplaced but not foolish. She knew of the reality of the Darkness. Had tried to teach Maiyen to listen there and not only to the Light of the Embrell Sight. Maiyen had refused, shocked at the suggestion. Like the Church, she would not even acknowledge its existence.

Pellary focused on walking. Goddess knew there was plenty of that to do. While there were many small animals around them, it was tedious going from one pair of eyes to the next. Pellary found herself mostly depending on the orientation of their points of light to navigate the trail. She could almost see it in the way there was an absence of the lights on the road itself, except for the occasional sunbathing lizard that would scurry into the scrub as they came closer. But as the bushy trees began thinning out, the surrounding critters did as well, making it harder to traverse. Even more worrying, she could faintly smell smoke in the air.

A short distance later she internally saw a small point of light approaching at a non-threatening speed. As it grew closer, she saw the vague outline of a dog and connected with it. There was a sudden pang of agony in her right side, and she broke the bond immediately, as if touching a hot coal.

Careful, she warned Maiyen, *she's injured.*

Yes, a burn. Saints and stars, it hurts! Oh, she's got bad eyes too, I can barely see.

Pellary connected again, better prepared for the pain this time, and saw Maiyen fall to her knees and hold out her arms. "What happened to you, girl?" she asked as the old dog found her hands and began smelling and licking them gently. Maiyen explored the animal with her hands, careful to avoid the side where she'd been wounded. Pellary bent and gave her a scratch behind the ears.

At the abbey, the novitiates would often provide service for the

Pyressa citizens with ailing pets. It was useful to know where and how they were in pain. Those service opportunities had taught Pellary that she got along better with animals than humans.

"Poor thing," Maiyen said. "We're having a hard day too, old girl. Where'd you come from?"

In answer, the dog circled them, burying her nose in their robes. Pellary grimaced at her own offensive body odor under the dog's superior sense of smell.

When they walked on, the dog loped along beside them, and Pellary could detect a different aroma. Smoke was in the air. It grew thicker as they walked, and soon, even with the dog's poor eyesight, they could see the source ahead: a blackened ruin.

They'd finally reached Bellawych.

CHAPTER 5

BESIDE THE RIVER

Near Lockwood

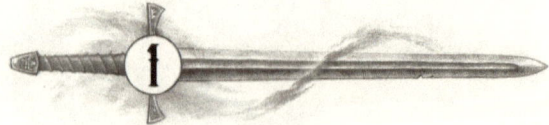

The boy was searching for a suitable stick and moving around too much for Daverell to add him to the drawing. Daverell sketched the trees and river instead. It seemed proper. He'd all but decided against capturing Crow in any other manner as well. Leastwise, not without his mother's permission. He'd try to convince her to see her boy the way he did, when the time was right. Maybe she'd believe. She was a faithful woman who lived her life by *The Song*. And her trust in Dav was growing.

She'd even allowed Crow to come on this little excursion into town. After delivering apples to Warrell's shop, Daverell and Crowan stopped at a little copse of shady trees by the bridge to allow the mules a drink from the Idryll River. Dav sat in the cart with his pencil and sketchbook. Crowan searched the wet and shallow banks with his pants folded high above his bare feet.

The talk at the general store was of the war and nothing else. Nearby Sentrial had been razed by the Uthiri, its people slaughtered. Some Lockwood citizens were fleeing for larger and more protected cities. The Vowery homestead was far outside of town, but there were rumors of similar places not being spared. The conflict was closing in. It all made Daverell wonder if perhaps the Goddess sent him to protect this family, not unite the boy with the faraway weapon.

"What about this?" Crow asked, holding up a fallen branch.

Dav shaded his eyes from the blaring sun and studied the boy's find. "Damn, kid. That's almost as good as a real training sword. It's got two stumps on the side like a crossguard and everything."

Crowan swung it around. "Yeah, I'm the best stick-finder in the county. Won a contest for it last year."

Dav squinted. "Really?"

Crow laughed. "Life's slow out here mister, but we still got better things to do than that."

Daverell smiled. "If you keep taking advantage of my ignorance of country life, I'll do the same to you for swordplay."

"But that's the main thing we do for fun," Crow said, and Daverell stowed his sketchbook before hopping off the seat of the cart.

"First things first," said Daverell. "You're holding it wrong. It's the pointy end that goes in your hands."

"Nice try, Dav."

"Alright, alright." Daverell stood in front of Crow. "Keep it pointed right around my center. Think of where my attacks might come from and keep it as close to the middle of that point as you can. You want one hand against the crossguard and the other down at the pommel. Remember to engage both to best handle the sword. Precision is your goal for now. I don't want to see any big swings from you yet, and don't practice on me. The tree over yonder won't mind you swatting it near as much. Pick out little features on the trunk and see if you can strike them with accuracy. Pretend it's an Uthiri raider."

"Or a demon," Crow suggested. "And I'm one of King Madros's knights."

"Even better," Daverell said, grinning.

He settled back and watched the boy, offering advice now and then. Crow wasn't doing half bad.

Sighing, Dav leaned back. A speckled falcon cut across the blue, riding the air. It landed not far from him, on the opposite bank, lost in the limbs of a lonely juniper, long dead. Its sharp, naked branches stretched in every direction like the warped claw of some buried behemoth. Daverell was half tempted to sketch the twisted tree when a shape at the base caught his eye and stole his breath.

It was her.

The ghost child, sitting in the shade. Her accursed shape silhouetted by the sunlit desert behind her. Despite the heat of the day still clinging to the landscape, a cold breeze rose up and made him shiver. She pinned him in place, spellbound. It was those eyes more than anything else. More than the pale and colorless skin under the filthy rag she wore or her long and tangled dark hair. More, even, than her legs that ended in bloody stumps just above the knee. Those eyes were every bit as blank and dead as they were hurt and accusing.

He watched her long enough that his fear turned to a deep, aching regret. It always did when she appeared to him for more than only a moment. He didn't flee from the shame. It was less—far less—than he deserved.

"Leave me be," he muttered under his breath.

"What?" Crow asked.

"Nothing," Daverell said, and it was true. When he turned back, she was gone, as he knew she would be. "Time to go."

It took some persuading before he could get the boy in the cart and speed away from the river. The uneasy feeling refused to stay behind and only increased when they passed another cart being pulled the opposite direction. The driver paid them no mind, but the passenger, a younger man missing an arm, fixed Daverell with an astonished stare. Were they coming from the Vowery's? An injured soldier sent home? Someone with a secret—his secret—to expose?

It was too soon. He needed more time.

He slapped the mule's backs, coaxing a little more speed from them. The closer he came to the Vowery homestead, the more certain he was that something was wrong.

"You alright, Dav?" Crow asked.

"Fair as flowers," Daverell lied.

Coming to Crow's home, he didn't see Ameryn at first. It was Romy's barking that drew his eye down to the river pool. Ameryn stood there, waiting for him with hands on her hips. Daverell and Crow approached to see she'd pulled Daverell's saddle from the barn and gone through his supplies.

"Crowan, come here, please," Ameryn ordered sternly. Crow glanced nervously at Dav before silently complying. His mother took his hand and guided him to stand behind her before she spoke again, to Daverell this time. "Just got a visit from Garrus Clay. Don't suppose you know him?"

"I...can't say..." he started.

"No need to keep lying. I already know you don't," she said. "He left for the war on the same day Tamiron did. Lost his arm in the accident that stole my husband. Turns out you weren't lying about that, even if you were about everything else. Garrus and Tam were side by side in all their short military service. He was sent home, wounded, from the front and came to pay his respects. So I says what a shame Dav isn't here to say hello, and he has no idea who I'm talking about. Told me he never saw anyone like you so much as trade words with Tam."

"Mrs. Vowery," Daverell said. "I can explain."

"But I carried on like a fool, kept describing you, and it's not until I mention your great brute of a horse that he asks with sudden realization if I'm talking about the great Daverell Kain, decorated war hero. But no, he says, it couldn't be him, because he's dead. Garrus

63

said the devastating news went through the military ranks just weeks ago. People was calling it the hardest blow the Uthiri had struck in the whole war."

"Mother," Crow said. "What are you—"

"So after he leaves, I got a mystery on my hands needs solving. I hope you can forgive me, going through your things, but I had to know if you were a fox in hen's feathers. Imagine my surprise when I came across a box full of medals—quite a few of them, I might add—and all of them say in big, engraved letters: Captain Daverell Kain." She paused, taking a few breaths. "Now, what in all the Midlands is going on here? And don't you dare lie to me again."

"I never lied," Daverell countered.

"You withheld pertinent truth and that's no different to honest folk."

Daverell fell silent, saying nothing—even with his expression.

"Why call yourself Dav? Why not something more common or completely different? You don't seem like a witless man, yet, even from the start, you risked me telling people in town all about Dav and his white horse staying on my land?"

"I knew I'd be discovered eventually. My aim was to delay it, not avoid it. I don't like lying, ma'am, especially not to decent people. I tried to fabricate as little as possible."

"So you lied to us enough to allow you to stay here for a time, but also not so much that your conscience got in the way?"

"Yes," Daverell said, feeling foolish.

"And the army doesn't know you're here. Thinks you're dead."

"Yes," he said again.

"I can't imagine how you got away. But of all places, why come here?" Ameryn asked. "When you never even knew my husband?"

"I did not know him, no. Not personally," Dav admitted. "But I met him. Even spoke with him."

"So you *did* talk to him?"

"Just once," Dav said. "In truth, I only ever asked him one question."

"What was that?"

"First, you must understand, I know the *Lyprakarum* prophecy better than anyone."

Ameryn blinked. "You...what?"

"It says, '*None may wield the Illumed, save one born within the mother's water, while Okgram's eye is blinded, within the Hunter's Year.*' The ancients believed the moon was Okgram's eye and the different phases were the opening and shutting of it."

"What are you talking about?" she asked, baffled.

Daverell went on as if she'd said nothing, "Everywhere the *Lyprakarum* mentions Okgram's eye as a new moon, it says 'closed' not 'blinded' as it does in the prophecy. Most scholars are convinced that 'blinded' refers to an eclipse."

Ameryn's jaw dropped. She went pale.

"Most think they know what '*born within the mother's water*' means," he continued. "Finding someone it's happened to is the hard part. It's very rare. Now, I would often sit at a different fire at the end of the day and just happened to choose the same one as your husband the night before he died. The men were swapping fireside tales, and he shared the story of a very distinctive birth."

"Hold your tongue!" Ameryn demanded.

"It happened during an eclipse of the moon, and the mother's water never broke. The child was born within the caul. The midwife ruptured the sac once the baby was outside the womb."

"Mother?" Crowan asked. "What's he—"

"Crowan, no. Don't listen to a word he says!"

"So the single question I asked Tamiron was what year this birth took place. He named it, and though no one else at the fire knew the significance of it—been a long time since most folk paid any attention to the old four-year cycle the ancients marked years by—sure enough, the year Tamiron named was the Hunter's."

"You're mad. Go!" Ameryn shrieked. "Get away. Go, now!"

"I can protect you and your son," Daverell protested. "The Uthiri are beyond their borders, burning everything. You can't send me away."

"Sleep with the rattlesnake to keep the coyotes at bay? No, thank you. We'll take our chances. Now leave, please."

"You think me a snake?"

"What should I think?" she asked, kicking a bundle out from one of his saddlebags.

She'd found it, taken it out of its wrappings. More than that, she must have pulled the Lagrim dagger out of its sheath and read the ugly words inscribed upon the blade.

Daverell picked it up, studying the exquisitely crafted scabbard and hilt as if it were the first time he'd seen it. In truth, it very nearly was. He'd wrapped it up immediately after receiving it and had not looked at it since. He couldn't figure what to do with it. But studying it now, he knew just what to do. Pulling it from its sheath, he held it aloft. The extraordinary weapon glittered, as if stealing more than its share of the afternoon light. It was the second most finely crafted blade Daverell had ever seen.

To his side, he saw Crow, gazing at the blade in adoring awe. Daverell wondered if the boy's worshiping eyes had noticed the same detail his mother's surely had. Like vandalism on a temple, along the narrow fuller were engraved the words, "Ever Bathed in Blood" and on the other side, "Ever Embedded in Bone." A mocking perversion of the holy adage, "Ever bathed in Light. Ever embraced by Truth."

"When it comes to this…this…*thing*," Daverell said. "You should at least know that I hate it." He squeezed the grip tight, wanting to crush it. "I *hate* it. The only reason I've not been rid of the damned gob of metal before now is that it's worth a fortune. But to me, it's a curse, and I think I've had enough of it." Dav turned and unceremoniously threw it. The dagger flew in a long arc and barely made a splash as it sliced, blade first, into the middle of the river.

Crow darted forward, plunging into the water after it.

"Crowan!" Ameryn shouted at his back and again when he surfaced. The boy ignored her and immediately dived back under.

Daverell wasn't sure what to do. "Mrs. Vowery, I never intended—"

"Why are you still here?" she snapped before turning her attention back to the water.

Daverell paused a moment before marching away. He saddled Druid, packed his things, and rode into the desert.

He looked back one more time to see that Ameryn had successfully coaxed a dripping and defeated Crow back to the riverbank. She was filling his ears with what appeared to be an impressive scolding. Crow's gaze was on him, however. Daverell turned away from it and kicked Druid into a canter.

Further on, he felt a different pair of eyes upon him—the legless girl's, watching from a rocky crevice—and pushed his horse into a gallop.

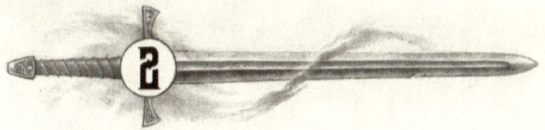

He wandered, aimlessly, with nothing but the oppressive sense of failure to keep him company. It had all gone wrong and gone wrong fast. Daverell tried blaming the Goddess, as if offering him purpose was a cruel trick she'd played on him.

Or maybe the trick had been from the demons in that Uthiri grove, and some hell-spawned creature was watching him even now. Perhaps through the eyes of his legless tormentor. Watching and laughing.

He became aware that, at some point, the sun had set. He was cold and hungry. Retrieving the flask in his pocket, he took a swig, hoping it was the fastest way to solving both problems.

Eventually, Druid grew tired, and Daverell was forced to stop for the night.

He spread his bedroll and fell into a fitful sleep. It wasn't until morning that he realized he had no idea where he was.

After a little hardtack for breakfast, he climbed a nearby mesa with a map in his hands to get his bearings. Where should he go? Back to the army? They might execute him. Could he explain his way out of a noose? Did he even want to?

As it turned out, the question ceased to matter when he looked over the edge of the bluff. Bad as his eyesight was for spotting things at a distance, the Uthiri war party below was hard to miss. Squinting, he could make out the red and black of their uniforms. They were maybe a half mile away.

There was precious little else he could discern from up there. Studying the map didn't help; Daverell couldn't make any sense of where he was. But of one thing he was certain, he, and these Uthiri butchers, were closer to Lockwood than any other town.

CHAPTER 6

ANKR PASS

Bellawych

At dusk, when the only star in the sky was the Goddess's, Pellary and Maiyen sang for Striker and the bodies strewn about the smoldering remains of Bellawych. In this ceremony, their voices were meant to replicate the pure singing of the Goddess and call the departed home. If any of the dead were listening, Pellary worried her weak and off-note warbling drove them away. Thankfully, Maiyen's singing wasn't too offensive.

"Do you think they'll find their way to the Embrace?" Maiyen asked.

"I hope so," Pellary said. Whenever she participated in a Singing Ceremony, she thought of the lost fourth Iress faction: the Opravics. Dedicated holy singers deemed unnecessary and discontinued by the Church hundreds of years ago. Their task was shared by all the surviving factions now.

"I wish there was more we could do for them," Maiyen said.

"As do I," Pellary agreed. "But it's best if we leave things undisturbed. The Uthiri may return."

That night, they huddled together in the corner of a shallow basement under a dirty blanket with their new dog friend at their feet. Maiyen and Pellary had cleaned and dressed the dog's wound as best they could.

Pellary was just beginning to nod off when a faint, moaning sound echoed over the ruins above.

What was that? Maiyen asked, as the dog lifted its head, alert.

I don't know, Pellary admitted.

It didn't sound like anything I've ever heard, Maiyen said.

The pass is supposed to be haunted, Pellary replied with a yawn. *The locals tell strange tales of the place. They've claimed to see ghosts or roaming lights and hear unnatural sounds. I read once that it was the one place the Tar Ishik purge never reached. The land was scoured of demons, but the exorcism never reached Ankr Pass. As if all the spiders had been swept from the room but one remained, hidden in the darkest corner.*

Aren't you afraid? Maiyen wondered. *I thought you believed in ghosts.*

Oh, I do, Pellary confirmed. *But that doesn't mean I'm scared of them.*

There was a pause; Pellary sensed Maiyen listening for another sound. None came. The dog laid her head back down.

I just thought of something, Maiyen said. *The Pathmaster told us to enter the Path eight days from the Setting. Tomorrow will be seven.*

Yes, Pellary mused. *I was wondering about that too. I don't like the idea of staying here another day with the Uthiri around.*

I think we should start early, I'd rather wait an extra day at the end of the Path than the beginning.

I agree, Pellary said. She suspected it might take them longer to get through anyway. And she was as eager to get the test over with as Maiyen. However, she knew that at the end of the pass stood Osgerath, one of the ancient demon towers. According to her research, it might just be the rotten core of the pass itself.

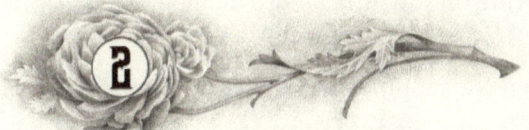

Maiyen must have fallen asleep at some point, because the bloody faces of the Uthiri soldiers watching her from the basement shadows could only have been a bad dream. In her first moments of being confidently awake, she noticed the dog was gone. Maiyen cast her mind and found the animal roaming the street above. Praying she didn't have her nose in something awful, Maiyen briefly connected with her and was pleased to see a bright sky overhead. Not yet the warm light of the sunrise, but the pale blue of its approaching.

She was less pleased with the dog having bitten off her bandages sometime during the night. At least it was less painful to connect with her than it had been the day before.

The two women rose and prepared for the long day. First, they discarded their robes and replaced them with outfits better suited for the trek ahead. Maiyen couldn't remember the last time she'd worn trousers. Their boots were already well suited for the journey and in good condition, but Maiyen laced them extra tight that morning. Last to be donned were their hooded cloaks and packs.

Next, they filled their waterskins to full capacity from the town well. It was much less than she would need, but the pass was, reportedly, the home to many natural springs that seeped right out of the rocks. Not to mention all the rain they'd be dealing with.

"Alright," Pellary said. "It's three or four days to the tower on the other side, as long as we don't get lost. We simply need to make it there without taking off the blindfolds. If we do that, I'm sure whatever spiritual task they have for us at the abbey in Andira will seem easy."

Maiyen agreed and gave her friend a tight hug before they started out. Before long, the sun broke over the peaks in front of them, and shortly, cold as she'd been all night, the sweltering heat of the day set in.

From the eyes of their four-legged companion, Maiyen watched the gaping mouth of the canyon yawning before them, waiting to swallow them up.

She routinely checked the landmark as they drew closer and was struck by how far away it remained. Maiyen trudged along, blindly, for what seemed like hours, thinking they'd surely reached it by now, until she checked and saw it still looming ahead. Once she was in the ravine, however, it felt too soon. The sharp rocks closed around them like a trap.

Thick clouds stole the sun, and it became harder to judge their direction. There was no river running out of the canyon, despite the constant rain that supposedly fell within it. The ground turned muddy and pungent, and the incessant buzz of flying insects surrounded them. She connected with the dog and was surprised to see herself and Pellary a fair distance ahead. Maiyen turned and invited the dog to follow them. She only paced and whined in response, unwilling to cross some invisible barrier that only she could feel.

No, that's not true. Maiyen thought, *I can feel it too.*

Yes, Pellary reflected in return. *It feels...wrong.*

This is an evil place, Maiyen decided. It was a simple observation, but there were no other words for it. It was as if some horrific act were being committed before her, and she was forced to watch.

"Come on, girl," Maiyen invited the dog again.

"Let's keep going," Pellary said.

"We can't just leave her," Maiyen protested.

"We have to at some point. Might as well be now," Pellary sighed. "I wish we could save her too, but she's on her own from here on out."

Maiyen watched herself from the poor creature's eyes as she

turned away. It looked, oddly, like she was abandoning herself.

Perhaps if we hug the rock on the side we'll get out of this mud? Pellary suggested with a slap to her face where something had bitten her.

It wasn't much better on the borders. Maiyen clambered over an unyielding stone but lost her footing on the other side, sliding into the fetid water and thorny bushes. Pellary followed her to the same fate. They were both so coated in mud they stopped trying to stay out of it and plodded straight through the sucking sludge. Each step was strenuous and nearly every heavy breath choked her with a mouthful of gnats. The muck was thickly infected with serrated brambles that caught at her clothes, forcing her to frequently stop and disentangle herself. She was tempted to remove her outer layer but feared what might happen to her bare skin. What little she had exposed—only her face and hands—was already covered in angry scratches.

Maddeningly, other than the clouds of tiny, biting bugs, there were no animals in the pass. Nothing to connect with. They were truly blind as they dragged themselves along, one step at a time. Maiyen had only the muddy edges of the marsh with which to orient herself, and she was, at the very least, confident that they'd not turned around. Their pace was agonizingly slow, and though she was sure they'd gone only a few miles thus far, they collapsed in the shallower mud on the edge for a break. Maiyen barely noticed the leathery taste of the water from her canteen as she relieved her raw throat and slaked her desperate thirst. Much as she didn't want to, they moved on once they'd caught their breath.

It began raining and continued to do so, on and off, for hours. They were the worst hours of Maiyen's life. She could not conceive of a more miserable environment. If the point of the Nimara Path was to test the novitiates with new challenges and hardships, then this was an ideal place to do it. That said, Maiyen was increasingly sure she was missing the point. Was she supposed to be feeling some emerging inspiration? Alighting upon some new insights about life? Communing with the Goddess in the absence of the distractions of civilization? Because all she thought was how profoundly she loathed this place. All she felt was pain and fatigue. All she sensed was unholiness.

The oppressively dark feeling of the place had increased and had become their best indicator that they were going the right direction. It took a fair amount of willpower to not turn and flee. Yes, to escape the insects and the thorns and the rain and mud and stink and heat of the dreadful place, but more than anything, to escape that feeling.

Pellary walked silently on beside her. Maiyen was too tired to even think a conversation with her. There was nothing left in them but to keep taking step after arduous step.

Around mid-day, Maiyen's stockinged foot came up, leaving the boot completely behind in the muck. As she checked her balance, her unprotected foot came down hard on something sharp under the water. A stinging pain ran up her leg, and she knew she'd cut it. Deep. She groped for her boot, ignoring the pain as best she could until she found it. It took pulling with both hands to wrench it free. As it came loose, she fell backwards, splashing into a sitting position in the reeking water.

The tears came then. She sat there for a while, unable to even use the opportunity to catch her breath through her sobs. Pellary's comforting hand touched her shoulder. Maiyen took it and held it tightly, crying into it. She might be wrong, but she thought she heard Pellary weeping as well.

"Come on," Pellary said after their tears had stopped. It was good to hear—actually hear—her voice. "Get your boot back on, let's see if we can't find somewhere dry to rest for a moment. I need to get out of this water."

"Yes," Maiyen answered.

Getting the boot back on was agony, as was every other step after that. They were able to feel their way to a boulder and climb atop it. Maiyen felt like crying again, even wished she would, but nothing came.

"Just breathe," Pellary told her, hopelessly out of breath herself. "Just breathe."

Maiyen did so. "We should eat something," she said.

"I've been swallowing insects all day without meaning to."

Maiyen sighed. "Me too."

The sun peeked through the clouds, and Maiyen found it comforting at first. Within minutes, however, she began feeling like a fish being steamed. The pause in walking brought to the surface all the aches she was trying to ignore. A biting, burning sensation throbbed on the inside of her thighs, under her armpits, and around her breasts—skin rubbed raw by wet friction. Worst of all were her feet. Beyond the laceration in her arch, there was a deep, pounding pain. Blisters covered her toes and heels. Blood was seeping into her boot, and her right foot was going numb.

"Can you walk?" Pellary asked.

"Do I have a choice?" Maiyen breathed.

"I think it's getting late in the day. Let's go a little farther and see if we can find a place to stop for the night. It can't all be mud and swamp, can it?"

Maybe we can get above it? Maiyen suggested.

I'm willing to try anything.

Saints and stars. This would be easier if we could share sight with something.

I think something about this place repels everything but these accursed insects. It's all I can do to keep from running away myself.

I know what you mean. Do you think it's because we're getting closer to Osgerath Tower on the other side?

I hope so, Pellary said. *When we're through and on the other side, we'll meet the Sister from Andira. She'll take us back to her abbey where some Curials will make us feel well again. Then we'll spend a year or two relaxing.*

This made Maiyen smile. *We'll be full Iress by then, of course. The novitiates there will obey our every command, which we'll issue from scented baths and soft, soft beds.*

We'll dine on fine foods and drink exotic wines.

I'll see my father again. He'll take me on one of his ships to some sunny coast where I can spread the Truth of the Goddess with warm sand between my toes. And you, Pell, can visit any library you wish.

Pellary managed a small laugh, then it was silent for a few minutes. Maiyen stood unsteadily on her feet and began moving again with a heavy limp. They climbed the steep, slippery walls of the canyon and found a ridge that let them walk above the swamp for a little while. However, were they to take another spill from up here—a very likely possibility—it could be much worse than it had been closer to the water. Because of this they scrambled along, almost as much on their hands as their feet. Maiyen had assumed there was no other exposed part of her body left to injure but, before long, her palms were as scraped and raw as everything else.

Even after the ridge ended, they were able to clamber along, hugging the side of the slope, only slipping when they hit some wet runoff. They continued this new strategy further down, closer to the water. Maiyen couldn't tell if it was faster or less tiring, but it was drier. That alone was a welcome change.

It was getting late in the day when an intense stinging pain burst in her left ear. With a shriek, Maiyen probed the painful spot but found nothing.

It was me, Pell thought to her.

What is it? Maiyen asked.

Something stung me, Pellary answered. *Goddess above, that hurts!*

The side of Pell's face grew very tender. Maiyen had been connecting with her occasionally to escape her own discomfort but stopped once the fire of the sting became more unbearable than her foot.

It keeps getting worse, Pell said with trepidation. *I'll bet I look an absolute fright. The swelling is so big. It must look like I've got an apple beneath my skin.*

The thought of fresh fruit made their sharp hunger ache even deeper, and they decided, at that moment, to stop for the night.

They ate a meager meal on another small ridge. Maiyen chewed and swallowed automatically. The food was tasteless, the air that had been so hot was now cold, she was soaked, and every inch of her body screamed as she lay on bumpy and hard-packed dirt. All the while, the ominous feeling hung over her so completely and cruelly, she was sure something was watching them. Casting her mind revealed nothing around her. The revelation wasn't as reassuring as she'd hoped. They were so, so alone. The only mercy to be had was the ease of sleep. Heavy weariness pulled her into senselessness, her body gratefully diving into the escape of a slumber so deep she didn't wake again until the sun was well in the sky the next day.

Stiff or not, she hurried to relieve herself. Despite her protesting and rigid joints, she felt a fair bit better once she had. Even her foot wasn't quite so painful when she walked on it. The sting on Pellary's ear was a different story. Even the faintest touch to the left side of her face was excruciating.

"At least I slept well," Pellary said.

"It probably helps when there's nothing, no hooting owl or chirping crickets, to rouse you at night."

"True," Pellary remarked. "A bit creepy though."

After a quick breakfast, they moved on, and the day began much as the previous day had ended, with the two women scrambling along the rocks. They hadn't really discussed it, but Maiyen assumed Pellary also preferred this method over trudging through the muck and swamp water.

Though Maiyen had been out of the water for nearly a full day, she still *felt* damp. It added a chilling layer of discomfort over the agony radiating from every bone, joint, muscle, and inch of skin she had.

By midday, the painful objections of her body had disappeared into numbness but were no less difficult to force into action. Every step was a battle, and she stole a small break after taking only two or three of them.

Just as Maiyen was getting the hang of moving sideways along the bank of the swamp, her hand made contact with a particularly muddy runoff and slid out from under her. Her face slammed into the rock and scraped along it as she tumbled into the bog. She was too exhausted to be upset about the sharp sting along her scraped nose and cheek, and there was even part of her that enjoyed cooling off in the water. That part swiftly disappeared as she started moving again, and the wetness caused every blistered and chafing part of her to burn anew. It made her cloak noticeably heavier as well.

She suggested they stop for a little rest and lunch while she dried out. Pellary happily agreed.

This would be much easier without the blindfolds, Pellary noted, chewing on a bit of dried apricot.

Don't even suggest it, Maiyen returned in shock.

The blindfolds are intended to help us develop our inner Sight, never meant to force us to stumble about, especially in such a hellish place without sight to share. Curials and Arrantines don't have to do it this way, Pellary grumbled.

We are not Curials or Arrantines, Maiyen thought to Pellary with a hint of pride. Embrells followed a more distinguished discipline with a richer legacy than the other two. Well, perhaps not Curials but certainly Arrantines. *Besides,* she continued, *they'd know.*

Would they? Pellary asked. *You think the seal is real? What if it's just a trick and the real test is to see if we're smart enough to take these things off out here.*

I can't believe you're seriously considering this, Maiyen thought.

I'm not really, Pellary sighed. *I just...it's never been more tempting than it is today.*

Don't forget the Twenty-Fifth Edict.

I'll let you remember it for me, Pellary said. *The Jophrat Edicts aren't scripture. We've enough rules as it is, you really don't have to search out more.*

If I didn't, I wouldn't be following Edict Eighteen, Maiyen thought with more humor than she would have expected she was capable of at the moment.

Pellary sighed again. Minutes later, they lifted themselves up on their wobbly legs and continued on.

They managed to avoid any more spills or injuries for the rest of the day. Maiyen guessed they were perhaps getting better at navigating the nightmarish place. Pellary's bite even seemed to lessen in size and discomfort by the time they stopped for the night.

She used the last of her strength to force down a carrot and raw potato.

At other times in her life, Maiyen had been exhausted. She'd even, on occasion, described herself as suffering from a bone-deep weariness at the end of a long day. Oh, to feel that level of exhaustion again! The bliss of it. What she felt now was so far beyond that, a month of sleep on a heap of feathers couldn't cure her. The notion might have coaxed a smile, but she hadn't the energy for it. The smallest movements were a chore.

Unexpectedly, Maiyen found herself thinking about her mother. She never thought about her mother, had barely known her. The memories were her earliest and most foggy. And most cherished. She wanted the comfort of those memories now, but they were too slight to support her need and that made her want to cry.

Pell, she reached out to her friend's consciousness, *tell me about your mother.*

There was a pause before Pellary's reply. *I think we might be tempting fate a bit too much with that conversation.*

What do you mean?

Seems like the sort of thing people talk about before they die.

At that, Maiyen did manage a faint smile. She took a long drink from her canteen and lay back on the hard but welcome stone. In moments, she was lost in as deep and dreamless a sleep as the night before.

Maiyen awoke with the same pressing need to urinate. If it had been hard to get her body to move before, it was nearly impossible now. She thought passingly about wetting herself and was shocked she'd consider such a thing, even briefly. She didn't do it, of course, but as even the slightest movements were white-hot agony, she barely managed. Pellary was in much the same state, and they both stretched and worked their muscles for quite a while before they could cope with walking at all.

Starting out that day, for the first time in the pass, the sun was not obscured by clouds and beat them full in the face as they walked. Maiyen was imagining how ridiculous she'd appear with a sunburn on only the lower half of her face—if indeed she was raised to full Iress and could remove the blindfold without dying first—when Pellary interrupted her thoughts.

Maiyen, cast your mind, up ahead.

She did and noticed something they'd not witnessed their entire time in Ankr Pass. Before them was a light, distinctly brighter than the tiny dots of buzzing insects surrounding them. Something alive and substantial. An animal? A person?

Perhaps it means we're almost out! Maiyen's excitement pulsed through Pellary's head.

Perhaps, Pellary responded with more caution. Though, the ground beneath her feet *did* feel less wet and slippery.

When she was close enough, Pellary connected but immediately recoiled, cutting it off. Whatever it was felt...wrong. She'd never bonded with anything so twisted and malicious. There was a darkness to it, something sick.

And it was watching them. Very closely.

Oh Goddess above, what is that? Maiyen cringed.

Pellary attempted to connect again, physically wrinkling her nose in disgust as she forced herself to maintain the bond. Through its eye—it had only one—she saw herself and Maiyen moving towards it. What shocked her more than their appalling state was what she sensed from the creature itself: a ravenous hunger. But not to fill its belly, only to kill. It was an ache, a heavy lust for carnage. The thing's heart was racing, and it panted with intense desire as it imagined ripping the two of them into shredded masses of bloody gore. Ripples of pleasure shuddered through its body at the thought. What kind of creature was this? She'd never come across a mind capable of conjuring such vivid imagery, while also being so wild. No, not wild. She'd shared the minds of animals before. Predators studied their prey with detached determination and cold indifference. But this thing *wanted* to kill, and for the pleasure only.

It's a demon! Pellary exclaimed.

That's absurd, Maiyen said.

Then what is it? Pellary asked.

There was a pause, and Pellary could sense Maiyen searching for an answer before giving up.

Why hasn't it attacked us? Maiyen thought. *It certainly wants to.*

It's waiting for us to get closer. Pellary nervously licked her lips. *I'll see if I can draw it away.*

Fooling an animal was more difficult than fooling a human, even for Pellary, as it required replicating a sensory experience she was unfamiliar with. How did this creature hear or smell? How did its mind interpret these processes? Connecting with it gave her some insight into those answers, but for an Embrell to replace sensations convincingly took far more familiarity than could be gained from a moment's link. Thankfully, even if an animal wasn't tricked, it was usually confused.

Pellary concentrated, altering the beast's genuine vision with a false version wherein she and Maiyen began running to the side.

The ruse worked. The beast bounded away from them, giving chase to a fleeing version of them that didn't exist. In actuality, they hurried forward as fast as they could.

Moments later, the beast passed beyond Pellary's range, and the illusion failed.

I can't reach it anymore, Pellary said. *Move quietly, maybe it won't find us again.*

Swiftly and silently, the two women stole through the mud. Before long, however, even the mud dried out, and Pellary walked on blessedly flat, dry ground again. Her excitement was short lived, however. She again sensed the presence of the creature, like a tingling on the back of her neck.

Pellary, Maiyen cautioned.

I know, she responded. *Just keep moving.*

Without warning, the creature's ghastly howl echoed through the pass. That otherworldly sound could not have come from anything but a Beloworld monster. It entered her range, fast. Connecting with it confirmed her fear. It had seen them and was giving furious chase!

Run! Pellary urged and they both began sprinting. Pellary desperately tried to raise more imagery to fool the thing, but she was panicking now, losing control. Running away required too much of her attention.

They watched their backs grow ever closer from the eye behind them. Ahead, their path dead-ended with a cliff edge, several hundreds of feet above the ground beyond. Built into the cliffside was a massive, black tower that extended above the ridge to a pronged crown.

Osgerath.

If we can get to it in time... Pellary sent.

The tower was just far enough away that the creature was going to reach them before they reached it. As if teasing them, she could see the tower door ahead, still intact despite its age.

Maiyen was outpacing her. Pellary was falling behind, and from further away than she would have expected, the monster leaped into the air and landed immediately behind her. A savage swipe from its taloned paw across her back sent her screaming and spinning. She shrieked again as she landed in the dirt, but the sound was cut short when a large, heavy paw pushed on her chest and forced the air out of her lungs. The monster roared in her face.

Pellary tore at her shirt front. Her fingers closed around her ericle, and she brought it out into the thing's view.

The beast leaped back, growling. A rush of confusing emotions passed through it, all of them obsessively focused on the charm. Pellary whipped the ericle off her neck and held it out before her. Maiyen was beside her now, helping her to her feet.

We need to get into that tower! Pellary shouted into Maiyen's mind.

That was impossible, however. As the demon had backed away

from the two women, it had done so in the direction of the tower and now hunched between them and the door.

Will the ericle drive it away, to the side, if you get closer? Maiyen wondered.

Pellary tentatively approached it, and the creature readied itself to pounce, feeling cornered. Pellary backed away.

No, that won't work, Pellary thought. *Is the tower the only way down the cliff?*

Hard to tell; that thing won't take its eyes off your ericle, Maiyen responded.

Pellary had always understood ericles drove demons away, but she observed now that it was more complicated than that. This thing was entranced. Almost hypnotized. It desired, as much as feared, the small medallion.

Maiyen noticed the same thing. *I think it will chase the ericle if you throw it. Do it and we can run for the door.*

I don't want to lose it!

The demon's attention on the thing was failing. It was considering killing them and claiming the prize once they were dead.

You may not have a choice! Maiyen argued in a panic.

Wait! I've got an idea, Pellary said. *There are windows on either side of the door.* Pellary circled the monster, keeping the ericle between her and it as she did so.

Careful! Maiyen warned. Pellary was only steps away from the sheer cliff edge.

Pellary could see, in the creature's field of vision, a window right above her.

Be ready to run. Pellary threw her treasured charm through the thick iron bars and into the tower.

The creature roared with covetous rage and sprang toward the window through which the ericle had disappeared.

Go now, through the door! Pellary directed. *I can reclaim it once we're inside.*

Pellary connected to Maiyen, feeling her hands on the old iron door, blindly searching for a handle. Finding it. Pulling. Pulling harder. Pellary joined her, and the two women heaved with all the strength they had left. The door was immovable.

Something else is coming, Maiyen said.

But Pellary had connected to the demon again. The creature slowly turned toward the two with fresh fury. She saw herself, frightened and small, in its ravenous eye.

Then, in an instant, the connection was severed. Pellary searched and saw the light Maiyen had mentioned. Something walking their way.

A low voice greeted them. "Novitiates," he said. "I've been searching for you. You were a little ahead of me, earlier than I expected. I'm glad I found you when I did."

"Who...who are you?" Maiyen asked in a shaky voice.

"My name's Ollett," the strange man replied.

"Stay back," Pellary ordered, her voice sounding broken and pitiful even to her own ears.

"That's a demon-inflicted wound." He pointed to Pellary's injured back. "You'll die without a Curial's aid. I can take you to one."

"You're from the Andira Abbey?" Maiyen asked.

"No." He shook his head. "There is no abbey in Andira, but there is one nearby. I can take you there. Please, you can trust me."

"How do we know that?" Pellary regarded him suspiciously.

"Let faith guide you in the places Light cannot reach," he recited.

That's the same phrase the Pathmaster gave us, Maiyen reminded her.

After a pause, Pellary nodded slowly. "Yes, alright. Thank you."

"Please, share my eyes," Ollett invited.

The first thing they saw when they did was a shower of blood as the man pulled his spear from the skull of the creature. It was their first good look at the thing. It appeared like a bear in size and form but twisted and monstrous. There were long quills jutting from its back and mottled, matted fur over the rest of its pale skin. Pellary imagined its single glassy eye appeared no less unfeeling in death than it had in life. Its menacing face was covered in scars of old wounds, one of which must have claimed its other eye. The thing's jaw hung limply open displaying an endless array of long, sharp teeth. They would be biting through her flesh at this very moment were it not for this stranger.

"What is it?" Maiyen asked.

"A demon," Ollett said, as he wiped his spear off on the carcass. "They find their way into the pass from the Beloworld sometimes; we're not sure how."

"I need to retrieve something from the tower," Pellary informed the man.

"It's gone. Trust me, even if we could get in, that place is worse than the pass."

"But—" Pellary protested.

"That door was sealed long ago and reinforced with holy blessings so the things inside couldn't lure people in. That's just at this top door, mind. Heaven help any fools that wander into the other entrance at the base." He noticed Maiyen was inspecting the sack in her hands and the large tear in the bottom. "Leave your things. You won't need them. Again, you must follow me."

Maiyen gladly dropped the heavy bag of rations.

The man rummaged in his own bag, producing some bandages. He turned to Pellary. "Let's dress your wounds with this for now."

Can you do it, Maiyen? Pellary asked.

Of course, Maiyen thought back as she took the dressing from the man's hand.

Pellary faced the tower door and lifted her shirt, exposing her back. The man modestly faced the other way, fixing his gaze on the surrounding terrain.

"Oh, turn around so we can see what we're doing," Pellary said in a huff. "I'd rather be embarrassed than dead."

"But mind your eyes and thoughts," Maiyen added. "We're sharing them both."

The wound was bad. The skin around the heavily bleeding lacera-

85

tions was turning gray as if from some poison or rot. Maiyen's hands were trembling as she bound up the gashes. Pellary kept gasping and hissing from the pain. When they'd finished, the two trusted the man more. They'd sensed nothing but concern from him.

"We best be in a hurry," Ollett said, leading them away.

Pellary hesitated a moment before joining the other two. Even though she couldn't see the tower, she glanced back in its direction, mourning the loss of her ericle.

CHAPTER 7

BATHED IN BLOOD

Near Lockwood

Crowan was angry with her, and she welcomed it. As long as he wasn't talking to her, he wasn't asking questions. Daverell had put dangerous ideas in his head.

Swimming became the boy's new favorite pastime. In the days that followed Daverell's departure, he stole every chance he could to dive under the surface of the river and search for the dagger.

It worried Ameryn, though it took her hours of rumination before she could rightly identify why. She herself bathed there regularly, and Tamiron had taught the boy to swim in that very spot. With the dam at one end, there was very little current and no threat of being swept downstream in good weather.

He might easily cut himself on the sharp brambles and fallen logs, especially those caught at the draining edge. And now, of course, there was a very sharp blade at the bottom somewhere that Crow's blind, waving hands and feet were searching for, but the potential danger was too thin a reason to forbid him.

There was the hunt itself, of course. The pool was large and deep enough that, while not completely fruitless, she doubted his chances of ever finding the knife. There was absolutely no visibility beneath the murky surface, and once the blade struck the pool, it might have cut through the water in any direction. The Goddess alone knew where it now rested. Whether he retrieved it or not, Ameryn found she didn't particularly care. They could sell it maybe. She'd forbid him to keep it, of course.

And that was the problem. If it came to that, she was certain she'd meet with her first real taste of youthful defiance from her son. He was upset with her for Daverell leaving and, of late, would pounce on any excuse to defy her. Well, let him keep trying. When it came to being stubborn, he didn't have the years of practice she had. Ameryn refused to lose her little, trusting boy so near the same time she'd lost her husband.

She was returning from feeding her old milk cow who was ready to give birth any day now when she saw dust being kicked up by an approaching rider. Her heart lurched with fear until she recognized Clim, the boy who made deliveries from the Lockwood post.

"Got a letter for you, ma'am," he said, holding it out to her from his mount.

Ameryn took it, confused—no one ever wrote to her except...she recognized the careful, boxy handwriting on the envelope and froze. Her whole body, from the hair on her head to the toes at the end of her feet, had momentarily shut down.

"You alright, ma'am?" Clim asked.

Forcing a smile, she composed herself as best she could. "Just...

yes...I...I wasn't expecting this."

"I just came from the Ayellas' place," Clim said. "Lerin says she made a pie from your apples she'd like to share. Asked me to extend an open invitation. Anytime, she says."

"That's kind of you, Clim. I've some coffee if you'd like, before you move on."

"Thank you, ma'am, but I've only a few deliveries left, and I'm anxious to return."

"Well, don't let me keep you," she said.

With a tip of his hat, he rode away.

She held the letter delicately. An aching desire to tear it open and hungrily consume the words overwhelmed her, but something else held her back. This was a rare gift. An opportunity to keep her correspondence with Tamiron *open*. Searching her heart, she realized she wanted that more than the words themselves. This letter may keep him alive, in a way.

Given the timing, this letter was likely written by Tamiron just prior to his passing. Maybe the day before or even the day of. Why hadn't she expected it? His letters were invariably short but regular; she had plenty of previous ones to read over again, and this letter was more valuable to her sealed tight and kept close. It might never leave her pocket.

The heat of the day was settling in strong by the time Ameryn was on the path to the Ayellas' place. She'd worn her hair up under her hat today, and a cool breeze at her back tickled her bare neck, making the temperature bearable, even pleasant. She'd almost driven the cart but decided a solitary walk was just what she needed.

Her thoughts wandered to Dav. His departure had brought back her worries for harvest time. It was coming on fast, and there was no way she and Crowan could handle the workload alone.

Another gentle rush of air blew across her. This time, it made her feel strangely uneasy and exposed. The truth of her lonesome situation unexpectedly pressed down on her. Before, it had been a temporary thing. Tamiron was gone, but he was coming back. She was holding out for a deadline. One with an uncertain date, true, but it *would* come. Daverell's presence had held this suffocating realization at bay. Now, it walloped her without anything to deaden the sting. She swiftly reminded herself of her favorite passage from *The Song of Saeris*:

Live not all thy days in one moment, lest sadness rule thy past and dread thy future.

But take ye, instead, each day as it is gifted to you: one by one.

One by one. She could do that. She *must* do that. For herself and for Crow and for Tamiron's memory. She'd work herself into a hardened shell of bones before giving up.

The Ayellas' homestead was just ahead now, their framed house tucked in among the sagebrush and lazily dancing ponderosas.

At first, the welcome sight gave her comfort, but as she approached, Ameryn became aware of a growing foreboding replacing it, though she could not identify the reason. Later, she would wonder if it was the lack of a dog barking or if she'd noticed a watering can on its side. Some element subtle enough to slip past her reasoning but alert her instincts.

She dismissed the anxiety as best she could, sure that once she knocked on the Ayellas' door, painted a cheery blue, Lerin would answer with her affable smile, and the feeling would flee like Darkness before a lidocrafted masterwork.

Ameryn rapped her knuckles against the hard wood in a friendly rhythm, and the door gave way beneath her fingers. It was unlatched. Instead of retreating, the unease mutated into a white-hot dread that gripped her heart. She swallowed and tried to breathe.

"Lerin?" Ameryn called out as she pushed the door inwards. "Hello?" Her efforts to keep her voice polite and free of worry failed, and at the sight of the scene within the Ayella home, all words, breath, even thoughts fled completely.

Lerin and her husband lay slaughtered on the floor in a pool of blood. Their bodies, stripped naked, were a sickly whitish gray, and each had deep slashes across their necks. The cut in Lerin's was so deep it had nearly separated her head from the rest of her. Mr. Ayella had accompanying stab wounds all over his torso, some deep enough that his innards had spilled out. Their dog had also been butchered, parts of him scattered around the room. The terror of the scene was punctuated by a silent stillness broken only by the buzz of a small swarm of flies around the corpses.

It was the sharp odor that broke Ameryn out of the stupor she was in. A foul aroma assaulted her nostrils, and she came to herself in an instant, bolting out the door.

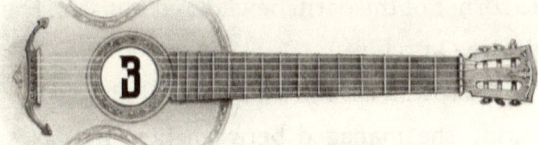

Ameryn ran for home. Ran as fast as she could, which wasn't nearly fast enough. Every pump of her frantically beating heart was a battle with her damnably weak body. Her throat was raw, and her legs burned; each individual piece of her screamed to stop, even threatened to give out. Ameryn screamed back, cursing her limbs and joints for being too slow, too weak.

She criticized her mind and decisions just as sharply. *The Goddess drops a warrior at your door, right when you need one, and you send him away days before the Uthiri arrive to kill you and your son. You fool! You absolute fool!* The image of her slain neighbors, blood everywhere, kept flashing in her mind, and when it wasn't, another image replaced it: Crowan. *His* throat slit, *his* blood spilling out. She forced it from her head, closing tear-filled eyes against the horror of it, but this did no good. It returned again and again, stronger and more vivid every time. She prayed it was only her excitable mind and not some premonition. If she returned to her home and was greeted by that sight, she would welcome the blade of the Uthiri across her own neck.

Why hadn't she ridden one of the mules? Why had she left home at all? How fresh was the scene of the murder when she came across it? Were the Uthiri behind her? In pursuit? Should she yell for Crow? Would that alert any enemies to her presence? Could she even find the breath to call to him if she wanted to? Was she, in fact, leading the murderers from the Ayellas' home to her own? Should she stop and try to hide herself?

Ameryn didn't pause to consider any answers, only kept running.

It was just like Pyressa. The fire. It had caught up to her again. The heat, the smoke, the death, that horrible feeling of helplessness.

An eternity later, she came within sight of her cabin and, at least from here, nothing looked amiss.

"Crowan!" she called. "Crowan!"

He darted around the corner of the barn, bewildered but safe. Her body collapsed, nearly plowing into him.

"Mother, what's wrong?" Crowan asked.

"The...Ayellas are...dead," she managed between heaving gasps. "Uthiri."

Crowan's mouth dropped open, and he struggled to say something. Ameryn spoke again instead. "Help...get the cart...we're leaving."

"Where are we—"

"Just go!" Ameryn shouted.

Crowan rushed away to get the two mules hitched up. Ameryn joined him once she could stand again and retrieved their wood ax and a few of her most priceless items from her home. Tamiron's letters, her mother's Star of Saeris, and the locket Tamiron had given her when he'd asked her to marry him—it held a lock of both her departed sister's hair as well as Crowan's baby hair. If all else was stolen or destroyed, she would be heartbroken but could survive.

In no time at all, they were both in the seats with Romy pacing nervously in the cart bed. She snapped the reins over the backs of Gooter and Gus and, sensing the urgency, they took off faster than usual. Ameryn steered them between the cabin and barn and onto the worn path that led into town. Then she pulled them to an abrupt halt.

Directly in front of them, blocking the road, were six dark figures in a row, each on a black horse.

Ameryn stared at them in shock. She'd never seen any soldiers from Uthir in person, but she had no doubt she was looking at some now. They looked so monstrous, she could hardly believe they were human men under that armor. The black metal was roughly twisted into sharp spikes atop their shoulders and heads. The parts of their uniforms that weren't black metal thorns were a deep red, including long cloaks that swept out behind them.

To Ameryn, they resembled the horned demons depicted in an illustrated *Lyprakarum* her grandmother had owned. Those images had always held a dark corner of forbidden terror in her heart. Her mind, struggling to believe the reality before her, brought them to the surface, flooding her blood with the kind of dread she'd not known since those childhood days when monsters were real and coming for her in the night.

One of the Uthiri moved his horse ahead of the group and opened a scroll. His harsh voice cut through the air as he began reading in an accent that suggested the Threyan language was demanding unfamiliar gestures from his tongue. "The Uthiri Empire has confirmed the Threyan treachery it long suspected."

Romy, no longer able to simply growl and pace in the cart bed, placed her front paws on the bench between Ameryn and Crow, and began barking at the men.

The one in the lead stopped reading and motioned at the rider on the far left who held a bow with an arrow already nocked. In one swift motion he raised, aimed, and loosed it directly at them. By the time Ameryn and Crowan ducked out of the way, the arrow had already found its mark. Romy's barks halted with a sharp yelp as she was thrown to the back of the cart. Ameryn turned to see the black shaft embedded through the roof of the dog's mouth and the serrated point jutting out the back of her head. She was twitching.

"Romy!" Crowan cried.

Ameryn grabbed his arm, urgently shaking her head with pleading eyes. They may just as casually kill a child for interrupting.

The man began reading again. "The Uthiri Empire has confirmed the Threyan treachery it long suspected."

While he spoke, the other Uthiri soldiers began riding forward. They would shortly be surrounding the cart. The one with the bow had yet to ready another arrow. Perhaps Crowan could get away.

"Crowan," Ameryn whispered in a gasp, "run!" Crowan remained motionless until she reached over and all but pushed him out of the cart, shouting, "Run! Now!"

The boy hit the ground and sprinted away. The invaders bellowed in a barbed language she didn't understand. The one in the center stopped speaking yet again and pointed at her fleeing boy. There was no need, his comrades were already giving chase, and on those big black horses, the chase wouldn't last long.

Ameryn slapped the mules into action and wrenched the cart to the side, creating an obstacle for the riders. The one with the bow fired another arrow more quickly than she could have imagined. Thankfully, Crow was bounding away in a crooked enough line that the arrow missed him by a hair. The bowman was readying another arrow and passing the cart when Ameryn, without thinking, threw herself at him. Launching off the cart, she plowed into the side of the archer. She didn't hit him directly, but as she fell, she clutched his cape and pulled with all her weight against it. It was enough to drag him backward as the whinnying horse bucked and flipped him fully off its back and on top of Ameryn. One of the large metal thorns on his left pauldron struck her right temple just below the hairline, and she was immediately dazed as blood spurted down her face.

The fallen bowman stood back up, screaming an ugly word she didn't know but could guess the general meaning of, and hauled her back to her feet. The world was an unsteady place for her, and she was tipping to one side when the back of a gauntleted fist hammered into her cheek and sent her crashing to the ground in the other direction. The armor on his hands had spikes as well. They bit into her face, slicing along the side. She tasted blood. Her tongue instinctively explored the side that had been hit. Her teeth were still there but she could feel

94

the stifling air through a gap in her skin. The cut had gone entirely through her cheek.

The soldier yanked Ameryn up again and spat in her face as he hurled more curses at her. She, in turn, spat right back and, in this at least, got the better of him as her mouth was full to the brim with hot blood. There was another blow to her nose that would have sent her sprawling for a third time had he not whipped her around and put a massive arm around her neck so tightly she could barely breathe. Further obstructing her airways was her now-bleeding nose; every exhale was accompanied by a spray of crimson that she had to push out with as much force as she could so she might inhale without choking on it. Even still, she squirmed and fought to break free.

All the blood and tears in her eyes made a blur of the world, so she heard more than saw the surrounding riders laughing and heckling their comrade as he struggled to hold her. They said something to him in mocking tones, and he answered with rage in his voice, punctuated by another punch to the small of Ameryn's back. She'd have crumpled again if not for the chokehold. He began walking her before him, driving her ahead.

Please, Goddess, she begged. *Let Crowan have gotten away. Let them kill me if it means he'll live.*

The archer bellowed at the others again, this time in a more authoritative voice, and two of them rode off to the side as she was still being pressed forward. Why hadn't they killed her yet? Where were they leading her? Blinking rapidly and wiping the blood from her eyes, she saw one of the men ahead, holding Crowan. He'd been caught near the banks of the river pool.

The man holding Crow drew his sword and held it at the boy's neck. In an instant, both he and Ameryn became compliant.

When they reached the river, she could see Crowan was crying. His sobs were interrupted by a sharp gasp when he saw her. "Mother!"

The man she assumed was the leader had dismounted and joined the group of four at the riverbank. He roared a sharp and short word that was clearly meant to silence everyone. It did. A heavy helmet covered most of his face, but Ameryn could make out his piercing blue eyes and black beard as he stood right before her. After a moment of stillness, he gave her the slightest hint of a smile and pointed behind him. The archer turned her head in the direction of her cabin. It was burning. Only a corner was alight now, but in minutes, the whole structure would be engulfed in flame and smoke. She could make out the remaining two soldiers, black figures with lit torches and bloodied swords setting fire to the barn as well. With another word from the leader, she was turned to face him again. He raised the scroll and began reading for the third time. "The Uthiri Empire has confirmed the Threyan treachery it long suspected. We are searching for our God, Vulsipher, imprisoned somewhere in your country. If you—"

Ameryn heard a sharp cry from the man holding Crowan. The boy had escaped again. Perhaps the soldier's grip had grown relaxed as the leader had started what was surely routine for them by now, and Crowan had seized the opportunity to slip away. He got farther than she would have expected. He made it to the flat rock he used to jump into the river and, like he had so many times before, leaped from it. Unlike all those other times, however, he was snatched by the back of his shirt and came down, splashing into the deep water at the edge.

The leader yelled something at the man who, grinning, changed his grip so he had Crowan by the hair instead and forced the boy under the water. Ameryn watched in horror as Crow's hands frantically searched for something to grab on to, but all he could find was the arm drowning him.

In that moment, Ameryn foolishly wished Crowan *was* some fabled warrior. If he were chosen by the Goddess for a greater purpose, he might be protected. But no, anyone who would defend the child was dead or absent. Any, except for her.

"Stop!" Ameryn cried, but the grip on her throat made it so the words carried no further than the man right before her, still holding the scroll. Scowling, he nodded to it. She understood his meaning, Crowan would not be let back up until it had been read in its entirety. Ameryn clamped her mouth shut and the man, after theatrically clearing his throat, began yet again.

"The Uthiri Empire has confirmed the Threyan treachery it long suspected. We are searching for our God, Vulsipher, imprisoned somewhere in your country. If you do not know where our God is held, you will die, beginning with the youngest. We will continue to spread death and terror throughout your country until we discover and liberate Vulsipher. Those within this country who know Vulsipher's location may reveal it and stop the massacre at any time. Are you able to lead us to Vulsipher?"

Ameryn glanced from the man to her son's still frantic arms in the river. There were surfacing bubbles among the splashes; he wouldn't last long. *This is madness,* she thought. *Randomly searching for one of the old-world gods?*

The man turned the paper over so she could see it. None of it was discernible to her except the words at the bottom which he was tapping. It read, *Yes - No.*

"Yes!" she shrieked.

The man tilted his head with disappointed skepticism. The chances of a woman and boy on the remote fringe of civilization knowing anything of their demon-god were so low it was the same as impossible and he, of course, knew this. She and Crowan were only supposed to listen and die. Their deaths, the Ayellas, and countless others before and to follow, were only a tool. A means to make whoever *did* know guilty enough to divulge the information. This man was simply sticking to the procedure his superiors had set him to. There was only one right answer, and it wouldn't save Crowan. At best, it might grant him one more small moment of life. A moment where she could tell him she loved him, and those words could carry him on his journey towards his father and the eternal Embrace of the Goddess. She would swiftly follow; they would all be together again, this very day.

"No! Damn you, no!" Ameryn wailed.

The Uthiri leader laughed now and called for the other soldier to let Crowan up. The man pulled the boy by his hair out of the water and set him roughly on the rock. Crowan sucked in the air with such distress he began coughing in heavy gasps. Ameryn looked at him for the last time, wet and struggling for breath in much the same way he had the very first time she'd looked upon him. Her heart shattered, the emotion so thick in her throat she could not force out the words she desperately needed to. Her boy. Her little boy.

No sooner had Crowan begun to finally breathe with more ease than the leader spoke an order to the boy's executioner, and he grabbed him roughly by the hair again.

"No!" Crowan pleaded.

Ameryn panicked and forced the words out in a sob. "Crowan, I love you! Be brave. We'll be with your father soon!" Before the last words had traveled beyond her bloodied lips, the man forced the boy under the murky surface again. However, this time he did not have as good a grip, and he brought his hand out, empty, and began searching the water. The boy had disappeared underneath. The leader barked an angry word at the man by the water's edge who gave a defensive reply.

The leader then spoke to the two still on the bank with him, and they traded places. The second man restrained Ameryn as the bowman nocked an arrow. He moved closer to the river, scanning the surface, ready to shoot Crowan once he emerged.

The scene persisted in tense stillness, broken only by the crackling inferno behind them. Ameryn studied, unblinking, the dancing reflections on the river's slow current for any change, any break.

It happened in an instant. A bursting splash of water immediately mixed with the gushing blood and screams of the man who'd been bending over the edge. Ameryn stared in disbelief. Crow was holding Daverell's lost dagger tightly in both hands. He'd embedded the blade in the Uthiri man's neck. With a yell of rage, Crow tried to push it deeper but only managed to push himself under the water again. This proved to be a good thing as in that same moment, the archer—who had also been staring—loosed his arrow. It ended up in the skull of the stabbed man, who had pitched forward. His screams suddenly ceased.

The grip on Ameryn loosened. She imagined the man holding her was watching the scene with as much disbelief as she was. She slid out of the hold and ran at the archer who was cursing and readying another arrow. The two men behind her were yelling, grasping after her, when the archer spotted her advance.

As he raised his bow to fire, a throwing knife struck him deep in the chest. Ameryn stopped, her eyes as wide as the man's before her. She turned, following the path of the blade to its source.

Daverell Kain stood there, ferocious and deadly, a ready sword in his hands. Both remaining Uthiri soldiers drew their own blades and charged at him. Daverell parried and ducked, expertly weaving through the simultaneous attacks. The Uthiri were clumsy amateurs against Daverell. Even with two against him, they were hopelessly outmatched and, within seconds, dead. The merciless lack of hesitation and practiced ease of movement with which Daverell decapitated them frightened her.

Ameryn turned away, only to see Crowan out of the water, holding Daverell's discarded dagger, watching in horrified fascination.

"Crowan." She ran to him. They embraced, and she held him tightly to her, barring him from the sight. To Dav she said, "There were two more. They set fire to the cabin and barn."

"I killed them," Dav said, "but there are more coming. Lockwood and the surrounding settlements are under attack. We need to leave."

"Of course, just let me…" she trailed off. Let her what? There was surely nothing left she could retrieve from the burning house. Her clothes, her guitar, her cookery—everything she owned was gone except for the few items still, thank the Goddess, in the back of the cart. Within one harrowing hour, it had all been erased from the world.

"Do you have saddles for the mules?" Dav asked.

She shook her head. "We've only ever used them to pull the cart."

"Well, today you'll ride them, bareback."

They hurried back to the cart to unhitch the animals, passing the bodies of the other Uthiri on the way. Gooter and Gus were unharmed and standing next to Druid. Ameryn retrieved her treasures, and Dav assured her there was room for them in his saddlebags.

"I was out in the wild when I came across them," Dav said. "I tried to get to town first to warn everyone, but they were too far ahead of me. When a contingent group joined them, I realized they'd already sent detachments to the outer settlements. I rode here as fast as I could."

Ameryn's mind was processing things slowly. She heard him, and she nodded but didn't think to respond until after a long pause. "Yes, of course," she said, before realizing that wasn't a correct response to what he'd said anyway.

"I'll do what I can about your wounds—but only quickly for now—then I'm afraid we'll have to move on."

"Where?" Ameryn asked. *And what does he mean about my wounds?* she wondered and then remembered all at once—her head, her cheek. She prodded them, and her hands came away bloody. Shouldn't she feel more pain?

"We can figure that out later," Daverell said, retrieving a cloth and some bandages from his saddlebags. He dampened the cloth with his canteen and began cleaning her face.

"I think I killed one," Crow announced.

"You found the dagger," Dav surmised.

"I swam to the bottom, and it was suddenly there, the grip in my hand. I'll give it back to you."

Daverell went from cleaning Ameryn to bandaging her. Without turning to Crow, he said, "No, I threw it away and you found it, it's yours now. Did you keep the scabbard?"

"It was in the house," Crowan said sadly. "I think I killed one of them," the boy repeated. "I was so angry."

"It's as good as I can manage right now." Dav addressed Ameryn this time. "It's not much, just field dressing."

Dav helped her up into the saddle of his sturdy charger, while he and Crow rode on the mules. Ameryn watched her little cabin collapse in the inferno as she rode away.

The fire had caught up to her again.

In the end, it always would.

CHAPTER 8

A NAMELESS PLACE

Somewhere in the Gray Mountains

It was hard not to whimper with every step. Her back was agony. Ollett assured her they were getting closer. Pellary shared his eyes and couldn't see a path or any landmarks he was following, but he trudged forward with confidence.

She was tempted to adopt the man's senses longer but didn't dare. Her training had been full of warnings and stories of Embrells escaping the full effects of some injury or illness by connecting to another person only to be further harmed—or even die—as a result of ignoring their own body's warning signs. Some even believed natural healing processes were stunted or confused when the mind was assailed with mixed signals. Not that she could escape her body completely. She always felt at least a whisper of the pain.

When she risked another peek, she saw, stretching before them, a stunning view of the canyon. She had not realized they'd climbed so high.

After another scramble up a steep incline, they stood in a relatively round and shallow bowl. It was enclosed by a natural stone border, supplemented with boulders and constructed walls anywhere that didn't span or rise far enough. Before them and down the center of the space was a neat path leading to an ancient, but well maintained stone building.

As they walked toward it, Pellary noticed six greenhouses, three on either side of the path.

"Are those lidocrafted greenhouses?" Maiyen asked.

"All your questions will be answered soon," Ollett said.

The path ended at the entrance to the main structure. Pellary wasn't sure what to make of it. It was too small to be considered a proper castle, but it also didn't appear to be a church or abbey. At least, it didn't conform to any of the traditional layouts she was familiar with. However, it did boast tall turrets on all corners of its crenelated walls. The style of architecture matched the very oldest sections of the Pyressa Abbey, those built before the emergence of the classic styles most associated with the Church. Despite what was obviously a considerable effort to care for the building, it bore the signs of age everywhere. The crenelations were chipped and rough. Metal frames around the windows were thick with rust. Brighter, newer mortar had patched cracks in the brickwork, and, on the roofs, new wood shakes replaced old ones. Countless rainstorms had produced long stains running from each corbel. The steps leading to the front entry doors were worn down and polished with centuries of use. There were sections where Pellary found it difficult to discern where the original, mountainous stone ended and the cut stones began. Looking at it filled her with the same acute sense of dread that had been her and

Maiyen's constant companion since entering the pass.

A woman in Iress robes, perhaps a decade older than Pellary, opened the door and ran to them.

"Ollett!" she said, wearing a wide grin on her round face. "They've arrived."

"Yes," he stated to her before turning to them. "I'll leave you with Iress Rin." He bowed to all three women before leaving them.

"How exciting," Iress Rin proclaimed. "We've been waiting for you. Your names?"

Maiyen and Pellary introduced themselves.

"I'll take you to Iress Lee right away," Rin said. "She's the Matriarch here. Are there any injuries that need immediate attention first? I'm a Curial. Oh, you may share my sight, of course."

They did so and saw she was holding the door wide for them to enter. As they stepped inside, Maiyen answered her question, "Novitiate Pellary sustained a terrible injury to her back from...something."

"A demon," clarified Pellary.

"Oh dear, demon-inflicted injuries ain't chicken scratches. Even a small one will kill you without a Curial's healing. It's a good thing you got here when you did. I can stop the bleeding for now, but you'll need more attention later. Come over by the window."

The Iress pulled an elegant Restorative from her robes. She manipulated the cylindrical collection of rotating rings and hinged arms— pulling out a lens here, tucking in a stencil there—and spread the sunlight into an array of patterns and holy runes that she repeatedly ran over Pellary's back. The wounds closed beneath the hypnotizing dance of light. Pellary returned to her own senses, enjoying the feeling of the pain disappearing.

"There," Iress Rin said, "that'll do for now."

"Thank you," Pellary murmured before drawing attention to Maiyen's foot.

The Curial performed a cursory healing on it as well. "I'll give you both proper attention in the infirmary, but Iress Lee will want to see you before that."

Pellary connected with the healing Iress again as she led them into the gloomy interior of the building. They meandered through shadowy passages with only flickering candles on the walls to light their way.

The place was almost deserted. Other than a smoky gray cat that eyed them passively from a corner, they passed only one other person as they walked. A woman, much closer to their own age, sat on a bench in an arched niche cut into the wall. She was reading a book and looked up to watch them. Rin didn't acknowledge the woman as they passed, but Maiyen gave her a small wave and smile. The woman with the book didn't return the gesture.

Iress Rin led them to an aged wooden door and gave it a polite knock. After a brief moment the door opened, and an old woman poked her tired and resolute face through the gap. She was about to say something when her eyes fastened on the two novitiates, and her eyebrows shot up so high they nearly disappeared behind the hem of her hood.

"Goddess above! Can it be?" she exclaimed.

Iress Rin laughed with delight. "These are novitiates Maiyen and Pellary. Ollett only just arrived with them."

"Earlier than we expected." The old woman closed her eyes and sighed. "I'm so happy you made it. You're very much needed here. I'm sure you're bursting with questions, unless Iress Rin here has already told you everything."

"Me? Not a word," Rin said.

"The Goddess provides miracles every day, Sisters," Iress Lee declared. "Novitiates, please." She stepped aside. "You may share my sight, of course."

They entered a small room with a desk at one end. It was brighter than the corridors, having one window that let in cool, natural light. Iress Lee sat at the desk and invited Maiyen and Pellary to take the other two seats in the room as she poured them each a glass of water from a pitcher on her desk.

Once they were all seated and the novitiates had drained the cups,

Iress Lee ran a Restorative over their faces. "Your seals are intact. Ankr Pass is a pitiless nightmare to navigate. To do so blind is quite an achievement. I congratulate you on having completed the physical trial of the Nimara Path. Now, tell me a little about yourselves."

Pellary and Maiyen introduced themselves more thoroughly. The old woman interviewed them, eager to learn about their education. Everything they said pleased the woman. Pellary found it all quite odd. They were clearly expected, yet no one seemed to know anything about them.

"Excellent," the Iress Matriarch remarked when she was satisfied she'd learned enough. "Pellary, well on your way to being a demonology scholar, and Maiyen, uncommonly gifted in the famously difficult skill of reading intention beyond the senses. The Jophrat Seat made the perfect selection in you two."

"Thank you, Iress Lee," Pellary said. "But selection for what? What is it you do here? I've never heard of this abbey."

"Indeed, there are precisely twenty-one people in all the world who know of this place. The Jophrat Seat himself, the eighteen people stationed here, and now you two. It has no name. Appears on no map. There is no record of it anywhere. Even the Jophrat, while aware of its existence, is ignorant of its exact location."

"Why?" Pellary asked in a shocked gasp.

"That has to do with your task here. I'm sure it can wait until after you've cleaned yourselves up, had a good meal and a sound night's sleep."

Pellary shook her head. "I'd much rather know now."

"As would I," Maiyen agreed.

The woman's gaze passed from one to the other. Pellary could feel her studying them.

"Are you certain?" she asked.

They assured her they were.

After another pause, the Matriarch said quietly, "In that case, listen to me very, very carefully. We, all of us here, are tasked with a mission of the utmost importance and secrecy: to kill a demon."

There was silence after this was spoken. No one seemed to know what to say at first.

"But," Maiyen said, "in the pass, we were attacked by something. That man, Ollett, killed it."

"I'm relieved you survived such an encounter. The lesser demons are powerful and wicked creatures. The thing we have here, however, is..." She rose to her feet. "I think it may be easier to show you. Yes, it's always easier to get the shock over with quickly. I'll take you to see it—and I mean really *see* it. Novitiates, at some point, I will ask you to remove your blindfolds."

"Remove...but Matriarch, we've not yet been Raised!" Maiyen gasped.

"No, you have not," she agreed. "This will, unfortunately, only be the first breach of common practices you'll experience at this place. Leave them in place for now, and please, follow me."

Moments later, Maiyen hurried behind the Matriarch down a narrow corridor. The walls of cut stone became walls carved out of natural rock. The hall ended at a steep stairway that curved slightly to the right as it led downwards. Despite a few evenly spaced, flickering candles mounted to the wall, the stairs disappeared into a thick blackness. Iress Lee produced a candle from her pocket and lit it.

"Remove your blindfolds."

Maiyen did as instructed with trembling hands. She opened her eyes slowly, almost *feeling*—as a vibrating and physical sensation—the light pour into them. Her eyes. Her very own eyes freely seeing for the first time in what seemed like forever. She and Pellary looked at each other for what was, in a way, the first time. They blinked and offered each other nervous grins. Maiyen wished she could stop and enjoy the moment.

"Very good. Now, watch your step," the Matriarch warned in a whisper.

The space only allowed for a single file descent. Pellary followed the Iress Matriarch, and Maiyen was last in line. The old woman was taking each step one at a time, one hand holding the candle aloft, the other lifting her robes out of the way of her feet. Even at this unhurried pace, Maiyen was out of breath. Her unease stole the air away before her lungs had their fill.

There was no sound in the passage but their own scraping, tentative footfalls. They echoed in a subtle way that made Maiyen sure someone was behind her. She glanced back and saw only darkness. They'd gone far enough that, with the curve of the stairs, she could no longer see the hallway above. Nothing but roughly hewn stairs behind her and the same ahead. It made her feel isolated and trapped. As though running in either direction would only lead to more stairs.

Before long, however, they came to the bottom. The three huddled together on a small landing with a single door. The door was constructed with the most ornate lidocrafting she'd ever seen. The metal embellishments of holy designs were artfully inlaid on every inch of the thick wood. It was old and significant, like a sacred artifact. Maiyen couldn't even guess at the exorbitant price something like this might have cost, nor the years it might have taken to build. As she drew closer, however, she noticed it was being eaten away by some sort of malignant decay. It didn't appear to be rust, but she couldn't say what it was, something black and infectious. It made her shiver to see so foul a thing eating away at something so profoundly beautiful.

The Iress Matriarch produced a key with her free hand and unlocked the door. "If you feel sick, please vomit directly onto the floor. It's cleaned regularly. Don't touch anything or let anything touch you. Stay close to me." She set the candle she was holding on a small shelf before unlatching the door and hefting it to the side.

The feeling of evil that permeated the place spilled out from the room beyond and hit Maiyen like an ocean wave. As though fighting the current of it, she trudged into the room. There was no doubt in her mind that this was the source of what they'd felt all the way back when they'd first entered Ankr Pass.

Beyond the entryway she found a round chamber roughly fifty paces across. It was well lit by a collection of candles and braziers. The walls, floor, ceiling—in fact nearly *all* surfaces—were covered in a tight network of sacred runes. Some were carved, some were crafted of various materials, all bore the same decay that the door did. However, it wasn't the space but the horrific scene playing out within it that seized all her attention, filling her senses like spiders crawling into an open wound.

There were six stone tables in the room, each bearing a severed body part of some monstrous, but still vaguely human-looking, creature. Two tables for the legs, two more for the arms, one in the center holding the torso, and the last one for the thing's head. Each piece of the form before them had been strapped down. All were twitching with movement. From each bloody, hacked-off section grew searching, rope-like tendrils that writhed like worms. The thin, veiny tentacles seemed to be reaching for each other, trying to reconnect the body.

There were six people in the room. They glanced up when she, Pellary, and Lee entered but didn't watch them for long. Everyone was busy. Two men wearing blood-soaked gloves and aprons moved from table to table. Maiyen watched one cleave the little wriggling worms in two with a large knife and sweep the ends into a wooden box he carried. From each stump of the body, and even more so from the newly cut tendrils, spurted and seeped dark red blood that pooled on the tabletops before cascading down the edges and draining into a series of grates built into the floor.

Maiyen identified two Iress among the workers. They also wore stained aprons and gloves. One was working on an arm. It had been sliced open, and the woman was peering into the cut, making a note of something with a pencil. She had a cart next to her holding small vials of viscous liquids and various knives and saws. The other was replacing candles that had burned low and coordinating the efforts of the last two workers in the room: the cleaners. They were scrubbing and washing the blood away. One took the full box of severed tendrils from the butcher and emptied the contents into a furnace at the opposite end of the room. The flames turned a sickly yellow-green, and the smell of burning flesh mingled with the already potent mix of putrid odors in the room. Maiyen guessed that was at least one reason why everyone was wearing a mask over their mouth and nose.

The creature itself, whatever *it* was—the torso was bare of any genitalia—was much larger than an average human. She imagined if it were put back together and stood on its feet, it would be eight or nine feet tall. The veiny skin was a pale, dead, gray-blue color that subtly shifted as it pulsed with life. The skin was secreting some sort of slime that gave it a sickly sheen. They were closest to the legs, and Maiyen saw each toe ended in a curved talon. She couldn't see the thing's face from where she stood, and even if she were closer, there appeared to be a lidocrafted helmet over most of its head as well as straps in place over its eyes and mouth.

Maiyen was so engrossed by the sight that she didn't feel her body's reaction until, all at once, her churning stomach pushed its meager contents out onto the floor. When she whirled away from the scene, she felt nothing *but* her reaction. Every shred of her was bursting with repulsion and trembling terror.

Maiyen glanced at Pellary. She'd not vomited, but all the color had drained from her face. Her wide eyes were still hypnotized by what they were seeing. She then turned to the Iress Matriarch, whose gaze was not on the alarming scene in the room but on them. She wore an expression of concern and pity under a mask of determination.

"I think that's enough for now," she declared, reopening the door.

Maiyen bolted out of the room and ran up the stairs in such a frenzy she tripped multiple times, scrambling to her feet again and continuing her mad dash. Needing to escape, to get outside, to be anywhere else.

3

Pellary and Iress Lee found Maiyen outside in one of the greenhouses. She was facing away from them, sitting on the ground, her head in her hands.

"Maiyen," Iress Lee said gently.

The trembling girl shrank from the Matriarch's voice as if it were ice. Iress Lee addressed her again, and Maiyen suddenly jumped to her feet, turning to face the old woman. "What in the holy name of the Goddess did I just see? Nearly the first time using my own eyes in more than four years and you show me *that*?"

Pellary ran to stand next to Maiyen.

The old Iress turned from them, picking green beans and dropping them into a basket she'd retrieved from near the door. "Help me, won't you?"

They didn't move, only watched her. "It's one of the great demons, an old-world devil. A living relic from the Age of Legends. Long ago now, when the Church and monarchy were indistinguishable from each other, the knights of the Tar Ishik purges discovered and captured it. They tried for years to kill the thing, and over time, their efforts have become our mission."

"You're trying...to *kill* it?" Maiyen asked.

"We are, yes. We don't yet know how," Iress Lee answered. "When it was discovered that this might be a problem that would take decades and a whole team to solve, this mountain fortress was built and fitted to that purpose."

"And that is now our task as well?" Maiyen assumed bitterly. "The task we must achieve before being allowed to leave?"

The woman nodded.

"And how long have you been trying to kill it?" Pellary asked.

Here, Iress Lee met their eyes. "More than three hundred years."

Maiyen broke into fresh tears.

110

"Maiyen," Lee said, "I know this is quite a lot—"

"You *don't* know," Maiyen spat. "We killed two men on our way here."

"You...what?" Iress Lee stammered, ashen-faced. "Who?"

"Uthiri soldiers. We were attacked."

"Uthiri in Threya?" Iress Lee's tone was incredulous.

"Do you not even know? There is a war going on."

"There's very little communication between myself and the Jophrat, and he's not told me much about it. Only that it's happening."

"We had to defend ourselves. I...did not like it. Killing. Now you want to make me a killer as part of a *mission*? The very First Edict says, 'Do no harm to any creature under Her sight, save in most desperate defense.'" Her voice was shrill and trembling. "This is a hideous perversion of all the Goddess represents. How could you do this to us?"

"Believe me, Novitiate Maiyen, what we do *is* in desperate defense. Were this thing to walk freely again, it would plunge us, all of us, into a fresh age of horror. Threya would become a barren wasteland of death and pestilence. With so much more to feed on, the demon would cut a grisly path of wreckage throughout all the world. The rivers would burst beyond their banks from the blood spilled."

"One demon might do all that?" Maiyen asked.

"It's not only a solitary creature but a channel to the Beloworld itself." The Matriarch stopped harvesting as her eyes took on the long look of remembrance. "Three years ago, Iress Em took a piece of it out on the grounds to examine how it reacted to new sunlight patterns she'd devised. It gained enough independent strength to summon a lesser demon. I saw it with my own eyes. A lump of flesh, no bigger than a festival ham, began vibrating and grew fat, as if it were about to burst. Poor Em thought she'd made some breakthrough. Instead, in a flurry of flames, a lesser demon was birthed from it. Two men were killed before Ollett managed to destroy it. Poor Iress Em—she's still wracked with guilt over the whole affair."

"The demon was slain?"

"Lesser demons, like that one, or the one that threatened you in the pass, while fearsome and destructive, can be dispatched much as any other living creature. The thing in our basement, however, is an Elder Demon. If it gets out, not only it, but countless feral creatures it commands, will be introduced to a world that no longer knows how to combat them."

Pellary cut in. "It won't burn?"

"Parts of it do, other parts—vital parts, no matter the size and heat of the inferno—simply refuse to be consumed."

"Have you tried cutting it up into little pieces?" Pellary asked.

The Iress Matriarch glanced back from her vegetable picking, giving her a humorless smile. "Believe me, we've recorded every attempt to end its life. We've gotten quite creative over the years. I can show you the logs; they've grown very thick and numerous."

"I suppose what I'm really asking," Pellary said, "is *why* does none of that work?"

"You saw it. Did you notice the blood issuing from each individual limb? The veins pulsing with a heartbeat? If we separate any part of it from another, that part might appear dead for a while, but soon each portion develops a heart of its own, keeps itself alive and growing."

"Like a sea star?" Pellary wondered. "Each piece growing into a whole new body?"

"No, thank the Goddess. It ever remains a single entity. If it's cut into pieces, the thing's wretched soul will eventually attach itself to one of them. The others will reconnect or die."

"But how is it sustained? Where is it getting fresh blood to pump? Fuel for the energy to grow and move?" Pellary picked a few green beans herself now.

"As I said, it maintains, or is itself, some kind of conduit to the Beloworld. From that place and through that connection, it somehow pulls whatever it needs for sustenance."

"Yes, the *Lyprakarum* supports that idea," Pellary noted thoughtfully. She glanced over her shoulder and shrank a bit from Maiyen's withering gaze. In another moment, however, she turned back to the Matriarch and asked, "Why keep it dismembered like that?"

"It is subject to its own corporeal rules as we are. Much as we can't control our own heartbeat, it doesn't seem to be able to override certain physical limitations, few though they might be. Over the years, it's been discovered that if we sever each limb and keep them close to each other, they attempt to reconnect instead of growing independently. It's still exhausting work, keeping them separated, but it's the best way we've found to make it manageable. However, the Jophrat Seat who first set us on this task, and every Jophrat after, has made it very clear that our mission, yours now too, is to find a path to success. We are not to become complacent and simply maintain the situation as it is; we must find a way to kill it."

There was silence for a few breaths.

"And what part do we play in this...mission?" Maiyen breathed.

"Every one of us fills a role. The monks take care of most of the basics, but we all pitch in where we can. We have one of the most skilled lidocrafters in the kingdom to replace the designs when they break down. Three soldiers who provide us with security. As for Iress, we have two Arrantines who keep everything clean and organized—we must invite the Light of the Goddess to this place as much as we can. Two Curials who do most of the research on the demon and introduce new threats to its life. Myself, I run things and newly sanctify the water beneath the basement room that all the foul blood drains into. And now we have you two who, I regret to say, have the most dangerous job of all of us, in many ways."

"Truly?" Pellary asked.

"Yes, you two must connect with it. Live in its head and search its mind. Discern its intentions. Our unkillable demon is a cunning thing. I was not gifted with the Sight myself, but past Embrells have said it's even harder to read than people or most animals. It has subtle ways of manipulation. You must be ever on your guard against it. It will try to use you to get what it wants."

"You want us to tell you what it's going to do?" Maiyen gaped at the Matriarch.

"Precisely," the old woman nodded. "You two will be instrumental in ensuring nothing like the close call we had three years back happens again. Warn us of its plans. The peace and welfare of all Threya depends on what we do here."

"Yet we're denied our Raising?"

"No," Iress Lee said quickly. "I told you; we do things differently here. If you accept the mission, you will be Raised and considered a full Iress in equal standing with the rest of us."

"When?" Maiyen demanded.

"As early as tomorrow," Iress Lee said. "However, it won't be quite the celebration it usually is. We're almost entirely self-sufficient and cut off from everything here."

"Almost?" Maiyen asked.

"Breek, our mute monk, takes a hidden road to Epiraff once every few months to procure some of the materials we cannot produce here. He delivers some very limited correspondence between the Jophrat Seat and myself, but that is truly the only connection we have. Which brings me to what may be the hardest news I have for you." She sighed, studying them both before continuing. "You are effectively dead to the outside world. You may never see, nor even write a letter, to your loved ones outside this abbey ever again. Unless our mission is fulfilled, of course. I'm so sorry. We agree to give our lives to the Goddess when we become novitiates. We rarely expect that gift to be so consuming as it is for those of us here."

Pellary said, "There were always rumors of those who walked the Nimara Path in Ankr Pass never returning; I suppose we know why now, Maiyen."

Because they die, Maiyen despaired in silent bitterness. *Like you. Like me.*

But this is an important task we have, came Pellary's answering thought. *A chance to change the world as we always hoped.*

From an ugly, isolated mountaintop that makes us feel sick, Maiyen countered.

The Iress Matriarch continued in response to their last out-loud words, "The bleak rumors of this place are something we indulge, not

114

that most people need a reason to stay away from such a miserable spot."

"We might have died before we got here," Maiyen huffed. "Yet you claim to need us."

"Others would have been sent if you hadn't survived the journey," Iress Lee said matter-of-factly. "The secret of this location is worth the risk to all our lives."

"What if I refuse?" Maiyen challenged. "If I don't participate in the mission, what happens to me?"

"When I told you there were no other Embrells here, it wasn't entirely true. Bryn is an Embrell novitiate who has made that very decision. She refuses to accept our mission or help us achieve it. She lives here, but it's a diminished, selfish life. One I urge you not to imitate."

"If she were to try to escape from this place?" Maiyen framed the question, but before the old woman could say anything she continued. "No, don't answer; I can see it in your mind. She would be killed, as would Pellary or I."

"Or me, Maiyen. Or me," Iress Lee stated. "Ollett and his men have uncompromising orders on this point." She paused. "You weren't exaggerating about your skill."

Maiyen looked away.

"It is entirely proper for you to grieve the life the Church has stolen from you. It is unfair. I felt the same way when I came here. I had a family, a son. I was a Curial, trained to heal, looking forward to a life full of helping people. I felt tricked into this place and resented it for a long time.

"But please, Sisters, don't focus on the unfortunate circumstances we live under here. There is much to love about our lives. We share a powerful bond, united in this fight against the Dark. This is a chance to fight, really fight, for the Goddess. Beyond that, we've all adopted enriching pastimes, and we teach each other new skills. It is not the life I would have chosen for myself, but it *is* a life worth living and loving."

"What about the oppressive atmosphere hanging over everything here, how do you live with that?" Maiyen asked.

"That is a challenge, for you Embrells more than the rest of us, sensitive as you are to the internal world. We all feel it, but it's more acute for you two."

"Is it the reason for all the lidocrafting throughout this place?" Pellary asked.

"Yes, it's all been built to contain the evil the demon exudes. Nothing but weeds would grow in these garden boxes without the lidocrafted cages surrounding them. The rooms have some extra protection, especially your quarters. Beyond that, you will get used to it, build a natural defense against it. We all have."

"The *Lyprakarum* speaks of the holy weapon, the Illumed Blade," Pellary mentioned. "Capable of destroying such a being, unless I misunderstand the words."

"You know your pagan scriptures well. It does indeed speak of such a thing." Iress Lee paused before leaning towards them. "It's here. The weapon it speaks of. A gleaming, glorious masterwork upon which all lidocrafted art is based. A gift from the realm of Light itself."

"Where?"

"Under lock and key, in a location only I know of. The faintest touch to it means death to all. Except the chosen one and the damned creature."

"But I thought—" Pellary started.

"Many attempts have been made on the monster's life with the Blade while holding it through protective coverings, but to no avail. It is only effective if wielded by the one the *Lyprakarum* speaks of, it would seem," Iress Lee said. "If such a one exists at all. Years ago, there was a young man who believed he matched the description outlined in the *Lyprakarum*. His claim was convincing enough he was brought here by an emissary of the Jophrat Seat. I've never seen such a breech in the privacy of this place before or since that day."

"What happened?" Pellary asked with intense interest.

"It...didn't work," Iress Lee remarked.

"May I see it?" Pellary inquired.

116

"No, I'm afraid you cannot. If you can think of a new way to use it, which itself would be quite a feat, it might—*might*—be allowable."

"There's something else I think you should know," Pellary said. "The Uthiri claim to be searching for their god, Vulsipher, who they say we've imprisoned somewhere within our borders."

The Iress Matriarch went pale and dropped the basket. "What? No. This is...the worst possible news. No one is supposed to know."

"So, the thing in the basement...?" Pell let the question hang.

The Matriarch nodded. "Is Vulsipher, yes. How could this have happened? All our precautions. How?" She fell to her knees and began putting the spilled beans back into the basket. "No, no, no" she repeated, again and again, clearly devastated.

"What does this mean?" Pell peered intently at her.

"It means...it *might* mean that we have a traitor here. Someone clever. They somehow discovered how to get word out, and all the way to the Uthiri...but that's impossible."

"The Uthiri claimed it was something they'd long suspected," Pellary said. "Might it be a coincidence? Nothing more than justification for their true aim in this war?"

"It's possible, but I'm afraid we need to proceed as if that is not the case. Do not speak a word of this to anyone else."

"I can explore the matter," Pellary volunteered.

"You will be very busy," the Matriarch said. "I can't have you distracted by an investigation."

"But—"

"*I* will look into this matter. You two will keep your minds focused on your vital part of our mission here. If, indeed, I can count on you to accept this mission and help us fulfill it?"

"Yes, I will," Pellary said.

Maiyen looked from one to the other. Pellary could sense in her a desire to scream, to run away, to do anything but what she eventually did: bow her head in heartbroken defeat and mutter, "Yes, Matriarch. What choice do I have?"

PART 2

CHAPTER 9

SILVER HILLS

Silver Hills

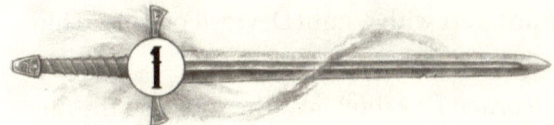

Silver Hills was the largest town on the frontier south of Red Chapel and was apparently worthy of the Crown's protection. There were soldiers posted at the gates and atop watchtowers. Daverell entered the city along with throngs of displaced refugees. He stayed deeply under the hood of his cloak and exaggerated his limp as he shambled into town. No one recognized him, especially without Druid. He'd ridden one of the mules to the gates before leading the animal through. They didn't attract a second glance among the crowds. The soldiers hadn't even asked for his identifying papers. Apparently, not being Uthiri was all it took to get into the city at the moment.

The first thing he learned was that the great Red Chapel Cathedral had been destroyed. Silver Hills was buzzing with the news, and Daverell found it as disturbing as anyone. The jewel of the Saerisian Church, gone. It cast a shadow over the already tense atmosphere.

After some asking around, Daverell was able to locate a wealthy weapons collector. The man insisted on taking Daverell through his prolific collection before even hearing Daverell's offer. When the canvas was pulled back from the blade Daverell was selling, the man nearly collapsed with shock. He'd never dreamed he might own one of the priceless daggers forged by Lagrim of Pyressa, the greatest of all Threyan bladesmiths. It took a fair bit of convincing on Daverell's part before the man believed it was both genuine and not stolen. Before long, however, Daverell left with a much heavier coin purse than he'd arrived with.

The man paid less than a quarter of the blade's true worth, but it was still enough to buy two saddles, plenty of rations, and two practical blades, along with a couple of wooden swords for practice. There was even a fair bit left over, despite every shopkeeper inflating their prices due to the war and influx of refugees.

After making the last of his purchases, Daverell returned to the streets of Silver Hills. It felt good to be well and truly rid of that accursed dagger. Crow wouldn't part with it until Daverell promised him something better in its place.

These won't fill that tall order, Dav thought as he strapped the new swords to the mule's back, *but I know of one blade that most certainly will.* There were very few people in all the Midlands that knew the Sword of Light was real. Even fewer who knew where it was. Dav was a part of both groups. *If it's the last thing I do with my worthless hide, I'll see that perfect weapon in the boy's hands.*

By the time Daverell left Silver Hills, his shadow was quite a bit longer than it had been when he'd arrived. Getting out of the city proved a bigger challenge than getting in. He was the one and only person exiting, and the soldiers stopped him.

"You sure you want to leave the city's protection, old-timer?" a man asked him. "It ain't forbidden but hardly advisable."

"Thank you," Dav said. "I'll be back before nightfall."

The young soldier didn't say any more, but Dav doubted he was convinced. He'd have noticed the generous supplies strapped to the mule's saddle.

The sun was just beginning to drop behind the tops of the distant Gray Mountains when Daverell returned to camp. Crow already had a fire going in a small pit. He'd placed rocks around it that were large enough to hide it from a distance.

"I did it just like you showed me," Crow declared.

"That's as fine a job as I've ever seen, Crow," Daverell compliment-ed. Ameryn was sitting at the base of a tree, facing away from them. "Mrs. Vowery," he called to her. She jumped at the sound but didn't turn. "The Goddess is making a real painting of the sky tonight, and I think we've got as good a view of it as any. There's a herd of buffalo on the move. The sun's turning their dust to fire. You really should see it."

She didn't stir.

"Were you able to sell my dagger?" Crowan asked.

"I was indeed," Daverell said, pulling the wasters free of Druid's back and showing them to Crow. Daverell might have been holding blades of grass judging from the look on the boy's face.

"Those ain't much better than that branch I found," Crow grum-bled.

"Just to practice with," Dav laughed, "until you're ready for this one." He pulled a finely forged blade from its scabbard and displayed it for Crow.

The boy studied it. "It looks like it's meant for someone more my size."

"Yes, but it'll probably still take some getting used to." Daverell held the hilt invitingly out to him. Crow took it and swung it around. "Oh, and there was some money left over." Daverell tossed the boy the bag of coins.

He barely caught it with his already-full hands. "It's heavy," Crow said with a smile.

The sight gave Daverell heart. Crow had been nervous and emotional in the days following the attack on his homestead, but glimpses of his old self were starting to return. Ameryn was another matter.

After setting a pot of beans and water over the fire, Daverell walked over to her, the other sword in his hand.

"Mrs. Vowery?" he spoke to her drooping back. "We've a spare blade here."

She turned to regard him.

"Seeing as how, earlier today, you granted me permission to teach the boy, I wondered if you wouldn't want to learn as well?"

"Yes," she said, accepting the blade and inspecting it in the firelight. There was resolve in her face. Cold as winter iron. Dav decided that was a good thing.

A short time later, the pot began bubbling. Daverell was no cook, but he had prepared enough meals on the road as to not embarrass himself. He added another generous sprinkling of salt before replacing the lid.

While the food simmered, he unsaddled Druid and brushed the horse's coat, mane, and tail before cleaning his hooves. While he worked, Dav began quietly singing an old Threyan army song.

Our Threyan King wants soldiers,
To fight on land and sea.
Take up your sword and join us,
And march to victory.

Defend your home and nation,
And keep our foes at bay.
To win your share of glory,

Come on and join the fray.

The thrill of war, once tasted,
And earned by taking part,
Will fortify your spirit,
Will never leave your heart.

Dav didn't even finish it. He'd not sung it in a long time, and he was unprepared for how cheap and hollow the words sounded to him now. Worse than that, the last verse struck him as a threat. *The thrill of war once tasted...will never leave your heart.* He'd only started singing in hopes it might coax Ameryn to join in or start a song of her own.

She remained silent.

"Dav?" Crow said, sitting on his other side.

"Yes?" Dav faced the boy.

Crowan paused before speaking in a hesitant voice. "I was wondering...what is the Year of the Hunter?"

"The ancient Threyans counted the years in four-year cycles." He stowed Druid's brushes back in his saddlebags as he spoke. "The Hunter, the Bee, the Fish, and the Bear. The hunter fears the honeybee's sting, the bee fears being eaten by the fish, the fish fears the same from the bear, and the bear fears death at the hands of the hunter—starting it over again."

"Fish eat bees?" Crowan asked.

"A honeybee getting a drink on the water's surface is among a trout's favorite meals," Dav confirmed.

"So people were afraid of anyone born a year before them?"

"It was more about personality assumptions. If your birthday was in the Hunter's Year, you were thought to be more clever. The Bee, more hard-working. The Fish, tenacious. And the Bear, ferocious."

Crowan nodded thoughtfully.

"They used to teach this in school," Daverell continued. "I reckon they don't these days."

"Or it was on a day I wasn't paying attention," Crowan confessed.

125

"There were a lot of those."

Dav laughed as he turned to feed the fire.

"Do you really think I could be the one from the prophecy?" Crowan whispered.

"I do," Dav said, glancing at Ameryn. She remained motionless, either not listening or too tired to make a fuss. Daverell regretted the confrontational method with which he had presented her with his assumptions about her son. Assumptions that, to his mind, had been all but confirmed after the miraculous recovery of the dagger from the river. When he attempted to convince her again—and he would—he'd be gentler.

After some time, the welcome aroma of the stewing beans leaked outside the pot. Dav tested them and found them suitably tender. After tossing in some more salt and pepper, he filled three bowls. He offered a prayer of thanks to the Goddess. Crowan bowed his head, but Dav noted that Ameryn, who he'd come to regard as steadfastly faithful, did not. Crowan ate hungrily and went back for seconds before Daverell had even finished filling a bowl for the boy's mother.

He startled her again, despite his efforts not to.

"Oh, thank you." She took the food he offered. "I forgot to ask. Silver Hills, what did you think?"

"Yes, I wanted to talk to you about that," Daverell said. "It's certainly better defended than Lockwood, and they're letting people in. We could wait things out there, though I worry about resources. Even today, I paid more than double the regular price for all the supplies I bought, and the shelves were already looking mighty bare when I left. The Uthiri could swiftly destroy the town just by cutting off incoming provisions. While I was there, everyone was talking about the Red Chapel Cathedral. The Uthiri burned it to the ground."

"Truly?" she asked, wide eyed. "The cathedral," she repeated in unbelief. "How? Why? Will they leave any beauty in the world?"

"If we want to wait things out in Silver Hills—"

"No," Ameryn said. "If Red Chapel isn't safe, how could Silver Hills be? Especially if they run out of food."

126

After a pause, Daverell said carefully, "I know of a place. Safe and secret. In the mountains."

She looked at him suspiciously. "How long will it take to get there?"

"About a week, I reckon," Dav said.

She sighed, placing a hand to her head. "It seems as good a plan as any. For now."

"As you say, ma'am. We'll move out in the morning." Dav managed to hide his elation. "Oh, and how's the dinner?"

"What?"

"The beans? What do you think?" Dav asked.

She took a bite. "Pinto. I make them with onions and add some sage, maybe garlic if I've got it."

"I'll keep that in mind," he said.

The bite had apparently reminded her body of its hunger, and she continued to eat, though automatically. He wasn't sure she was aware of his presence, and he didn't care. She was eating and she had spoken to him, if only a little. It was a small victory, but those were the only ones to be had in situations like this. He took her empty bowl and traded places at the fireside with Crow, who went to his mother. Her arms folded around the boy in what was likely as natural a movement for her as the eating was.

It was under that comforting observation that he turned to stare into the flames for a spell. A sharp crack from the blazing wood sent a spray of embers upwards, where they briefly shared the sky with the eternal stars.

CHAPTER 10

ABOVE AND BELOW

The Nameless Abbey

Pellary and Maiyen knelt at the foot of the altar in the chapel.

Pellary's heart carried a wide array of colorful emotions while Maiyen's was heavy with only one. If Pellary was forced to name a feeling that overruled the others, it would be guilt. She'd never dared dream the way Maiyen did, but if she had, she might have hoped for something just like the situation she found herself in now. A secluded life with her dear friend and a fascinating subject to explore together. But the fact that these circumstances brought Maiyen such pain stole the pleasure. It seemed wrong to be happy.

128

"Novitiate Maiyen, born Maiyen of Ariat of Porth Arth, Threya," spoke Iress Lee from the other side of the altar, "and novitiate Pellary, born Pellary of Olk of Knatalar, Uthir."

The guilt sharpened to a sudden pang. She wasn't connected to Maiyen at that moment but knew her friend would feel at least a little betrayed that she'd never known Pellary's origins. Pellary had revealed it to no one save the Matriarch this very morning as a part of her Iress interview.

"They kneel now, before these gathered Iress and the Goddess above, having learned the ways of Saint Embrell and followed the steps of the Prophet Jophrat upon the Nimara Path. They have been judged worthy by the Church to become full Iress. To join our Sisterhood in service to the Goddess by, in their turn, serving all who dwell over the world of Shadows beneath us and under the realm of Light above."

Here, Iress Lee paused and Pellary heard some faint rustling as two Saercandles were lit. This part was different for each discipline. Embrells had simply to remove their blindfolds and look upon the flame before blowing it out. Arrantines extinguished their own handcrafted Saercandle. Pellary had read that Opravics used to sing the flame out with the breath of their voice. Curials were the most unlike the others; they had to *light* the candle by focusing sunlight through a Restorative before also blowing it out.

"Remove your blindfolds," Iress Lee said.

Pellary untied the covering over her eyes and stared at the Saercandle before her. Holy designs had been molded into the pure beeswax. The wick at its center was infused with substances that made the flame burn a brilliant white, meant to mimic the Light of the Goddess. Once Pellary drank her fill of the sight, she blew out the candle. The flame lived in her now. A servant of the Goddess.

Pellary turned to smile at Maiyen, but Maiyen remained facing forward, tears in her eyes.

"Rise now as servants of the Eternal Mother, Iress...?"

"Mai," Maiyen said in a small voice.

"And Iress...?" The old woman motioned to Pellary.

"Pell," she said, having chosen the single syllable version of her name years ago when her training had begun.

They rose together and faced the small gathering of witnesses behind them. There were only four additional Sisters in the chapel, but the other women did their best to make it a rousing celebration.

An hour later, the two new Iress sat alone in the dining hall.

"I'm sorry, Mai," Pell said.

Mai only looked back. For once, the more silent of the two.

"Do you not want to talk to me because…I'm Uthiri?" Pell asked, afraid of the answer.

"No. No, I just…I thought we were close."

"We are," Pell assured her. "Close as sisters."

"Then why did you not tell me?" Mai asked.

"I'm not sure," Pell said. "It's not as if I grew up there. I don't remember it at all. I was just a baby when my family fled the country."

"Why?"

Pell took a deep breath before answering. "Please keep this just between us," she whispered. "My grandmother was an Embrell, though in Uthir they called them Porsheks, the Uthiri word for 'listener.' They employ the Sight differently than we do in Threya, but it's the same gift. She was uncommonly talented and served in the royal court under the previous king and even helped raise his son, Orugos, the current king. Orugos, even in his youth, was sinful and arrogant. A religious zealot who reveled in chaos and suffering."

"I'm afraid I've been raised to believe that an apt description for any and all Uthiri," Mai said apologetically.

"I know it seems that way to a Threyan," Pell said. "But most Uthiri are good people. They've been raised to fear and respect the Dark, but with no understanding of the Light. The opposite of the Threyans, who, I believe, have an imbalance the other way. If the Uthiri weren't held back by the corrupt royal family, they would be a great nation.

"When he was a young man, Orugos forced himself upon one of the court attendants who worked under my grandmother. She came upon the act as it was happening, drawn by the girl's screams. My grandmother threatened to expose Orugos's crime. He just laughed and, right then and there, killed the attendant. Stabbed her in the heart with a dagger as my grandmother watched. Even had he not, the word of two women, especially against someone of the royal family, is worth very little in Uthir. My grandmother alone didn't stand a chance. Based on nothing more than his word, she was accused of the murder he committed, and the court soldiers sought to execute her for it.

"She and my parents took me and fled, seeking refuge in Threya. They eventually settled in Fullina. The forests there are similar to the ones in Uthir. It felt like home. When I showed promise at being a Porshek, my grandmother was overjoyed. She had always wanted a student from her family, and so she became my eager teacher. I learned much about the old ways and mostly forgotten magic"

"How did you end up joining our faith?" Mai asked, petting the cat that had leaped onto the bench next to her. She and Pell had learned his name was Mr. Drizzle—but most called him Drizzy.

"When I was fourteen, we were visiting the Red Chapel Cathedral as a family. My father was always interested in architecture, and its reputation was well known, even in Uthir. I'll never forget it."

Mai nodded. "Yes, it is—*was* incredible."

"I never thought anything could be so beautiful. I visit it in my mind every night as I fall asleep. I've never been so in love with a place. The sacred vibrations are in the very air."

"I see why you were so upset when we heard it had been destroyed."

Pell smiled sadly. "I heard, with my heart, the voice of the Goddess there. She called me by name. Whispered that she had a Path for me to walk. I set myself upon it that day and haven't looked back since. Well, maybe once or twice, in sorrow, at my family. They disowned me when I told them. My grandmother wouldn't even say goodbye."

"Oh Pella—Pell, I'm sorry," Mai said.

"I left home and found a place working in the Oberon Abbey until I was old enough, and found to be talented enough, to train in Pyressa. While in Oberon, I received a letter from my family, wanting to reconcile. I was overjoyed until, that same day, word came to me that assassins from Uthir, hired by Orugos himself, had tracked down and slaughtered them."

"That's awful. How have you never shared this with me?"

"I hardly like thinking about it, let alone talking about it."

Mai placed a sympathetic hand on Pell's arm, and they stayed like that for a moment before Pell spoke again.

"My service to the Goddess has only led to increase. Initially, I lost my family because of it, but if I'd remained with them, there's a good chance I would not be alive today. And since then, I've gained a dear friend in you and even, in this place, a new home and purpose. I know you feel the opposite. Your service feels like it's only taken from you, and things have turned out so differently than you wanted them to. But please, Mai, let's try to make something new of ourselves here, as Iress."

"You've never opened up to me like this," Mai reflected. "It gives me strength. Perhaps this is only a temporary hardship and, though I don't know how, I can find my own way to home and purpose."

"I will help you," Pell said, "any way I can."

"I'll do the same," Mai promised back.

The sound of approaching footsteps. They looked up to see the Iress Matriarch enter from the hall.

"Well, Iress Mai and Pell," she said. "It's time to begin."

Forcing her feet, Mai entered the cellar room at the bottom of the stairs. At least Pell was with her. The Matriarch allowed them to serve their first session together. After this, they would do so separately.

Iress Mai decided—as was her privilege now—to wear her blind-fold while performing her duties. She was determined to never see the lower room again. She wore a mask over her mouth and nose which helped on the assault to her other senses. Worst of all was the palpable misery, thick in the room, and there was no escape from that.

Mai allowed herself to be led by Pell, whose eyes remained uncovered, until they were in front of the thing's head. Mai cast her mind before her and saw its consciousness. The little spark of life looked hardly different from any other. Only a little amplified by the helmet surrounding it. The ornate metal had been lidocrafted in a way to enhance, instead of restrict, the flow of Light.

You ready? Pell asked.

I suppose so, Mai replied.

Let's just get a taste, Pell said. *We can talk about what we find after we've disconnected—don't communicate with me while it can listen in.*

They reached out together and made contact. With the help of the helmet, it was so easy. And the creature did not resist the bonding. It seemed indifferent to the Embrells. Mai had been expecting something similar to the creature they'd encountered in the pass, chaotic and angry. Instead, she found a distant, colorless void. It was as if she were adrift on a vast, impassive ocean with no hint of land in any direction. No stars by which she might gain her bearings. Nothing to even provide a sense of the familiar. She was lost within something vast and unknowable.

For once, finding her way back out was harder than finding her way in. She had to intentionally retrace her steps, following a thin and flickering line back to herself.

Mai, finally. Pell's relieved awareness entered her mind.

How long was I connected? Mai asked.

It must have been nearly ten minutes.

Really? Mai was shocked. *I didn't realize...*

I don't blame you, Pell said. *One could definitely get lost in there.*

Yes, Mai agreed.

They discussed their findings, which were essentially identical, though Pell compared it to being lost in an expansive and strange forest. They made a few more exploratory voyages into the thing's head and, by the end of their time there, Mai was all but convinced there was no way to do what was asked of them. The thing was impenetrable. Pell shared her assessment.

How can we read what it's planning when there's nothing there to observe? Pell wondered. *I could detect no line of reasoning, no thought at all. No emotions. Nothing.*

I think I was beginning to at least feel anchored, Mai said as they left. *Though now that I say that, I'm not sure what I mean by it.*

The Matriarch, who controlled all entrances and exits to the chamber, led them out, shutting the lidocrafted door behind them. Mai felt like a huge weight had been taken off her shoulders when the dark atmosphere was diminished.

I'm sure you made more progress than me, Pell said. *Perhaps you could teach me to be better at reading intention.*

There's no secret to it, Mai returned. *I think I just understand people.*

Probably not much hope for me to learn it then, Pell said as they climbed the stairs.

But we're not trying to read a person, Mai reminded Pell. *And if anyone can understand the mind of a demon, it's...* Mai trailed off, not wanting to cause offense. She removed her mask and blindfold to see Pell watching her with an amused look on her face.

At the top of the stairs, the Matriarch briefly interviewed them about their first shift in the chamber. She saw through their polite answers to their true, hopeless feelings but urged them to keep trying.

"All our Embrells have a hard time at first," she said. "Do your best. Breakthroughs may happen when you least expect them."

4

Pell convinced Mai to help her find the library.

"Iress Em told me about it," Pell said. "But she didn't tell me where it is. I thought it would be fun to search for it."

Iress Mai thought it would be much nicer to return to the baths they'd visited the day before. After visiting that cellar chamber, she could really use a cleaning, though she didn't feel *quite* as dirty as she had after going through the pass. It was a wonder what the tub of warm water and the attention of the Curials in the infirmary had done to refresh her the day before—though there was little either could do for her mood. However, there was some definite enjoyment in watching Pell peer into rooms and around corners. She clearly loved the dusty old castle.

"Here it is," she announced finally, pulling open a thick oak door banded together with iron. Stepping inside, her shoulders fell. "Not very big, is it?"

"It looks big to me," Mai said. "Just not the endless maze that the Pyressa library was."

Pell nodded and began looking over the shelves, pulling down the occasional book and flipping through it. Even smelling it sometimes.

Mai turned down a different canyon of tomes that dead-ended in a wall of volumes that coaxed a smile from her on Pell's behalf.

"Iress Pell," Mai called her over.

Mai watched Pell's face as she walked between the shelves, her eyes widening more and more as she came closer. There was one subject of which the nameless mountain abbey boasted more volumes than likely any other in the world. Before Iress Mai and the gaping Pell was the most comprehensive collection of books on demonology, witchcraft, and dark magic than either had ever seen.

"They have every volume of Sykros's *Tar Ishik History*," she exclaimed excitedly. "And *Dark Magic of the Ancient North*." She continued looking through the shelves and naming more titles Mai had never heard of, as if she were describing priceless jewelry. She gasped. "The original Uthiri translation of the *Lyprakarum!*" She hefted the thick book from the shelf and gingerly turned the pages.

"What makes this better than any other version?" Mai asked, looking over her shoulder.

"Look." Pell pointed to the words. "You can see it was copied by hand. There are famously only a few of these in existence. I've never seen one before. It's from before the Kanvaras translation—that's the version they printed. The one everyone knows."

"Aren't they the same?" Mai inquired.

"No," Pell answered. "For example." She pointed at a passage. "This preserves the original anaphoras that the Kanvaras translation eliminated to make the text more efficient and accessible."

"So...it's even *more* tedious to read?"

"More fascinating," Pell insisted.

"If you say so," Mai said. "I can tell you're going to be here a while. I think I might go enjoy another bath. I still have bits of Ankr Pass under my fingernails."

Iress Pell shut the door to her room and enjoyed the added lido-crafted protection it offered, along with the rune-etched walls. There was no better place to escape the oppressive feeling in the air.

She dropped the old copy of the *Lyprakarum* onto her table and began leafing through it. What a treasure! And Iress Lee said no one had looked at it in generations, as far as she knew. Apparently, it had been a long time since there was anyone at the abbey who understood Uthiri writing. Lee had even given Pell permission to keep it in her room. She was toying with the idea of doing her own translation into Threyan since the Threyan version was translated from the Kavaras.

Good night, Pell, Mai's thoughts drifted to her from the room on the other side of her south wall. Each of her room's walls bore runes that disrupted the flow of Light except that one. It allowed them to converse without obstacle.

Sleep well, Pell answered back.

She stayed up reading but would connect to Mai from time to time. Freed from the distractions of the day, Mai descended into despair again. She sobbed herself into a fitful sleep full of vile and horrific dreams.

While Mai was disturbed by their current situation, it was old memories that haunted Pell that night. She'd never told anyone the story of her past. It had been relegated to a corner of her mind so isolated it couldn't hurt her. Doing so had been vital for her survival. It had once dominated her thoughts. She used to spend her nights imagining what revenge she might exact on King Orugos for his betrayals. How sweet it might be to return as the last surviving member of the Olk family, whom he'd thought he'd destroyed, and deliver some equally vicious fate to him.

By the time she'd arrived at the Pyressa Abbey, she'd left such fantasies behind. Her hunger for it hadn't abated, but she was old enough to recognize the laughable absurdity of a trivial girl finding her way to one of the most important men in the world. It was a foolish dream, especially now. This may be the only bed she'd ever sleep in again.

CHAPTER 11

RANCE

The Frontier

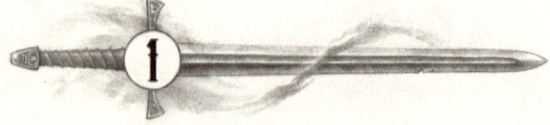

Daverell found Crowan to be an enthusiastic student. Like most beginners, he was overly focused on banging the swords against each other at first. An hour later, under Daverell's direction, he was fast improving.

Ameryn preferred to watch and listen only—for now.

The sun was fairly high before they left their campsite. The riding was much easier for the mother and son now that the mules were saddled. It would take them a few days to reach Rockmond. From there, they'd head west to the mountains.

"Someone's coming up behind us, Dav," Crow observed not long after midday.

Ameryn started. "Uthiri?" She spun around so fast she yanked on the reigns and Gooter or Gus—whichever one she was riding, Dav couldn't keep them straight—gave a whinny in protest.

"I see him," Daverell said, squinting. The figure was close enough he could make out some features. "He ain't Uthiri. Not dressed like one, at least."

Daverell waved at the man, who waved back and kicked his fine Mearethan steed into a canter to meet them.

"Hello there," the stranger called when he was close enough to be heard. "Wasn't sure I'd run into anyone today." He was a young man in a pressed shirt and dark slacks, all under a white, beaver-fur hat.

Dav called back, "What's your name, friend?"

"Rance of Berrellitt," he said, with a tip of his white hat.

"Well met, Mr. Berrellitt," Dav welcomed the man. "Name's Dav. This is the lady Ameryn of Vowery and her son, Crowan."

"Well met, Lady Vowery, Crowan, Dav," he addressed each of them in turn. "May I ride with y'all a spell? These roads get mighty lonesome."

Daverell turned to Ameryn for an answer.

"Oh," she said, "yes, of course."

"Thank you much, ma'am." Rance tipped his white hat again as he fell into pace with them. "In truth, I thought I'd be meeting a fair bit more out here than I have. There ain't enough people in the frontier to be choking the roads, of course, but with the Uthiri on the rampage, I figured more people would be trying to escape to Taggeroth."

"Most seem to be gathering in the larger cities instead of heading south. I suppose some might be on the road between Lockwood and Marker," Daverell said. "Though Lockwood was hit recently; that might be steering folk away."

"You seen them at all?" Rance asked. "The Uthiri?"

"Yes," Dav answered.

"Truly? I ain't seen them myself yet," Rance continued. "Met a man in Silver Hills had a run-in with them in Lockwood. As he tells it, he barely got away and only 'cause they let him. Those Uthiri are in for a surprise when they try to tangle with me. I ain't yet met a bladesman this side of the Grays can best me."

He patted a sword strapped to his saddle. It was at the rear and on the wrong side if Dav had the man's dominant hand rightly figured. It was a Haggerand sword. They were popular these days due to their flashy design but, while they handled well enough for training and show, they were woefully lacking in a real fight, despite their high price.

"I'm coming from Lurie Beach myself. Most folk from there are leaving on boats, and my pap paid for my passage to Brockett Island. He's going to be awful sore when I don't show up." He laughed at the thought before continuing. "Me and my friends used to ride down this way to Andira. Great town for getting into some trouble. I know a serving girl there that I'm hoping will wait things out with me in Tag." He leaned over to whisper to Dav, "She's got tits and legs that'll make you weep, mister. Told her I was a soldier about to be sent to the front a few years back, when the war first broke out. That story got those legs to spread like a cheap book, and I figured, even if she won't come with me to Tag, I could use the situation for a few more reading sessions, if you catch my meaning." He winked at Dav.

"That so?" Daverell said.

"Not sure what I'll tell her this time. The soldier angle might not work again seeing as how the war is still on and all. Think I might pretend I got sent home, make it out like I really do have the injury my pap told the army I had when they tried to conscript me." He giggled like this was a tremendous joke.

Daverell let out a sigh. Any hope that Rance Berrellitt might be a pleasant traveling companion was swiftly dissipating. As they rode along, Rance threw tale after tale at him—and only him. The young man barely gave Ameryn or Crow another glance. Daverell learned of every man Rance had ever bested in a fight and every woman he'd conquered in bed. When he wasn't wagging his jaw, he'd whistle a slow, aimless tune that Daverell found no less grating than his conversation. Over time, Dav was only half listening, and soon after, not at all. A creeping realization wormed its way into his thoughts. Rance reminded Daverell of any number of young swordslingers he'd met in his life. However, more than anyone else, Rance reminded Daverell of himself in his younger years.

True, Daverell had thrown himself into military service instead of avoiding it, but that was a difference of circumstance, not nature. When he'd been somewhere between the age of Crow and Rance, his life's purpose had failed, and he needed something that would provide him with a new one. The military failed to do that, but it gave him structure, and that was better than nothing. A newly humbled Daverell Kain embraced the warrior's life and found it was a good fit. Very good, in fact.

He had even earned some measure of immortality over the years. After he was gone from this world, his impressive feats in combat would be recounted by military men over many a round of drinks for generations. There might even be a woman or two who would think fondly of him, but only fleetingly and only enough to draw a faint smile. None would truly mourn him, not like Ameryn mourned Tamiron. He'd never guessed at the breadth or depth of legacy a good man might leave, even in an obscure place. Tamiron, and others like him, had died. Meanwhile, men like Dav and this Rance fellow were free to roam, and anyone who lived this empty life of theirs for long enough grew to resent it. Rance would, if given the chance. Daverell certainly did. He couldn't stop his mind from returning to the incident in Kratoa. The girl. After that…after her, he hated his skill for dealing death.

The memory drew a shudder, and Daverell glanced about, feeling her at the edge of his vision.

He had been certain there was no coming back from that. Neither was there drink strong enough, or woman's company pleasurable enough, to make him forget. He was hollow. A shell. Or had been before Tamiron's fireside tale and the slaughtered horse in the woods.

141

Before Crowan.

The boy was the key to Daverell leaving some mark on this world beyond death and violence.

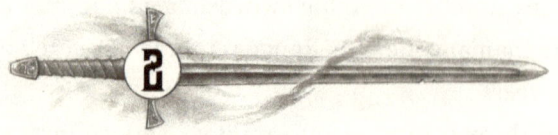

When they stopped for the night, Rance invited himself to join them. Neither Daverell nor Ameryn argued with the idea, though Daverell was already looking forward to their paths diverging once they crossed the canyon. They made camp in a sparse grove to the east of the road. Crowan went in search of firewood, and Rance accompanied the boy to help, though it appeared to Daverell that Rance had adopted more of a supervisory role.

"That man is insufferable," Ameryn muttered.

"Wasn't sure how much of that bilge you heard," Daverell said.

"Enough to be sure he's filling my son's head with poison and nonsense right now," Ameryn said. "If I weren't in such need to be rid of his company, I'd follow them and try to hold it back. Not that the presence of a lady does anything to discipline his tongue."

If nothing else, Rance's presence had prodded Ameryn back to herself a bit.

"How are you healing up?" Dav asked.

"Oh." Her hand rose to her face. "All right, I suppose."

Dav studied her. "The swelling in your nose has come down by a fair margin, and I think you'll be able to remove that bandage from your head soon. Your cheek is the nastiest one. I'm afraid my crude dressing will leave you with a scar."

Ameryn shook her head. "Don't fret about that; my face was never one to shame the stars." She stepped away before he could protest, going through one of the mule's saddlebags. "I'll make dinner tonight. If you want to help, go find some hemlock. It's poison but looks just like carrots. Mr. Berrellitt will never suspect a thing. Until it's too late, that is."

Dav laughed, even more encouraged to hear her joking. At least he *thought* she was joking. She wasn't wearing the humor on her face.

"Hey, Dav!" Crowan called to him.

Daverell looked up. "Yes?"

"Rance says I'll fight like an old man if I keep learning the sword from you." Crow was grinning.

Rance cackled, waving at Dav.

"Tell him the old ways are the best ways," Dav shouted back, then spoke so only Ameryn could hear. "Hemlock, you say?"

Ameryn sighed. "In truth, it only grows west of the Grays. I suppose we'll have to endure him a little longer."

After the night had closed in around them and they'd filled themselves with some hot food, a weary silence prevailed over the group as they all clustered around the dying fire. It shimmered and snapped while the crickets made music in the dark behind them. Dav went back for a third helping of beans, an undeniable improvement over the same meal he'd prepared the night before. Ameryn had made plenty, but there was very little left now. When Daverell settled back down, he saw that Crow had fallen asleep on his bedroll. Before long, Ameryn also noticed and rose to tuck the boy in. She gathered the messy dishes from each of them afterwards.

"No," Daverell said, pulling his bowl back. "You did the cooking, leave the cleaning to me."

"You've been doing both for the last few days. I'll do both tonight," she insisted. "Besides, I'm feeling restless, might wander a bit when I'm done."

"As you like," Daverell said. "Thank you."

Ameryn walked away, and Rance watched her with eyes like a wolf.

Pulling a flask from his coat pocket, the young man took a swig before leaning over and whispering, "You ever pummel those petals, mister?" He nodded in Ameryn's direction. "She doesn't look too old yet, for a frontier woman. Hopefully her body's a might more pleasant than that face. What happened to her?"

Daverell swallowed his instinct to answer Rance's inquiry with a hands-on demonstration of exactly what had happened to her. Instead, he said, "When we first met, you asked if we had crossed paths with the Uthiri."

Rance whistled. "They did that? I'd say she's lucky then. Got away and only lost her looks."

"She lost a great deal more than that."

"The boy says you're teaching him to swing a sword."

"Yes, well, some of the *older* techniques."

"Hey now, I was just having a bit of fun, old-timer," Rance said. "I suspect you may even be a decent teacher."

"Oh?"

"Sure, you look like a fella who knows his way around a blade. Why, you might even be as good as...," he trailed off before looking directly at Dav across the fire, "Daverell Kain."

Daverell stared silently back.

Rance chuckled to himself. "Don't worry, Captain. The Uthiri won't hear it from me."

Now Daverell was confused. "The Uthiri?"

Rance laughed a little harder. "You don't even know, do you?" When Daverell remained silent he continued. "I told you; I shared a few drinks with a fella in Silver who had a run-in with the Uthiri just outside of Lockwood. This was after they burned the place down and killed near everyone in town, mind you. This fella thought he'd got away, but they caught up with him eventually. Asked him a bundle of questions about a homestead where no less than five or six of their men were killed, including their leader's brother."

"That a fact?" Daverell asked.

"All I know is the Uthiri told this fella they'd let him go with his head still attached if he could clear up the situation for them. And Goddess above, did he sing. Told them all he knew. Town gossip said there was a man in town returned from the war, and that man recognized Daverell Kain out on that homestead. He said the leader of the war party looked none too pleased, seemed to take it personal." Rance took another drink from the flask he was holding. "This man in Silver

Hills said he'd sure hate to be you about now. Said this Uthiri fella appeared ready to hunt you down and hang you from the highest tree in all Threya."

"How many Uthiri were there?" Dav probed.

Rance shrugged. "He didn't get too particular, and I didn't ask. Described them as a mob though, so however many that is." He smiled and settled back on his bedroll.

"Any idea where they are now?"

"No sir, just that they were in Lockwood near a week ago, but damn near the whole valley knows that at this point, I expect."

Dav nodded, thoughtfully.

"Ain't too many places to hide on the frontier," Rance remarked.

"You've got a real talent for giving voice to the obvious, don't you?"

"Easy mister," said Rance with a grin. "You ain't cornered...yet."

Daverell settled into a glower. He would not be getting much sleep tonight. Not only did this news set his mind alight with worry, but it seemed he'd also have to keep a close eye on Rance.

In the morning, Dav gave Crowan another lesson in sword fighting. At least, he tried to. Rance interrupted constantly with his thoughts on nearly every direction given. By the time Ameryn slipped away, her poor boy looked so confused he could barely move. She wished him luck but refused to stay. If she attempted to practice with her blade there and Rance gave her some advice on how to do it better, she just might kill him.

Once she found a secluded spot, she pulled her sword from its scabbard and swung it around, cutting through the air, trying to remember and follow the advice Dav had given Crowan.

She liked the blade Dav had chosen for her. It was just the right length and weight. She wielded it clumsily but only due to her inexperience, not lack of strength. Years of frontier living had toughened her. It wasn't long before she gained more control over it. Control and confidence.

Minutes later, however, she dropped her arm limply to her side, feeling foolish instead. Tamiron had surely practiced in much the same way, thinking it might protect him. Ameryn had worked long and hard to create a home, expecting it to last.

She sat on the trunk of the fallen tree and took the unopened letter from her pocket. Her fingers ran over the words and along the sides, cherishing the texture. Tamiron had touched this. Sent it to her. It had made its way to her somehow, despite the war tearing her country apart.

Ameryn remained like that, handling her treasure in the warmth of the new day when she heard Dav call to her.

"Mrs. Vowery," he said. "We're ready to move on."

She quickly wiped at her eyes and pocketed the letter as she stood up. Dav glanced at her pocket but didn't say anything as they walked back to camp.

Everything had already been packed. Once they were all on their mounts, they left the small grove behind, returning to the road.

Dav studied the path in either direction, and Ameryn followed his gaze. It was empty to the south. To the north, however, a black mass was kicking up dust and glinting sunlight back at them.

"Any of you see Threyan blue on that party coming our way?" Dav asked.

The others all turned, angling the brims of their hats to keep the sun from their eyes.

"I think..." Ameryn's brow wrinkled with worry. "I think I see red."

"Have they seen us?" Crowan asked.

"Party that big's likely got scouts out ahead of them," Dav said. "They might have discovered us an hour or more ago. Even if they didn't, they've seen us now. If you're seeing red instead of blue, that's our Uthiri war party. We can stay ahead of them, even warn the people of Rockmond." Dav urged Druid forward. The rest of them followed, moving quickly.

Ameryn rode up beside him. "Should we try to lose them instead? Surely Rockmond has people watching the roads. They'd likely already spot them by the time we arrive. We're not that far ahead."

Dav considered. "We can't do either until we cross the canyon bridge."

"It's another day's ride, but we could cross the open country to the Marker Road. Go south from there, avoid the bridge altogether."

"That area's impassable," Rance commented.

"What if they have someone waiting at the bridge already?" Ameryn asked.

"They'll be a smaller group than we've got behind us," Dav said. "Make for the bridge, and we'll deal with whatever we find there."

After a full three hours of hard riding, they halted on a craggy hill that gave them an expansive view of their surroundings. The horses and mules huffed heavily and had worked their sweat into a thick lather. Ameryn was worried the animals were getting thirsty. They'd stopped once to briefly feed them hay that had been soaked in water, and were doing so again now, but they'd need a real water source soon. The closest one was the river only a few miles away, but it was at the bottom of an eight-hundred-foot drop. Ameryn had heard there were public troughs at the bridge, but now she could make out a group waiting there, just as she'd feared.

"Bad news, Cap," said Rance. "Looks like the lady was right. I see a group ahead of us, at the bridge."

Dav squinted into the distance. "Your eyes work as well as your mouth?"

"I see them, too," Crowan said.

"Uthiri?" Dav asked.

Crowan just shrugged.

Ameryn glanced over her shoulder. The ominous stain on the horizon was no further away. Thankfully, it was also no closer. However, the trap was rapidly closing around them.

"What's to the east of us?" Dav inquired.

"Durado Canyon. It sweeps all the way back up to Silver Hills along the Idryll," Rance answered.

Dav swore in frustration.

"Why don't you just take the old road down into Durado?" Rance suggested.

"What?" Dav asked.

"I ain't used it for near a decade, few do anymore, but it should work for us."

"Why would you have used an old path instead of the bridge?" Ameryn asked.

"The bridge is where the Crown taxes incoming goods from Tag. Those inclined to avoid that brand of robbery take the old road."

"Why didn't you mention this before?" Ameryn struggled to control her irritation.

"I figured you knew about it. Most around here do, even if no one uses it."

"Why don't they use it?" Ameryn asked.

"It's not exactly what you'd call well maintained. Or safe. Precipitous is the word I'd use."

Dav turned to face Ameryn. "Might be the best of all our poor alternatives."

"I don't trust him," Ameryn whispered.

"Neither do I," Dav replied. "But I think we're quickly running out of options."

She wasn't happy about it, particularly as it placed them in Rance's duplicitous trust, but, reluctantly, she nodded.

Dav turned to Rance. "Will the Uthiri see us leave the road?"

Rance smiled. "That's the best part, Cap. You follow a little gully that the road passes through, takes you right to the trailhead. Unless someone's nearly on top of you, they can't see a thing."

"Lead the way," Dav said, watching the young man closely.

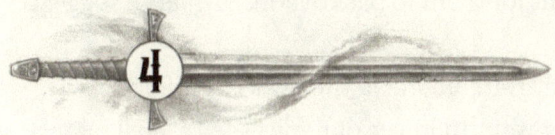

4

It was an hour or so later that they found themselves along a small, winding path that had been worn down and cut out of the side of the canyon wall.

Daverell hadn't thought twice about the trail itself. He'd been in narrow and high places before. At least, he'd *thought* they were high. He reconsidered those conclusions now that he was inches away from a sheer eight-hundred-foot drop. Every other step Druid took sent pebbles tumbling down the precipice, and Daverell couldn't stop himself from watching them fall. He didn't even hear the impact when they finally struck the bottom far, far below.

They were riding single file. Rance insisted on going first since he'd ridden this trail before. Crow and Ameryn followed, while Daverell took up the rear. In the time they'd spent on the trail, they hadn't descended nearly as much as Dav would have hoped.

Worse yet, the bridge was just ahead, and the path wound its way directly between the footings.

"Rance," he called to the young man ahead of him, "why didn't you say this path switches back under the bridge? All they'll need to do is look over the edge to see us."

There was a pause before his answer came. "I suppose that's true."

Daverell cursed inwardly and appraised their situation.

"Maybe they won't look down?" Rance offered.

"You think that out of their whole party not a single one will look down as they're crossing? A bridge as high over the river as this one, I'd do little else *but* look down."

"Even if they do see us what can they do about it?" Rance argued. "It'd take them a powerful long time to circle back around. We're out of reach down here."

"You ever heard of arrows?" Daverell asked.

"We'll be harder to spot if we're directly under the bridge. We

149

should stop there and wait for them to pass over us," Ameryn suggested.

"Yes," Daverell agreed, grateful one of them was thinking clearly.

"Additionally, we may want to lower our voices for a spell," Rance called over his shoulder.

The bridge was just ahead. Tense as he was, Dav marveled at the engineering of the thing. Long, straight beams were connected by steel housing and thick nails into an intricate lattice. It was straight and wide, the top about fifty feet above their heads.

It was hard to tell with the sound of the wind in his ears, but Dav thought he could catch the occasional babble of human voices above him.

They stopped in the shade of the bridge and carefully dismounted.

"We wait here for them to move on," Dav whispered.

They quietly fed the rest of the soaked hay to the horses. Thankfully, the mules were less interested. Gooter and Gus might have nothing on Druid and Rance's horse when it came to speed and strength, but they were better suited for endurance traveling like this. Dav could sense that the thirst in Druid remained unslaked after all the hay was gone.

A commotion arose at Daverell's back. He whipped around to watch a stone spilling down the cliff. Rance winced at every impact the rock made on its long journey to the ground and mouthed "sorry," before moving to a more secure spot further from the edge. Everyone waited, tensely listening, when an alarmed voice sounded from the deck of the bridge.

It was a man shouting something in the Uthiri language, which Daverell hadn't learned enough of to understand. Dav tensed, his hand going instinctively to his sword, though he had no idea what he might do with it in this position.

There came a thumping of feet on the bridge. Shortly, that sound was replaced by the low thunder of many approaching hooves. The main war party had met up with the group at the bridge. There were voices above, talking. The conversation quickly devolved into an argument. One voice was clearly displeased that the scouts waiting at the bridge didn't know what had happened to the group they'd seen on the road. Dav had been on the receiving end of such tirades and had little patience for military leaders who blamed their subordinates for mistakes that were as much or more their own fault.

The dispute grew more heated, and there was a scuffle. With a sudden, clear scream, one of the Uthiri fell from the bridge. For an instant, Dav thought the soldier had simply been thrown over but realized when his body swung back towards them, crashing into one of the beams face-first, that he had a noose around his neck. Apparently, the commander decided an execution was suitable punishment.

Dav and the others shifted away in the opposite direction, sure some of the men above would look over the edge at the sight.

Ameryn hid Crowan's face as the rope stopped swinging. The choking man, in his gasping, final moments spotted their quarry, hidden under the bridge. He tried to alert the soldiers above, gesticulating wildly, but if anyone was watching, his movements were indistinguishable from the sharp twitching of any other strangling man. Dav held the Uthiri's frightened and enraged stare as his eyes became bulging, bloodshot, and glassy orbs set in a purple face. Eventually, all movement ceased as the voice above began roaring again.

A moment later, the ground beneath Dav gave a little as he sent a stone spinning into the gorge to follow Rance's from earlier. By that time, it didn't matter. Dozens of hooves were striking the wooden bridge above as the Uthiri began riding across it. They were showered with dust for a moment as the chaotic drumming traveled beyond them.

They waited in silence until Daverell turned to them and whispered, "They likely left a few behind to watch for us. Hopefully they'll be expecting us from the north and not look into the canyon itself. Either way, I think we should continue on as quietly as we can."

Remounting, they silently set out under the unblinking gaze of the dangling corpse.

Step by step, they made their way along the narrow, dizzying trail.

Daverell remained on high alert, scanning the surroundings and listening for anything out of the ordinary. When the trail switched back in the direction of the bridge, he searched for faces spying over the edge. He saw none there, but in a cavity in the cliff face, someone *was* watching him.

Daverell looked away, shaken. Would he ever be spared her gaze? Perhaps at all times and in all places he found himself, if he paused and searched long and thorough, he'd find her. If he took the time to peer between the floor slats, into the tree hollows, below beds, or over his shoulder, would those eyes of hers be always looking back?

He shifted his mind away from the girl. There was enough to think about without her damming up his thoughts. He needed to focus on the problem before him.

Daverell was fairly sure he could find the hidden castle again, but convincing Ameryn to allow her son to take up the Sword was another matter. By now, he'd abandoned the idea of leaving her behind—was ashamed he'd even considered it. But Ameryn thought only of protecting the boy and not of the good he might do for the world. She considered only the negative consequences, not the positive ones. He would have to persuade her.

Of course, he would never get that chance if he fell off the side of this canyon wall. The ground refused to get any closer. Every time he glanced down—something he did infrequently—it remained so far away, it appeared more like a painting or some imaginary dreamland. Visible but untouchable. Eventually, however, the view finally appeared like a real place, and not long after that, the trail widened, grass and shrubs appeared on either side, and the sound of rushing water filled his ears.

Daverell dismounted and led Druid to a shallow bank where the horse plunged his mouth into the cold river water and stole a long drink. Daverell patted the horse's neck gratefully.

"Well, Cap," Rance said, walking up to him. "Even with that target on your back, we managed to give them the slip. Maybe traveling with you wasn't such a bad idea."

This caught Ameryn's attention. "Target on his back?"

Rance covered his mouth and looked at Daverell with wide-eyed amusement. "Sorry, Cap, didn't know we were keeping secrets."

"Secrets?" Ameryn glared at them.

"We...I'm not," Daverell said, annoyed that now it would appear as if he very much was. He quickly explained the situation to Ameryn. Crow listened too.

"So the Uthiri are trying to find us?" the boy said when Daverell finished.

"No," his mother told him before turning to Daverell. "They're trying to find *him*." She paused in silent thought a moment. "I think it best if we parted ways once we get out of the canyon. It'll be safer for both of us. We're only slowing you down and making you easier to track."

"We've lost them," Daverell protested. "They're not on our trail anymore."

"For how long?" Ameryn wanted to know.

Daverell had no answer, and so asked a question of his own, "Where will you go?"

"We'll return to Silver Hills. Take refuge there."

"You told me you didn't trust that Silver Hills was safe."

"That was before we had an Uthiri war party hunting us down."

"We're safer together," Daverell insisted. "They could be waiting for you along the road back. Even if you want to go north again, Marker makes the most sense."

"Yes," she said thoughtfully. "We'll go to Marker, at least. As you say, it's along the best route back north anyway."

When the horses were satisfied and everyone was rested, they crossed the river at a section just upstream that was wide and shallow before beginning their ascent. The sun set as they climbed, and before they were halfway up the cliff, it was fully dark. It was a clear night, and they had the light of a half-moon overhead, but Daverell couldn't see much at all. He was almost grateful for the dark. It made the extensive fall harder to see. An Iress Embrell had once told him horses

153

saw nearly as well at night as they did during the day. With every step Druid took along the dangerous path, Dav hoped it was true.

Rance was casually whistling that slow tune of his as they went, and it was fraying Daverell's already taut nerves. He wanted to tell Rance to stop, but he didn't dare lest he startle anyone or their mounts. As they came closer to the top, Daverell's fear turned from falling off the cliff to the possibility of the Uthiri waiting for them at the end of the trail. Rance had assured him there was very little chance the Uthiri had learned of or found it, but still, Dav could vividly imagine coming just over the rise and seeing the entire war party leering at them, bows drawn.

Thankfully, the only sight that greeted them when they arrived at the blessedly flat terrain of the southern side of the gorge was the empty, moonlit desert.

"Well, Cap, Crow, ma'am," Rance said, his white hat bright in the moonlight as he nodded to them, "I figure this is where our ways part."

"I hope you stay clear of the Uthiri," Dav said.

"Same for you, friend," Rance returned before riding away. In moments, he was lost in the gloom.

"We should use the cover of night while we have it," Ameryn said.

"Yes, ma'am," Dav agreed. "We ride west." He turned Druid, leading the way along the canyon edge. They'd reach Marker sometime tomorrow. So little time. He had until then to convince Ameryn to keep following him instead of taking Crowan north.

CHAPTER 12

UNDER THE SKIN

The Nameless Abbey

Pell entered the small dining hall in search of breakfast. Only a quick bite. She was eager to get to her shift in the chamber. She had something new to try on the demon.

Mai was sleeping in, so Pell ate alone, watching the room as others filed in and out. Iress Gan was playing her guitar by the fireplace, the cat, Drizzy, at her feet. Her plucking fingers sent lovely music through the hall. The instrument looked as beautiful as it sounded. Gan told Pell it had once fallen into disrepair and she'd been devastated until it was restored by Master Halvett. The result was something like a lidocrafted instrument. Pell had never seen or heard of anything like it.

Iress Lee entered the room and approached Pell.

"There you are," the old woman said, sitting across from her. "I went to your room this morning and you weren't there."

"Apologies, Iress Lee. I went to the library for a book," Pell explained.

"Of course you did," Lee said.

"You want to ask me about Iress Mai."

"Embrells," the old woman huffed. "Yes, I do. Would you like to tell me why I want to ask you about her?"

"I'm afraid I'm not as good as Mai at that sort of thing."

"I'll just speak it then, shall I? How is she coming along?"

"Not well," Pell sighed. "Is she having a harder time adjusting to this place than the average Embrell?"

"Well, no. In that, *you* are the deviation. Most who come here, especially Embrells, are alike in her reaction, but I still worry. This place...it'll devour us if we're not careful."

Pell nodded. "Perhaps I might take her afternoon shift in the basement in addition to my morning one? Grant her some respite?"

"No, I'm worried about you too," Iress Lee said. "Your first few days here, she was the more tired-looking of you two—nightmares, she told me—but lately, she's appeared more rested than you. Are you not sleeping?"

Pell shrugged. "Late night reading."

"I'd like to get the both of you involved in some of the hobbies we all enjoy here. It really helps us maintain some balance in our secluded lives."

"Reading is my hobby."

"Clearly. But I highly encourage you to take on something else. Something creative. Iress Rin leads a knitting circle, Gan teaches guitar, Ahl cultivates flowers in the greenhouses. We must do all we can to keep the Darkness at bay."

"I will consider it."

"See that you do," she said, getting up. "It's time to begin your work for the day."

Iress Pell followed the old woman, along with Iress Em and a group of monks, to the basement.

Over the week she'd spent here, she'd grown somewhat callused to the oppressive evil that permeated the abbey. However, the thickness of it that accompanied her daily introduction to this particular chamber never failed to make her dizzy—even when wearing a blindfold, which she'd decided to do today. She pulled a scarf over her mouth and nose as well to protect against the smell. The points of light and faint outlines of the exhausted night workers filed past her while she and the rest of the day laborers walked in, immediately setting about their tasks.

Pell shared Iress Lee's sight as she walked to another door across the room and unlocked it with yet another unique key. How many keys did the woman have to keep track of? The door leading to the altar pool wasn't nearly as ornately lidocrafted as the entry door, but it was enough to cut off Pell's connection to Lee once she shut it behind her. None but the Iress Matriarch saw the room still lower than this one, though Iress Lee was happy to describe it to anyone who asked, which Pell had. More than once.

According to Lee, after another short, curving stairway there was a small room directly beneath the main chamber. It was circular and held an altar in the center. There was a natural spring flowing into and draining out of the space. The unholy blood that dripped through the drain in the floor of the room above fell onto the holy altar and streamed into the surrounding water. In addition to all the tasks she performed as the abbey's Matriarch, it was her charge to bless the water and altar each morning, that it might dispel the wickedness within the foul blood.

Pell wanted to see it. The central grate was an elaborate lidocrafted design that blocked her inner Sight but had gaps wide enough she might be able to peek through it physically. She was daily tempted to do just that. However, indulging such childish curiosity was beneath an Iress, especially if it required her to crawl about, sticking her face

157

on the bloody floor.

Reluctantly, she turned her attention to the far end of the room where the thing's head rested. For a moment, she couldn't see the point of light representing its consciousness. She shook her head and looked again. Yes, it was there, pulsing and active.

She connected with it. As usual, she saw and tasted nothing, heard the same sounds she would with her own ears and felt nothing but a sharp prickling sensation at the places where its limbs had been severed. There was no emotional reaction to any of these things. Its mind was more unfathomable than even the more unusual animals she'd connected with. Creatures without any calculating reasoning behind the puzzle of their brain. One could only share their sight and observe. So it was with Vulsipher. Except, in this case, there was *something* under the surface. Something watching back.

The Iress felt for the strap over its eyes and undid the clasp, revealing the only view it had presumably seen for hundreds of years, the ceiling of its ineffectual execution chamber. On her first day with it, Pell had wanted to introduce stimuli to the thing while observing its reactions. She was far from the first Embrell to attempt this but wanted to try anyway. Frustratingly, it had revealed nothing thus far. She'd present holy relics, plants, rocks, drawings of all sorts of objects and places. All to no effect. Not only could Pell detect no reaction, but it didn't seem to even look at them. It only looked at her.

The first time she pulled back the band over its hideous eyes, they had been staring directly back into hers. They hadn't darted from elsewhere nor glanced about the space before settling. They were already fixed. On her. The eyes themselves were a milky, sour yellow, laced with purple veins twisting around the reddish irises featuring ill-defined edges. And the pupils. More like a snake's than a human's. Whatever umbilical connection to the Beloworld that supplied it with endless fresh blood must also keep its eyes moist. It never blinked.

Retrieving the book she'd borrowed from the library, she began flipping through the pages, holding the old ink drawings of hellish monsters and wicked rituals before its eyes. Again, it was looking past the book at her.

But no, she sensed something. The slightest stir of excitement at the sight of the picture held open before it now. She noted that image and attempted to plunge beyond its senses, into its deeper consciousness.

It felt like falling into an endless cave, leaving her with a sense of smallness, of being cornered. Taking a few deep breaths to steady herself, she tried probing at what she found. It was an ever-shifting labyrinth in both breadth and depth. She'd been exploring it nearly every day and was no closer to making any sense of the snarled web of the creature's mind.

If she could understand it better, she could feed it images the way she had the demon in the pass or the men that had attacked her and Maiyen on the road. However, this being's mind was far from the simple one of the bestial or the familiar one of her fellow humans. The Goddess alone knew when, or if, that would ever be a possibility.

Something *did* feel different this time, but what? She spent the rest of her time in the basement trying to discover what it was or to recreate the subtle reaction she'd detected earlier, but it was all to no avail.

Finally, she replaced the strap over the demon's eyes while removing her own eye-coverings and breaking her connection. Whenever she retreated from the thing's mind, it was with the distinct feeling of having been violated somehow. Her hands trembled for at least half an hour afterward. Every time.

"Anything?" Iress Em asked.

Pell shrugged. "I thought I noticed something, but…now I'm starting to doubt myself. What are you attempting today?"

"Breek obtained some caustic soda. They use it in Demerra for cleaning. It's said to be quite poisonous, but it may as well be honey for all it seems to affect this thing. I've tried feeding some to it, stuffing a generous portion down its throat to its superfluous stomach. Just now I've been pouring it directly into open wounds at different locations, including right into its heart. Nothing."

Iress Pell held back her own ideas. The first time she had worked a shift with Iress Em, she had assailed her with endless suggestions about things she might try. As the Matriarch had warned her and Em informed her that day, the Curials had been very imaginative and thorough over the years. Every kind and combination of stabbing, crushing, incinerating, and infecting had been tried. Pell had studied the almost daily entries in the logs, going back hundreds of years. She found that even her most unconventional ideas, and quite a few she never would have considered, had been attempted in the past. Iress Em and Rin were now steadily working their way through toxins, coating and injecting them into every organ and muscle of the thing's body. Em and Rin remained hopeful that some rare poison might be the key to its demise. They had to try something.

Pell was sure the solution lay in the Holy Sword hidden somewhere within the walls of this abbey. She didn't have many ideas beyond what had already been tried with the creature, all well documented. The most obvious thing that had *not* been tried was finding whoever might wield the Illumed Blade and let them kill the Elder Demon with it. But how might you scour the land for such a one, especially without turning it into a debacle? Many a fool would die trying to hold the weapon.

The biggest reason to avoid making the search public was to keep the associated truth of the imprisoned demon from getting out. Of course, that had possibly already happened. They were at war with Uthir over that very thing. Perhaps, with the flour already spilled, this was the best time to seek the chosen out more openly. Pell had even run the possibility by Iress Lee. The old woman maintained hope that the war would fizzle out.

Iress Lee had also forbidden her from spending any time trying to find the person who had betrayed their secret to the world. Officially, she was honoring that directive for now. Inside, however, she thought about it a lot. She had no idea who might have done it, but she had at least one idea of how it might have been done.

She was letting herself be distracted from the task at hand. Pell spent the rest of her shift staring at the page in the old book that had elicited a reaction from the demon.

160

It was an old drawing done in cross-hatched ink. The strokes came alive under the ever-shifting firelight in the room. It depicted a terror-stricken man lopping off his own hand with a hatchet for fear it had been possessed by some evil. Pell read the caption on the opposite page. It was a passage from the *Lyprakarum*:

When wicked spirits roam free, trust neither person nor thing. Thine own flesh may betray thee.

Odd. Pell could think of no reason for the demon's mind to find this interesting above any of the other images in the book. Perhaps the creature found the idea of possessing someone or something appealing? Did it like seeing the twisted, clawed hand so similar to its own? If so, why not respond to the depictions of fully rendered demons in the book that resembled it better and more fully? Maybe it enjoyed the sight of humans maiming themselves? No, there were many other examples of that in the book, some much more dramatic.

Eventually, the Iress Matriarch unlocked the door again, letting them out. Iress Pell felt as if a heavy burden was being lifted off her shoulders and passed on to Mai, who stared at her as they traded places.

Take heart, Sister, Pell sent to her. Mai gave her a brave half-smile in return before donning her blindfold and reluctantly entering the chamber.

Iress Pell removed the mask she wore over her mouth and nose before rubbing her neck and walking down the hall. She started when she saw Bryn sitting in an alcove. Pell couldn't imagine why she'd been shocked. In all her time here, she'd rarely seen Bryn anywhere else. Sometimes reading a book but often simply staring into space. Today, she had a book in her hands.

"Oh, Bryn," Pell said. "Hello."

Bryn only stared back at her.

"What are you reading?" Pell asked, automatically probing her mind.

Bryn's face darkened. "You're supposed to ask permission when you make a new connection," she seethed.

"I'm sorry." Pell severed the bond. "I was a novitiate at the Pyressa Abbey not long ago; I'm still used to more open sharing."

"I think it's time you break that habit," Bryn said. "If you don't, I'll tell the Matriarch."

"But usually, between Embrells, we—"

"Does the Fifth Edict not apply to your fellow Embrells?"

"It does," Pell replied, unable to keep the chill out of her voice. "Again, I'm sorry. I was only asking about your book."

"It's a story," Bryn said. "The epic of Omron. If you want to know what it's about, read it yourself."

Pell nearly laughed. She had never seen Bryn with anyone else at the abbey and had assumed she'd been socially rejected as a consequence of her refusal to participate in their shared mission, but perhaps she was simply an insufferable twit. Pell had been withholding judgment on the young woman, but her opinion was solidifying very quickly.

Saying nothing further, Pell resumed her walk, wondering how the woman could live like she did. If Pell had made the same choice as Bryn, there was no way she could be so idle. Bryn's level of isolation was beyond what even Pell could endure. It bothered Pell that Bryn might be fine with it. Shouldn't there be some punishment for the self-ish choices she had made?

None of this occurred to Iress Mai. The next night, Pell sat next to her at dinner as she watched Bryn with pity in her eyes. Moments later, Mai's expression became one of resolve. She stood and walked over to the lone woman, sitting down and engaging her in conversation. Pell was too far away to hear, but it appeared to be a fairly one-sided affair. Bryn was nodding and providing, at best, one-word answers. At least Bryn didn't seem to be as hostile with Mai as she'd been with Pell. Pell wondered if that even mattered. Iress Mai would defend an outlaw who'd taken her hostage—try to understand and make peace with him. If there was any avenue at all to some sort of friendship with the woman, Mai would find it. Pell decided she wouldn't try to stop her.

"Iress Lee won't like that," Rin said, next to her.

"She wants to keep Iress Bryn isolated?" Pell asked.

"Not necessarily. She'd be more worried about Bryn rubbing off on Mai. Maybe convince her to give up the mission as well."

"Iress Mai is a more dedicated person than she seems," Pell defended her friend. "She simply can't abide to watch anyone be lonely and can't conceive of anyone truly wanting to be."

"Even if they deserve it?"

"Mai doesn't believe there's a single creature under the Goddess's eyes who deserves that."

"Well, as long as she continues to fill her shifts in the lower chamber..."

"She will," Pell promised and prayed she was right. She understood Mai better than anyone else in the world, but could she truly say what her friend might do when their circumstances had changed so dramatically in so short a time?

For now, at least, Pell was correct. Over the next few days, despite Mai's increasing friendship with Bryn, she continued to dutifully fill her role at the abbey. She even began making a little headway. During one of their late-night conversations, Mai admitted she'd begun to understand, if only a little, how the thing's mind worked. She couldn't yet read its intentions but could sense a hint of its thoughts. Unlike Pellary, who had continued her tests with visual stimuli, Mai had focused purely on the connection and navigating the labyrinth of its brain. With her help, even Pell had begun making sense of its mental landscape.

What confounded her most when it came to the demon was the reaction she'd sensed from the drawing. It was consuming her thoughts again when she stepped into the chamber one morning, blindfolded. She saw the points of light belonging to everyone in the room except, as had happened days before, the creature at the center. She thought she'd imagined it then, but now she was sure something strange was going on. It couldn't have died, could it? She glanced about the room and saw it, but only for a moment before it was back where it was supposed to have been in the first place: its head. But where had it been a moment ago? It was well documented that to do this it needed an empty vessel. Something either freshly dead or...of its own biology.

"Iress Rin," Pell called to the Curial who was working with her today.

"Yes?" Rin asked.

"Check the right arm for rogue organs, I think you'll find brain tissue."

"You think it's possessing a different part of its body?"

"Yes."

Rin turned towards the right arm and let out a small scream. Pell watched from Rin's eyes as long, serrated teeth sprung from two places under the arm's skin. They bit through the leather belts holding it down. Rin jumped at it, bringing her dagger down on the stone table, just missing it as it scurried away.

"Catch it!" she shrieked.

Pell tore her blindfold off and stomped towards the disembodied arm. Again, it was too quick. The fingers had rotated unnaturally to the side and carried it about like the legs of a spider. Pell lunged again with more success. The shoulder end was caught beneath her foot, but it squirmed out before Rin, or anyone else, could get at it. This time, the arm turned on Pell, flinging itself at her by swiftly extending the elbow. It latched onto her leg. Pell swatted at it, and its mutant teeth found her hand, biting hard. She yelped in pain, then again in fear, as it clawed up her chest, settling around her throat. The fingers were twice the size and length of the average man's and more than that in strength. Pell's hands went to her throat, attempting to pry the slimy,

164

hot fingers away as lights popped in her eyes. Through her terror, she was vaguely aware of others crowding around her. Of more fingers at her neck, trying to wrench the demon's hand free.

After a few terrifying seconds, Pell was able to draw breath, and her blood pumped back into her head. She staggered back, watching Rin and three monks wrestling the thrashing appendage back to its table. It was covered in lacerations, spraying blood about as it squirmed.

"Ring the bell!" Rin cried.

One of the monks was already in the corner, pulling at the string that signaled everyone in the abbey above of an emergency. Once the monks had the arm more or less under control, Rin rushed to Pell.

The Curial looked her over. "We didn't cut you by mistake, did we?" she asked.

Pell shook her head. "I'm fine."

"You're not. Your hand is bleeding," Rin said, handing her a cloth. "Bind it."

Pell had scarcely finished wrapping her hand before Iress Lee was there with Ollett and his men. Rin began explaining everything as she sliced through a tangle of tendons and muscle in the demon's arm. Once she found the web of nerves and brain matter, she wrenched the stubborn substance and all the teeth from the twitching arm. An attendant was waiting with a platter. Rin piled the material on top and, once she was certain she got it all, nodded at the man holding it. He walked to the incinerating fire and tossed it all in.

Iress Rin filtered the sunlight streaming through the large infirmary window onto Pell's hand.

"It's been a while since it tried to escape like that," Rin noted.

Pell said nothing. Rin hadn't been on the receiving end of the attack, nor had she been connected to the thing's mind afterwards. While Pell hadn't sensed much from the demon, she was sure of one thing: it wasn't an attempt at escape, but an attempt to kill her.

Pell watched her injuries close and felt her emotions also recover. If one could call shock curdling into anger a recovery. Up to that point, she'd been approaching killing Vulsipher as something of an academic challenge. But now she craved its death and questioned Rin about the demon with renewed determination.

"So it's done this before?" Pell asked. "Changed its anatomy?"

"Yes," Rin said.

"And it always changes back?" Pell asked. "How long will that take?"

"It might be back to normal already."

"It can change so fast?"

"Oh yes." Rin made a few alterations to her Restorative before running the Light over Pell again. "One hundred years ago, it possessed the body of a dead pig that had been brought in for an experiment. That was one of the closest it's ever come to escaping. After they strapped the animal down, it mutated from the pig back into its regular shape and size within days." Iress Rin pulled the Restorative away and began closing it up. "Have you been sleeping well? You look a bit worn."

Pellary ignored this last comment. "But this mutation—what it did to its arm—must have taken more time."

"The pig's body changed into something that was natural for the demon. The form embedded in its biology," Rin said. "Growing a brain and mouth in its arm goes *against* its natural design, which takes it much more time and effort. Praise the Goddess that it does."

"How did it possess the pig? Why does it not possess any of us?"

"Vulsipher is, ultimately, still a corporeal and embodied being. It's bound to its physical form. It could possess the pig because the animal was dead and came in contact with the thing's blood, which created enough of a biological link for it to leap into the brain of the corpse."

"Surely a pig, even one possessed by a demon, would be fairly easy to subdue or kill."

"If only it were," Rin replied sadly. "Whatever supernatural power that keeps it so stubbornly alive moves with it to whatever frame it inhabits and makes it strong and unkillable. I'd be happy to show you the records that detail all the experiments and attempts made throughout its captivity."

"I've seen them," Pell said. "I've even read enough of them that I'm embarrassed I didn't see what it was planning sooner. It seems obvious now."

"We've had much closer scrapes than this. With more time to mutate, who knows how much worse it might have been. You saw through its plan before it was ready."

Iress Rin's feelings were shared by her fellow Sisters. As Pell went about her day, she was frequently stopped and congratulated for her quick thinking and heroics.

"I'm so glad you're alright," Iress Mai said to her outside their doors at nightfall.

"Thank you, Mai," said Pell. "Be careful, I think it sees us as a threat."

"I will," promised Mai. "And get to bed. I can tell you haven't been sleeping well."

They wished each other good night and retired to their separate rooms. Pell tried to work on her *Lyprakarum* translation, but her mind was too active. She connected to Mai next door and found she'd already fallen asleep and was in the middle of a ghastly nightmare. She'd been suffering from them every night.

Pell closed her eyes and pictured a cool breeze running through an open meadow, making wildflowers dance under a bright sun. She fed the image into her friend's mind, replacing the nightmare, and felt her calm down, relaxing into a deep sleep. Projecting didn't even take Pell's total concentration as it normally would have. The dreaming mind was considerably less critical of the imagery. It allowed her to keep thinking, and, after considering the day, she was certain of one thing: Vulsipher was, in its own way, afraid of her.

Now, if she could only figure out why.

CHAPTER 13

THE MOST DANGEROUS THING

Marker

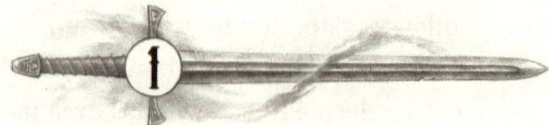

"Dav, I've been thinking," said Crow.

"Have you?" Daverell replied.

"You bought these saddles with coin from *my* dagger, true?" Crow tapped the saddle horn.

"That's a fact," Daverell said, squinting into the distance. He should be able to see Marker soon.

"And same story for the food we've been eating?"

"I suppose so."

"Well, that makes me the leader of this here expedition," Crow declared.

"How you figure?"

"I'm paying for it, ain't I?" Crow said with a laugh. "That puts me in charge."

"Not when you've got your mother along with you," Ameryn remarked. "Plus, that's *my* mule you're riding."

"That makes you boss of the mules," Crow argued. "Not the journey."

"Alright," conceded Ameryn. "You're the leader."

"Thank you kindly," Crow said.

"As long as you do what I say," Ameryn added.

Crow sighed before turning to Daverell. "Was it like this in the army?"

"Authority disputes? Oh yes. It's the burden of leadership, I'm afraid," Daverell said. He was fairly certain he could make out some shimmering shapes on the horizon. "Tell me, boss, you see a town up ahead?"

"Sure do," Crow said. "That Marker?"

"Must be," Daverell said. "Even better, it appears to have been spared Uthiri fire."

It took them nearly another hour to reach the frontier town. Daverell felt more trepidation than relief at having arrived. If he was to convince Ameryn to allow Crow to take up the Sword, it would have to happen sometime during the night they spent in this town. This was his last chance.

Marker was little more than a single street boasting naught but the most essential of establishments. It was also completely empty. Their only greeting was the echoing sounds of their own mounts and the moaning whistle of the wind that carried away the dust they kicked up. Any other sounds made them jump and turn their heads, but it was never anything more than a swinging sign squeaking on its pole or a loose fence slat clapping against its rail.

"Ain't a soul left," Daverell whispered.

"Mom," came Crowan's voice from behind him.

169

Ameryn gasped, and when Dav turned, he saw why. The boy was pale and listless.

"I don't feel well," he said, but even more worrisome was what came out of his mouth next—nearly everything he'd eaten that day.

Daverell was off his horse in a moment to catch the boy who fell limply into his arms. Ameryn was at his side, her hand to Crow's forehead.

"He's on fire," she said. "Let's get him inside."

They made for the nearest building, which happened to be the Marker saloon, and laid his shivering form on a table.

"Get me a blanket," Ameryn requested.

Daverell ran out and retrieved one from Crow's saddlebags. After delivering it to Ameryn, he moved Druid and the two mules to the stables in back where he made sure they had hay and water before he returned to the saloon. Ameryn had placed the blanket over Crowan's body and a cold, damp rag on his head.

"That was sudden," Dav said.

"It often happens like that with children," Ameryn said. "He'll be fine in a day or two. He'll be fine."

Daverell knew her well enough to hear the worry beneath her steady voice.

Ameryn huffed angrily, "I'm sure he caught something from that... that...," she paused, searching for the right word before giving up. "From Rance," she finished.

"How can I help?" Dav asked.

"See if there's a proper bed upstairs, maybe more blankets and a well in town," Ameryn replied. "He'll need lots of clean water as he sweats out the fever. Eventually, we'll have to find some foods that are gentle on the gut."

"I'll see what I can dig up." Daverell hurried out the door.

They relocated to a room above the saloon as night closed in.

By the light of a single candle, far from any windows, Ameryn watched her son sleeping. She placed her head on his chest and listened to his breathing and heartbeat for a moment before replacing the blanket. The boy's breath caught, and he had a brief fit of coughing before settling back into the rhythm of slumber.

"I can't tell if it's reached his lungs or not." She stroked his forehead. "I'm afraid he's getting worse."

"Let's pray he doesn't," Daverell said.

After a long pause, she murmured, "I don't think I can."

"Pray?"

She gave no answer.

"Ain't that the way of things," Dav mused sadly. "Your son's destiny restores my faith while eroding yours."

"Please, Dav, I've had enough of that," Ameryn said. "My boy is not some…"

"He's important, Mrs. Vowery. The Goddess will protect him."

"She's never protected anyone I love," she snapped back. "If…*when* he gets well, I'm taking him back to Silver Hills. We'll wait out the war there, then use the money left over from the dagger to begin rebuilding the cabin. Just as it was."

"You wouldn't change anything?" Dav asked.

"I used to want a framed house, but not anymore. I'll have our little cabin restored—exactly the way Tamiron built it—beam for beam, if I can. Somehow, I'll have my old life back."

"It's not always best to hang on too tightly after they're gone. We have to say goodbye, at least for now. That's what I've found, and I've a lot of practice at losing people."

"I'm sadly well practiced at that myself."

"Who else?"

"You remember the great fire in Pyressa?"

"Hard to forget a thing like that."

"My mother, father, sister...all perished in the flames. I only escaped by luck and timing. There was nothing left of our home by morning."

"Same as the Uthiri did to your cabin."

"Yes, but it's different this time. Out there, on our land, I can live with Tam. With his memory. I said goodbye to him when he left for war, and that's the only time I'll need to. Nothing has to change simply because he's not coming back. Crowan and I will go back and rebuild."

Ameryn blew out the candle, punctuating her words and pitching the room into blackness. Dav might be well-intentioned, but he'd only ever known resilient systems of order. Everything she'd ever believed in had collapsed from under her. But memories never changed, and building a life on them was the only thing that made sense anymore. That, and defending her son. If that was even possible.

"Is there any way to protect him?" Ameryn asked, surprised she'd spoken the question aloud. The total dark blurred the line between her thoughts and her words. Now that it was out there, she clarified, "Is there any way in all the world to be truly safe?"

After a long pause, Dav spoke. A floating voice in the black. "There's a man I remember from my early training, a mean, old varmint. Can't recall his name or anything that he told me—save one thing. It was after my first battle. I'd been scared witless the whole time, and I think he was trying, in his way, to comfort and encourage me. He took me aside and said, 'Kain, there ain't but two ways to not feel fear in a battle. One is to be mad as a midnight moon bird. The other is to be the most dangerous thing on the field.' I've always tried to be the latter." Dav took a breath. "You put a sword in Crow's hands, Mrs. Vowery. *That* sword. Let me train him. Not a soul in all the Midlands will be safer than one wielding a blade capable of killing demon-gods."

"Demon-gods," she laughed humorlessly. "Do you know if the Sword is good against anything other than monsters long gone from the world?"

"Even if they *are* gone, anything that could kill such dark creatures could stand up to everything else. If I could only see him hold it, my life would finally make some sense."

"You're asking my boy to fix your problems. That ain't fair. Not to either of you. I'm no perfect mother, but every choice I make is to try to protect or help that boy."

"Including a diminished existence, living only in a memory?"

"Pursuing the past is better than chasing delusions," she countered.

"You saw him find the dagger in the river. That was a miracle."

"It's not enough to put him at further risk," she said. "I know what the prophecy says happens to those who touch it but ain't meant to."

A silence followed. Ameryn thought Dav was going to argue some more, but instead he began softly singing. It was one of Ameryn's favorite hymns. In his voice, she detected an invitation. He wanted her to join in or sing the second verse. She wouldn't.

Watch over me, O star above, and drive away my fear.
The storm is passed, the rain is gone, the evening night is clear.
Of all the souls beneath Thy sight, please spare some Light for me,
O Mother of this sleeping world, I send this prayer to Thee.

His voice faded completely before resuming in spoken form. "On the trail, around the fire, and as we're falling asleep, Crow and I sing," Dav commented. "Even Rance had that damnable whistling—but aside from that one night at the riverside, you never do. And you, with an angel's own voice. Why?"

"I used to never stop. I drove my family mad with it," Ameryn recalled. "But I...I no longer like the feelings it conjures. I can manage a frivolous song occasionally, but I won't sing anything with real meaning. Not unless I'm among family."

"Is there no time or place in which you might sing again?" Dav asked. "For someone who ain't family?"

"Perhaps in a Singing Ceremony for Tamiron. If I'd been offered that chance, I'd have taken it. Though in some ways, it's a mercy it never came my way."

"Why?"

"Because I'd have seen his vacant body. I'd know, really know, he's gone. Our separation would be more absolute than it is. I don't want that."

"What would you have sung?"

"There was a song we liked," she said. "It was a simple thing, but I think it would have been just right."

"Would you let me hear a little?"

A taut and fragile stillness was the only answer she gave.

"Not family?" he ventured.

"You have only been, and remain to be, a stranger to me," she stated, angry again. "You've been in my house, met my late husband, spent time with my son, even knew the names of my chickens. Just now, I shared something personal, yet you've shared nothing with me that I didn't have to drag out of you. You keep asking me to trust you. I can't trust you—I don't know you. There's that haunted look that takes you at times. Scars upon scars covering your body. That blade Crowan pulled from the river. Everything about you is a mystery."

He sighed, heavily. "You're right," he admitted. "I think I'm used to being a captain. Trusted as a matter of rank. Not as an…exchange. I owe you some honesty."

"Let's start with the dagger," she suggested. "The one you threw in the river. I don't think you're an evil man, so how did you come to possess such a foul thing?"

She could feel his discomfort, hear him shifting. His resolution to be honest with her was only seconds old, yet she suspected he was already regretting it.

"It was a gift from King Aesrik."

"You know the Holy King of Threya?"

"'Know' is too generous a word, as is 'holy,' for that man. He was aware of me, yes. Called me out by name whenever he'd attend our victory feasts after battle. Told all within the considerable range of his voice I was the best in the kingdom. Nearly the perfect soldier. How much better I'd be, if only I could learn to be as ruthless as some of the other men and stop holding the battle rage back. He gifted me that priceless knife once he thought I'd learned that lesson."

"What happened?" Ameryn asked. After a pause, she asked it again.

Reluctance was heavy in his voice when he continued. "The Uthiri first began raiding beyond the border a few years ago, started by attacking Kratoa. We were sent to drive them back. I led the group. You've seen the Uthiri's appetite for destruction with your own eyes, and Kratoa was no exception. It was in ruins and overrun when we arrived. The invaders were no match for us, however. Those we didn't kill, we chased out of the town. It was the sort of 'glorious battle' I'd participated in many times before, and I expected to be drinking with my friends that night—as we always did, after such...valorous feats," Daverell scoffed. "But first, we had to search every corner for survivors as well as any Uthiri rats who might be hiding.

"I was searching a small barn. It had a floor dug a few feet lower than the outside and was full of hay from which a man sprang upon me with a knife. As I fought him, several more men took the opportunity to jump from their holes and flee out the doors. I dispatched the knife-wielding man quickly but heard what I thought were the running footsteps of one of the fleeing men outside the barn walls." Daverell paused before he continued. "Every day since then I've wondered why I didn't recognize the lightness of the footfalls, the smallness of the strides. I can still hear it in my head now, and it seems obvious. But at the time, I instinctively swung my blade between the horizontal barn slats. The gap was barely wide enough to allow the steel to pass through, but with the exactness I'd gained from a lifetime of sword-wielding, I managed a long, clean sweep at the shape I could just make out on the other side. I knew immediately, by the feel of it, that something was wrong. Even before I heard the screaming.

"I ran out to the side and saw her. A filthy little girl with no more than five winters behind her. I'd cut clean through both her legs." It sounded to Ameryn as if Dav had buried his face in his hands, shutting out the world that he already couldn't see. "I've done some wicked things, ma'am. Things that had already robbed me of ever feeling much respect for myself. But nothing compared to when I looked at that girl. The shock on her face as she stared at the bleeding stumps, the sounds of her sobs as she reached for her little legs, lying in the mud...the pleading in her eyes when she looked at me. I stood there, unable to do anything but watch as the life drained out of her. Her movements grew slow and clumsy, eventually stopping altogether. Her eyes never left me as she died. They've never left me since."

He paused here and the silence was heavy. So was his voice when he resumed his account. "Word of the incident got back to the king. When we returned, he wanted to celebrate the moment. Finally, Daverell Kain had succumbed to bloodlust. I was as merciless as he'd always wanted me to be. The perfect soldier. He made a big ceremony of it, found it all quite funny, presenting me with the dagger and making me read the inscription: 'Ever bathed in blood. Ever embedded in bone.' A mockery of holy words used by common cutthroats. I thought being a soldier for the Crown meant more. I guess the king doesn't see it that way.

"I left shortly after the feast started; no one even noticed. I vowed that night, the only blood and bone that blade would taste would be my own, when I used it to end my miserable existence. I was about to do that very thing when I saw her. The girl, legless and pale in the moonlight, sitting in the courtyard, watching me. For whatever reason, under her gaze I couldn't bring myself to do it.

"To this day I see her sometimes. I don't know if she's a real specter or something from my head. I suppose it doesn't much matter."

After a pause, Ameryn said thoughtfully, "All that, the fruit of a life spent trying to be the most dangerous thing."

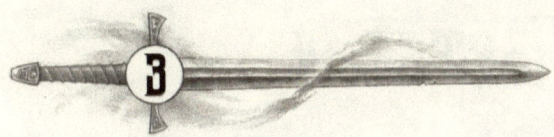

Her words cut deep. Worse, in that instant, Daverell felt the chance to train Crow and lead him to the Sword slip away. She'd take the boy to Silver Hills. Maybe she was right to do so. He'd failed.

Daverell turned to leave.

"I'm sorry," she said. Whether her apology was meant for what she'd said or what had happened to him, he didn't know and couldn't bear to stay and find out.

She said it again, as he left. "I'm sorry."

Those same words were the next Daverell spoke, but not until he was in his room, alone. No, not alone. Even in the total darkness, he could feel the eyes of the girl, watching him from the corner. Daverell met those eyes with his own and didn't look away this time. It was then that he said the words. Again, and again, and again.

CHAPTER 14

CATACOMBS

The Nameless Abbey

1

Iress Mai pulled the three heavy volumes off the shelf and heaved them onto the table. The sound was loud enough that Drizzy, loafing in a little island of sunlight streaming through a window, decided he'd rather be elsewhere. He stood and padded out of the room with his tail in the air.

"Wait, don't go. I'm sorry," Mai said in his direction. She was ignored, and he disappeared through the door. Mai almost followed the feline to drag him back but decided not to. Despite her efforts to make friends with the gray cat, he was always rubbing up against Pell, who barely acknowledged him and only ever offered a distracted scratch behind his ears. Perhaps that was the better approach? Yes, Mai would pretend his affection didn't matter to her. She turned away and sat before the pile on the table. "What am I looking for?" she asked, leafing through the book on top.

"The term 'chaos echo' or 'chaos call' or anything similar," Iress Pell said.

"You sure you don't want to talk more about reading the demon's mind?" Mai asked. Pell had wanted to talk of little else the last few days.

"I think I need to step away from that particular puzzle for a moment," Pell replied.

"Yes," Mai said. "Iress Em told me what happened the day after the attack."

"It was nothing." Pell brushed it off.

"Did you really try to stab its eyes out?" Mai asked.

"No, I did not. I only stood over it with the knife imagining what it might be like if I did," Pell said. "I wanted to hurt it but decided that devising a new way to kill it was the more proper action."

"Have you thought of one?"

Pell looked at her miserably. "I thought I did. I wanted to bore a hole in its head and pour molten metal into it. Checking the records, an Iress Jen tried that very thing ten years ago. Then I thought of removing its brain and cutting it up like a loaf of bread. It so happens that was tried by an Iress Heth one hundred years ago. They wrote that there was some core like a peach pit that couldn't be breached, and the brain tissue just regrew around it. Everything I think of has already been done. And *nothing* works."

Iress Mai placed a hand over Pell's. "We're still new here," Mai assured her. "We have plenty of time."

"Yes, of course," she said. "You're right."

"Now, what in all the Midlands is a chaos call?" Mai asked.

"It's a little known Uthiri ritual," Pell related, "wherein a corpse is mutilated to create a channel to the Dark."

Mai's nose wrinkled. "Lovely. Do you think that's how someone exposed the secret of this place?"

"Yes," Pell whispered. "And if we can find a reference or description of it, we'll know how the traitor learned of it."

"Pell, the Matriarch forbade us from looking into this. We're to focus on our assigned task."

"Yes, but she is misleading about even that. I asked her a few days ago if I might have extra time in the chamber to practice and study the demon and she refused. Why would she want to limit our time with it? If *I've* sensed some secrecy from her, then I know you have."

"Well, yes, but I'm sure there's much about this place she must conceal. You've never trusted anyone in authority. Do you really think she's the traitor? That she leaked the secret by mangling a body?"

"I don't know," Pell admitted. "Maybe it's Bryn."

"Saints and stars, Pell. Don't hate her because everyone else does," Mai said. "She's quite a nice person, beneath her awkwardness."

"Like me?" Pell asked. "You took me under your wing once in much the same way, but I was never a brat."

"I recall you arguing with our fellow Embrells—teachers and students alike—telling them we could listen in the Dark the same way we listen in the Light. Back when they called you 'ghost girl' instead of 'demon girl,' remember? It wasn't until they threatened to kick you out that you stopped. I think there might have been one or two of them that would have called you a brat."

"Well, they were wrong about that *and* about listening in the Dark. I can still show you how."

Mai shook her head. Her teachers at the Pyressa Abbey had warned them against trying. The idea frightened her. "I'm more interested in learning to project. You promised to help me," Mai said.

"Yes, of course, I'm sorry. I'm in your debt for all you've done to help me with reading the demon," Pell said.

While they'd been chatting, Mai had been studying the pages. She flipped now to the most relevant sections and scanned each paragraph finding nothing remotely like what Pell had described.

She kept searching until it was time to leave. After saying goodbye to Pell, Iress Mai exited the library. She had the first shift in the lower chamber today and was looking forward to it. The chamber itself was still a horror. But connecting with the vast and neutral void of the demon's mind was almost meditative. She'd begun to enjoy getting lost within.

Pell, alone in the library, pushed the books away in frustration. Mr. Drizzle had returned and was stroking himself on her legs. She bent and combed her fingers through his fur.

She was making no progress on the demon or on finding the traitor. Additionally, something Mai had said was distracting her. She'd gotten so out of the habit of turning her ear to the Dark that she'd not even tried since she'd been here. This old castle, of all places, must have *something* hiding in the emptiness.

The Embrells were quite skilled at connecting with waking minds running through the living world of the Light. The space of illumination, connected to the Above, was one of abundant substance, varied in voice and deep in feeling. But the other side of the spiritual landscape, the Dark and its connections to the Below, had long been denied by the Saerisian Church, though it had not always been so. Only after the Tar Ishik purges, when its leaders had foolishly claimed victory over Darkness itself and abolished all references to it. That act was made doubly foolish now that Pell knew it was done by men aware of this abbey and its secret. The thing in the basement, immortal evidence of the Dark, hidden away.

However, the Uthiri remembered. They knew how to listen to the Dark. Pell's grandmother had taught her. Growing up, she'd hear voices in empty places.

Iress Pell decided, immediately, it was time to try. She stood and walked out to the empty hallway. It was impressed upon her, as occurred every time she walked the corridors, what a lonesome place this was. In this corner of the castle, not a soul could be found. Pell stepped lightly, the echoing tap of her footfalls the only break in the silence. They brought her to a solitary nook she liked. Tying her blindfold into place, she cast her mind into the world of Light. It was mostly empty here, save a spider creeping along its web in the corner. Turning one's Sight to the Dark was a simple, but unintuitive, thing. It was no surprise that her fellow Embrells didn't do it accidentally. She shut her inner Sight while opening her inner ears. One didn't *see* the world of Darkness; there was nothing there but shadows. But one could hear the things lost within it.

The most shallow depth was called the Hollow. This was where one could listen unaided. Any level deeper required the sort of wicked ritual Pell suspected had been performed by someone here. The Hollow was where the souls of the dead wandered if they'd died in Darkness. As the name implied, it was *supposed* to be empty, and usually was, except in places with an unhappy history. Places where some tragedy had occurred.

Places like this one.

Whispers. Faint echoes surrounding her. Residual vibrations coming off the very walls. Above it all, however, something newer. A sobbing from a ghost who had not been dead long. A lingering soul stricken with an injury so deep it endured beyond death.

Pell began moving, running her hands along the stones, following the weeping woman. Pell was getting closer, but the ghost was moving now. She chased it, turning and weaving through the interior of the castle until her hands impacted on a solid door. She lifted her blindfold to see where she was. The front gate. Pell swung the obstacle aside and moved on, only to find the sound of the specter had disappeared over one of the hills surrounding the tiny valley. Iress Pell sprinted to the spot, but by the time she arrived, the spirit had fled beyond her senses.

"Iress Pell," came a voice behind her, "is everything all right?"

It was Ollett. "Yes, Captain, thank you." She peered through the break in the craggy, elevated border of the shallow bowl housing the abbey. There were sheer cliffs to the west and south of the plateau. She and Mai had first entered from the east, but she'd never, until this moment, observed what lay to the north. It was a rocky slope, steep but traversable. It almost looked like a trail. "Is there anything down there?"

"Why do you ask? What brought you out here?" he asked.

"Just a sense," she answered. "I can feel something in that direction."

"It ain't exactly a secret or anything. Just...we don't talk about it."

"What is it?"

"The catacombs," Ollett said. "Old tunnels carved right into the cliff just down yonder. The place where you and I and everyone here will one day be buried. Where everyone who's ever served here in the past *has* been buried."

"I see," she said, thoughtfully. The enduring dead often stayed near the final resting places of their bodies.

She returned to the abbey and to her shift in the lower chamber. She could hardly focus on the demon's mind. Instead, she watched Iress Ahl. The Arrantine was supervising some of the cleaning and making notes of the things in the room that would need replacing. One of the altars holding the creature had been chipped on one side, and the network of lidocrafted runes covering the ceiling had begun to wear away in one area.

"Iress Pell, are you alright?" Iress Em, the Curial working with her that day roused her back to attention.

"Yes, just having a hard time focusing today," Iress Pell said. "Have you been to the catacombs?"

"Oh, many times," Em replied.

"Where is it?" Pell asked.

"In a network of caves to the north of the dell." She was more eager than Ollett to elaborate. "It's a fascinating place. Some of the space has been carved out manually but others are part of a natural cave system. The seals over the niches that hold the bodies often have beautiful en-

183

gravings and epitaphs on them as well. I'd be happy to take you when we're finished here."

"That would be wonderful," Iress Pell responded.

"I'll get the key from Iress Lee once we're finished here and meet you in the courtyard."

Pell waited for Iress Em near the lidocrafter's shop. It was a small building outside the main castle, and the workspace was an open-air studio from which poured rich, oily aromas and the soothing sounds of tools being expertly used.

Master Halvett was an immensely talented artisan. He was also generous with his time and patient in conversation. Pell liked him almost immediately. While he could always be found fashioning something interesting and lovely, today he was working on his masterpiece.

"What sort of wood is it made of?" Pell inquired. With her eyes, she traced the elegant lines of silver running over and through the sweeping grain of the finely finished wood. It would one day replace the door to the cellar chamber. Pell felt her gaze unworthy of the exquisite sight, though she did not turn away. It deeply pained her that this triumphant work of art would be admired by so few and was ultimately fated to be slowly eaten away by the infectious Darkness ruining the current door.

"Bristlecone pine," Halvett answered cheerfully. "They're rare and sacred. Cutting one down is punishable by death. Without permission, that is. They live thousands of years in the highest, driest, and most exposed places. Some even seem to thrive around this place. Bristlecones make for the most effective lidocrafting wood, and the older the tree, the better its warding power."

"Bristlecone," Pell said in wonder. She'd heard of small things—a personal Star of Saeris, a ring, or an ericle made of the wood but never—*never*—anything so grand as a full door. "How old was this one?"

"Four thousand years, or thereabouts," Halvett said in a tone she'd expect at a graveside. "The old girl had nearly gone when we cut away a large, dead part of her and hauled her here."

"Four thousand years," Pell reflected. "What might she tell us?"

"Well, if she's anything like the old ladies I know, it's to keep our mouths closed when we chew our food," he quipped.

Pell laughed, then fruitlessly searched the courtyard again for Iress Em.

"Have you any lidocrafted weapons?" Pell asked.

"Oh yes," Halvett said. "A whole rack of them, some from the Age of Legends. Wait here a moment."

He disappeared into the back room of his shop and returned with a wooden box from which he pulled a graceful dagger. He held it before her. "You ever see such a pretty thing?"

Pell had not. She marveled at how the light glinted off the holy symbols that artfully and seamlessly fused with the lines of the hilt and blade. It was like an exotic snake, as alluring in its lithe beauty as it was fatal.

"Puts a spell on you, don't it?" Halvett asked.

Pell met his eyes. He'd been watching her.

"Why don't they make weapons like this anymore?" Pell wondered.

"We no longer fight demons—except in this place, of course. A man can be just as easily killed by any old blade, and these cost a heap more to make." He placed the dagger back in the box. "Of course, then there's that thing in the cellar. Lidocrafted or no, makes no difference."

Halvett snapped the box shut.

"May I borrow it some time?" Pell asked. "Might be useful to see how the creature below reacts to the sight of it."

"For that you'd need the Matriarch's permission."

"Of course," Pell said.

She turned to the still-empty courtyard. The hour was more than twenty minutes old. Iress Em wasn't coming.

Pell said goodbye to Master Halvett and began walking in the direction of the catacombs, determined to find it herself. Ollett and his men blocked her way.

"Sorry, Iress," Ollett said. "Iress Lee says no one is to leave the premises today."

Pell sensed he'd been asked to stop her specifically. Without a word, she turned and went to find Iress Em or Iress Lee.

Upon entering the abbey, Pell nearly collided with the Matriarch.

"Why don't you want me to visit the catacombs?" Pell demanded immediately.

"Excuse me?" Iress Lee said.

"When Iress Em asked you for the key, you must have refused to give it to her. Ollett acted strange when I asked about it this morning, and even more so just now. What is it you don't want me to find?"

"Watch your tongue, Iress Pell," the Matriarch warned. "There's nothing to see there. Why would you want to visit?"

"To pay my respects to those who've passed on. Those who rendered service to this place."

Iress Lee shook her head. "No, I'm afraid not. It's not the sort of place we regularly visit. We keep it locked at all times. Except when interring one of our own, of course."

Pell could tell the old woman was not lying exactly, but there was some withholding, an element of deception in her answer.

"You'll have to trust me, I'm afraid. Visiting that place will do you no good."

That was a true statement. At least, Iress Lee believed it was.

"Very well," Pell said, before stalking away.

Three nights later, Pell was in Mai's quarters tutoring her on projecting.

"Remember, keep the image as clear as you can in your head," Pell instructed. "Imagine so vividly you believe it. Convince yourself that you're seeing it with your *own* eyes, not mine."

Iress Mai nodded, licking her lips. Pell couldn't see her friend's brow under the blindfold she wore but knew it was tight with concentration. Pell turned, staring at the blank wall of Mai's room, waiting.

A shape fluttered by, over her head.

"Did it work?" Mai asked hurriedly.

"It looked like a bird flying across the room."

"That's what I was trying to make you see!" Mai exclaimed. "What kind of bird?"

"It was too blurry to really tell," Pell confessed.

Mai's shoulders fell. She brightened a moment later. "Well, it's a start."

"And we can try as many times as you want," Pell said. "When you've done it successfully with me, we'll find a volunteer for you to work on. Someone with a mind you're less familiar with."

"It would have to be Bryn," Mai concluded. "The other factions are not supposed to know we can do this."

"I don't see why it matters up here," Pell said. "But yes, I suppose so."

"Do you think the other factions have anything like this?" Mai asked. "Secret ways to defend themselves?"

"I know Curials can make Light patterns with their Restoratives that hurt instead of heal. Do you suppose Arrantines could arrange furniture so poorly it drives enemies away in disgust?"

Mai laughed. "Maybe. And back when the Church had dedicated singers, the Opravics could make your ears bleed with poor singing."

They continued practicing, and Mai showed some improvement. She could convincingly make small adjustments to the ordinary environment: a brick out of place or a bottle on the floor. However, a more complicated image was always hazy, though Pell could often guess what it was.

"How about this one?" Mai asked.

The indistinct shape appeared before Pell.

"A fir tree? Growing out of the floor of your room?"

"Yes!" Mai said. "Alright, one more."

Pell watched the scene before her and suddenly saw the shimmering, shifting image of bodies on the floor. They were lying in blood, covered in lacerations and pierced with arrows.

Pell pushed Mai out of her mind and turned to look at her blindfolded friend. Mai wore a strange smile.

"Did you get it?" Mai asked, giggling. "No? It was your family."

Pell tried to speak but it took a few tries before she was successful. "Mai, why would you...are you alright?"

Mai broke into tears. "I'm so sorry," she sobbed. "I don't know why I did that."

Pell connected with Mai and found her friend's mind a more unstable place than she'd ever known it. In the next moment, however, it was as it had always been.

"Are you well, Mai?" Pell asked.

"Yes, I'm sorry," Mai said. "I think I'm just tired."

Long after she had left Mai's quarters, Pell walked alone through the narrow corridors of the abbey. She was determined to find the catacombs, even if she found nothing but a locked door and walked away with no better understanding of why the Matriarch wanted to keep her away. If she could find a way in, however, she might confirm her suspicions that a chaos call had been performed. Perhaps find some clue as to who had performed it.

If nothing else, once there, she would turn her ear to the Hollow. She might learn some vital information from the wandering souls within. They would be easier to hear at this time. It was the earliest hours of the morning, the darkest hours. To the faithful, they were the shrouded hours, the frightening gap between the setting of the Star of Saeris and the rising of the sun.

Pell's boots were in her hand instead of on her feet. The light tapping of her footfalls over the cold stones wouldn't travel far. Still, she made them as faint as she could and kept her breath shallow.

Despite her focus on stealth, she was distracted by the incident with Mai earlier that evening. Pell could make no sense of it. It was so unlike her.

A sound broke both the silence and Pell's musings, pulling her mind back into the lonely hallway. Pell retreated into the shadows and held her breath as a black shape rushed past her in a rustle. She couldn't be sure, but Pell thought it was Iress Em—and she seemed as eager to avoid being seen as Pell. Once Em disappeared around the corner, Pell moved again. An Iress was allowed to be up and about at any time, but few of the faithful would do so during the shrouded hours. Pell hadn't expected to see anyone. What was Iress Em up to?

Pell decided to worry about that another time. She tried to push Mai from her mind as well. If she was going to slip past the men patrolling the grounds, she needed to concentrate.

There were two on watch, Rykard and Jos. She watched them patrolling the border but didn't connect with them. This would be easier if she could; she'd walk right past them while convincing them there was no one there. However, it was likely the two had been trained to recognize an Embrell connection. She'd have to go without that advantage. Thankfully, she had another. Having spent a lot of time blind to the world, she was comfortable moving about in the darkness.

Pell slipped out of the gate and stole forward across the stone walkway that split the courtyard in two.

Crouching in the darkness near the center of the dell, she waited for one of the guards to pass farther beyond the northern break in the wall that led to the catacombs beyond. When he was far enough away, she rushed across the dirt and through the gap.

On the other side, she pulled her boots onto her feet but still walked as quietly as she could until she was well out of earshot of the men on watch. After that, her footsteps sounded loud as thunder in the unnatural stillness. She'd already forgotten how truly otherworldly the terrain surrounding the abbey was. No drone of crickets, no far-off howl of coyote, no leaves fluttering in the wind, nothing.

The trail led her onto a narrow shelf that jutted out of a steep cliff face. Pell clung to the rock wall with each careful step, stopping occasionally to feel for the tomb entrance. It was slow going, and as the time wore on, Pell worried she'd passed the door somewhere in the impenetrable gloom. Only moments later, however, her searching hands met flat wood instead of stone. Her exploring fingers confirmed her find as a doorway cut into the cliff face. She found the handle and tried the latch.

As expected, it was locked tight.

Em had told her the tombs were, at least partially, part of a natural network of caves. If that was true, there was very likely a natural entrance somewhere around here. It had surely been bricked up, but she had to check.

Pell eased her way along the rocky ledge, past the entrance. As she felt along the wall, she was aware of the slightest increase in light. Whether it was the clouds thinning above and admitting moonlight or the sun preparing to rise, she could not yet tell. Either way, it helped her locate a few natural tunnels that might have allowed her entrance if they'd not been filled with bricks, as she'd suspected they would be. Once she was beyond the sight of the door, around a corner, she nearly tripped on some loose stones at her feet. She might have assumed these bricks had fallen out of place as a natural result of age and disrepair if not for the obvious drag marks along the ground. They'd been moved. *Recently* moved. And there was enough space in the newly exposed passage to crawl through.

Pell bent and carefully entered the small gap. It was tight, but, shuffling forward on her stomach, she was able to push herself beyond the opening. The tunnel abruptly ended once she was fully inside. For a moment, she assumed it was a dead end until she pushed her back against the roof and it lifted. With a heave against what proved to be aged wood and not stone—though still quite heavy—she was able to scramble her way up and over an expertly fashioned concrete ledge and onto the floor. She was inside!

Pulling a match and candle from her pocket, Pell set the wick alight

190

and held the dim flame aloft. She had emerged from a stone sarcophagus. It had been built along the wall over the natural entrance she'd entered from. She wondered where the previous occupant was now. Her imagination answered with images of the corpse having broken out, wandering these dark corridors or the hills outside.

She was holding her breath and tensely listening. No shambling footfalls reached her ears. It was perfectly silent. She was alone, unless she counted the hundreds of remains all around her. From the stillness of the air, Pell concluded the bodies continued their long rest undisturbed. At least, here in the living world. Would these halls be so silent were she to turn her inner ear to the Dark and the realms of the dead Below? At least one ghost wandered both the abbey and this place. She would be surprised if it did so alone. There was so much hurt here. So much madness and death.

Under the flickering light, Pell crossed the narrow hallway and studied the niches carved into the walls. They were five high and all occupied on the left side. A few tall and thin windows were also carved out of the exterior wall, though the day was still too young to be casting any light through them. This had initially been a natural passage but was dug out in some places and supplemented with masonry in others. Even then, the angles in this place, while they appeared to have an intended order, were just misshapen enough to make menacing shapes of the shadows.

Pell read the inscription on the wooden seal over the recess closest to her: *Iress Ett, 280 – 309 JR*. Beneath this was the Embrell emblem. Iress Ett had been of the same Iress discipline as Pell. She said a silent prayer for the woman—dead now more than three hundred years—that she might rest in the Embrace, forever in peace.

Iress Pell took a few steps further down the hallway and read the next inscription: *Iress Sen, 287-321 JR*, also an Embrell. Below her was *Iress Tal, 294-336 JR*, an Embrell. The one beyond her was an Embrell as well. For a moment, Iress Pell believed this to be an Embrell-specific section of the tomb, but, even as she considered this, she saw a few further inscriptions were for Curials and Arrantines. They were just mostly Embrells laid to rest here.

Taking a side passage, Pell studied the niches carved into this corridor as well. The bodies here were all from the three hundreds. Embrells outnumbered the other factions in this section also, and she noticed each one had died fairly young. Most in their forties. In the next corridor, it ceased to feel like a coincidence.

She moved at a hurried pace now, down another branching passage and another. She was desperate to find some clue that this was not the constant truth in this place, but everywhere she looked only confirmed it. Embrells outnumbered any other faction by more than double.

Additionally, the problem worsened over time. The closer the dates got to the current one, the younger the Embrells were dying—in their thirties, even twenties.

Now that she considered it, she might have wondered at the fact that she and Mai had been called together. There was no Embrell here when they arrived. No aged woman ready to pass this responsibility on. There was Iress Bryn, yes, but she had decided not to participate. Had she discovered this secret in the catacombs? Or witnessed what happened to the last Embrell Iress here?

What *had* happened to her? To all of them?

If Pell could locate the last Embrell to have died, perhaps she could...what? Did she have it in her to study the corpse and determine the cause of death? She thought she did, but she'd find the body first before deciding.

A few turns later brought her up to the present date. This section boasted newer seals and empty niches beyond. The gaping cavities in the wall were waiting and ready for their eternal occupants. Which would be hers? Which would be Mai's? Might they fill the next two?

Step by step, she walked further into the corridor. She pulled a handkerchief out of her pocket and held it over her mouth and nose to block out the odor. The bodies here were not yet dust and bones.

Pell found the last seal. Expertly carved into the wood by Halvett's exacting hand, she read: *Iress Rún 582-623 JR; Ever In Our Hearts, Ever*

192

In Her Embrace. She'd lived longer than most Embrells around her, though there was no telling how old she had been when she'd arrived. Perhaps she and others who'd lasted into their forties had arrived in their late thirties. How long had they lived after arriving? How long did Pell have?

Holding the flame close, Pell studied the seal to see how she might break into it without leaving a trace. Her eyes widened.

The seal was already broken.

Eight lidocrafted brackets held the wooden seal in place over the recess, and the silver nails that connected the brackets to the wood had been wrested out. Whoever had done it had hastily tried to cover up the violation but had not done a very good job.

Forgive me, Iress Rún, Pell thought. With trembling hands, she slid the wooden seal aside and squinted against the foul air it released. It was situated high enough that Pell had to stand on the tips of her toes to peer inside.

She saw nothing in the inky cavity until she raised her little flame. She'd only ever heard the ritual described to her, but what she saw before her was exactly what she'd imagine a chaos call would look like.

Rún's body had been dismembered and disemboweled. Each organ, each tooth, each toe and finger, every individual piece had been intentionally misplaced in a way that was a sick mockery to a body's rightful design. Whoever had done this had offered a ritual prayer to Okgram and watched shadows cover the remains as if they were black liquid. Then the individual placed their face into the amplified channel they'd opened and spoken into the Dark at a depth that allowed their voice to travel long and far.

The sight gripped her. Pell remained frozen in place until a sharp pain in her hand pulled her back. A drop of hot wax had dripped down the candle and burned her.

She began backing down the hall, afraid to turn her back on the remains. It was little wonder why Rún's ghost wandered and wept in the empty land of stray souls. Was she here?

To answer this, Pell turned her inner ear to the Hollow and fell to her knees, hands clasped over her head. Assailing her from all sides was a cacophonous blare of sorrowful wailing and mad screams. Lost spirits churned about her, sweeping her away in white, violent rapids of grief. In the maelstrom she could make out a few voices.

"It binds us!" one shrieked.

"Feeds upon us all!" sobbed another.

"It blocks the way," a voice was repeating, again and again. "It blocks the way!"

"Help us!"

"Free us!"

"Help us!"

"HELP US!"

The seals over the niches began shuddering, splintering under violent pounding from within. Each soul begging for salvation. For release. For any existence but what they had.

Pell shut the connection off, instantly returning her to the stillness of the living world. The seals, save Rún's, were undisturbed here. The cave's silence was broken now by only one sobbing voice, her own. She didn't know how long it took to gain control of herself, only that it wasn't until she was breathing in small hiccups and her cheeks burned from dried tears that she was able to move again. She groped for the candle she'd dropped and lit it again. Wearily, she got to her feet and began walking back to the exit. It was a meandering, distracted journey, but she eventually found herself back in the first area she'd entered. Crawling, once again, through the sarcophagus tunnel, she emerged into a bright morning.

Pell returned as quickly as she dared. By the morning light, she could see how precipitous the path really was.

CHAPTER 15

DESERT SNAKE

The Frontier

She'd not slept well. Every move Crowan made, each catch in his breath, every rustle, brought her leaping out of slumber. Even now, Ameryn had her hand upon his head. He was still hot.

An urgent knock at the door made her jump. "Mrs. Vowery!" called Dav on the other side.

Ameryn dashed to the door and swung it open. "What is it?"

"The Uthiri, coming this way, fast," he said, crossing the room to check the sight out of the window.

"What?" Ameryn stared passed him, through the dirty glass. They

195

were there, a distant blemish on the horizon.

"They'll be here in ten minutes, fifteen at the most," Dav said. "They must have ridden all night. How's Crow? Can we move him?"

Ameryn swallowed, forcing her breathing to slow. "No, he's only gotten worse."

"Then stay here. I'll draw them away." Dav marched back to his room and began hastily packing. Ameryn followed. He had a map laid out on a small table in the room. Before folding it, he pointed at the head of the river. "There's a waterfall where the Durado comes out of the mountains. If you still want to wait out the war in the mountain sanctuary, meet me there in a few days, but I'll understand if you want to take Crow back to Silver Hills."

Ameryn blinked, she'd expected more argument from him. "You aren't going to try to convince me?"

"I know when a battle's lost," Dav acknowledged, and she heard the honesty behind his words. He would no longer bring up the Sword.

"What will you do if we fail to meet you at the falls?" Ameryn asked.

"Don't know, but I reckon I'll be just fine on my own."

"How do you know where this…sanctuary is?"

"I was there once before, as a boy," he said. "There's more to that story, but no time for it now."

"What if the Uthiri come here?" Ameryn asked.

He paused. "I don't know, but I'll do everything I can to keep that from happening. Don't worry, ma'am; if I'm good at anything, it's pissing people off enough to chase me halfway across the frontier. I just got to stay ahead of them."

He hefted his bag and sword and walked out into the hallway where he paused and turned back to her. "If you decide to meet me, but I don't show up within a week, you'll know I didn't survive this. Then, Silver Hills is your best option. But be careful, this can't be the only war party on the rampage. The roads aren't safe. I know I don't need to tell you to take care of Crow, but take care of yourself too. If this is the last I see you, I pray the Goddess watches over you and yours…and I'm sorry for any grief I brought you."

With a tip of his hat, he bounded from the hallway and down the stairs. Ameryn followed him as he burst onto the streets. She stood there until he rode by at a steady trot. By the time the dust cleared, she couldn't even see him anymore. Just like that, he was gone.

Ameryn walked back to the room she was sharing with Crowan and peered through the dust-caked window at the approaching soldiers. She felt a sharp need to be doing more than only watching and hoping. It wasn't much, but after a moment more, she dropped to her knees and sent a prayer to the Goddess.

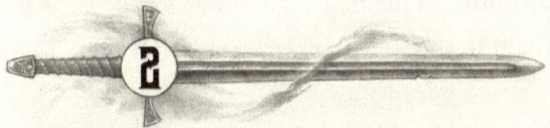

It would seem suspicious if Daverell baited them into a chase right away. It had to appear like they caught him by surprise as he was setting out for the day.

"Looks like we get to be soldiers at least once more, old boy," Daverell said, patting Druid's neck.

He rode to a spot where the Uthiri would be able to see him plainly and made a show of taking a drink out of his waterskin. Just a man in no hurry at all, taking in the morning. He glanced over his left shoulder and gaped at the approaching soldiers for a heartbeat before hastily stoppering his bottle and kicking Druid into a gallop. It was a good thing, too. Not a moment later, an arrow pierced the ground where he'd been only moments before. He'd thought he was out of accurate range. He would not underestimate them again.

He guided his horse in a wide arc, leading his pursuers east, along the canyon.

As Dav rode, he mentally listed the disadvantages he had in the current situation. The group chasing him were about fifty in number, far too many to attack directly. He was unfamiliar with the area. He had neither bow nor arrows and, even if he had, wasn't especially good with them. Any long-range engagement would come from the Uthiri only.

It wasn't all bad news, however. The Uthiri were equally unfamiliar with this landscape, and, with greater numbers, they would be slower and less reactive. There was little chance any of their mounts could outrun Druid. The rising sun would be in their eyes, once he had the chase going eastward. Of course, it would be in his as well, but he'd kick up as much dust as he could to give them the worst of it. Additionally, Daverell and his warhorse were well rested, while the Uthiri had been traveling through the night. Their commander was acting rashly. He was either a fool or so obsessed with revenge he wasn't thinking clearly. Hopefully both. He needed them mad as hell, or they might decide to stay the night in the shelter of Marker and take up the chase the following day.

Daverell pulled Druid back and forth into unpredictable movements, avoiding the arrows falling around them. By the time they were parallel to the sheer edge of the canyon, the chase had spread out, with only a few still close enough to pose a threat. Easing back, Daverell allowed one of the Uthiri riders to draw even with him on his left side. Once the man was riding between Druid and the gaping canyon, Dav pulled his horse's reins to the side, forcing the Uthiri soldier dangerously to the sheer edge. The man drew his sword, taking a wild swing at Daverell, who parried with his own blade and stabbed the man in his armpit. He screamed as Daverell yanked on Druid's reins, hammering into the soldier and his mount, sending them over the edge. It took an equally hard wrenching in the opposite direction to keep himself from pitching off the side after them. Druid whinnied loud in protest.

The falling man's screams echoed off the canyon's walls, and Daverell hoped the Uthiri heard them too. He hoped they liked that fellow. He hoped they were vowing to hunt Daverell down, even if it took all day.

A dry gully feeding into the greater canyon appeared in front of him. Before Daverell had time to react, Druid was sailing over the fifteen-foot gap. Daverell had never taken his steed over such a long jump, but the beautiful beast managed it, landing in a scramble as the loose ground beneath them gave way. Leaping and flailing, Druid's hooves clambered back to the surface. As they darted out of the gully, another Uthiri soldier and his mount came crashing down into the gap behind them. One of the vaulting horse's legs snapped with a sharp crack, followed by agonized shrieking as it fell back onto its rider who also cried in pain.

The rest of his pursuers lost time as they took the long way, around the small gully.

Dav turned south, hoping to further thin the enemy's numbers or momentarily lose them in the steep plateaus and rocky bluffs that lay in that direction. The war party had fallen enough behind at this point that Dav eased his horse into a canter, careful to stay within range of their eyes but not their arrows. Druid was breathing and sweating heavily, despite the cool morning air. The Uthiri slowed as well, and Dav disappeared into the craggy terrain.

He immediately came across a steep hill with loose gravel on one side. The backside of the hill provided a safer way to the top, which Daverell used. No sooner had he reached the summit than he was spotted and fired upon. Daverell tried to appear panicked as he dodged the arrows by swiftly riding down the back side of the hill. He stopped when he was just out of sight and listened. Some of their group gave chase, straight up the gravelly side, as he hoped they would. Halfway up the incline, the Uthiri horses lost their footing. They slid and tumbled into a tangled heap at the base. Dav dismounted, risking a peek over the ridge and got his first good look at the leader. He was a large man with a red and angry face behind a long black beard. He was shouting at his men, separating them into groups and pointing them in different directions.

Hurrying back to Druid, Dav rode cautiously down into a shallow ravine, sword drawn. The place was a maze of boulders, bluffs, and sandstone channels. They'd find him before long, but in smaller groups and in an environment unfavorable to ranged combat. Daverell glanced about, trying to see in every direction at once. Any moment, he expected to hear an Uthiri shout they'd found him, calling the rest of the wolves.

Moments later, however, he spotted *them*. A group of four at the end of the same ravine he was hiding in, their backs to him.

Daverell charged; he'd have to fight to get through. They heard him before he reached them, and one sent an arrow Daverell's way. He cut it out of the air and swung his blade into the man's helmet. The blow was enough to knock the man off his mount and into the dirt, dazed.

The next soldier was raising his bow and drawing an arrow back. Daverell cut through the tip, and more than a few fingers, before the archer could fire. The man howled in pain as Dav kicked him off his horse as well.

Dav left the last two with superficial wounds before slapping each of the riderless horses with the flat of his sword. The animals ran, panicked and wild, in different directions.

That should keep you busy, Dav thought, kicking Druid hard, riding past them. However, almost immediately, he pulled back on the reins. Another group of Uthiri were ahead of him, no doubt drawn by the sounds of the scuffle.

He was trapped, Uthiri at either end of the gulch. He searched for a way out; the walls were only nine feet high, but they may as well have been ninety for how sheer they were. He rode back the other way and noticed, to his left, a small gully connecting to the gorge that, while still quite steep, might allow him to scurry out. Daverell leaped off the back of his charger into the narrow flume and scrambled up, whistling for Druid to follow. The horse looked at him like he was mad for a moment before placing his front hooves at the entrance and leaning into the space. It was barely big enough for the horse to fit but with Dav pulling at his reins, Druid clambered up. Shouts of the Uthiri on either side followed them as, somehow, shakily, Dav and his white steed managed to climb up and out. Just as Druid was clearing the gully an Uthiri sent an arrow after them. It struck Druid in the rump, and the horse whinnied in pain, bucking as Dav climbed into the saddle guiding him out of the enemy's line of sight. Dav didn't have time to examine the wound but feeling at it as they rode away convinced him it hadn't gone deep. The archer must not have had time to fully draw.

"Don't worry, boy," Dav said. "We'll make them pay for that."

Druid sailed over the gap of the gulch and the Uthiri below, carrying Dav down the other side.

It was time to get out of here. If he didn't have the enemy soldiers spitting mad now, he never would, and his luck would only last so long in a region with so many places for him and the war party to surprise each other.

Further on, the terrain flattened into a wide, unbroken expanse. It took the Uthiri time to spot him and regroup outside of the rough section, which allowed Daverell to get ahead. When the chase continued, it was a slower one, each side content with keeping the other in their sights for now.

For Dav, it was only a matter of pulling them south. Far enough that, if they needed to resupply, it made more sense for them to hit Rockmond or Andira and not Marker. Riding until the end of the day should do it. Then, he could slip away in the dark.

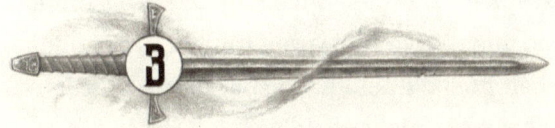

As the day was drawing to an end, Daverell made a show of stopping for the night. When the Uthiri rushed in, he rode away. He did this twice more until, finally, Dav and the war party entered a stalemate where all involved wordlessly agreed to stop for the night.

He settled under an outcropping of rock that would block any arrows from raining down on him—as long as none of the Uthiri crept close enough to shoot from a more forward position. It was a decent campsite. Shame he wouldn't be there for long. It was time to slip away and do so in a way that fooled the Uthiri into believing he'd gone further south.

Daverell always carried a little pitch tar in the event he had to make a torch. He set some alight in his firepit. Enough to burn for an hour, making it appear to anyone watching that he was still at his encampment, feeding the meager flame. He even piled his saddlebags and bedroll near the campfire to cast a vague shadow on the wall. At the distance his enemies maintained, he expected that, even with a spyglass, it would appear he was sitting at the fire. Something he'd much rather be doing than what he was about to.

"Stay here, old friend," he said to Druid. "You'll help convince them I've not left. If they injure you any further, I'll not rest until the cold carcass of every one of them is on the insides of the local buzzards." Once they'd stopped, Dav had removed the arrow from Druid's backside and dressed the wound. Now, he hobbled the horse and dropped a few apples at his feet.

Daverell crept away to the sound of Druid happily crunching on the sweet fruit. The Uthiri had almost certainly set a lookout. Daverell would have to kill the watchman before he could slip away, or they'd just take up the chase again. Sneaking up on a fellow was more a matter of patience than anything else. Most men lacked the restraint to move as slowly as it took to not make a noise and the composure to wait long enough for suspicions to pass once they did. And sound wasn't the only thing that might give him away tonight. The moon was high and more than half full. Without a whisper of clouds in any direction. It was nearly as bright as night could be.

Getting closer, Daverell lowered himself to a crawl, as much on his belly as a rattlesnake. The thought made him suddenly extra thankful for the frigid desert night. If he crossed paths with a rattler, the cold would put it in a less aggressive mood.

Stealing silently through the sagebrush in a wide arc along a low ridge, he eventually found himself behind the enemy camp. He slowly rose, searching for the man or men with the unenviable job of keeping watch. They were likely taking shifts, which complicated Dav's timing. If Dav dispatched one right before another came for their turn as sentry, the body would be discovered too soon and ruin his escape.

Perhaps they were all asleep? It wasn't an implausible hope. After riding all the previous night and day, the war party would be exhausted to the point of collapse.

Dav had left his sword behind, carrying three hidden daggers instead. It made him feel a bit naked. He was a soldier, not an assassin. He preferred direct conflict—a fight against an opponent in uniform. But a soldier was also adaptable, and this was not his first time sneaking into an enemy encampment.

But, Goddess willing, it will be the last, Daverell thought, hoping his days of soldiering might be coming to an end. However, today had not felt like as much a return to his old ways as he'd feared. In the long and hot ride leading the Uthiri away from Ameryn and Crow, there had been plenty of time to consider why.

All his life he'd operated under orders. And while he was close with his fellow soldiers and fought for them, the homes and families they defended were abstract things. Oh, he loved his country, in a general sense. He had also loved, and been loved by, a few women in his time, but only ones with as transitory a lifestyle as his own. But now that he'd tasted of rooted family life, he finally understood what it was he'd been defending all this time. More than that, he wanted it. It was a foolish thing to hope for, old as he was, but if he could save the boy and his mother from the war, maybe he would deserve it. A little.

Daverell was getting close now. He stilled his already slow movements. Just up ahead, as merely a shape in the moonlight, one—and only one—of the Uthiri men kept watch. The man was facing away from him, towards his own far-off campfire.

Barely breathing, Daverell edged forward, even more cautiously than before.

As he prowled closer, the desert silence was broken by the low throbbing of dozens of snoring men and the occasional stir of their horses. Daverell sneaked a peek to his right and saw them, sprawled out along the ground, every last one asleep.

To Dav's surprise, the man who was supposed to be on watch was also adding to the chorus of snores. His chin was on his chest, which rose and fell in regular rhythm.

Now that it came to it, cutting a sleeping man's throat from behind

203

didn't sit right. If the man had been alert, Dav could better justify it. Matched in a battle of watcher and watched, he would have lost fairly to Daverell, but with the man asleep—*fast* asleep—it required blood much colder than Dav's to execute him. What if Daverell simply left? He could sneak back to Druid and slip away under the man's snoozing ignorance. But he didn't like the idea of that either. The man, or whoever was set to replace him, was liable to wake up at any moment and spoil his escape.

Daverell settled on the only option left. If these were the cards he'd been dealt, he'd have to play them the best he could.

Easing a hand over the man's mouth, Dav pushed a dagger against his throat. The sentry's eyes sprung open, and he stole a sharp breath through Dav's fingers.

"Don't move," Daverell hissed directly into the man's ear. "I'll cut your throat if I sense so much as your toes twitching without my say so, got it?"

Dav didn't expect the trembling Uthiri man to understand him, but he managed a slight nod.

"You understand Threyan?" Dav asked.

A small nod again.

Dav pressed the blade even tighter against his neck. "Did I tell you to move that blistered head of yours, stranger? Blink once for yes, twice for no. Understand?" Daverell shifted his position so he could see the man's eyes. He very deliberately blinked once, and Dav could read so much more than the 'yes' in those eyes. They were wide and terrified; whoever he was, this man was no soldier. "Are any of your fellow child-killers relieving your watch soon?"

The man blinked twice.

"Okay, then you're coming with me," Dav said, lifting him into a standing position. "Walk. Quietly."

Daverell kept his hand over the man's mouth and the knife at his throat. It made moving slow and difficult, but he didn't trust the man, nor were they far away enough yet for Dav to attempt to remove it. When they finally were, Dav pulled him to a stop and whispered, "If

I take my hand off your mouth will you make a ruckus and try to call your friends over?"

The man blinked twice.

"Listen close, stranger," Daverell continued, "if you do, I'll focus my life's final moments on leaving you so painfully mutilated, you'll wish I'd left you a tongue with which to beg for a swift end to your pitiful life. Understand?"

One blink.

Daverell eased his hand off the man's face. The Uthiri stayed quiet as a fish and was so fearful he breathed little better. Dav waved his dagger in the direction of his camp. "Walk in front of me; make for my fire. Quietly," Dav muttered as they crept forward.

The pitch he'd set alight in the distance was beginning to burn out but still made for an adequate destination. It took them much less time to get there than Daverell had taken in the other direction, given the lack of care Dav was now taking in favor of speed.

He kicked out what was left of the fire when they reached it. "Name?" he questioned his prisoner.

"Leifal," the man answered.

"How you know the local language, Leifal?"

"I am Gyorick's interpreter," he replied. His accent was thick, but Daverell understood him just fine.

"Got a weapon on you?" Dav asked, already patting the man down.

"A small knife in my trousers pocket," he said. "I am never using it for anything but cutting food."

Dav found it, and nothing else, on the man. He pocketed the blade and ordered Leifal to pack his saddlebags for him. The captive did so under the reproachful eyes of Druid, whom Leifal was reluctant to get too close to. Dav would have preferred to pack himself but didn't dare turn his back to the man; he kept having to instruct Leifal where to put things.

As he was finishing up, Leifal spoke, "Listen, Captain Kain, you should know something—"

"Tell me once we're moving," Daverell answered.

Daverell helped Leifal onto Druid, who huffed at the situation, but Dav gave him their last apple before climbing on the horse's back himself. He urged his mount to the south, and they slipped away into the wild silence of the desert night.

"You were saying?" Dav asked the man sharing his saddle.

"Gyorick has men waiting for ambushing you in Andira," Leifal said.

"Gyorick? He the leader of your little war party?" Daverell surmised.

"Yes. And even if you are avoiding Andira, they will be catching you on the Dune Road. You will have to be stopping at the outpost; it is the only place having water between Andira and the border of Taggeroth. Gyorick is knowing this."

"Let me make one thing solid as bedrock, Leifal. I'm not interested in hearing anything you have to say, and even if I were, you could tell me it was raining in the middle of a hurricane, and the fact that it was you saying it would make me doubt my own wet head."

Leifal stayed silent after that. Daverell did likewise. He was unsure how detaining this new traveling companion would affect the days ahead. Leifal would complicate things, that was certain. Still, he'd already proved to be of some use. If he was telling the truth, then the Uthiri commander already assumed Daverell was making for Taggeroth. They might have even thought they were chasing him that direction. They'd learn their mistake by the time they reached Andira, but Daverell planned to either be hidden in the mountains or returning to the army by then. He'd find something to do with this Uthiri man before that.

Daverell did all he could to make the hunting party think he was continuing south. Once his horse had left some evidentiary droppings and hoof prints, Daverell changed directions and followed more stony paths northwest.

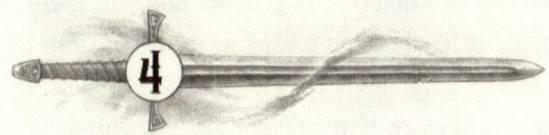

They rode well into the morning and didn't stop until the sun was high and the heat of the day was setting in. Daverell and the Uthiri man took refuge in a small cave carved out of the rocks by the harsh desert weather.

"I want to sleep through the day," Daverell told Leifal. "Soundly. Which means I'm going to tie you up." He pulled a rope from his saddlebags. "You need to take care of any necessaries before I do?"

Leifal finished the long drink he was taking from the water skin that Dav had thrown at him moments before. "Yes," he breathed.

"Don't be about it too long," Daverell said.

He tracked the Uthiri man's movements without keeping too close an eye on him; there was nowhere to run to out here. When he returned, it was with his hands held in front of him and close together. Daverell didn't have much experience with prisoners, but he guessed Leifal was one of history's most submissive.

"Please tie me in a way that allows me resting as well, I have not been having more than a few minutes of sleeping for days and days. Just keeping my eyes open now is taking all the strength I have."

Indeed, the man's words were slurred, and he was swaying with exhaustion. Daverell made sure the knots were good and tight. Leifal was asleep before Daverell even had his own bedroll spread out.

He was still sleeping when Daverell awoke. More than an hour passed before Leifal groaned into the waking world with him.

"Morning, princess," Daverell said from the mouth of the cave. He'd been sitting there sketching some distinctive rocks.

"You are allowing me sleep through the whole day," Leifal remarked, sounding grateful.

"You're just lucky I want to travel by night as much as possible," Dav commented.

Leifal grunted in pain as he lifted himself into a sitting position.

"I will never be getting used to sleeping on the ground. Did you know in Uthir I was sleeping in a feather bed? Soft and scented bluegoose feathers from Demerra."

"You slept just fine, and I told you before, if you must bore me with stories, do it once we're moving. We've got to get back to the river fast."

Leifal swayed as he worked himself into a standing position, gasping at his stiffness.

Dav laughed. "Nothing like spending hours on a bouncing horse to loosen you up."

Exiting the cave, Dav whistled for Druid. He'd left the horse grazing on what little grass there was when he'd gone out earlier to convince himself of their isolation. He studied the horizon again now, grateful that Druid was the only thing cantering towards him. Once the horse was saddled and Leifal had relieved himself, they set out just as the stars began appearing above them.

Leifal, now well rested, was eager to pass the time with conversation. "Gyorick is never being the best master," he said, "but ever since the emperor was inviting him to lead this campaign, he is becoming a nightmare. He was experiencing some success on the battlefield, in his youth. Though never as a leader. Gyorick thought this was his chance at becoming the commander he was always dreaming of. I am from Uthir, but I was taught in Meareth where I had to be learning the common tongue you speak also here in Threya. I wish I did not know it. Then Gyorick would not be taking me along. It has been unbearable, my time with them. They are ruffians, every one. Then after you were killing his brother—an awful man, Gyorick is only speaking of him with contempt—but he is taking it as a personal insult."

"And turned this whole campaign of his into a vendetta against me?"

"Oh yes, very much so. He is pushing us after you so hard we are useless with exhaustion. He is never being a great leader. When he was arriving here at the beach, it was with more than two hundred men."

Dav grunted. Most of this he'd guessed, though he'd underestimated their losses. "Why were you the one on watch that night?"

208

"They are making me do anything they do not want to," Leifal spat. "Gyorick is needing his fighting men well-rested, he is saying, but I am only the interpreter."

"And how did you track me to Marker?"

"There was a young man who is coming to Rockmond while we were there. He was asking Gyorick if he could be expecting compensation for some clue to your location."

Dav pulled Druid to a dead stop. "Did this young man wear a white hat?" Dav asked, though he was already sure of the answer.

"Yes."

"Do you know what this young man told him?"

"Oh yes, I was interpreting the whole exchange. He said you were heading to Marker where the rest of your group was planning on leaving you behind and going north. He was being unsure of your plans after that but was saying you might be interested in going west, possibly to the mountains."

Dav winced. He'd rather the Uthiri not know that part.

"You said he had men waiting in Andira."

"That is before the young man's information is leading us west. Gyorick is deciding to be leaving them there for now, in case you are changing your mind, or they could be driving you that direction."

Dav nodded. Hopefully, that's what he'd left them believing. "Gyorick thinks the rest of my party is heading north from Marker?"

"Yes," Leifal said. "But he isn't caring about them. Besides, General Foroka is having a war party patrolling the crossroads between Silver Hills and…Coyote, I'm thinking it was."

Another war party along the very path Ameryn was planning on taking? That was not good. He had to get back to Marker before she and Crow left.

"What happened to this young man?" Dav asked, nudging Druid back into a trot.

"He was paid." Leifal shrugged. "And as he was riding away, Gyorick was promising the money to anyone who is putting an arrow in him. The body was looking like a pin cushion last I was seeing it."

So, Rance was dead. Despite his betrayal, the news made Daverell sad. He'd hoped Rance could be granted the same opportunity he had: to grow old enough to see himself for what he was and learn to hate it. But he reckoned that was no great ending either. "None of that answers the one and only question I've had since I first saw you."

"What is that?" Leifal blinked curiously.

"What specter of foolishness would possess an educated man with thinning hair to step foot under the frontier sun without a hat?"

"Ah, yes." Leifal sounded a bit embarrassed. "I am wearing the official uniform of an interpreter. In Uthir we are favoring hoods over hats, and are seeing less sun generally, but an official like myself usually is conducting business indoors."

Daverell nodded. "Well, were I you, I'd place procuring a hat at as high a priority as your next breath."

"I see." Leifal contemplated. After a pause, he asked, "Are you having an extra, by chance?"

"Afraid not," Dav said.

CHAPTER 16

CALL TO THE DARK

The Nameless Abbey

Iress Mai, blindfolded, entered the lower chamber and walked as calmly as she could to the area next to the thing's head. Hungrily, she connected with it and breathed a sigh of pleasure at the sensation. At least, she thought she did. She couldn't really feel her body anymore. Mai floated away beneath the surface of the endless waves and into the bizarre world of this mind's landscape. She used to explore it but didn't even try anymore. There was no use. It was different every time. She just let herself drift. This was the only escape one could find in this awful place, and Mai let its currents bear her away. They'd taken her further every time. Deeper. So she could hardly see the surface.

This time, however, she felt something on the other side. She'd sunk so far that she could detect a bottom. No, not the floor, but another surface. Was this mind like a globe? Had she been carried to the other side? She began swimming towards it, curious.

When she burst through this new plane, she entered a new level of the creature's consciousness. Without meaning to, she'd broken into the reasoning part of its mind, and the whole of its mental universe was visible to her. What she found shocked her.

Suffering. *Only* suffering. The whole of its being had been reduced to a single concept. A plea that consumed it...and her now.

Help!

The poor, hurt thing. This profound ache was the only thought in its head. Mai could detect no deception. No hunger. No reasoning. Nothing at all beyond its single, desperate need: help. Help!

She retreated, tracing her tether back until she was out of the thing's mind and into her own—small and plain. She was crying.

"Are you alright?" Iress Em asked.

"No, I don't think so," Mai answered. "I need to leave."

"You need to stay here and stop wailing like an ill-tempered child," Em said.

"How can you be so hateful?" Mai shouted, rounding on her.

"What?" Mai sensed genuine confusion from Em. A trick. Em was playing games with her. They all were.

Mai marched to the door and began pounding on it. "I have to get out of here."

A hand took hers, and Em's voice sounded in her ears again. "Iress Mai, what is wrong?"

"Don't touch me!" Mai spat, pulling her hand away.

Iress Em called for the bell to be rung. The Matriarch and guards were there moments later. Mai tried to force herself past them, but they held her back and flung questions at her. She forced herself to calm down. Explaining herself was the fastest way to escape. She told them she'd suddenly felt unwell but was already improving. She could hear the annoyance in the Matriarch's voice when she said Mai's shift was nearly over anyway and urged her to catch her breath outside. But walking up the stairs, Mai knew she needed to talk to someone.

Iress Pell would be starting her shift soon. Mai had not even seen her that morning; the Matriarch had confined Pell to her room for some reason. Bryn might be the only other one that would understand.

She was sitting on the alcove bench where she spent nearly all her time. Mai sat next to her.

"Iress Mai?" Bryn looked up. "What is it?"

"I don't know," Mai said.

"Tell me," Bryn urged.

"It...it spoke to me...in a way."

"What did it say?" Bryn asked as if this was unsurprising.

"Only one word," Mai replied. "Not even a word, really. Just a notion. A plea. It was so sad and desperate, Bryn. Help was all it said. Help."

Bryn leaned forward, her face inches away from Mai's. "You sensed no malice? No evil?"

"Only helplessness," Mai stressed. "Why would a demon seek not to harm but only to escape?"

"What if..." Bryn whispered before glancing about, ensuring they were alone. "What if it's not a demon?"

After her shift, Pell returned to her room and began working on her translation to pass the time. For the most part, Pell didn't mind Lee's imposed confinement for her trip to the tombs, but she'd welcome a visit from Mai or Drizzy. She suddenly realized it had been a few days since she'd seen the cat.

There came a knock at her door. Pell answered, finding one of the individuals she'd been hoping for.

"Are you allowed visitors?" Mai asked, looking shaken.

"Yes," Pell said, pulling Mai in and shutting the door. "I just can't leave my room. Mai, what's wrong? You're trembling."

"Why did the Matriarch confine you to your room?" Mai inquired.

"You first," Pell insisted.

"Something happened," Mai said before relating the whole experience to Pell.

Iress Pell, after listening closely, spoke as sensitively as she could. "It must have been a trick, Mai. Don't forget, it tried to kill me."

"No," Mai protested. "It was only trying to escape. After today, I know it."

"It's toying with you, trying to mislead us."

Mai shook her head, striking the table they sat at with a fist. "You're not listening. I only sensed all this after breaking through layers of complexity and could see more clearly into its mind. It didn't force the communication on me. I observed it."

"It could have fabricated all of that."

"I've never felt any threat from it. Remember the demon in the pass? It was *nothing but* hunger and bloodlust. The thing in the basement is so different."

"What we encountered in the pass was a lesser demon; Vulsipher is one of the Elders, mentioned multiple times—by name—in the *Lyprakarum*. It's like comparing a hunting hound to its master."

"Bryn believes it might not be a demon at all," Mai said. "She thinks…she thinks it may be an angel."

"What?" Pell was dumbfounded. "That's absurd."

"It's not." Mai had tears in her eyes. "Why must the Beloworld be the only realm to trespass into our mortal lives? Why not the Above? We fear demons far more than we hope for angels. Why must that be so?"

In this, Pell was not well equipped to respond. She'd been raised to believe in and fear Darkness with no space given to the Light. A divine force of goodness had been a new idea to her when she'd converted. However, to imagine that the creature in the basement might be an angel? "What does Bryn think angels look like?"

"*The Song* never describes them, only says that any encounter with one left mortals fearful. I was afraid of it too, at first."

"You fear it no longer?" Pell asked.

"My fear is turning to pity."

"And what of the feeling surrounding the thing? The heavy sense of sickness that permeates this whole area?"

"*The Song of Saeris* says that Darkness follows chaos. Dark deeds lead to dark feelings. What could be more evil than what's being done here? Especially if it's not a demon from Below, but an angel from Above? Would this not be the most wicked of all acts? Would it not generate this oppressive sense in the air?"

"It very well may, but...an angel?" Pell shook her head. "*The Song* also says that the Light is knowable, but none can fathom the Darkness. The mind of that thing is truly inscrutable."

"It's not, Pell," Mai insisted. "I'm seeing it more and more. I can teach you how."

"I'm not sure I want to delve any deeper."

Mai laughed at this. "And even if it is a demon, do you not wonder if all this effort to kill it is worth it? The Age of Legends sounds like a scary place with its roaming monsters, but now that they're gone, have we inherited a paradise? Death and fear are still in the world. Perhaps we were all better off with a common enemy. Maybe it's even how the Goddess intended it."

Pell wanted to respond, but the words caught in her throat.

Mai continued, "Knowing the creature is there, seeing it with my own eyes—whatever it is—it's forced my faith to be more real. I've always held my beliefs at a safe distance; I didn't even realize it before coming here. It's not that I didn't believe the stories in the scriptures, but they were all from so long ago. Having to *really* believe...it scares me. But it comforts me too. Makes me feel like I am one of the people from those scripture stories. Like I can do something significant, as they did."

"By killing it," Pell pronounced. It wasn't a question, but the silence that followed made it clear Mai was considering her answer as though it was.

"Iress Bryn told me she's heard the whispers of the Goddess," Mai said softly. "Urging her to set it free."

"Bryn has too much empty time and too idle a brain to be trusted."

"Don't hate her like the others," Mai shouted. "Simply because she made a decision we all contemplate making every day."

"It's not that, it's—"

There was a sharp rap on Pell's door. Pell stood and eased the door open, meeting the stern expression of Iress Lee.

"Iress Pell," Lee said. "Come with me."

"Where are we going?" Pell asked.

"Nowhere you haven't already been," she huffed.

Iress Pell turned to Mai before leaving. *I'll find you later. We can keep talking.*

Don't bother, Mai answered, exiting the room as well. *You don't believe me.*

"Iress Mai," Lee greeted her as she walked beyond them.

"Matriarch," Mai replied coldly.

We'll talk more later, Pell called again. Mai didn't answer.

It wasn't until they were outside the abbey walls and in the courtyard beyond that Iress Lee started explaining the situation to Pell. "I was thinking of your little excursion and decided it might be a good idea to inspect the catacombs—be sure the lock held firm and nothing was out of place. I took Ollett with me."

Pell remained silent as Lee escorted her to the path that led to the catacombs. The scene of Pell's crime, as Iress Lee saw it.

"He found...well, I suppose I don't need to tell you what he found, do I? You broke the Thirteenth Edict when speaking to me yesterday."

"I never said I didn't gain entrance," Pell stated. "You drew your own conclusions."

"Which you did nothing to dissuade me of, despite knowing they were false. That's the same as lying. Now, not only have you damaged an old and sacred place of rest, but the bones of Iress Ven are missing from the sarcophagus you crawled in from. Where are they?"

"I don't know where her bones are."

"Already gone, were they?" Lee asked skeptically.

"Yes," Pell insisted. "And the bricks walling it in from the outside were already loose when I found them."

"Ollett says they were forcibly removed, not fallen away with age. I suppose you know nothing of that either?"

"I swear by the Goddess above, someone broke in before I did. I was following their tracks."

At this declaration, the Iress Matriarch halted her progress and fixed Pell with a hard expression. "If only I were an Embrell," she said after a moment.

They made the rest of the short journey in silence and found Ollett waiting for them when they arrived at the door to the tombs.

"Well, Captain?" Lee asked. "Anything else?"

"I'm afraid so, Iress," Ollett said. "Iress Rún's seals were broken."

"Goddess above, no." The Matriarch grew pale. "Her body?"

"It's in there but...something's wrong." Ollett shifted uncomfortably. "Didn't look too closely to be honest."

Iress Lee took the lantern from his hand and made for the entrance.

"Matriarch," Ollett cautioned, "I should warn you—"

"Thank you, Captain, I'll take it from here. Iress Pell, with me."

Ollett nodded and gave Pell a sickened glare as they passed each other.

The Iress Matriarch, knowing exactly where she was going, walked to the final resting place of Iress Rún in much less time than it had taken Pell to reach it the day before. It remained as Pell had left it; the seal was slid open along the broken brackets leaving the cavity exposed.

Iress Lee lifted the lantern up enough to peek inside and immediately stumbled back as if the sight had physically slapped her. "Goddess above," she gasped. Her hand was over her mouth, and she looked lost for a moment. Her eyes searched the room before landing on Pell. "You'd best start explaining things and fast, Iress."

Pell bit her lip, caught between her distrust of the Matriarch and her need to share all she'd discovered. She'd wanted to confide in Mai, but now she wasn't sure that was a good idea. Could she lie? Give an account, other than the truth, that explained everything? She didn't think so, not without more time. She was cornered.

"May I share your mind?" Pell entreated. "I need to know I can trust you."

"Yes," Iress Lee said. "Take a good long look. The only thing I've ever tried to hide from you is in this place."

Pell connected with the old woman and searched as thoroughly as she could the Matriarch's intentions and emotions. She was able to go deeper than she might have without a subject so willingly open. By the time she retreated again, Pell felt more comfortable being honest with the old woman.

The words tumbled out of her mouth. Iress Lee listened, quiet and attentive. The old woman learned of Pell's training at the hands of her grandmother, sorceress of the Uthiri royal court who, shamefully, participated in such shocking practices as chaos calling. Pell told her of the existence of the Dark or the Hollow. How, just as the Light of the Goddess acts as a flow between the living, the Hollow is a channel to the Beloworld where lost souls wander. The Matriarch knew, of course, how the Church had long ago cut off any official acknowledgments to the Dark and denied its existence.

"But it is real, Iress Lee," Pell promised. "I can hear it."

"You can hear it?" Lee asked.

"Every Embrell could, if taught how," Pell said, bracing herself for the lecture that had been leveled at her every time she brought it up.

The Matriarch only nodded. "I've always suspected as much; we acknowledge the existence of it with our practices, even while denying it with our words."

Pell's mouth fell open in shock. "Precisely."

"And you're saying only an Embrell can perform this ritual?" the Iress Matriarch asked.

"No," Pell said, "any man or woman can call to the Darkness, but only an Embrell could listen to responses."

"How?" the Matriarch inquired. "How is this chaos call performed?"

Pell pointed a shaking finger to Iress Rún's niche. "Like that."

"Mutilation of remains?"

"After they've murdered the victim, yes."

"You're saying Iress Rún was murdered?" The Matriarch focused hard eyes on the sundered remains.

"Nothing draws the Darkness more effectively," Pell said. "How did she die?"

"We thought she'd thrown herself off a cliff."

"She was pushed," Pell declared with certainty. "Who found the body? Was there anyone with her when it happened?"

"No, but you're saying that after we laid her to rest, the murderer came here and did *that* to her body?"

Pell explained the particulars to the Matriarch.

"I thought Embrells couldn't form bonds from more than a few dozen feet away," Lee said. "That the inner voices didn't travel far."

"In the Light, no. The Light is a full and vibrant thing. But in the Dark, the emptiness—especially at the depths which this act opens to one—there is nothing to impede the message. Even the wails of the dead don't reach that deep."

"It might even reach Uthir?"

"I think so," Pell said. "But it's understood the messages need to be simple, short. Like calling across an open canyon, the longer the message the more lost it gets in its own echoes. My guess is that this is why the Uthiri knew Vulsipher was alive but not where it was."

The Iress Matriarch nodded thoughtfully, expression troubled. "As long as the traitor did this only once."

"You have reason to believe it was done a second time?"

219

"Possibly. Would an animal be a sufficient sacrifice for this ritual? A cat?"

Pell gasped, her hands covering her mouth. "Mr. Drizzle?"

The Matriarch nodded. "We found the poor thing two nights ago, just outside the grounds, in pieces. Ollett feared we had another demon prowling the pass, but he could not locate anything, and Osgerath's door remains locked tight, thank the Goddess above. But there was something about the way the cat had been cut apart that appeared too careful and intentional to me."

Pell wiped at her eyes. "Performing the ritual with a cat would limit the voice from going as deep or traveling as far, but with the Uthiri within Threya—and doubtlessly listening—it wouldn't have to."

"So, it's likely that a second message was sent," Lee said grimly. "Our location may have been revealed. What does someone need to do to hear this call?"

"To hear it, the person *does* need to be an Embrell or Porshek. They must perform a similar act of desecration. It requires a less significant life, even to listen at the deepest levels. Owls are a popular choice, I understand. However, with the war on, I suppose there's no shortage of human bodies they might access."

"And are they always listening? The Uthiri sorcerers?"

"Yes, it's a daily mark of piety for them. It even makes sense that they'd be listening for a message from Threya. It is how they once listened to the words of the demon-gods, and they've long believed Vulsipher was hidden or imprisoned here somewhere. They've been listening, all these years, for its call and it appears they finally got one... maybe two. If not from the thing itself, then from its servant."

"Why has Vulsipher not called to them itself, do you think?"

"Its voice cannot reach beyond the network of lidocrafting it's contained in."

"So, you believe this is how someone got word out to the Uthiri?"

"I think what's been done to Rún's body, and Drizzy's, proves it."

"And how," Iress Lee's voice quavered, "did someone here learn of such a hideous thing?"

"That I don't know," Pell said. "I thought it might have been referenced in one of the books in the library, but if it is, I cannot find it. My only thought is, well, there is one here, other than me, that surely knows of this."

The Matriarch understood her meaning and shook her head. "Impossible. The demon never speaks. The closest thing we get to communication with it is through our Embrells, and we were without any when this happened. At that time, Iress Rún was the only one capable of listening to it, but she could hardly have done this to herself."

"What about Bryn?" Pell asked.

"She's never connected with it," Lee stated. "She's only been in the chamber once."

"Are you sure Vulsipher never speaks?" Pell pressed. "Physically, I mean."

"There's no record of it uttering a single word aloud. Never once. Though, again, some of the Embrells claim it speaks to them inside."

Pell thought of Mai.

"Let's get out of here," the Matriarch said, moving past her. "We need to get back."

"Wait," Pell spoke to Iress Lee's back. "I've told you all I know; now it's your turn. Why do Embrells die more frequently here than any of the other Iress disciplines?"

The old woman's shoulders fell. "You'd have discovered it eventually; I was only hoping you'd be more established before that day came. Have you told Iress Mai?"

Pell shook her head. "Not yet."

"Please, Iress." The Matriarch turned to face her again. "Keep it from her until she's not so fragile. The both of you are doing such exemplary work so far. I truly believe you may be the ones we've been waiting for. Vulsipher's demise may soon come with your help. Please, wait to tell her. I'd hate to see either of you take Bryn's course."

"Why are there so many more Embrells interred here? Tell me that first."

Iress Lee looked miserable, her weathered face drawn and sad as she met Pell's eyes. "I'm sorry, Iress Pell. It's the reason we were not suspicious of poor Iress Rún's death. The Embrells here eventually and invariably, go violently mad...and kill themselves."

"And it's getting worse," Pell noted. "Happening faster over time."

"Yes." The Matriarch looked ready to cry. "We don't know why. The early Embrells went years and years before the madness started to take hold, but now..."

"I think it's already taking Iress Mai."

"I worry about that too. At her shift today...Iress Em said she was reacting in ways that didn't make sense."

"Perhaps she could take a break from connecting to the creature," Pell suggested, before realizing something herself. "Wait, that's why you didn't want me to spend more time with it than I already was."

"Yes," the Iress Matriarch admitted. "And limiting Mai's time with it is a good idea, but we cannot neglect it too much. You've no idea how tense it can be here when we're without an Embrell. Nearly every escape attempt has been thwarted by one gifted with the Sight. You, especially, should know this, having already done as much."

Pell nodded.

"I'm afraid I must place more responsibility upon you. Not only with the demon but with finding our traitor. You and I will solve this. Come, we must return."

Pell followed the Matriarch through the winding halls, her mind puzzling over the previous issue. The one the old woman had no answer for. The one upon which Mai's life depended. Something about connecting with the demon was driving Mai mad, as it had the previous Embrells. But why was the problem getting worse over time?

The words of the spirits returned to her mind.

It binds us!

It feeds upon us all!

It blocks the way!

CHAPTER 17

CROSSROADS

The Frontier

From the moment he'd woken up—feeling well but still a bit weak—Crowan had been arguing with her.

"You didn't think to ask how I felt?" Crowan complained as they rode across the bridge north of Marker. The canyon here was nowhere near the depth that it was at the other bridge to the east, but it still made her a bit nervous in crossing.

"You were asleep and feverish," Ameryn said. "And you're only eleven years old. Too young to be making decisions for yourself."

"I don't even get a say?" he protested.

"Of course you do," she said. "But what were we supposed to do? The Uthiri had found us, and Dav had to draw them away."

"We should wait for him, try to find him. What if he needs our help?"

Ameryn hadn't even told Crowan that Dav had offered to meet them at the falls. Looking down at the river, she considered how simple it would be to follow it west and meet him. But traveling with Dav meant sharing the target the Uthiri had painted on him. It was only a few days to Silver Hills, then this would all be over.

"Mother!" Crowan pulled his mule to a stop.

Ameryn did the same and turned to face him. The boy would not give her a moment's rest if she didn't talk it through with him. "What did you think was going to happen?"

"What do you mean?" Crowan asked.

"Even if Dav could lead us to that sword, even if you are the one to wield it, what then? Would you sweep across the countryside, killing Uthiri and driving them from our land?"

"With Dav's help, why not?"

"Because you're a child. The war is not your problem to solve. Nor mine."

"But shouldn't we do what we can?" Crowan asked. "Dad did. He tried."

"And look what happened."

Crowan bowed his head, silent a moment. "I just...don't want to go back."

"To Silver Hills?" Ameryn inquired. The boy didn't stir. "Home?"

He nodded. "It's not the same, knowing he won't be coming back."

"We won't be there straight away," Ameryn said. "Although—without us to look after—maybe Dav will help win the war in no time. We'll go home and make it just as it was. For now, we just need to get to Silver, son."

"It'll be worse in the city," Crowan grumbled. "We'll still be getting guarded by soldiers. Just not ones as good as Dav."

The memory of the night before Dav left stung her. She'd accused

224

him of using Crowan, instead of caring genuinely for the boy. She wasn't entirely wrong in her assessment. However, Dav's actions on the morning the war party had arrived proved she wasn't entirely right either. He'd left so willingly, thinking only of protecting them.

"I'll bet Silver is so full, they can barely fit anyone else in anyway," Crowan continued.

Ameryn sighed. "It's not as if I haven't already considered all this, son. I'm no fool."

"You're acting like one," Crowan growled.

"Crowan Vowery! For your sake, I hope I misheard you," Ameryn snapped back. She fumbled for some punishment, but their situation was so desperate she could think of little to make it worse. "We go north, and I'll not hear another word of protest. Now, get moving."

Wordlessly, he complied and stayed silent for miles after, speaking only when he needed to. His cold company made the familiar slap of exposure strike her hard. They were alone out here. Truly alone. With every step her mule took, the feeling strengthened, not lessened. It made no sense. The mule was bearing her closer to the city, to protection...but further from Daverell. Why should that bother her? It was what she wanted. But no, it wasn't so simple. The truth was, her mind was split on the man. Split as sure as one side of the Durado Canyon from the other. He was danger. He was safety. Both were true, and no amount of tossing the problem about in her head would give her any clarity beyond that. She'd chosen a path away from him, and she would follow it.

They spent a chilly, black night in the desert sand. Ameryn forbade Crowan from building a fire. They huddled together, waiting for the darkness to pass and wishing that sleep came easier.

The next day, they saw riders on the road ahead.

Mother and son hid in the shadow of a bluff where Ameryn prayed they hadn't been seen. When she opened her eyes, she caught Crowan peeking around the boulder that hid them.

"Move away from there," she whispered.

"They ain't doing nothing," Crow breathed before shuffling back to her. "Just watching the road, I think. They haven't moved."

"Uthiri?"

"Hard to say," Crowan answered. "They're a ways off, and this wind's kicking up half the desert."

Ameryn crept to the edge and peered around it, unable to discern anything more than her son had.

"Who else would just be watching the road and not riding it?" Crowan asked.

"Travelers taking a break? Waiting out this wind?"

"Maybe," Crow conceded. "What do we do now, Mother?"

Ameryn bit her lip, looking around her as if she might find the answer in the sage or sky.

Falling in two flows for hundreds of feet, the waterfall was an impressive sight. Daverell assumed it had a name, but, if it did, it wasn't on his map. It was not that, however, that demanded most of his attention.

Ameryn and Crowan hadn't been in Marker, and they weren't here.

Nor did they arrive the next day.

Daverell had told himself he was fine with the possibility of them moving on without him. He might have even believed it while he was occupied by the war party, but now that he was here, waiting, his eyes were constantly pulled to the east. His mind replaying every moment he'd spent with the woman and her son.

If they don't come, what do I do with myself? The army didn't seem like the right place for him anymore, but without the boy and his mother, what else was there? He would be unable to watch good men die and do nothing. He feared it was his only path forward, and he had no choice but to follow it, but not yet. Not for a few days.

Late into their second night at the falls, Leifal shook Daverell awake.

"Captain!" he whispered urgently. "They are finding us, riders are approaching."

Daverell bolted upright and drew his sword from his pack next to his bedroll. "Where?"

Lit by the moon and the embers in their fire pit, Leifal pointed into the darkness beyond toward the sound of hoofbeats.

Daverell's heart leaped with as much fear as it did hope. One of the emotions completely gave way to the other when he heard a voice ring out in the darkness.

"Dav?"

"Crow," he called back, almost melting with relief as he ran to meet them.

Ameryn said nothing, and in the dim lighting, Dav could feel rather than see her cautious expression. Crowan dropped from one of the mules and surprised him with a hug.

"All better?" Daverell asked.

"Yes," Crow answered before noticing Leifal and jumping back a little. Crow and his mother both fixed the Uthiri man with a suspicious scowl.

"This is Leifal," Daverell explained. "He's my prisoner. Took him with me when I slipped away from the Uthiri."

"He's Uthiri?" Ameryn exclaimed.

Leifal raised his hands, palms out. "Please, madam, I am never meaning harm to anyone. I am no soldier."

"He was the interpreter," Daverell said. "I've made it clear what ill fate he can expect if he does anything that displeases me."

Leifal continued, "I assure you—"

"He'll behave," Daverell stated confidently.

"Keep your distance from us," Ameryn told Leifal, dismounting.

After seeing to the mules, Daverell led Ameryn and Crow along the river.

The moon lit their path away from the dull roar of the waterfall, and it occurred to Ameryn what a lovely place this was. Downstream, they settled in a tight circle on a flat riverbank rock, and Ameryn spoke first.

"Alright, Dav. Start with the Sword of Light," she said. "You say it's real?"

"I've seen it." Dav sounded as though his voice itself were handling something delicate. "There are no words for it; it's beyond exquisite. As though forged from starlight. Remember, Crow, when I told you about expert lidocrafting? How some folk say it might be done so skillfully it glows? True to its name, the Illumed Blade does. Shimmers with its own pure Light. Like the sun reflecting off a mountain stream. Elegant and eternal. I'll never forget it, yet I've tried to sketch it hundreds—maybe thousands—of times and can't recall any of the specifics. It's like trying to remember a dream."

"Where did you see it?" Crowan asked.

"Deep in the Gray mountains, beyond Osgerath Tower to the south, housed in an old castle. I only ever saw the inside of one room. The closer we got, the more they hid the way from me—even blindfolding me in the end."

"Who took you there? Why?" Ameryn asked.

"It's the reason I'm so familiar with the prophecy, know it by heart," Dav said. "There were some who thought, once, that *I* might be the chosen warrior it speaks of."

"What?" Ameryn and Crow breathed.

"I was born as my parents were traveling. The labor pains came on my mother unexpectedly. She was from Meareth where the custom is to give birth in a body of water, lest the child live a cursed life." Dav laughed sadly. "She found a mountain spring just in time, and I was born in it, under an eclipse of the moon in the Year of the Hunter."

"But," Crowan said, "the water?"

"It wasn't until later my mother found out the ancients had called that very spring 'Mother's Water.' It was a sacred place to them."

"Born within the mother's water," Crow whispered.

"Even then, they'd not thought much of it. My parents weren't spiritual scholars. When I was seven or so, a sickness ran through Imiggan—where I grew up—and my father died. Needing help, my mother turned to the Church. She began studying to become an Iress, found she had a gift for the Curial arts and became a healer. Everyone knew about the prophecy, of course, but she didn't think much of it until she had to study it. The more she learned, the more the pieces fit. Once she was Raised, she informed her superiors of her suspicions about me. I was thirteen by then. She was surprised to find that the information made it all the way to the Jophrat himself. She never thought it was real, not at first. But the Church quietly arranged to take me to the Blade."

"This place in the mountains?" Ameryn inquired.

"I've searched every map of Threya, old and new, and those from different countries…I've found nothing save Osgerath, the tower guarding Ankr pass from the eastern side and, while that was along our journey, it's not where the Sword was. But it's up there," he said, gazing at the soaring peaks above them. "Somewhere."

"I would never have imagined the Church would take an old *Lyprakarum* prophecy seriously," Ameryn remarked.

"The Church acknowledges the *Lyprakarum* as scripture, in part. One just needs to separate the old culture from the revelations. That, and the antiquated language makes studying it a little cumbersome, which is why few reference it anymore. But Grath's prophecies are considered true by many scholars; if you ignore the talk of High Heilaroth, the Blade fits with the mention of the Goddess's gift mentioned in *The Song*."

"And you," Ameryn said, "you…saw it."

"I held it," Dav declared.

"Truly?" Crow exclaimed.

"When they presented it to me, they asked me to take it in my hands. Anyone who had touched it before me had been killed instantly."

"And you?" Crow asked.

"I remember shaking, so afraid but…excited. I took the grip in my hand and immediately felt a surge of power, like holding the sun. All at once, I knew what it was capable of. No threat could stand in the face of such power; it could be the key to the first real, lasting peace. But then, in another flash, it hurt me and…" Dav opened his fingers, hands empty. "Nothing. I woke up in a Church orphanage a week later being watched over by a man and an Iress Curial I didn't know. The man said he'd follow me all my days and kill me if I ever spoke of the experience." Dav paused and looked around them, a faint smile on his lips. "I expect he's no longer dogging my steps, but in my youth—the years that followed my experience with the Sword—I would see him occasionally, watching from shadows. He needn't have bothered. Until this moment, I never spoke a word. There was no reason to. What had happened was no mystery. I'd been struck down. Denied. Close enough to the prophecy's requirements to not lose my life, but not enough to wield the Sword."

"How did your mother feel?" Ameryn wondered.

"I don't know," Dav said. "The last time I saw her was in the room with the Sword."

"What?" Ameryn asked.

"That place was such a secret. While they didn't keep me there, they never let her leave."

"And you want me to take Crowan there?" Ameryn demanded in shock.

"The same won't happen to you," Dav assured her. "My mother was already promised to the Church. They do not hold the same authority over you. They'll let us stay *and* let us leave. At most, someone will be sent with you to protect the boy and ensure you keep the oath they'll make you take: to keep their secret intact…and perhaps to return when you think Crow is ready."

"I'm ready now," Crowan protested.

"What if we say nothing at all of Crowan or prophecies?" Ameryn ignored her son. "Beg for sanctuary only?"

"That might limit what leverage we have for both staying and leaving. Crowan gives you a connection…a right to the place and a powerful reason for them to keep you safe."

"And makes them aware of him," she said, looking at Crowan. She trusted the Church, more or less, but she didn't like them thinking they had some claim on her boy.

"Do I get a say?" Crowan asked, reading her stare as permission to speak. "Y'all are talking about me like I ain't here."

"Go ahead then," Ameryn responded, a little stiffly.

"Let me try, Mother," Crowan said. "I think I'm ready, but if you don't agree, it can be another time. But the Church should know I might be able to. I *will* try someday."

Crowan's reasoning nearly convinced her, but she could tell he didn't mean it. Not all of it. "Didn't you hear what Dav said, Crowan? People have died touching that thing."

"He didn't." Crowan pointed at Dav. "And neither will I."

A silence followed. One filled with searching gazes. Ameryn considered her options and found this was far from the worst one.

"Alright," Ameryn said with quiet finality. "Perhaps one day, when you're older. When you're ready. But it may not be until the day I can't stop you."

"*His* mother let him try." Crowan gestured to Dav again.

"She's not your mother, I am. And I forbid it." Ameryn turned to Dav. "I'm sorry, I know it's not what you hoped for."

"No apology needed, ma'am. That is no longer what I'm seeking. When the Blade rejected me, I felt lost. I couldn't understand why I'd gone through all that, but now, I finally do. The experience prepared me to recognize the signs. I'm not the hero but the man meant to find him. To bring him to the Sword. Maybe not to end our current threat but a greater one years from now—I don't know. I trust the Goddess as far as all that goes."

231

"But what if you weren't wrong?" Crowan argued. "What if I can help people now?"

Ameryn was about to reprimand the boy yet again, but Daverell spoke instead.

"I'm honored to play a part in your story, boy. But your parents were a part of it before me. Before even you."

"Father would have wanted me to do it," Crowan claimed.

Ameryn thought that might actually be true, but he wasn't here. "You don't know that," she remarked. "The Church knowing will have to be enough for now."

Crowan folded his arms and settled into a scowl.

Ameryn disregarded the boy and focused on Dav. "Very well, what do we do next?"

"Tomorrow, we make for the tower ruin," Dav answered.

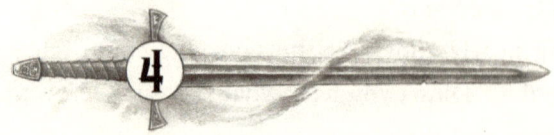

Ameryn and Crowan continued bickering all the next day as they rode beside each other. The boy answered his mother's every request with some show of defiance. Even Daverell sensed less warmth from him. He couldn't blame the boy, understanding all too well what it was like to be denied adventure. Especially when it offered an escape from grief and mundanity.

On their second day traveling, Ameryn asked to borrow Daverell's *Lyprakarum*. As they rode, she read the prophetic passage again and again, handling the book almost as much as she had her little envelope the previous day.

Daverell had almost asked her a few times what it was, but some inner sense compelled him not to.

Leifal remained with them, taking turns riding Daverell's horse and Crow's mule. The man wouldn't last more than a few days alone under the frontier sun, and Daverell wasn't sure what to do with him. Leifal, for his part, spent most of his time and energy on telling them all about the fine things he'd owned back home. He was telling Crow about the lovely collection of porcelain finches he'd received as a gift from some dignitary when Ameryn surprised Daverell with a question.

"Why might the Goddess give us prophecies? Why seed the world with notions of what may one day happen?"

"I assume so we'll be watching for it."

"But doesn't it seem a cruel trick? On you, if none else? How different might your life have been if you'd been spared such powerful rejection at a tender age?"

"It prepared me to recognize the signs in Crowan. Under the wide view of the Goddess, my life is only a small thing. A single soldier in the greater war. Besides, most of my suffering is of my own doing. I'll not blame Her."

"I once thought," Ameryn recalled, "hoped, that She saw things differently. That the little things, individual lives, were *more* important than the grand scheme. *The Song* says, 'She sees the wildflower that blooms in the desert and the thrush that falls in the river.' But I suppose that only means She follows the details in Her plan. We're all players in some greater work. Do we have a choice? If we do, a prophecy is a reckless thing. What if Crowan were a murderous tyrant?"

"I suppose that's why She made sure to provide him with a good mother."

"While killing his good father?" she snapped and blinked, appearing surprised at the surge of anger. She sighed. "If I ever was a good mother, I'm not anymore. It used to come more natural. Now my only thought is to keep him safe."

"And you're doing just that."

"No, *you're* doing that. I can do nothing to protect him."

"There's more a boy needs than physical defense. Even—maybe *especially*—in these times."

"I can't find it in myself to mother him, and when I try, I make a mess of things, and we both end up angry."

"You love him, yes?"

233

"Maybe too much," she said.

They were silent a moment. Dav cursed himself for never possessing the right words to speak. "I've no answers, Mrs. Vowery, I'm not a parent, and I don't pretend to know how life works. I believe we're masters of our own lives but also that the prophecy is true. How those pieces fit, I can't say."

In that moment, Leifal, up ahead, made a startled exclamation. Dav spun to the east, searching the horizon, afraid he'd see some evidence of the Uthiri war party. But no, that was not the reason for the clamor. The man and Crowan had begun arguing about something.

Dav gripped Druid's reins, readying himself to investigate the disturbance up ahead but turned to Ameryn one last time. "As the son of an imperfect but good mother, knowing you are—or were once—powerfully loved can do much. Even when all else fails."

Kicking Druid into a canter, he caught up with Crow and Leifal. "What's the trouble?" he demanded.

"I don't know," Crowan cried. "I mentioned we were going to the tower, and he went mad."

"Osgerath?" Leifal shouted, wide-eyed and out of breath. "You are taking us to Osgerath?"

"Yes," Dav answered.

"It will be our tomb!" he wailed.

"What would you know about old Threyan ruins?" Dav asked.

"All Uthiri are knowing of the old towers. The five structures that were housing the Elder Demons. Vulsipher was once ruling this land from Osgerath."

"Even if that's true, it's been empty for hundreds of years."

"You fools are not understanding," Leifal said before wincing. "That is, you are wise, Captain, but...but you are forgetting the old ways in this land."

"I know the old stories; lesser demons die like anything else."

"Death is different in the Ishik towers. There are two such towers in Uthir, and when the demons were dying there, their ghosts...festered. Becoming something else. The pilgrims that were visiting the

234

sites began disappearing. The spirits within were hungry. In Uthir, we are offering them a sacrifice every year just to be keeping them sated. Walking into Osgerath will be like waving fresh meat before a lion that has been dining on only cabbage for years."

"You're in a frenzy over nothing," Dav said. "We're not going inside."

"We...we are not?"

"There's a secret way around, cut into the cliffs. A path we'll take to the pass above without ever stepping foot in the tower."

Leifal cleared his throat, regaining some composure and making an embarrassed expression. "I see."

Ameryn had caught up to Daverell as Crow and the Uthiri man moved on.

"Do you really know a way around? I once heard there was no way into the pass without going through the tower," Ameryn whispered to Dav. "It's why no one crosses the Grays through Ankr Pass."

"It's there," Dav answered. "I remember a hole in the northern end of the wall outside the tower; beyond it was a hidden road. It was the last thing I saw on our journey before they blindfolded me—and they did so without realizing I'd already seen that much. I can find it again."

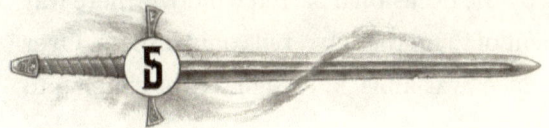

Their first glimpse of Osgerath came the next afternoon. It stood like a dormant giant. They were miles away still, though Daverell guessed he'd be able to see it from many more were it not so solidly nestled in the rocky terrain. But surely nothing so massive could remain erect alone. It needed the sheer cliff at its side to lean on. The single, tapering turret appeared like the rotting trunk of an impossibly colossal tree. It rose higher than seemed possible. Anyone who came to it from the pass in the mountains would find themselves near the pronged crown that extended just beyond the precipice at its top. Daverell and his small company approached the wide base from the opposite side.

The view held them in place, all except Leifal who had hopped off the horse and knelt, muttering fearfully and making sweeping praying motions. It took Daverell a fair bit of convincing to get the man back in the saddle. They were a ways off yet, but, if they hurried, they could reach the wall and hidden path by nightfall. Daverell would urge them to keep moving through the night. While not as terrified as Leifal, he was eager to leave the ruin behind.

The terrain required them to climb down and around the ridge of a wide plateau. The tower was mostly hidden from view for more than an hour until they rounded a corner and it was again revealed. Much closer.

It stood directly ahead, looming over them. Though it was a repugnant sight, Daverell tried to burn it into his mind to draw later. The shape and size of each brick were of such a wide variety that some were taller than Daverell—even atop Druid—while others were small enough to be held in his hand. It was a wonder the spire didn't topple given the chaotic placement. Helping hold it together were thick, iron bands running over the surface, imprisoning the stones that appeared eager to escape. The metal was interrupted here and there by long spikes and the brickwork by the occasional barred window. There was no method to the placement of them that Daverell could discern. Over everything, the whole surface, was a black, malignant rot clinging to the walls.

The sun was lowering, disappearing behind the mountains and casting a long, dark shadow from Osgerath. Daverell found himself riding to the side, avoiding straying into that darkness. It soon made no difference as storm clouds gathered over the mountains, cutting out the light entirely.

Leifal, riding with Daverell again, had renewed his praying. It was an unbroken, frightened murmur that raised in volume and desperation as they advanced. Dav didn't understand the words, and it soon became a rake over his nerves. A flash of lightning and roll of thunder preceded a buffeting wind that helped drown it out, though not enough for Crowan, apparently.

The boy whirled around, facing Leifal. "Quiet! You're—" he stopped, his mouth hanging open and eyes wide, staring at something behind them.

Dav followed his gaze to the Uthiri war party riding hard towards them. The soldiers were readying their bows.

"Follow me!" Dav shouted, kicking Druid into a gallop. Leifal glanced behind them and gave a shriek. He seemed as unhappy to see the Uthiri as the rest of them.

Osgerath stood at the dead end of a canyon, hugging the cliff on the south side. Running from the tower on its north side was a huge stone wall with pointed, metal crenelations that met with the opposing cliff face. The gap in this wall was to their far right side. Dav rode for it, closing the distance fast despite holding Druid back to keep from outpacing the mules.

Drawing nearer, Dav's heart plummeted. The gap had been filled by fallen stones; some rockfall within the last forty years had blocked it off completely.

"We can't get through!" Ameryn yelled in a panic as rain began falling.

"Hurry!" Daverell shouted. "Make for the door!"

"Inside the tower?" Ameryn blurted.

"We've no choice!"

Even then, as Druid regained his speed, a clatter of arrows struck the wall beside him. Dav blessed the gusty wind throwing off the Uthiri's aim and prayed the rain would swiftly soak their bowstrings. Until that happened, they'd be under nearly as many falling arrows as raindrops. Coming to the gate, Dav steered Druid directly into it behind Ameryn and Crowan. The darkness of Osgerath swallowed them all.

In that moment, Daverell didn't pause to consider how unlikely it was that the old portcullis had remained open throughout these long years. Nor did he give much thought to the man sharing his saddle who would surely have preferred the retribution of his unforgiving master to the fate he believed awaited him inside the tower. Dav did, however,

237

acknowledge the crushing feeling he had when he sliced through the rusty chain just beyond the arch, sending the heavy iron door slamming into place with a resounding boom. It felt less like blocking the war party's entrance and more like blocking his little group's exit. Less like sanctuary and more like the jaws of some enormous, ravenous creature clamping shut, trapping them in its gullet.

CHAPTER 18

VOICES

The Nameless Abbey

1

"You're not listening," Mai shouted, pacing around Pell's room.

"I am listening," Pell insisted in a voice so calm it made Mai even angrier. "I just don't think it's a good idea to allow myself to drift aimlessly inside that thing's head. It'll take me where it wants me."

"No, it's the fastest way to reach its reasoning. Please, Pell. I want you to see what I see."

"Are you sure you're not seeing what you want to?"

"What I…why would I want to see it the way I do, Pell?" Mai's voice was rising.

"So it wouldn't be evil. So you'd have something to save."

"Instead of something to kill? Is that what you see? Because it's what *you* want?"

Iress Pell paused. "Let's not talk about it. In fact, maybe we should take a break from even connecting with the thing. I worry it's toying with our minds."

"I barely have time with it anymore. The Matriarch has seen to that. And after I was making progress."

"She's only looking out for you," Pell argued.

"What? You used to be more suspicious of her than I am, but now you two are inseparable. You think I don't see you? Whispering in corners. Bryn has noticed too."

"I don't care what Bryn thinks."

"Why not? According to you, she's the most stable of the three of us. She's *never* connected with the thing. Maybe her opinion should matter most."

"Can we please focus on improving my intention-reading?" Pell requested. "You've become quite accomplished at projecting, and I have some catching up to do."

"There's no point," Mai said, making for the door. "You won't listen anyway, and I can tell you're distracted. I'd know what about if you weren't being so deceptive."

"You think *I'm* being deceptive?" Pell asked.

Mai didn't even say goodbye, only walked through Pell's door slamming it on the way out.

"Mai," Pell called after her.

Mai ignored her. She didn't want to go to her own room where Pell could still reach her internally, so she walked the halls. Before she even knew where her feet were taking her, she found herself at Bryn's alcove. She was there, of course, and looked up at Mai in alarm.

"Iress Mai," Bryn said. "Is everything alright?"

"It's Iress Pell," Mai complained. "I thought if she could connect better with the angel, she'd see it for what it was."

"She's been indoctrinated like everyone else here," Bryn said.

"Don't worry. In hardly any time at all, they'll all see."

Mai nodded. "Yes, soon."

"Come," Bryn patted the spot on the bench next to her. "She always makes you feel better."

Iress Mai had wanted Pell to share this experience as well, but she'd been sworn to secrecy. It wasn't meant for Pell. But, as Bryn had said, Pell would understand soon. Mai sat next to Bryn and closed her eyes. The voice came to her, and she knew in an instant that everything was going to work out perfectly. She sighed and smiled.

In the dark of the next morning, Iress Pell walked through the narrow corridors. The Iress Matriarch waited for her at the front gate. The two women exited the castle and began walking across the courtyard.

Mai had not been wrong when she'd called Pell distracted. She was wrong about many other things, but not that. Pell wanted to know why the spirits here suffered so and could think of little else. The Iress Matriarch agreed to allow her back into the catacombs to search for answers. Talking to the lingering dead was impossible, as far as she knew. But if she could listen to their lamentations longer, perhaps she could understand their situation better.

There was a wind tonight. It made the lamp held aloft in the Matriarch's hand swing, casting ever-shifting shadows around them. To Pell, more than once, the light struck the craggy rocks in ways that turned them into leering monsters. She was grateful when they arrived at the catacomb door.

The Iress Matriarch unlocked the entrance and followed Pell inside. The howl of the wind became a murmur when the door was shut.

"You say the barrier between our world and theirs is thinnest during the shrouded hours?"

"That's what I understand," Pell said with a shrug. "But the first ghost I heard here was wandering the castle halls in the light of day."

The Matriarch nodded thoughtfully.

"Is there a place I might sit down while I listen?" Pell asked, worried she might collapse.

"I don't think it would be too wicked a thing to rest upon Iress Ven's sarcophagus since it was emptied by whomever broke in."

Pell sat and the Matriarch settled beside her. Iress Lee took some paper and a pencil from her pocket. Pell was to speak aloud whenever she heard something, and the Matriarch would write it down. Pell closed her eyes and took a deep breath, noting that the air tasted vaguely damp and moldy before she turned her inner ears to the Hollow.

Immediately, she was in the tempest again. Swirling voices of despair surrounded her.

"It is always with us," whispered one.

"It holds us," screamed another.

"It killed us," sobbed a woman. "And kills us again and again."

"It hurts us! Empties us!"

"Feeds upon us."

Just as Pell wished she could ask them who or what it was they spoke of, more voices cried out.

"Vulsipher."

"The Unholy Flame!"

"The Long Shadow!"

Iress Pell could take it no more and shut off the connection, coming back to herself. She was crying. The scratching sound of frantic writing met her ears. Pell waited for the Iress Matriarch to finish before speaking.

"I think I understand," Pell said. "Somehow...Vulsipher is trapping these souls and gaining sustenance or power from their continued suffering. The Uthiri even believe something like this, but the demon has to kill them to gain command over their spirits. I just didn't think...I mean to say, these victims killed themselves..."

"But if the demon had driven them to it..." the Matriarch suggested.

"Then, yes, I would say it killed them."

"We'd thought," the Matriarch said, sounding hopeless, "for all these years, that we'd contained the destruction the demon was capable of. Instead…"

"We've only ever stopped it from committing the type of destruction we can see."

"You said it gains power from this misery?"

"Yes," Pell answered.

"The kind that might let it damage the minds of our Embrells here more swiftly over time?"

Pell hadn't made that connection yet, but it fit. "I think so," Pell concurred fearfully. "Iress Mai has been affected faster than any before her, according to you. Even after you've limited her time in the cellar, she's only gotten worse."

"With the extent of this pain, I'm not surprised," the Matriarch said, looking at the words on her paper before meeting Pell's eyes. "How can we fix this?"

Pell could do nothing but look back.

Hours later, Iress Pell was in the basement chamber with the thing. Not since the morning after it had tried to kill her had she been so tempted to attack it. She hated it. Wanted so badly to wound it in some way. Instead, she connected with and talked to it.

I know why you tried to kill me, she asserted. *You must have read my mind as I was trying to read yours. You discovered that I know how to listen to the Dark, and that it was only a matter of time before I learned of the suffering souls under your control. And it will only be a matter of time more before I learn how to take them away from you. That's been your dark secret all this time, but now we know.*

She sensed nothing from the creature. Not a single reaction. She nearly screamed in the face of its continuous blankness. She began frantically searching for its reasoning but refusing to let herself drift into it like Mai suggested. To let it show her what it wanted. An act put on by a talented performer. Pell scoured the endless corridors of its psyche until she felt the vague echoes of someone shaking her body.

It was Iress Rin. "Our shift is over, Pell. Time to go."

Over already. It made her sick. Where did the time go while she was within the demon's mind? Had the creature begun infecting her more than she suspected?

It took effort, but Pell left the chamber rejecting the sense of failure waiting to take her, clinging to determination instead.

In the hallways above, Pell pulled the scarf she'd used to block out the noxious smells of the basement chamber from off her face and enjoyed the clean air for a moment before strolling in the direction of the library. Perhaps she could find a book that might contain a clue as to how an Elder Demon's soul slaves could be set free.

She passed Mai and Bryn sharing the alcove bench, both with books in their hands. Pell, wanting to avoid an awkward social exchange with Bryn present, connected to Mai to send her a greeting. Maybe she could apologize for earlier. However, what she observed caused her to stop dead in her tracks.

The first thing was that Mai was only pretending to read. Her eyes were on a book, but her mind was not. Instead, she was listening to a voice. A beautiful voice. Whether it was from Bryn or Mai's own mental dialogue, Pell couldn't tell. If it was Bryn's internal voice, it didn't match her physically spoken one. Interior voices didn't have an identifiable sound, but they were no less unique and generally matched the individual they came from, at least in character. This voice was old and immense while also feeling comforting and intimate.

Soon, daughters, the voice said. *Soon.*

It was clear Pell had trespassed on some private moment. She would have withdrawn in an instant but didn't have the chance as Mai fiercely ejected her from her mind, rising angrily.

"How dare you!" she screamed, marching over to Pell's position.

"I'm sorry," Pell faltered, shocked.

"I warned you before," Bryn said to Pell, also leaping to her feet. "Yet, again, you connect with someone without permission."

"I...I..." Pell was unsure what to say. "Mai, we've always..." Pell looked to Mai for support, but found her friend scowling back at her.

"We'll see what the Iress Matriarch has to say about this," Bryn said, looking over Pell's shoulder. Pell followed her gaze to see the Matriarch approaching. She'd just finished facilitating the shift change below. "I know you've become her little pet lately," Bryn whispered at Pell's back, "but she can't ignore such a breach of the chief edict of our order."

"What is going on?" the Iress Matriarch asked.

Mai pointed accusingly. "Iress Pell connected against my wishes."

"Iress Pell, is this true?"

"Yes, I did," Pell admitted. "I said I was sorry."

"And that makes it acceptable?" Bryn retorted.

"Easy, Sisters," Lee soothed. "I'm afraid I have to confine you to your room, Iress Pell."

"And be sure she stays away from me. In *every* way," Bryn called.

"Yes, yes, Bryn, thank you. You may return to whatever it is you do here," the Matriarch said.

Pell could feel Bryn and Mai glaring at her back as she was led away.

After turning down a side corridor, Pell quickly relayed the whole bizarre experience to the Matriarch.

"What do you think the voice was?" the Matriarch asked.

"Perhaps it was Bryn's own, internal voice that she was making sound more grand," Pell proposed.

"For what purpose?"

"I've no idea," Pell answered.

"What was it saying?" Iress Lee asked.

"Soon, daughters. Soon."

"Soon?" the Iress Matriarch repeated, wearing a troubled expression. "I'll ask Ollett to watch them closely. If they do anything out of the ordinary, we'll confine them."

"Mai could project on him and slip away," Pell objected. "I should watch her; I will know if she's replaced my senses."

"Ollett has been trained to recognize this as well," Lee said. "Besides, tonight you'll be restricted to your room. I will have to follow through with that, I'm afraid. I'll send someone up with food."

"And some books?"

The Matriarch sighed. "Give me a list."

Pell flew through every volume that might be even remotely relevant, searching the pages for a reference, even a clue, to help the abbey's imprisoned souls. Again and again, she found nothing, but there was always another book to explore, more pages to scan. Until there wasn't.

The only remotely pertinent passage she found was from *Dark Magic of the Ancient North*. The section on Elder Demons described them as simultaneously existing in the mortal world as well as the Hollow and Below. In some bizarre way, Elder Demons were already dead, while also being alive. Pieces of them out of harmony with the rest.

Most of this Pell had already guessed. What she really wanted to know, and what the book said nothing about, was how to sever its bonds to those realms. She knew a common weapon could cut the creature's link to life, a *lidocrafted* weapon could cut the link to the Below, but what could cut the link to death? What made something, or parts of something, less dead...so it could be killed? What did that even mean? And would severing the creature's link to the Hollow allow its spirit slaves to wander free? Pell was convinced that cutting all three links was the key to ending its life. If nothing else, she had finally landed upon something that had never been tried. Now if she could only find the missing piece. But book after book, and her own frantic mind, refused to provide her with an answer.

She stood and walked to her window. It was raining, and she

watched raindrops race each other down the panes of glass. When that became tiresome, she paced the length of her room. It proved to be no more helpful, and finally, she lay in her bed. She would confront the problem with a well-rested mind. It was her best idea that day, but sleep, it seemed, was determined to reject her as well.

Ultimately, she ended up working on her *Lyprakarum* translation. She intended it to be a distraction but figured she may as well work on a relevant section. She opened the book to Notix's demon descriptions and was pleased to find the exercise swiftly lulling the busy beehive of her mind into something more meditative. Her eyelids even began feeling a little heavy. Seconds later, however, they snapped open, and she leaped to her feet.

It was a piece to the puzzle! She gripped the book, holding it closer to the flame of her candle, reading it again and again. It was not *the* piece—not the complete answer she was looking for—but it was *something*.

Notix Chapter Six verse eleven had always, in every translation, read: *From the great devils, the song of the Faithsingers will free captive hearts.* It had always been a mild point of confusion among scholars why Notix, the most literal of all the *Lyprakarum's* authors, would use a metaphoric device like a captive heart. And that was before even deciphering what it might mean.

However, in this original version it read: *From the great devils, the song of the Faithsingers will free the captive dead.*

Had the Kanvaras translation been miscopied? Had this one? No, this was closer to the original source. This must be the authentic wording. If so, it might mean that Vulsipher's throng of imprisoned spirits could be liberated by the song of a Faithsinger, or as they'd been called more recently: an Opravic!

As Pell had suspected, they were not without purpose as the Church claimed. It had been wrong—even dangerous and cruel—to discontinue their order. Especially as an appeal to the pride of the Tar Ishik conquerors. They had declared the Dark defeated. Any element that, in practice, acknowledged its continued existence could not be allowed to survive. Not in this new Age of Light. The fools.

Hymns were sung within the nameless abbey's chapel twice a week. Pell suspected that, if there were an Opravic among their number, she'd have set the spirits free—even without meaning to. If a Singer could be found, Vulsipher's power would be greatly diminished. Mai would be free of its influence, and Pell would have decades to find a way to kill it. Decades of life left, not years. Or, in Mai's case, weeks. Maybe days. She'd been acting so strange. That voice...

Iress Pell decided it was worth another reprimand to leave her room and get this information to the Matriarch. Iress Lee could get word to the Jophrat. The Church could find an Opravic. In the meantime, they had to work on ways to cut the demon off from the different realms. Lee had been a Curial once, perhaps she'd have some ideas on how to cut the demon off from death.

Just as Pell turned to the door, there issued a knock from it. She answered, expecting Iress Mai. Instead, she found Bryn on the other side.

"I think I owe you an apology," Bryn said with a nervous smile.

Pell looked around the landing, it was empty. Bryn had slipped away from Ollett. "No, thank you," Pell replied, trying to shut the door.

Bryn pushed against it, holding it open. "Please, let's just talk for a minute."

The two politely fought over the door for a moment until Bryn squeezed in, closing it behind her. Pell backed up, cautiously.

Bryn was grinning, circling Pell like a wolf.

"Please leave, Bryn," Pell said.

"I suppose it's my own fault for being distant." Bryn walked towards her. "I've never felt much at home here. I thought we might get to know each other; Mai speaks so highly of you."

Pell kept her distance but made her way back to the door. "If you don't leave, then I'm going to." Pell's gaze dropped to find the doorknob, when it returned, Bryn was rushing at her, a knife held high in her hand.

With a gasp, Pell ducked just fast enough that the blade sliced across the top of her head. It struck the door behind her, pinning Pell in place by her hair and the hood of her robe. Bryn was above her, trying to pull the blade free. Pell recovered enough to kick Bryn hard in the gut, flinging her backwards. The knife went with her, tight in her grip. With a mad shriek, Bryn was on her again. Pell shoved her away. Bryn was sent flailing but not before leaving Pell with another wound. She hissed at the sharp sting from a cut just above her left breast.

Pell fumbled at the doorknob again, managing to throw the door open. The dining hall was just down the hallway at the bottom of the stairs; she'd find help there. However, as she was exiting the room, another stab hit her lower back. Pell screamed, as much in fury as pain, but was able to slam the door behind her. Her shaking hands attempted to lock Bryn in, but by the time she retrieved the key from her pocket and pushed it into the keyhole, the door burst open again. Bryn emerged, knife first, and sliced Pell deeply across her outstretched arm resulting in a spray of blood and another intense bite of pain.

Pell turned to run, but her robes were grabbed from behind, and she was dragged back into the room. Bryn thrust her across the floor. She came down hard and watched as Bryn locked the door from the inside. She stalked towards Pell, slowly now, as a cat might advance on an injured mouse. Pell had only been angry up to this point. Now, she was scared, more of Bryn's face—contorted into a blotchy and maniacal knot of hate—than the dripping knife clutched tightly in her whitened fist.

Pell, on her back, tried scooting away from the approaching Bryn but slipped in her own blood. She was swiftly losing feeling in her arms. She couldn't catch her breath. Desperately, Pell attempted to force a connection with Bryn and project false sensations on her, but her head was swimming, and dark shapes were popping in her vision. She was finding it hard to concentrate. Why had she not done it sooner? Bryn had come upon her so fast.

The menacing woman knelt over her now, knife held above Pell's heart, ready for a final plunge that would end Pell's life, when the door to the room opened. Pell looked beyond Bryn to the shocked faces of

Iress Em and Ollett rushing inside. They were too late. Bryn drove the knife into Pell's chest. It remained there, even as Bryn was pulled off her. Pell studied the hilt protruding from her sternum. It was one of the nicer kitchen knives that the cook was so protective of. *He will be furious*, she noted as she collapsed.

CHAPTER 19

DARKNESS

Osgerath

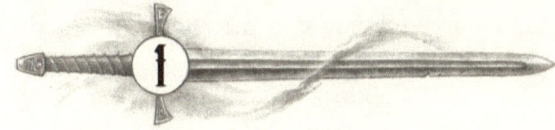

Leifal pounded on the door, loudly lamenting something in Uthiri.

"Why would you block our way out?" Ameryn yelled at Daverell.

"Would you rather the Uthiri follow us in here and slaughter us?" Daverell asked in return, matching her volume.

"Maybe there's another way out!" Crowan interrupted. He was holding the reins of the mules, both of whom were whinnying and stamping their feet. Even Druid, whose bridle was in Dav's hand, was agitated.

Ameryn ignored her son, pointing at Leifal. "You think they would have followed us? Look at him!"

"Not every Uthiri is as superstitious as our foolish friend here," Daverell said. Though, in truth, it was a shaky assumption; every Uthiri he'd met seemed *very* superstitious. "Besides, they're watching the exit, arrows at the ready."

"Stop!" Crowan shrieked.

"What are we to do with the horses? Can they climb the tower?" Ameryn asked. "Did you see the size of this place? We may be lost in here for days."

Leifal ceased clawing at the unyielding iron. "You are dooming us to a far worse fate than we would be suffering at the hands of Gyorick! He was laughing in triumph when he was seeing us enter. We are as good as dead!" The man withered, falling to his knees. "He will give up this chase and be taking the rest to the field."

"Leifal, I've had my fill—" Daverell was interrupted by a deep, deafening boom sounding around them and shaking dust loose from the ceiling.

"Oh, gods below!" Leifal gasped. "They are coming for us!"

"You fool; that's thunder from the storm outside," Daverell stated, hoping he was correct.

"It was so loud," Crow remarked. "Maybe lightning struck the tower?"

A flash through the single barred window in the room preceded another resounding roll of thunder, mixing with the cold sound of rain slapping the stones on the sill.

"Thunder," Dav said again. "Hopefully lightning strikes your friends outside."

"Why are you still worrying about them?" Leifal whined. "They are not mattering anymore. Demons will be killing us all in minutes. We are doomed!"

"Settle yourself! *If* demons ever were real, they haven't been for a very long time," Ameryn said to Leifal, though to Dav's ear it sounded like she was trying to calm and convince herself more than anyone else. "That sudden attack and now this dismal tower has us worked

252

into a craze."

"Yeah." Crow's eyes wandered around the room. "Look at this place."

Everyone did, silent a moment. The space was large, made of stone, and empty. Every surface was thickly layered in dry dust, tangled cobwebs, and the black moldy substance that also covered the outside. It had a high ceiling supported on a series of intersecting arches. Everything was constructed with the same messy brickwork as the outside. There was enough order to keep the structure standing but none beyond.

Crow kicked a loose rock across the floor.

"Don't disturb anything," Ameryn instructed.

"I found a skeleton!" Crowan cried with fascination.

"Don't touch it!" Ameryn told him.

"I knew it," Leifal said. "This *is* a tomb. Our tomb. You are marching in here unprepared, no protective ericle, no human sacrifice—"

"Oh, I think we can provide one of those," Daverell interrupted, looking meaningfully at Leifal, who shrank with a pitiful whimper.

"Maybe even the ghosts have left this place," Crowan whispered. "I would, if I were them."

"You Threyans." Leifal shivered. "These are not wandering human souls but demon ghosts, bound forever to this place and mad with hunger. They will not be just tearing our bodies apart but dragging our souls to hell."

"You say they're bound to the tower?" Dav asked.

"Yes," Leifal answered. "They cannot be leaving, thank the gods, but that doesn't help us."

"Why do your people worship them then?" Crowan regarded the jittery man quizzically.

"Worship?" Leifal replied. "No, we are *respecting* their power and trying to keep them sated. Some are worshiping them I suppose, but most of us are only reverencing the Dark forces...out of fear."

"Seems like just an old empty ruin to me," Crow observed.

"Me too," Dav agreed, willing it to be true. "Enough Uthiri delusions. We move on now. Unless you'd like to spend the night here."

"I couldn't sleep here if I wanted to." Ameryn shuddered.

"Me neither," said Crow.

"I think—" Dav began.

"Or me," Leifal agreed.

"We all might have assumed that." Daverell gave Leifal a pointed look. "Besides, you're not part of this decision. We're all agreed; we push on through the night. All we need do is scale the tower. Sounds simple enough."

Daverell made a torch from one of the bones Crowan had found, some cloth, and pitch—his supply of which was running low.

There was only one door—other than the impassible front gate—in this room, and they all walked through it. It delivered them into a long hallway in much the same state as the room preceding it. There was enough space that Daverell walked beside Druid, leading him by the reins. The sounds of the thunderstorm faded; either it was blowing itself out, or they were moving away from any outside windows. Soon, only the clopping of the horse's and mules' hooves broke the silence.

Daverell waved the torch before him, burning the cobwebs that sometimes spanned the entire width and height of the passage. He wondered what size of spider might spin a web so extensive, or might it have been many small ones working together? Neither possibility was particularly preferable to the other. Dav had never been afraid of spiders, but given the tension he was feeling here, a butterfly might make him jump out of his skin.

Occasionally, they would pass a door leading to some other chamber or passage to the left or right of them. Many were barred shut with heavy iron rods, but others had their doors ajar, and a few had no doors at all. Whether they'd fallen away with age or were torn from their hinges he couldn't say and was in no mood to investigate, but the thought of those open doorways behind them made him nervous. What might be watching, or now following, from the impenetrable darkness beyond?

The hallway ended with an entrance into a large, cylindrical space that extended vertically beyond their discerning, both up and down. They were standing on a landing with a spiraling ramp leading up on their left and down on their right. In the center was a frayed rope.

"Is there a lift, perhaps?" Dav wondered, peering over the precipice. There was no rail of any kind.

"Even if there is and, by some miracle, it's still intact, would you trust that rope to hold us?" Ameryn eyed the dangling cable warily.

"Not for a second," Dav said. "But it would suggest that this channel was once used for transporting supplies."

"To the top?" Ameryn asked.

"To the exit," he confirmed. Turning, he saw Crowan approaching the edge holding a rock. Dav reached out and placed his hand over the boy's. "Believe me, Crow, I'd love to drop that rock off the edge and see how long it takes to hit the bottom too, but I'm afraid we'll have to live without finding out. Best to disturb as little as possible."

Crowan nodded, reluctantly setting the stone back on the floor. Dav turned to Ameryn and caught a grateful look from her before leading Druid and the rest of them up the ramp. They huddled against the wall as they went, as far away from the crumbling edge as possible.

Their footsteps, in this vast chamber, caused echoes upon echoes. Several times, Daverell stopped and swung his torch around, peering behind them, sure he would find something coming up the slope from below. The light from his torch didn't extend far, and if something were waiting in the darkness just beyond its reach, he'd be unable to tell. It made him nervous. Grimly, he searched for something to talk about as they moved.

"Leifal, what about the field?" Dav asked.

"Field?" Leifal shook his head in confusion.

"Back at the entrance, you mentioned Gyorick was going to the field."

"Oh, yes," Leifal said. "Right before you were snatching me away, he was getting word that all Uthiri soldiers were to be meeting at Tannis Field."

"That's on the other side of the Grays," Ameryn noted. "West of here."

"And the fastest way to get there from here is through Ankr pass," Dav said. "Will your friends be waiting for us there after we make our way out of this place?"

"They would not be daring to come any nearer than they already have," the interpreter insisted. "Nor consider taking that cliff road you were speaking of, even if they could be finding it. Just passing by a demon tower is terrible luck."

"Then they'll have to take either the mountain pass to the north or go around the range to the south. Either way it'll take them weeks. Why there? There's nothing at Tannis."

"I do not know," Leifal protested.

"How're they passing orders?" Dav asked. It was something the Threyans had always wondered. The Uthiri had enjoyed superior communication, and the Threyans were baffled as to why.

"I do not know," Leifal repeated. "A sorcerer is always traveling with each party; he is receiving the orders. I am not knowing how."

Daverell remembered seeing the man—other than Leifal and Gyorick, he was the only other in the war party dressed differently than the soldiers. Black robes. Was it some dark magic that let them pass information immediately over great distances?

"Why did you not mention any of this before?" Dav inquired.

"You were never asking me anything about our orders or plans beyond tracking you. I am having no idea you are even interested," Leifal griped. "It does not matter anyway, we're all—"

"Yes, I know, we're all going to die here," Dav finished for him, falling back into scowling silence.

Each full revolution they made around the ramp brought them up another floor. There was a flat landing each time they completed a lap, and sometimes one in between. Usually, an iron door stood at each landing, but sometimes there was only more brick wall. Daverell tried counting the levels as they ascended but the inconsistencies made it hard to keep track. In any case, he wasn't sure how many floors up they had to go, nor did he expect the structure to have been designed

256

with much reason behind it. Before long, he gave up his attempt to determine their progress.

The door he passed now was in even poorer condition than most. Not only had it been devoured by flaky rust, but deep claw marks marred the area around the small, barred window and the arched frame. He could also detect a foul odor pouring from beyond the barrier, and a mass of black liquid seeped underneath, forming a pool. He guessed some creature had been trying to escape. Perhaps it had died, leaving its rotted stink and a puddle of blood or drool or whatever it might be at the base of the entrance. Dav stepped around the wetness and gave the door a quick tug as he passed, happy to find that, despite the state it was in, it was locked tight.

Leifal began his distressed, whispered praying again. This time it didn't even sound like Uthiri but some other, sharper tongue. The hushed tones of the man echoed enough that it sounded as if it were more than one voice speaking.

"Leifal," Dav snapped, turning to face the man, "will you please silence that damnable whining?"

Even before Leifal answered, Daverell could see the man's mouth hadn't been moving.

"It is not me!" Leifal objected.

"I can hear it too," Crowan said.

"It is the demons!" Leifal squeaked. "They are all around us."

Daverell wanted to disagree. Claim it was their own sounds being distorted, but it was untrue. Finally, he said only, "Keep moving."

But within just a few more paces, they reached a large, crumbling gap in their path where the ramp had long ago fallen away.

"What do we do now?" Crowan asked.

"We'll have to retreat a bit. Head back to the last landing and go through the door there, if we can force it open," Dav said.

"You think we can find a side staircase or some other way to the floor above? Meet back up with the ramp?" Ameryn suggested.

"Well, we can't jump this." Dav held the torch out, only barely able to make out the continuing ramp on the other side of the gap.

Dav passed the torch to Crowan. "Give this to your mother," he said. "The walkway isn't wide enough for us to safely turn the whole party around. You're in the lead, Mrs. Vowery."

It took them all a tense moment to turn the horse and mules before they could begin following Ameryn back the way they had come. She suddenly halted, and it took him a moment to see why. She'd reached the clawed door. It was open wide.

"Dav?" Ameryn glanced at him, alarmed.

"I don't think we have much choice," he answered and pulled his sword from its scabbard. The blade in his hand failed to grant him the surge of confidence it usually did.

"This is only the beginning," Leifal breathed. "They will be toying with us and torturing us before killing us. Oh gods below, make it quick for me!"

"Silence!" Ameryn glared over her shoulder before placing a hand atop her mouth and nose. "Ugh, that smell," she said, before creeping forward holding the torch shakily before her, peeking around the edge before she entered.

"What do you see?" Dav asked.

"Nothing," she answered.

Gooter, Gus, and Druid all hesitated at the doorway, shaking their heads and swishing their tails. They had to be forcibly pulled through.

The party gathered in a wide but low corridor beyond. It was indeed empty save for more of the black fluid dripping from the ceiling and even oozing from the walls. Dav couldn't help getting some on his boots as he walked through the puddle on the floor, but he did all he could to avoid it drizzling on him.

"What is this stuff?" Crow asked.

"I'd rather not know," Ameryn said. "Don't let it touch you."

Crowan inclined his head and smelled at the pool of it on the floor and shrugged, not finding a trace of anything beyond the foul odor already permeating the air.

Ameryn wordlessly handed the torch back to Daverell. It was pitiful, having burned nearly all its fuel.

"We're going to have to relight it," Dav said. "We'll have a moment of darkness. Stay close. Crow, get your starter ready." Daverell waved out the flame and, in total darkness, coated the cloth end again with pitch. He had to scrape the sides of the vessel to coat it well enough. Once it went out again, it would be out for good. "Alright, Crow, give me a light," Dav said. A few sparks later and the torch blazed with renewed life. *But for how long?* Dav wondered.

"Where's Leifal?" Crow asked.

Dav spun around, searching the group. Their Uthiri companion was gone.

"He's here," Ameryn said, inclining her head.

Dav followed her eyes to the shape cowering at her feet. "Get up, you fool," he said.

Trembling, Leifal slowly stood, not nearly as embarrassed as he should have been in Daverell's estimation. Though in truth, even the military captain wasn't feeling as brave as he appeared. The ghostly whispers persisted and were straining his nerves.

"I wish we had more than one torch," Crowan said.

"I wish it, too," Daverell agreed. "We're not very prepared for this place, are we?" He caught Crow's eye and gave him a little smile.

Crow managed to grin back. "Nope."

Daverell started forward, going as fast as he dared. The low ceiling gave little room for the smoke of the torch to escape, and they were all, mules and horse included, hunching to get to the better air near the floor. Despite Dav's best efforts, some of the dripping black liquid fell onto him. He did his best to ignore it, at least they'd left most of it behind at the entrance and he was no longer having to walk through it. They came to a door in the hallway to their right.

"We'll have to search the rooms," he said. "See if we can find some stairs." Daverell pushed on the ancient iron, and it swung open with a rusty groan. He swung the torch into the room beyond.

"Nothing here," he said, hoping no one else had seen the hundreds of bones littering the floor.

"There's another doorway ahead," Ameryn noted.

That one was an open archway leading to an empty room.

They continued on, searching the space and finding only side rooms with nothing in them except the occasional piles of old bones. Bones that were all much too old and dusty to be causing the fetid stench assaulting them.

Eventually the hallway ended in a larger, exterior room. It had small windows that let in traces of moonlight. The storm had passed. This space was tall enough it allowed them all to stand upright. Even better, the floor above had collapsed in one corner, and the resulting mass of bricks and splintered beams made a crude slope to the floor above.

"There." Daverell pointed. "I think we can get up there."

They started walking towards the debris when a call from Crowan stopped them all.

"Dav? Mother?" he said.

Daverell whirled the torch around to see the boy searching the floor behind them.

"What is it?" Ameryn asked.

"I think the black puddle is...following us," Crow said, pointing.

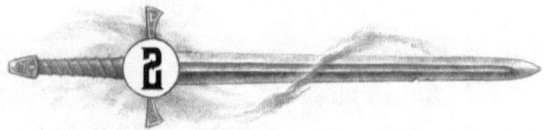

Dav moved to the side of the boy and lifted the torch. There it was. Much bigger than it had been before. It couldn't have been another pool of the stuff unless it had only just formed behind them; Dav would have remembered walking through it. Had it really...*followed* them?

"Oh gods! Oh gods!" Leifal cried.

Daverell grabbed the man by the neck. "Shut that mouth before I gag you. They jump at puddles where you're from?"

"If they be moving on their own, yes!" the man wheezed through Dav's grip.

Dav pushed the Uthiri man away. "We move now," he said. "I'm—"

"Crowan, no!" Ameryn shouted as the boy tossed a stone into the puddle.

It landed with a goopy splash and everyone tensed, waiting in breathless silence.

Nothing happened.

"I'm going first," Dav said, turning back to the pile of debris. "With Druid. Once we know it's safe, the rest of you follow." He pulled at the horse's reins, leading him over to the base of the pile and handing the torch to Ameryn. "I need to free up this arm."

Ameryn nodded. "Good luck."

Daverell took his first few steps, each one met with a deep creak from the beams beneath him or the skittering away of a loosened stone. Druid liked the rickety incline even less than Dav did, but in the end, they both managed to cautiously climb atop it to the floor above. They were now in a room much like the one beneath. Dav peeked out one of the windows, trying to assess how high they'd climbed, but it was too dark to tell much of anything.

"Leifal," Ameryn said patiently, "why don't you go next. Seeing how you don't have a mount to lead, take the torch, won't you?"

He turned away from the black substance and numbly took the torch from her. Wordlessly, he clambered up the rubble and handed the torch to Daverell when he reached the top. Dav held it out over the edge, giving as much light as he could to those still below.

"Crowan, you and Gooter next," Ameryn said.

Crowan licked his lips and worked his quavering way up the pile. The mule proved to be more sure-footed than Druid, and before long, Ameryn and Gus were the only two left on the lower floor.

"Come on, Mother!" Crowan called down. "It's easy!"

Ameryn began her ascent, more cautiously than her son had, being sure each foot was well planted before she moved the other one. Daverell waited at the top, his hand outstretched. Just as she reached out and took it, they both froze.

The clatter of a single, falling rock filled their ears. This was not something she'd knocked loose from the pile, however; the sound came from the upper floor. Searching, Daverell noticed a stone at his feet. It was still rocking back and forth, having not quite come to rest from being tossed up at them. It was coated in the black liquid, and, somehow, he knew it was the same rock Crow had thrown into the puddle.

The whole group craned their necks to peer at the room below. The pool of black sludge was now at the bottom of the slope, and a dark figure stood in the center of it.

With a jolt of alarm, Dav recognized her. The legless girl, but she was...different. She'd always been sitting before, unable to stand, but now she was somehow upright, without legs...floating. Below the stumps was nothing but a steady stream of her dripping blood. And she was...smiling at him. An unnatural rictus that split across her face. Twisted and predatory.

Beside him, Ameryn whispered, "T-Tamiron?"

Crowan and Leifal were watching with wide-eyed expressions as well. What were they seeing?

When Dav looked back, the child ran a finger across her neck. Her stare and smile didn't falter, even as the skin was split along the path her finger traced. Clumps of black dirt along with writhing white worms and maggots fell out of the slit. He turned away and wasn't the only one. Ameryn cringed, her eyes filled with tears of pain.

The thing below began laughing.

"Come on, Mrs. Vowery," Dav said.

Ameryn tightened her grip on his hand, and he pulled her up.

With a loud, reverberant snap, one of the heavy beams beneath the incline broke, and the pile of debris came down with a deafening crash. Gus fell with it, shrieking as he tumbled backwards. Ameryn, still clutching the reins, nearly followed him down as they were ripped from her grasp. However, Daverell's grip held fast to her other hand, and he clasped her, dangling over the edge. Daverell paused in that position, transfixed by the scene below.

The poor mule ended his fall with a splash directly into the waiting puddle. The legless, spectral figure was dashed away by the impact, as if formed from the liquid itself. The sludge immediately reformed into spidery tendrils that crawled over the panicking animal as he kicked his legs furiously. The black tar became a snarled web of clawed arms and skeletal teeth that began ripping the mule's body into pieces. The sounds and sights of wet cracks and crunches amid a geyser of blood finally brought the animal's horrified shrieks to an abrupt end before a new, more terrible sound filled the space.

Daverell watched the muck become a host of skeletal, horned heads, blood dripping from each fanged maw as they gurgled out an otherworldly bellow. It began as many lonely voices but came together in a dissonantly harmonic howl. Like a pack of undead wolves, ready to hunt.

Daverell broke out of his stupor and heaved Ameryn, who'd been equally spellbound by the unholy sight, up with the rest of them.

"Run!" he shouted. "Run! Run!"

They bolted down the hall as the profane baying echoed all around them. It was like the walls themselves were joining in. Leifal, at the head of the group, tore through the door at the end so swiftly he almost pitched right over the edge when they reached the landing in the tall, cylindrical room again. He teetered, arms flailing, until Crowan yanked him backward.

The group began scrambling up the ramp again. Daverell slammed the door shut behind him but had no confidence it would hold the thing back.

"Pray to the Goddess we don't come across any more gaps!" Ameryn exclaimed.

And Daverell did pray for that, as earnestly as he could while also running for his life. They were poorly situated now; Dav still held the torch but was at the back of the group. He held it high, hoping it would provide enough light for Leifal and Crowan at the front.

A scream from behind brought their attention to the monster as it erupted through the door. The tar-like knot of reaching, swelling limbs was now so large it hardly fit through the passage. It was forced to make itself long and thin, slithering through like a giant, writhing centipede.

It was fast, much faster than they were. In a moment, it was right behind them. Daverell brandished the torch at it to no effect, then pulled his sword from its scabbard and swung it too. While the creature showed no fear of the blade, the steel was effective at splitting the clawed hands that reached for him in two, even if they immediately reformed into new ones that reached for him again.

Daverell passed Ameryn the torch. "Keep going!" he commanded. "I'll try to slow it down!"

He tried, but even with all his concentration and skill, he was only barely keeping it from swallowing him. And he was growing tired—very tired, very quickly. While he was only barely able to force it to a slower pace than the group was keeping, ultimately, they *were* pulling ahead of it. However, as they did, he was losing the light of the torch, making it even harder to hack away at the roiling mass.

He made a rash decision, bursting into the next side door and running into the darkness beyond. The thing followed him as he'd hoped it would. It was focused only on him now.

He sprinted blindly down the hall and felt on each side for another door. He tried three that were immovable before one gave way, and he threw himself into the room beyond. He closed the door behind him and explored its surface for a lock or bar to block it shut.

He stopped when he realized how quiet everything had become and pressed his ear up to the door. Had it turned around, deciding to follow the others after all?

Something began pushing against the door. Daverell pushed back with his entire body. His hands, braced against the iron, met with the shape of a bolting mechanism. After forcing the door into a latched position, he slammed the rusted, screeching bolt into place.

There was a panicked knocking before Ameryn's frightened voice reached him from the other side. "Dav? Is that you?"

"Mrs. Vowery?" he asked.

"Let me in," she pleaded. "I was separated from the others. Hurry, I think it's coming back!"

His hand was on the bolt, but something stopped him from sliding it back.

"What are you waiting for? It's coming!"

If it could mimic the girl, he expected it could do the same for Ameryn.

"Dav, it's here, please!" She was screaming now.

Daverell began backing away, and some of the sludge struck his face as though, from around the edges of the door, it were dripping sideways into the room. It burned where it touched the skin, and he wiped it off quickly on his sleeve. It was seeping in through the crevices. Crevices being made wider as the metal groaned, buckling under pressure.

"Dav, Dav!" it continued in Ameryn's voice. "Let me in, hold me. Kiss me! We can do whatever we want now that the brat is gone."

Its imitation broke down, twisting the sound into something foul. Daverell frantically ran his fingers over the walls, searching for something, anything, that might save him while cursing his useless hide for trapping himself.

A brick came away in his groping hands and fell, clapping on the floor. He shoved hard against the wall, and more stones came loose. The wall was crumbling away here. Timing his actions with the pounding of the demon's, he rammed the wall with his shoulder until it gave way. Crawling through the opening, he found himself in the adjoining room. The door to this room had been locked, but now that he was on the inside, he slid the bolt back easily.

He opened the door tentatively, creeping into the hall. As far as he could tell, the thing remained fixated on the first door.

Sightlessly, Dav moved back down the hall on the toes of his boots, sure at any moment the creature would seize him from behind. However, the racket it was making was, indeed, fading. Perhaps he'd fooled it.

He entered the central chamber again and easily found the light held by Ameryn, high above now. They were all still rushing upwards. He raced to catch up as, echoing down the hall, the sound of the creature breaching the door followed him. He prayed it might be confused for a moment by his escape and investigate before returning its attention to this area.

He forced himself to keep running, hoping his feet wouldn't trip on some fallen stone or fall into a gap in the ramp. He was gaining ground on the group ahead, rotation by rotation growing a little closer until, finally, Ameryn at the back heard him and spun around in a panic.

"It's me!" Dav called out as loudly as he dared.

"Dav!" she breathed in relief.

There was a clicking sound from below. Ameryn leaned over with the torch, but the light revealed nothing in the abyss.

"Keep going!" Daverell bellowed at all of them.

"There's another gap!" Crow said. "But I think we can jump this one!"

Ameryn shouted, "Crow, wait!" But he had already taken a leap, landing safely on the other side. "Back away," Ameryn warned her son. "It'll be weakest near the edge."

Crowan followed her directions, making room for the rest of them. Druid and Gooter made the jump easily, as did Ameryn. Even Leifal managed it, sobbing with terror. Daverell leaped the gap last, flailing as some stones under his feet fell away when he landed. His heart stopped a moment as he clambered to the more solid section of the platform.

"Move!" he ordered.

They climbed and climbed; it seemed like the ascending spiral might never end. Especially with the host of demonic voices once again closing in on them. Soon, Daverell could see it as well as hear it. The many heads leering as it closed the gap, crawling straight up the tunnel instead of upon the ramp as they had to.

"Dav, look!" Crow yelled.

The boy was pointing to the ending of the ramp above. They'd almost reached the top.

Daverell climbed that last little bit slower than the rest as he once again had to turn, hacking away at their pursuer. It cackled at him as he stabbed and sliced at it.

With a broad cut that severed three of the grasping limbs, he turned and followed the rest at a sprint through the arched entryway and down the hall. The thing's many-voiced laugh followed him to where Ameryn was waiting, holding the door open. She slammed it into place once Daverell was inside.

Crow and Leifal were struggling with another door on the other side of the room.

"It's locked or rusted shut or something!" Crow said.

Daverell ran to it and found that, even when combining his efforts with theirs, it was immovable. There had once been a keyhole, but it had been long ago filled with molten lead—picking it was not an option. There was also no bar holding it shut, nor any other obstruction, and it was too thick to break down. The open night air beckoned on the other side of the windows next to it. They'd reached the point where the tower met with the top of the cliff. The exit. They were so close.

Yet they couldn't get out.

"Help me barricade the door!" Ameryn pleaded.

Daverell rushed to her side and began piling heavy beams, stones, and whatever else they found in the wreck of the room against the interior door while Leifal and Crowan continued to push and pull at the exterior one.

Daverell had noticed how confidently the thing pursued them. Now he knew why. It knew that even if they reached this room alive, they'd still be trapped.

In the spaces where the interior door met its frame, the black muck began bubbling through while the door itself groaned under the pressure, and the wicked voices filled the room.

Dav ran to the exit, handing Crowan the torch. It had nearly burned itself out again. He could get through the door, there just wasn't enough time.

"Leifal," Dav ordered. "Go help Mrs. Vowery hold that thing back!

Crow, hold the torch up where I can see the hinges."

"The hinges?" Crowan asked as Daverell grabbed a rock from off the floor.

"If you're trying to breach a door that's locked tight," Dav explained as he wedged his sword's edge under the head of the pin, "the weakest point is the hinges." He began hammering on the weapon's hilt with the rock forcing the pin a half inch out its housing. "If I can get these pins out, we can escape."

"Uh, Dav," Crowan said, studying the door, "there are *six* hinges."

The continuing roaring and laughing were momentarily lost in each thunderous boom that shook the space, sending flurries of dust drifting from the ceiling. More of the tar glopped into the room as the door bent. Ameryn and Leifal backed away.

"Dav," Ameryn said, "it'll break through any second."

Daverell was still trying to remove the first pin. It had moved easily at first but was now stuck. If he had something thin enough, he could knock it out from within the hinge itself.

"Crow, see if you can find a nail, search the floor," Dav directed.

Crowan began scanning the floor with the flickering torch while Dav tried the next hinge. It shattered when he struck it. His heart flared with hope for a moment, and he struck the rest, but they all, unfortunately, were in much better condition than the second.

A sudden scream from Leifal made him turn. A ropey tendril of sludge had worked its way around the door and across the room. It was dragging the Uthiri man towards itself by the leg. Daverell ran to his side and hacked through the slimy tentacle which splashed to the floor and immediately began reforming. Leifal continued wailing in agony even after it let go. It had made a burned and bloody mess of his leg. Daverell grabbed the man and began pulling him further into the room when, with another powerful shock, the door was forced inwards so violently it broke loose the very stones forming the arched doorway, leaving an uneven hole in the wall. They all shielded themselves from the spray of sparks, splinters, and grit that exploded over them in a cloud.

Daverell fell to his knees, and before he could even react, Leifal was ripped from his grip. Through the haze, Dav watched as the man was pulled into the swirling mass of blackness. He was grateful for the dim light as he could only just make out the horrific sight of the Uthiri being split up the middle, his ribs cracking open like an egg and his insides spilling onto the floor where dozens of eager mouths gobbled them up.

The darkness didn't hide the grisly sounds, however.

Cutting through all this chaos was Crow's voice. "I found one!" he exclaimed. But it was too late. They'd all be dead in moments. The boy bounded to his side, holding the nail triumphantly. It was long and straight, perfect for the job in every way, except that it hadn't been discovered in time.

"I also found this," Crow said, lifting into the uneven light of the torch a small copper charm.

Dav stared in wonder. "Where?"

"Under the window, over there." Crow nodded over his shoulder.

Daverell took it from the boy and stood, facing the mass of demons that had finished devouring Leifal and was now approaching them slowly, relishing its victory.

Daverell held the ericle before him and watched the thing recoil even as it entered a sort of mesmerized trance, all its attention on the lidocrafted charm.

"Crow," Dav called. He handed the ericle back.

"What is it?" the boy asked, holding it out as Dav had, between them and the demon.

"An old demon warding charm; it should hold that monstrosity at bay for long enough." Dav set to work on the door again.

Daverell placed the nail inside the hinge, against the underside of the pin. With one strike of the rock the top pin popped out.

Ameryn stood, paralyzed by the chaos of the scene. She watched in horror as her son approached the writhing mass of demons. She tried to force herself to move, to stop him. In the moment she succeeded, her shock froze her into place again.

Through the haze of dust and smoke, she saw Crowan holding a magnificent sword before him. The blade was graceful and glowing and, most importantly, driving the demons back. They shrank in the face of the divine beauty. Crowan looked taller, stronger, more confident. Where had the sword come from? She was so captivated it took her a moment to realize Dav was calling her name.

"Ameryn," Dav called from the door, "gather the horses. Get ready to run once I get this open."

She blinked, staring at him a moment before rushing to the reins of Dav's horse and Gooter, guiding them to the door where Dav worked frantically to remove the pins from the door's hinges.

"Dav?" her son said. She turned to see him backing up, nearly joining them against the outside wall.

The demonic muck was growing more aggressive and agitated. What confused her more was that the sword was gone. Crowan was holding a small charm instead.

"Almost there!" Dav replied, and after struggling with the bottommost pin for a moment more, he stood and kicked the door. It sprung open the wrong way. "Out!" he shouted.

They all raced through and into the open night.

Ameryn fell in exhaustion and savored both the feel of the cool night air and the enraged yowling of the creatures behind them, bound to their ancient, cursed tower. She breathed deeply but coughed as an offensive odor filled her nose. The rotting carcass of some beast lay ahead, barely visible in the moonlight.

"What is it?" Crow asked.

Ameryn had no idea. Was it an animal? A Beloworld perversion of something like a bear?

Dav didn't seem to know either; he shook his head. "No idea," he said. "But I don't like the look of it."

She agreed. It made her shudder. Were there demons roaming outside the tower as well? "Those monsters…" Ameryn faced the tower, trembling. "Demons," she mouthed, as if tasting the word. "They're real."

"I think this is another one," Crow guessed, leaning over the dead creature.

Ameryn's eyes went from the creature to the charm in her son's hand. She turned him towards her, looking into his eyes. "What is this? Did it turn into a sword?"

Crowan stared back, confused. "Sword?"

"You were holding a sword."

The boy shook his head. "Only this." He lifted the charm to show her.

"It's an ericle," Dav said. "I've only ever seen a few. People used to wear them as defense against the Darkness, protection from demons. How it ended up in that tower room is beyond me. But Crowan found it. Of course he did."

"He saved us," Ameryn whispered. "Again."

"She thought I was holding a sword," Crowan told Dav.

"I saw…" Ameryn began, "In the tower, as he held the ericle before him, for a moment through the dust and the darkness…it looked like he held a great, glimmering sword."

Crowan laughed a little uneasily while Dav nodded knowingly. "A vision."

Is that what it was? Ameryn wondered to herself.

"Alright," Dav said, "let's get out of here. I'll not be able to rest until we're free of the sight and sound of that wretched tower. Tomorrow, we begin searching the mountains. First for fresh water, then for the castle."

"Gus was carrying much of our food," Ameryn mentioned. "Will we starve to death out here?"

"Wait." Dav inspected a bag he'd spotted on the ground. "The Goddess smiles on us; we've got supplies here. Dried fruit, beans, rice... in addition to what your mule and Druid are carrying it could last us weeks, even more."

Ameryn stared at the bag. "It's a miracle," she said, then looked at her son again. "Two miracles."

The boy was facing the tower now. When he turned back to her, even in the night, she could see tears on his cheeks.

"Gus. Mister Leifal..." Crow's voice was thick with emotion.

His mother hugged him tight. "I know." Her voice broke too. "I know." She reached for Dav and pulled him into the embrace. She enjoyed the closeness, the honesty between them all in that moment.

"Come on," Dav said after they broke away from each other. "There's a lot to do yet before we can rest."

"Yes," Ameryn agreed. She wanted to find the castle, and not only for the sanctuary it offered. The tower had proven to her that there were still demons roaming the Midlands, and the world still needed someone who could destroy such beings. Perhaps, if the Uthiri were to witness what she had seen, a boy wielding a weapon capable of killing their evil gods, they would flee back to their own country, ending the war. Dav had been right. "Tomorrow, we'll begin searching for the castle." She looked into Crowan's eyes. "We need to get you to that sword."

CHAPTER 20

UPON THE ALTAR

The Nameless Abbey

Pell stepped out of the darkness a little at a time. She was aware of the light, aware of herself, but not sure if she was awake or asleep. Alive or dead. She was floating, motionless. Slowly, she became aware that her body ached and that her eyes were closed. Why were they closed? She opened them and realized she was in a bed, a bed she'd been in twice before. Both Iress Rin and Em were there. Rin was knitting something, but Em was looking at her, excited.

"Iress Pell," she exclaimed. "You're awake."

Rin glanced up from her knitting. "I'll tell the Iress Matriarch," she said, before stowing her yarn and needles in a bag and walking out of the infirmary.

"I thought I was dead." Pell was surprised by how weak she sounded. Taking a deep breath caused a sharp pain in her chest, and she began coughing. They were small, shallow coughs, but they still hurt.

"Don't try to talk just yet," Em advised. "Bryn punctured your lung and broke a few of your ribs in addition to all the other damage she did. She only just missed your heart. Even then, she was very close to injuring you beyond our aid. Had to use a Saercandle until the sun came up. As it is, thank the Goddess above, you're alive and should be for years to come with little more than a few light scars—and most of them in places only a lover would notice."

So they will never be noticed then, Pell thought, surprising herself again, this time with how sad the thought made her feel. "Bryn?" she asked in a whisper, which hurt less.

"She's in a dungeon cell," Em said. "Been a while, since before my time, that anyone's occupied one. I told you not to talk."

"How did you get in my room?"

Em made a face as her request was ignored but answered the question. "I was just sitting down to dinner when Ollett asked me if I'd seen Bryn. It was then we heard you scream and ran to investigate. Your door was locked but the key was in the latch, so we let ourselves in. It was quite a shock." She shuddered.

"Why?" Pell asked.

"Did Bryn do it? She isn't talking. The Matriarch is with her now, though she wanted to be notified when you woke up."

"What day is it?"

"Oh, it's the following day, almost lunch time," Iress Em answered, pulling out her Restorative and filtering the sunlight over Pell's chest. "One more pass should do it."

Pell watched the sparkling colors dance across her skin in holy patterns and designs. It was hypnotic. Pell's mind was being lulled into a daze when, suddenly, she bolted upright.

"Restoratives!" she shouted.

"What?" Em said, raising the tool in her hand.

The answer was obvious; Pell felt like a fool. She also felt very dizzy and fell back onto the soft pillow. If a lidocrafted blade could cut the demon off from the living level of the Below, then a Restorative was just the thing to cut it off from the dead one.

"Iress Em," Pell whispered urgently. "How do you heal a hereditary condition? Not an injury but an abnormality, like a clubfoot?"

Pell was grateful Em's enthusiasm for explaining her craft out-weighed the confusion she appeared to be experiencing. She answered the question Pell asked of her instead of asking the ones she obviously had for Pell.

"Those are the hardest maladies to treat, and the ones in which we have the most ground still to cover," Iress Em said, running the purifying Light over Pell's wounds again. "We have to understand, *really* understand, the reason behind the problem. If someone is born blind, we can't simply heal it unless we know why, and there are a lot of potential causes, many of which we can't identify by just observing them."

"But if you could," Pell urged, a little impatiently.

"Then it's a matter of Lightwork with a Restorative," she nodded to the one in her hand, "while first visualizing the problem as it is, then becoming as it should be. It's more time consuming, and the Light-work is more complicated too. We're not healing an injury. The body *wants* to heal injuries. We're coaxing the body to go against its own flawed pattern. It's a fairly new process, and there are so many ailments we have yet to understand—"

"What of Vulsipher?" Pell asked. "Are there things about it that don't make physical sense? Do you understand its body well enough to fix it?"

Em looked puzzled again. "There are many things that seem wrong, but it always heals essentially the same way, even in the wrong ways."

"Do you think you could coax its body to change those things?"

"I've...never tried," Em said, sounding intrigued by the idea. "It would have to be out in the sunlight and...I don't think it's a good idea to take it out of its chamber. The lidocrafting keeps its connection to the Below weak enough that it can't spawn lesser demons."

Pell remembered the story Iress Lee had told her about one of Em's experiments that had gone tragically wrong.

"But if we did it in one of the greenhouses or something, could you do it?"

"Yes, I think I could," Em answered.

At that moment, the door opened and the Matriarch marched in. "Iress Pell, thank the Goddess above you're all right. Iress Rin and Em, would you give us the room?"

They didn't want to; Pell could see it in their faces, but with a few small bows, they exited.

The Matriarch spoke immediately, "Well? Tell me everything. Bryn is refusing to speak."

Pell shook her head. "She said nothing to me, only attacked, took me by surprise. Matriarch, that doesn't matter now. I think I know how to kill it."

"Vulsipher?"

"Yes," Pell said. "We need to bring it into a state of Light and Order, cut it off from the Dark. Iress Em was just telling me that a Restorative might be used to *fix* its body. The parts of it that are wrong or dead. I believe those parts allow it to exist in the planes of the dead, and cutting its access to that realm has never been tried."

Iress Lee was nodding thoughtfully. "It's an interesting idea."

"We'd have to do it in daylight, in a lidocrafted cage or one of the greenhouses."

"And we would have to let the body restore itself," Lee cautioned. "Bring the limbs together. It would be dangerous."

"We'd shape the body into something more...right. Iress Em and Rin could use the Restoratives—"

"And myself, Iress Pell. I'm a Curial."

"Yes, of course," Pell said. "While Ollett and his men stand ready to execute it with some of the holy weapons from Halvett's collection."

"And you and Mai would be maintaining a connection, watching and warning us accordingly." The Matriarch was sounding excited.

"Yes, Iress Pell, yes!"

Her elated expression changed to one of vexation when the door opened again.

"Who's there?" she barked.

Ollett was standing in the doorway, Iress Em and Rin behind him.

"We told him you were busy," Em called.

"It cannot wait, Matriarch," the man insisted.

"What is it, Captain?" Iress Lee asked.

Ollett entered, flushed and dirty. "May we talk freely in here?" he asked, with a glance at Pell.

"Yes, of course."

"We killed a man, scouting around the area, searching the pass. He was very good, even against two of our watchmen. He killed Rykard and left Jos injured."

"Rykard?" Her hand went to her chest. "Dead? And at the hand of an outsider? That is grave news and a heavy loss."

"Jos thought there might be more. He swore he saw three people yesterday, searching just past the grand fold."

"So close?" Iress Lee questioned. "Do you know why?"

"I checked each end. The door to the tower has been opened."

"Again?" the Matriarch asked. "I thought we'd finally fixed that problem."

"What I found to the west was even worse," he said. "From the sun ridge, I saw out to Tannis Field. There are two armies gathered there, both of them vast. Even from the ridge I recognized the red and black of the Uthiri and the blue and brown of our own Threyan soldiers."

"Tannis? Why?" the Matriarch wondered.

"I don't know, but I think the scout is from the Uthiri army."

"He was Uthiri, then?"

"Wearing the uniform at least," Ollett answered.

"Were they fighting? The armies?"

"Not yet," Ollett said.

Iress Lee darkened. "I do not like this."

"Nor I," Ollett agreed.

"Two armies at our very doorstep? Not a convenient battlefield for either side. Unless they know their demon is in the pass."

"How would they know that?" Ollett inquired.

Looking knowingly at Pell, she said, "Unfortunately, there is a way. I'm quite certain they're searching for this place and planning to attack once they've found it. I'll fill you in on a few things, Captain. After that, we need to prepare. We're going to attempt to kill the demon tomorrow."

"Do we not try to do so every day?"

"We're trying something new."

"Tomorrow?"

"It will take us time to prepare, but the sooner the better."

"Let me help!" Pell started to rise.

"Your task remains unchanged, Iress Pell," stated the Matriarch. "Stay in that bed and recover. You'll have plenty to do once you're up and about. Come, Ollett."

"Wait," Pell called.

The Iress Matriarch turned to her.

"There's more," Pell remarked. "From the *Lyprakarum* I'm translating, I learned that a Singer can set free the demon's soul slaves."

"Singer?" the Matriarch asked. "An Opravic?"

"If our attempt tomorrow does not work, we must find one. Without the spirits to feed on, the demon will be greatly weakened."

"How could the Church have been so wrong? Discontinuing the Opravic faction when they provided such a vital task?"

"They might not have known," Pell said. "The Opravics voice reached those dead and lost in the Hollow, calling them to the Embrace. They may not have realized they were also regularly stealing souls away from the Elder Demons."

"Even if that's the case," the Matriarch observed, "for the Church to abandon those who have died in the Dark because it made their supposed victory over it appear more complete...it's unfeeling. If we fail tomorrow, I'll send word to the Jophrat Seat."

"How long will it take?"

"To locate and reinstate someone to an order that the Church has lost for centuries and find a way to send them here? I've no idea. Maybe years. It may be too late with this army on our doorstep." The Matriarch sighed. "Oh, Iress Pell. If only we'd had you sooner. Come, Ollett."

They left Pell to her thoughts. She looked out the large infirmary window at the perpetually cloudy sky. They must succeed tomorrow. They *must*. The Matriarch had said it might take years to get an Opravic to them, and that was *if* the Church believed they needed one. Pell worried she might not last that long and was certain that Mai would not.

The bare stone against her feet was cold. Why was she barefoot? She didn't know. Didn't care. Only lifted herself onto the very tips of her toes. She'd always liked tiptoeing. It made her feel like she was dancing. There was a grace to it if one did it right. It was so much better than simply walking. She hated walking. She hated corridors. And what was there in this place but those two dreadful things? Mai had been reduced to something small. Something that took sad pleasure in changing the way she moved. Wandering through this endless maze of stone and dark and brick and black and hard and cold and cruel and small people living small lives in this small and endless place.

She used to dance. Really dance. With an angel, in a way that made her feel beautiful, floating and spinning and escaping from corridors and walking. Then the Matriarch had barred her from even that. That horrid old crone had stopped her, over and over, from her refuge. From drifting and drifting and drifting away. Every tale had its adversaries, even hers.

But her happy ending was coming. The Matriarch, Iress Pell, everyone would see the truth.

Poor Pell.

Bryn had nearly ruined everything. Trying to kill her? Pell wasn't supposed to die; Mai had been assured of this. They only needed Pell occupied. Which Mai supposed she was. Not dead, only recovering, thank the Goddess above.

Coffee. It was in the air, mingling unfavorably with the scent of some stewing vegetables. She was near the kitchen but would not go in. Whispers were wafting from that room too. She heard them, talking about her. Cruel words and watching eyes. Keep watching. Watch. See.

But Bryn had allowed herself to be captured, ruining everything. Mai couldn't do it by herself. Thankfully, it had only been ruined for a little while. The Goddess had fixed it. She fixed everything. Now Mai had the vial and all was ready. Even *she* was ready.

Ready to do something wonderful and big like she'd always wanted to. Something important. Something heroic. Something worthy of a story. Something…something…

Iress Mai wished she could do the something now. It meant connecting again. Being one with the angel. How she longed for that feeling. Carried away on graceful wings. Born upon gentle waves. Moving together, away from the pain, floating like lace on a breeze. At one with the grand openness…forever.

Then she would not just dance and drift.

She would fly.

There were two things Iress Em assured Pell she *could* do to hasten her recovery: sleep and drink water. Her mind was too busy with information to do much of the former but the latter she did with admirable frequency and in impressive quantities. This meant the almost musical ringing sound she created with the brass chamber pot became a regular sound in the room that day, and each time she got out of the bed to make it, she felt better—and not just from the relief it brought.

She'd nearly collapsed the first time she stood, but by evening her head, arms—everything really—seemed almost back to normal.

It took some convincing, but, in the end, Iress Em allowed her to leave the infirmary. Pell told her that she really only wanted to sleep in her own bed for the night, and that was mostly true. However, there was something she needed to investigate first.

One lingering question Pell had was the strange voice she'd heard speaking to Mai and Bryn. In her abundance of recovery time, Pell's mind had given birth to a suspicion. Something she needed an answer to immediately.

It was late. Everyone had apparently retired for the evening, and Iress Pell stole through the silent hallways and steep stairways alone. She took the long way to her destination as it brought her by the Matriarch's office. She wanted to ask how the day's preparations had gone and tell Iress Lee of her latest surmise. Unfortunately, the door was locked for the night. Cursing her bad luck, Pell continued through the winding corridors, stopping at the ground floor bench set in the arched recess. Bryn's, and lately Mai's, constant sitting place.

Pell took it now. Perching on the edge of the seat, just as Bryn had been the first time Pell had seen her and nearly every time after that.

She closed her physical eyes as she opened her inner ones, searching the area around her.

While chewing on her thoughts and anxieties in bed, the one notion she failed again and again to swallow was the voice of the Goddess speaking to Bryn and Mai. Eventually, she remembered the day Iress Gan was on duty with her in the lower chamber. The Arrantine had commented on how the protective runes, in one part of the ceiling, had faded. Pell knew that cursed room so well she could easily picture everything's place in it. She suspected that, if she were to draw a straight line from where the demon's head lay to the very spot she now sat, it would pass directly through the worn-away runes.

With the Sight, Pell couldn't see the demon's life light from here, but that didn't necessarily mean she might not make a bond. She reached out, let her consciousness wander in the direction of the thing in the basement. The barrier blocked her, but after some mental prodding, she indeed broke through and made the connection. Her mind settled into the foul brain with which she was all too familiar.

Though it had been her suspicion, the realization came as a shock. The voice Bryn and Mai had been listening to was definitely *not* from the Goddess.

The demon's sudden reaction at her intrusion hit her. It was furious.

I found you, she thought. To her immense shock, it spoke back to her.

Iress. It responded in a voice that sounded simultaneously like a thunderous roar and a seductive purr. *What a shame you're still alive. I'll succeed where the incompetent child has failed and come for you, daughter. Soon.*

In a deluge, Pell's mind was flooded by a series of sickening images and sensations. A profane, discordant harmony of carnality and grisly, bloody filth. She was suddenly exposed, naked while the slippery tendrils of the demonic monster were exploring her, wriggling within her every crevice. Tightening around her throat, her heart.

She screamed, a deep howl so forceful she thought her throat might tear in two. Unsure if she even had control over her body anymore, she tried to push herself off the bench to the floor and outside the thing's line of sight. It must have worked. She came back to herself, on hands and knees, the taste of blood in her mouth and the feel of rising bile in her chest behind her savagely beating heart. Echoing at the edge of her consciousness, she could hear it laughing at her. A confident, mocking cackle that brought to the surface every embarrassing moment, every fear, every vulnerability that had ever made her feel small and disgusted with herself. She hated herself, wanted to die.

"Iress Pell?"

She looked up; it was Ollett, on patrol. "Did I scream?" she asked, feeling foolish.

"Did you...yes." There was terror in his eyes. "Goddess above, I wasn't sure it was even human."

282

"Something's wrong," she said. Vulsipher had felt so confident. Why would it have risked revealing itself to her like that? "We have to get into the lower chamber."

Pell raced down the steps.

"It will do no good, Iress," Ollett called after her as he followed. "The nighttime monks are under strict orders to never open that door. No one is to open it ever, save the Matriarch."

Pell pounded urgently at the door anyway, but, as Ollett had said, it was to no avail.

"Where is she?"

"The Matriarch? Sleeping, I imagine, as you should be."

"We have to find her."

"I—yes, Iress," Ollett relented, looking confused as he marched swiftly away.

Pell kept pace behind him, and in minutes, he was knocking on the Matriarch's door. They waited before he knocked again. No answer came.

"The dungeon," the man suggested. "She wanted to try talking to Bryn again after dinner."

Pell nodded and followed Ollett, who moved with even more urgency now. While Pell had thoroughly explored the abbey, she'd never seen the dungeon cells. Ollett led her past a thick, iron door and down a spiral staircase to a hallway so dark it seemed to consume the light of his lantern before it even reached the floor.

"Iress Lee!" he shouted. "Bryn?"

No answer.

He led her to the only occupied cell. Pell was afraid they would find the door open and the cell empty. She let out a breath of relief when the lantern light revealed it was shut tight, locking in the dark bundle in the far corner.

"Hello there!" Ollett called. "Bryn?"

Her shape remained motionless. Ollett tried the door. It was locked.

"Have you a key?" Pell asked, but Ollett was already reaching into

283

his pocket.

She took the lantern from his outstretched hand while he unlocked the cell. He took the lantern back, and the two of them approached the shape. Was she asleep? Had she found a way to kill herself? She had been connecting to Vulsipher for years without knowing it and was certainly deranged when she'd attacked Pell. Had she finally gone mad and taken her own life? As Pell drew closer, she noticed they were Iress robes. Bryn had never been Raised.

Ollett turned the shape over, and they recognized the face of the Iress Matriarch in the flickering light. Ollett checked for a pulse.

"She's alive," he said. "Pulse is faint, I think she was drugged. Iress Lee?" Ollett began gently slapping her cheeks.

Pell found a tray of food in the other corner and poked her finger in the cup to see if it still had water in it. There was a little. She took the cup to Ollett who took it, thanking her. The captain dipped his fingers into the water as well and ran them along the old woman's head, blowing on the wetness, hoping the coolness would wake her.

She stirred a little, taking a quick intake of breath before her head dipped again. Pell took the cup back and splashed the rest of its contents in her face.

Her eyes opened with a gasp. "What?" was all she replied.

"Iress Matriarch," Ollett said, "where is Bryn?"

"Bryn?" It took her a moment more before her eyes gained a sense of place and recognition. "Ollett, Pell, what are you doing...where are we?"

"The dungeon—what happened?"

"I...yes, I came down here after supper; I wanted to talk to Bryn one more time. Iress Mai came with me; she thought Bryn might be more willing to talk to her, but I started to feel faint..." She paused. "I think Iress Mai put something in my drink. At dinner she was sitting next to me..." The Matriarch sat up, panicked. "Where are they? Where are..." She fumbled with her robes a moment, searching her pockets. "The keys!"

"The lower chamber," Pell guessed. "I think they're there. Is there a backup key?"

"Yes. Help me up, Captain," Lee requested.

"There's no time," Pell said. "Tell me where it is."

The Iress Matriarch nodded. "Yes, Captain, go with her. It's under a brick in the floor. The one beneath the lower right leg of my desk. Hurry, I'll be fine. Go!"

Pell and Ollett sprinted to the Matriarch's office. Ollett had been fumbling with the keys as they ran, and when they reached the door, he unlocked it straightaway, swinging it wide. He was so fast Pell almost didn't even have to slow down as she ran passed him into the office. She pushed the desk out of the way and flung the rug aside before working her fingers around the loose brick. Ollett knelt beside her, and they both lifted it, setting it aside. In the space underneath was a small canvas bag that held two keys around a ring.

"Go and wait for me by the door," Ollett directed. "I'll return with Jos. Do not enter until we join you."

Pell grabbed the bag and ran to the curving stairs as Ollett ran for the outside. Pell took the steps two at a time, each footfall putting her in danger of tripping over her skirt and tumbling to the bottom. She didn't care; it would only get her there faster. Somehow, she reached the bottom without injury. Pell tried the first key, then the next one. It slid effortlessly into the lock. She stayed, poised and ready to unlock and open the door. Time had never passed more slowly. She watched the emptiness of the stairs, willing the men to appear. She also looked at the door, wondering what was going on behind it. Were they too late? Would Pell fling the door aside and find Vulsipher staring back? How did Mai and Bryn expect to overpower the monks on shift? Did Jos and Ollett have any hope of stopping the creature? And what the hell was taking them so long?

Minutes passed in agony. Finally, she heard footsteps rushing towards her. Ollett and a limping Jos emerged from the darkness, armed with lidocrafted swords. Pell turned the key and yanked the beautiful door aside.

Beyond, she drew blank stares from all the monks on duty that night. The pieces of the creature remained strapped down and nothing looked amiss. That was until she spotted an Iress facing away from her, near Vulsipher's head.

"You!" she shouted, rushing towards the figure.

A moment later, however, Pell's path was blocked by one of the monks. "What are you doing here?" he asked. "How'd you get in?"

"I used the Matriarch's key," Pell answered.

"The Matriarch is down below, giving the nightly blessing on the water."

"She is not," Pell said. "You've been deceived."

"But, but I saw..."

"It was an Embrell projection," Pell explained. "Stand aside."

The monk, all the monks, hesitated, unsure what to do. Pell wasn't in the habit of pushing aside large men wearing aprons covered in blood and holding sharp knives, but that night she did just that. Thankfully, none fought her, even when she grabbed the woman's shoulder and swung her around. Bryn's hateful face glared back at her. Pell slapped her, hard, before walking to the other door in the room.

"Ollett, watch her!" she commanded the captain.

"You can't stop this!" Bryn screamed at her from behind. "The Goddess wants her angel set free!"

Pell said nothing as she unlocked the inner door with the key that hadn't worked on the outer one. She jumped through, slamming it shut behind her, cutting out Bryn's ravings.

It was very quiet now. Pell found herself on a small landing with a stairwell bending to the side as it went down, much like the wider one above. Slowly, Pell began taking the steps, one at a time.

"Mai?" she asked in a very shaky voice.

No answer.

Step by step, she descended. Weak caustic reflections were being thrown on the wall as the light from above spilled through the central grate and bounced off the water. When she came across the sight of the cramped room itself, it wasn't the light, but the steady stream of the demon's blood through the grate that most caught her eye. Until she saw the figure on the altar in the path of both.

Oh no. No, no, no, Pell thought in despair.

Mai lay there, on her back, surrounded on all sides by the holy water of the spring. She had removed her robes and was in her shift only. It had been stained crimson. Her skin, however, was gray, and she was completely motionless.

Dead.

Pell checked with the Sight to be sure and found only emptiness. Mai was gone. There was an empty bottle in her hand. She must have drunk the rest of whatever they'd drugged the Matriarch with. Enough to kill.

The demon's dripping blood had coated Mai's body and was trickling, almost slithering, into her mouth, her eyes, her ears. Any opening it could find.

Oh, Maiyen, why? Pell lamented, unable to bear the sight any longer and turning away. But no, she had to do something. It hadn't possessed Mai yet. If she could push the corpse in the pool, maybe the blessing still clung to the water enough to...not kill it, of course; Pell had read a number of accounts wherein holy water was used and it only ever managed to weaken or contain the devil. Maybe that would be enough. She spun, ready to leap into the pool.

And froze.

Mai's body was now in a crouching position atop the altar.

The features of the face were hidden in shadow, but between the curtains of long hair were eyes that reflected the dull light, like a wolf's. Focused on her. Ripples of movement under the skin writhed like worms, already shifting this new body to match the one it had abandoned above. Though it was making as little contact with the lidocrafted altar beneath it as it could, curling vapors and a mild sizzle emanated from the thing's toes as they burned against the holy designs.

With a small cry of terror, Pell backed away, scrambling up the stairs. She had to get to the lidocrafted door above and lock it in. Even if that meant trapping herself in with it. She didn't get far before the thing pounced. It struck her back with its full weight. Her face slammed into the wall, and stars flashed in her vision. The creature threw her aside and, tripping, she fell into the frigid water. It was moving towards her again but immediately recoiled as the liquid touched its feet with a hiss and a puff of smoke.

It reached for her, but Pell crawled, splashing to the far side, praying the demon was weak enough in its new body that the consecrated water would act as sufficient deterrent to keep her safe. In the dancing reflections of the pool, she could see its face. It was Mai, but it was not. Like a puppet or crude sculpture, a ghastly and demented version of her friend.

A low voice scraped past the dead girl's lips. "If it makes your failure any more complete," the thing inside Mai said, twisting the tongue into foreign sounds and shapes. "Your little plan would not have succeeded. People would have died tomorrow, though not as many as will die tonight."

"It's a lie," Pell sobbed through chattering teeth. "I can sense your fear."

"And from you I can sense that I have an army awaiting me at the base of these mountains. We will leave this country buried under bones and blackened ash."

It looked as though it wanted very much to begin its spree of killing with Pell, but it also wanted to avoid touching the water.

"You cannot stay in there forever," it gloated, turning away and running up the stairs to the room above.

Pell was left in such motionless shock, she didn't even hear the screaming at first.

After recovering from her initial daze, Pell connected to the creature's mind through the open door and watched the destruction and massacre in the room above. It was no longer focused on hiding from her, and Pell could see into it as she never had before. Its expansive consciousness was capable of more evil and cruelty than any mortal man or woman with their finite minds. Pell lost herself in its seething hatred for the chamber. The shuddering ecstasy with which it brutally killed all within. The repellent reaction it had to the lidocrafted weapons and door.

Ollett and Jos fought bravely but fell tragically short of thwarting its escape. Bryn was the last to die. She watched the scene with a smile on her face. Vulsipher waited until she unlocked and opened the door before crunching her against the wood as it stalked past her. The beautiful door was left in bloody splinters and twisted silver.

At the top of the steps, the Iress Matriarch, running from the dungeons, was attacked. It went for her throat. It was the last thing Pell saw before it passed beyond her range.

But it was not the last thing she heard that dreadful night. Pell stayed in the icy pool, shivering and praying, for what seemed like hours. Even from so far below, the screaming reached her, echoing throughout the narrow halls.

At some point, after all went quiet, it bothered her that she'd only cowered in the pool throughout the massacre. She hadn't even considered leaving its safety to help. It might have filled her with guilt, but she knew there was nothing she could have done except be killed with everyone else. Maybe that would have been best.

How much time passed, she couldn't say. She knew only that her nose had stopped bleeding and her body was going numb before she finally crawled out of the safety of the mountain spring. The cold would kill her as surely as the demon if she stayed in it much longer. She pulled off her sopping robes until only her shift was covering her. She was trembling so violently she could hardly control her limbs, and each step to the room above was a burden.

The execution chamber was deathly still and completely silent. The furnace had gone out. The limbs on the tables lay limp and still. And the people...Pell tried not to look at the bodies or the blood, but she could not ignore the slippery squelch of each footstep.

The abbey was silent as she stole through it on the tips of her toes, peeking around every corner, averting her eyes from each fresh corpse. Eventually she came to her room and locked the door. She should be safe. The doors, the walls, even the window had lidocrafted designs. She hadn't been in it since Bryn had attacked her. Someone had cleaned the blood and straightened things up. She stripped out of her wet shift and into a dry one before huddling under the covers of her bed, waiting to get warm.

She must have fallen asleep.

By the feel of her raw cheeks, she must have wept as well. Tears had never come easily to Pell, but they did that day. Hopeless and so alone in her room, she sobbed as the weight of Mai's loss pummeled her.

In time, Pell pulled on some clean robes and ventured out into the halls. By the quality of the light outside, she guessed it was early afternoon.

What was she to do now? A part of her wanted to bolt back to her room and never leave. Another part wanted to run far away from this place. Still another wanted to remain and search for survivors. That was the most sensible option, but did it even matter? The destination at the end of all her options was death. If the demon had left, it would return. If it was still here...

She surveyed the scene in each room and hallway. Vulsipher's rampage had been extensive. How much worse might it have been if the demon hadn't been housed in the body of a young woman but within its own massive frame? Would even the walls be left standing? And how long would it take for the demon's form to complete reshaping Mai's body into its own? She prayed it was away and would stay away for a time. Remain in some mountain shadow as its body grew and changed. But what would happen when it was done? Would it return right away? Join the army waiting for it in the field below and *then* return?

"Iress Pell?" a shaky voice rasped behind her.

Pell turned to see Iress Em; she was pale-faced, and her eyes were swollen from crying, but she was free of injury, as far as Pell could see. The blood on her didn't appear to be her own. "Iress Em," Pell breathed, "you're alive."

She nodded. "And Halvett and Breek. Rin was...until an hour ago or so...I tried to save her...I tried..."

"Anyone else?"

"Iress Lee," Em said. "But not for long."

Pell started. "Lee?" She'd walked right passed the old woman, thinking her dead like all the others. How could anyone survive the attack she'd watched through the demon's eyes?

"Breek helped me move her to the infirmary; I made her as comfortable as I could, but she won't last through the day." There were fresh tears on Em's cheeks.

"You saved me from a stab to the chest," Pell reminded her. "*And* an attack from a demon."

"Inflicted by a normal blade and an average demon. Not Vulsipher. And your body is younger, more responsive to treatments. Poor Lee, she..." Em shook her head, failing to dispel the emotion that had taken her. After a pause, she asked, "What happened, Pell?"

"There's no time to discuss it now," Pell said. "How did you live through the night?"

"I was in one of the greenhouses. I sometimes sneak out for a late-night snack, just one of the small tomatoes or some sugar peas. I was in there when I heard the screaming from the abbey; I didn't know what was going on, but I shut the doors and stayed where I was. Eventually, I saw the monster barge through the main gate. I hoped it would run right past me. Instead, it stopped and watched me through the spaces between the designs. I have no doubt it wanted very much to destroy me—I've spent years trying to destroy it, after all. But you know the greenhouses, they're lidocrafted; it wouldn't enter. I'm sure that's how Halvett escaped, surrounded as he is by warding art. Poor man, he slept through it all. Breek was the only one smart enough to stay in his room, behind a lidocrafted door. Eventually, the demon ran off. I stayed in the greenhouse until morning. If I hadn't, there's likely more I might have done, lives I might have saved. Curse me for a fool and a coward!"

"I'm both the greater coward and fool," Pell admitted. "Especially knowing I walked right past the Matriarch when she was still alive."

"There's nothing you could have done for her. I wonder if Vulsipher purposefully wounded her just enough that her death would be painful and lengthy while still being beyond aid. The Goddess knows she's been here longer than any of us. Perhaps it hated her most."

"May I see her?" Pell asked.

Em swallowed. "She was in such pain, I sedated her. She won't wake for hours, if at all."

"Oh, Goddess above, what have I done?" Pell sobbed. "Hundreds of years it stays imprisoned but escapes shortly after I arrive."

"This is not your failure, Pell. That burden belongs to all of us," Em consoled.

The survivors gathered together, and Pell told the small group everything she knew about the situation and how it had gone so terribly wrong the night before.

"I thought...I thought it looked a little like Mai," Em breathed with a shudder. "She asked me only a few days ago about the various poisons and their effects. I took her on a tour of our extensive cabinet, told her about all of them. She must have taken one. We usually keep it locked."

Pell was sure everyone in the room shared a similar sense of guilt, but she knew, miserably, that most the blame fell on her own shoulders. All the pieces were before her, yet she failed to fit the puzzle together in time.

Not knowing what else to do, they went about the distressing task of collecting the bodies strewn about the abbey and gathering them into one place. Nearly all of them were in the hallways. Drawn by the commotion, everyone had left the safety of their rooms with their li-docrafted doors.

Pell wondered whether the demon had used a blade or had grown claws but was in no mood to investigate the corpses closely enough to tell.

The four remaining bodies were in the courtyard, still in the twisted positions they had died in, except for Rin whom Em had tried, and failed, to save. They laid them flat, side by side, and carried the rest out. Pell and Em pulled sheets out of the linen closets and off the beds to wrap them in. Em and Halvett worked together, while Pell was paired with the mute monk, Breek. They all went about the work as silently as he did.

The last and most difficult corpses to be taken out were those in the cellar chamber. As she made her way up the staircase, holding the feet of the last one, Pell turned her inner ear to the Hollow. She heard faint weeping behind her. She could pick out two voices in particular. Mai and Bryn. More souls for the demon to damn and rule.

Pell grasped for some narrative or context to dampen grief's sting, but there was nothing. She didn't even have the body of her closest friend to say goodbye to. This struck her more viciously outside as she looked over the collected remains of everyone else. There were so many. *But this isn't even all,* Pell thought. *There were eighteen victims, but Mai's body is gone forever, and Iress Lee has yet to join them.*

"Can you sing for them, Pell?" Em asked. "Call their souls to the Embrace? I'm afraid I've not the voice for it."

"Neither do I." Pell shook her head. *It would only comfort us and do no good to them anyway,* she thought, but kept this to herself. "Breek is a mute. I doubt very much Master Halvett, despite his many talents, can reproduce the voice of the Goddess."

"Are we to fail our Sisters and Brothers in even this?" Em asked.

"We'll do our best," Pell said. "Perhaps the Goddess will lend her voice to ours." As they had worked, Pell had been thinking and said suddenly, "I'm going after it. Halvett, have you a lidocrafted cage we could put the thing's severed head in and bring back here?"

"One of the old helmets could be modified, I suppose," he surmised.

"I don't think that's a good idea," Em said. "Have you read the accounts of how hard it was to get it into the state we kept it in? It took a whole company of trained soldiers—"

"We have to try something," Pell protested. "If we can get to it before it's body is fully restored..." She didn't know how to finish that sentence, and no one did it for her. All were equally at a loss as to what could be done.

Pell clasped her hands together and bowed her head. *Oh, Goddess above...* she started and stopped, not knowing what to petition for. *Help,* she prayed simply. *Help.*

She dropped her arms to her sides when another concerning observation struck her. The demon was gone, had fled the area, yet the dark feeling still hung heavy in the air. It had diminished, but only slightly. Perhaps Vulsipher was still near? She reminded herself that she'd first felt it all the way at the opening of Ankr Pass, miles and miles away. But no, even then, it was still stronger than it should have been with the thing gone.

"We can't sing over them until dusk," Halvett observed, his sad gaze still on the bodies. "We should wait in one of the lidocrafted rooms, just in case."

"Do you think it will come back?" Em inquired.

"Yes, eventually," Pell said.

"What of Iress Lee?" Em asked.

"We'll take her with us," Halvett suggested. "Iress Pell, your room is most protected, or the greenhouses."

"Yes," Pell agreed. "And at the first light of morning, I intend to go after it. I'll stay up all night thinking of something if I have to."

They entered the abbey and walked together. They'd nearly reached the infirmary when everyone stopped in their tracks.

Echoing through the stone corridors came the distinct sound of a forceful knock at the abbey's main door. Pell thought she'd imagined it until she saw the sudden alertness of the others around her.

"Did it come back?" Em squeaked before bowing her head, embarrassed. "No, why would it knock?"

"It might," Pell reckoned. "To deceive us."

"The door is locked, yes?" Em looked for confirmation.

"For all the good it might do against Vulsipher," Pell said.

"If it ain't the demon," Halvett breathed, "might it be...might it be one of them bodies come back for us?"

"A restless spirit?" Em gasped.

"Or a survivor we mistook for dead?" Pell supposed.

The knock came again, louder this time.

Everyone was looking at Pell. *How did I become the one making the decisions?* she wondered. "Well, whoever or whatever it is can't make our plight much worse," she said. "You are free to wait in my room, but I'm going to answer the door."

She spun and marched through the halls, displaying a confidence at great odds with the terror gripping her heart.

The knock came again just as she entered the small reception hall. She took a deep breath before pulling the heavy bolt aside and easing the door open just a crack.

She didn't know what she had expected on the other side, but it certainly wasn't what she found.

Three strangers stood there. A man, a woman, and a boy.

PART 3

CHAPTER 21

THE LIGHT
THAT PIERCES

The Nameless Abbey

"Who are you?" the shadowed shape beyond the door asked. It was a young woman's voice. "How did you find this place?"

"I am Daverell Kain," Dav answered. "This is Ameryn Vowery and her son, Crowan. I have been here before."

There was a pause, and the door opened a fraction more. "How? When?"

Daverell eased his grip on his sword's hilt, sensing no danger. But what in the holy name of the Goddess had happened here?

"Long ago," Dav replied. "When I was just a little older than the boy here." Dav nodded to Crow. "It was thought I might be able to wield the Illumed Blade. I could not. This boy can."

"What? Are you sure?" She came forward, studying them closer.

Dav did the same to her. "Yes," he stated. "May we come in? I will be more than happy to answer every question you have."

The Iress hesitated, her expression confused. "I...yes, certainly." She stood aside as Daverell entered after Ameryn and Crow.

Inside, another Iress and two men watched them curiously. Daverell nodded at them with a weak smile, trying to appear friendly. It did nothing to lessen their expressions of wide-eyed suspicion. Dav could not blame them. There was blood and sweat staining their clothing. So many freshly fallen corpses outside. Had they been attacked by some of the Uthiri from the field below?

"Breek," the Iress who had answered the door addressed one of the men. A monk by the look of his robes. "Perhaps we have something we can feed these weary travelers?"

The man only nodded and walked away.

"I'm Iress Pell," the Iress said, turning back to them. "This is Iress Em and Master Halvett." The man and woman next to her nodded. "You've come upon us at an unfortunate time, I'm afraid."

"The bodies in the courtyard?" Ameryn asked in a whisper.

Iress Pell nodded sadly.

"Have you any injuries?" the one named Iress Em inquired as they began moving through the hallway.

"Only scrapes and bruises. My son sprained his ankle. Any help will be greatly appreciated, Holy Sister," Ameryn answered.

In the dining hall, Iress Em worked her healing art on Crowan and Ameryn before moving on to Daverell. He was used to having Curials work on him after a battle, and it never failed to amaze him how whole he felt afterwards.

"That's about as good as I can do in this waning sunlight," Iress Em said, stowing her Restorative in her robes.

"It's amazing," Crow exclaimed, jumping on one foot. "Like I never hurt it in the first place!"

Breek brought them plates of cut vegetables. Daverell, Ameryn, and Crow all ate gratefully.

"All right, Mr. Kain," Iress Pell said. "You told me you had answers."

"You need only ask," Dav replied. "But please, before you do, will you answer a question for me?"

"If I can," Pell offered.

"Was there ever an Iress here, a Curial, named Iress Lee? Once Taralee of Kain?"

"Yes, our Iress Matriarch; she is in our infirmary on the brink of death even now."

Daverell was on his feet. "She's alive?"

Pell's eyebrows pinched. "Do you know her?"

"I...did once, yes. May I see her?"

The holy women led him to the infirmary, through the door, to the old woman's bed.

"The sedative should have worn off by now," Iress Em said. "But she may lack the strength to wake."

Daverell barely heard her. He stood motionless at the sight of his mother. She was covered in blood-soaked bandages, but her head and long hair were bare. Before entering the room, had he been asked if he could remember her face from more than forty years before, he would have honestly answered no. But with her before him now, her features were so familiar, it was as if he'd seen her every day between then and now. Time had exacted its price, but beneath the wrinkles, papery skin, and gray curls was the first face he'd ever loved.

He was unsure what to do. Take her hand? Try and wake her? Talk to her? If what the Iress had said was true, she may die at any moment. Dav was unprepared for this. Every eye in the room was on him as he approached the bed, kneeling at her side, listening to her weak breathing.

He decided he wanted to hear her voice.

"Iress?" He spoke softly, "Mother?" His hand was on her forehead.

It was the touch that roused her. She gasped, eyes fluttering open, unfocused and fearful.

"Hurts," she groaned. "Oh, it hurts."

"Mother," Dav said again.

He'd been sure she wouldn't know him, but her eyes flooded with recognition when they met his.

"D...Daverell?" Her voice was barely audible.

"I'm here," he answered.

She appeared and sounded so frail it surprised him when she tightly gripped his arm and spoke more clearly. "Daverell, of course you are. Here to save us," she murmured tearfully. "You're ready, I can see it in you. It will work this time."

She was wrong. Dav opened his mouth to tell her so, but the words wouldn't come. Purest hope was shining in her eyes, and he could not kill it in her final moments. It took all his strength to not look away. He was unworthy of the regard she was paying him, had forgotten what it was like to feel loved like this. He would have done anything to deserve it, including live the long years of his life over again, better this time. As it was, though staring into the sun might prove less painful, he held that gaze until the light drained out of it, her grip went limp, and she exhaled for the last time.

The world was silent and motionless; time itself did not exist until the sounds of muted weeping behind him brought it back. Dav wished he could join them in the emotion, but she was almost a stranger to him now. A gift once taken and now only cruelly hinted at, not returned. His only reaction was cold anger.

Daverell stood, keeping his gaze on the old woman's body. "What happened here? What killed her?" he asked.

There was a hesitant pause before Iress Pell spoke. "Vulsipher, the Elder Demon."

Daverell turned now. Iress Pell was the only one still in the room and in the process of exiting herself. The group had left him to grieve alone, but Daverell Kain was well practiced at holding his mourning for when time allowed.

"What did you say?" he asked.

"Vulsipher," she repeated seriously.

"Where is it?" he growled.

"We don't know," she said.

Daverell joined her and the others in the hall as the young Iress recounted a frightful tale of the demon-god. Vulsipher, the very being sought by the Uthiri, had been held prisoner here since the Age of Legends, subjected to a centuries-long execution that never succeeded. And now it had escaped, dooming the world to Darkness.

"I imagine it's waiting in some mountain crevice for its body to fully reform before it returns here or, more likely, joins the army waiting for it in Tannis Field and sweeps across Threya in a wave of fire and blood. I read its intentions and the beginnings of a plan before it fled."

"Why would it bring an army and not return alone?"

"It would be easier for mortal men to breach our lidocrafted walls."

"Is that why the Uthiri have been gathering at Tannis?" Daverell asked. "Waiting for it to join them?"

"Perhaps not." Pell shrugged. "We know they've sent scouts into the mountains, presumably searching for this place. I've no doubt, had they found it, the Uthiri would overrun us here to free Vulsipher."

"How did word reach the Uthiri from this isolated place?"

"By an evil process I'd rather not speak of," she answered.

"Please, I must know. The Uthiri have managed to outdo us again and again on the battlefield, and superior communication is the only explanation."

With a heavy sigh, the young woman described a ritualistic practice to him that, horrific as it was, explained much. He'd even seen it before in the grove with the dead horse.

"Iress Pell," Dav said when she was finished, "it seems the need for Crowan and the Blade is greater than I could have imagined. I'm sure the Goddess has brought us here for this purpose. He is young but already adept with a blade; take us to it, and I will take him to the demon. Together, we will kill it."

Crow, standing as tall as he could, nodded seriously. "I'm ready."

"Tell me why you think this boy can wield the Light That Pierces," Pell insisted.

"You know the prophecy?" Daverell asked her.

"Grath Twenty-Two, fourteenth and fifteenth verses," Pell answered. "Shall I quote it?"

"No need. I memorized it long ago, and it's never left me," Dav said. "I was born in the Year of the Hunter during an eclipse of the moon within a sacred spring in the heart of the Avender Mountains called 'Mother's Water.'"

"Yet the Blade rejected you," Iress Pell pointed out. "The boy?"

"Same circumstances as I, save the water." Daverell looked at Crowan and Ameryn. "He was born of Ameryn, in an unbroken caul."

"I've heard of that," the Curial gasped. "It's exceptionally rare."

"Yes," Ameryn agreed, placing a hand on Crow's shoulder.

"You know the price you may pay if you are wrong?" Iress Pell pressed Ameryn.

Ameryn paused, looking at nothing for a moment. "Twice before, we found ourselves on the edge of life or death. In both situations, Crowan miraculously saved himself and helped to save us with a blade in his hands. Once, as a vision from the Goddess. I dare not defy Her in this." Ameryn met the Iress's eyes. "He can, he *must*, wield the Sword."

"There's no time to waste," Daverell said. "We may still catch the demon before it returns to full strength. Where is the Blade?"

"I'm afraid," Pell responded sorrowfully, "the Iress Matriarch has taken that knowledge with her; she alone knew its location. Unless..." She looked at the other man in the group. "Master Halvett, did you perhaps see it? An inspiration for your work?"

He shook his head. "Always wanted to," he reflected. "But Iress Lee was particularly guarded on that secret. One touch of the thing'll kill you."

"I may recognize the room," Dav said. "Unless the Sword's been moved."

"You wish to test the boy against it now? We were hoping to sing the souls of our dead home at twilight."

"There is time enough before that, if Crowan and his mother agree." Dav looked to them, and they nodded. "I would like to see the

Sword in his hands as soon as possible. We may yet get to the demon before it reaches the army."

The Iress took a deep breath. "Very well," she said. "What did the room look like?"

"A chapel," Daverell recalled, trying to picture it. "There were pews before an altar and a window beyond it."

"Yes," Iress Pell said, her eyes brightening. "The abbey chapel. Follow me."

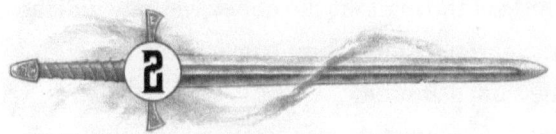

To Daverell, it was like stepping into a distant memory. It surprised him, how familiar it all was. He knew the faceted pillars and the arched ceiling. Even the way the fiery sunlight streamed through the prismatic planes of the window at the far end. Briefly, he was a young man again, full of hope. It was as though everything that had happened between then and now had been a dream, and he had only truly existed here. The sensation didn't last; it passed like a breeze, the sort that stirred leaves to life for a short while before moving on and leaving them more motionless than they'd been before. He was old again. The years of hard military service and harder drinking, of fleeting friendships and convenient women, of a little girl robbed of her legs and life, and a mother's dying love he didn't deserve, came crashing back into him. Unworthy of this place, unworthy of this quest, he reminded himself again of all that happened to bring him here. The Goddess had chosen him to bring the boy to this place and time. Of that, at least, he was sure, and it would have to be enough.

Everyone watched closely as Daverell walked to the altar at the other end of the room. It was here, somewhere around this altar. When he'd been here before, it had already been opened. Dav attempted to pull on the lip of the top slab. It shifted slightly, but something was holding it in place. Dav went to his knees and began inspecting the surface of the altar closely.

"Master...Halvett, was it?" Dav turned to the craftsman.

"Yes?" the man answered, stepping forward.

"You're a lidocrafter?"

"I am," he said with a small bow.

"Would you take a look at this? I'm wondering if there's a switch or a lock keeping it shut that your expert eye will see."

As the man studied it, everyone else in the room approached, watching as he ran his fingers attentively over the designs. If the level of lidocrafting Dav had noticed throughout the abbey was any indication, Halvett was a true master in a long line of true masters.

"Found something," he said, grinning.

Daverell followed the man's gaze but saw nothing but the same unbroken pattern. "Where?"

"Whichever of my predecessors built this—my guess would be Master Deulis—designed the pattern with these repeating circular discs. We need to press one to open it. My guess is every wrong one we press will only lock it further, and the right one will only work if none of the others are pressed."

"There are so many. How might we pick the right one?" Dav examined them closely. "Perhaps a slight discoloration of the finish or wear marks on the edges?"

"You'll find neither; it's too cleverly designed and too rarely opened. However, there are seven of the repeated elements on the sides and twenty-four on the face. The scene depicted on the altar is of Arama gifting King Belorok the lamp."

"Of course," Ameryn suddenly said. "In *The Song of Saeris*, the *Book of Onakus*. In the Seventh Chapter, twenty-fourth verse it reads... something about 'the Light reveals and opens the way forward.'"

Iress Em quoted the verse, "The Holy Light of the Goddess will reveal truth to thine eyes and open the way for thine heart."

"The word 'open' is the fourteenth in the verse," Iress Pell noted.

"So if we count fourteen from the leftmost edge," Master Halvett calculated, counting them with his finger until he reached the fourteenth disc.

"If we're wrong?" Dav questioned.

Halvett shrugged.

Daverell waited, thinking as his gaze passed from person to person. Everyone appeared unsure, but no one protested the idea, which was good enough for him.

"Do it," Daverell said, grabbing the edge of the slab again.

Halvett pushed the disc in, and Dav heaved; the marble slab came free. It was heavy. Ameryn, Crow, and Iress Pell rushed in to help him place it gently on the floor.

Inside the hollow altar was another slab of fine stone with a handle carved into it. It weighed nearly as much as the first layer, and no one could help him until it was over the edge. Despite the recent meal, Dav was feeling weak from lack of food and barely managed it. They placed it beside the top.

Under this second slab there was nothing. The altar was empty, save for a layer of sand dusting the solid and immovable stone floor at the bottom.

"What now?" Crowan asked, pushing and pulling at various parts and pieces in and around the altar.

"I'm not sure," Dav replied absently. The memory of the Sword itself was so commanding that, while he remembered the room and was certain the altar was open, he couldn't remember much else.

"Perhaps it was relocated," Iress Em suggested.

Crowan shoved at the stones that bordered the platform on the window side; to his surprise, they slid back a little.

"Yes," Dav exulted. "You've found it, the border stones!"

He and Crowan pushed the stones back; they slid easily into the cavity of the altar now that the secondary slab no longer blocked them. Under these stones was another series of bricks with carved handles. One by one, Dav lifted them and set them aside until he had uncovered a long but shallow space below. It held an ornate wooden box. Everyone in the room gathered around it. The two Iress, Ameryn, and the craftsman were praying, though their eyes were open and focused on the holy artifact.

Daverell held his breath as he unlatched and opened the box.

The Sword of Light. The Illumed Blade. The Light That Pierces. It lay, blade naked, next to a matching scabbard, and filled the room with its brightness, shaming even the light of the sun. Each gleaming highlight was alive with shimmering opalescence. Impossibly, however, it wasn't overpowering, nor did it hurt their eyes to look at it. If it had, they'd surely have all gone blind, as it was unthinkable to turn away. It was exquisite. Every element, from point to pommel, was perfectly balanced. Embellishments, so graceful and elaborate they seemed impossible, punctuated the sweeping and angular design of the blade and grip. If there was a break in the material from one part to another, it was impossible to discern. Each section effortlessly flowed to the next. In all its glory, the Sword was a reverent thing. Not a shout, but a whisper.

"Goddess above," Halvett prayed, "as long as I live under Thy Sight, I shall never call another work of mine lovely again. Nor even the sun and the stars, save Thine."

"It's...it's..." Iress Em stammered.

Though it had proved to be an elusive memory, Daverell gazed at it now as if he were intimately familiar with every elegant curve. It called to him still, but this was not his moment.

"Crowan." Daverell gingerly hefted the box out of the space and held it before the boy. "It's time. Take it."

Crow stepped forward; he was trembling and breathing heavily. Everyone leaned closer. The air itself was on edge. The world, motionless.

"Have faith, Son," Ameryn told him.

Crowan lifted his hand. It hovered over the hilt of the Sword before slowly, so slowly, his outstretched fingers inched forward until the tips touched it. The boy explored the delicate shapes for a moment, and Dav wondered if the surface was cold or warm to the touch—he could not remember. Crow took it in his hand, grasping it fully and raising it before him.

Everyone watching gasped.

Crow's eyes widened, and his boyish face took on an expression of enormous wonder. Dav thought he saw the boy's hair stir and skin ripple as if a gust of power radiated from the Blade.

"I knew it," Dav breathed, and all was suddenly made right. His life finally made whole. Around him were cries of awe and prayers of thanks. It was a beautiful moment.

And then that moment ended.

Crow made a whimpering sound. Before Dav's eyes, the boy's expression contorted into one of intense pain and he screamed. The howl echoed off the walls as he dropped the Sword and flew backwards as if struck by a giant hammer. Ameryn caught him with a shriek. Crowan's body went slack in her arms, his eyes rolled into the back of his head.

"Crow? Crow!" Ameryn cried.

Daverell dropped the Sword's box. *No!* he thought, desperately. *No! No! Not again. Not to him.* He ran to the boy's side.

"Get away from him!" Ameryn snarled.

Her eyes held so much raw pain and accusing anger, he shrank from them, slumping to the floor, bowed and slack. Defeated.

Iress Em dropped to Crowan's side, feeling at his neck and in front of his mouth. "He's got a pulse and he's breathing," she reported. "It didn't kill him. He'll be fine, miss. He'll be fine."

Daverell stared at the scene, dumbfounded. He'd been so foolish. So childish. Dragging Ameryn and her son across the wildest parts of the country to achieve a sad vision of his own salvation...and it had all gone wrong. All been for nothing.

Aside from Ameryn's sobs, a tense stillness ruled over the chapel for a long while. Daverell stayed on his knees, glaring helplessly at his empty hands until his gaze lifted to the Sword. It lay where it had fallen. Forged starlight. Still shining. Still perfect.

Still calling to him.

To his mind, the call was a cruel trick. His heart refused to agree, and the beckoning urge began to sound like his mother's final delusions.

You're ready.

I'm not, he answered.

It will work this time.

It won't.

He could not take it, could not be trusted with it or what it might make of him.

The most dangerous thing.

His head was in his trembling hands; he was trying not to look at it, seeing it still. This thing had hounded him through his life. More than the army he'd tried to escape from. More than Gyorick and his revenge. More, even, than the legless girl. It had injured him deeply enough, the scar had never stopped hurting, and now, it robbed him of his last chance at peace. It called to him because it remained unsated. It wanted more. It wanted to take everything from him.

Why not? Dav asked. *It nearly killed me once. It only wants to finish what it started.*

He imagined he would die if he held it for a second time. But now that he thought about it, he didn't much care.

In a single, swift movement, Daverell grasped the hilt and stood, lifting the Blade before him. The wave of power he remembered as a youth hit him. Starting from the hand that held the Sword aloft, Dav felt a galvanizing surge rush through him. He waited for the following bite of explosive refusal but did so without wincing. If he were to die at the hand of the Goddess, he would do so fully confident and on his feet.

He waited...and waited.

The blow never came.

Instead, the pulsing strength from the Illumed Blade continued moving through him. Welcoming him. Embracing him.

It...*She* had chosen her champion.

A poor choice. Daverell regarded the Sword, Ameryn's tear-streaked face, and Crow tightly in her arms. This should not have been the way of things. He'd wanted so much to leave his old self behind. To live peacefully. It was perhaps his first truly virtuous desire, yet the Goddess refused to grant it. Time and time again, he found himself

310

with a sword in his hand. And now it had been placed there by the Goddess herself. He could not escape.

Hot rage burned through him. *So be it*, he thought bitterly, *if my life is to end in blood, let it end in blood.*

When the Sword refused to push him away, even after this dark thought, Daverell bent and retrieved the scabbard. He slammed the Sword into it and strapped it to his waist. The Iress had said the demon was going to the battleground at Tannis Field. If he didn't hurry, it would be a bloodbath on the Threyan side. His days of war were not yet over. Again, always and forever, it seemed, he was a soldier.

Daverell stormed out of the room.

"Wait," Iress Pell called, chasing after him. "Where are you going?"

Dav didn't answer.

"Wait!" she called again.

Dav continued without pausing when, in an instant, a flaming skull erupted into the air before him, flying at his face. He pulled the Sword from its housing and slashed at it, to no effect. He ducked as it flew over his head, watching as it dissipated before the Iress following him.

Where are you going? Her voice thundered in his head.

He looked at her with fright and fury. "Stay back, witch." How had she conjured that...whatever it was?

Where are you going? she repeated.

Daverell had heard that Embrells could speak within one's mind but had never experienced it.

"To the field. You need not worry," Daverell answered before spinning and resuming his brisk exit. "The demon will die." If he was to be a butcher for hire one last time, it may as well be in service to the Goddess. When he sliced Vulsipher to pieces, however, it would not be for Her, but for himself. For the mother and the life the creature had stolen from him.

The footsteps of the young Iress continued at his back, but she didn't stop him this time.

"I may be able to help you," she said. "I know how to read its thoughts and intents."

"I cannot stop you from following me, nor, it seems, can I stop you from invading my head. Do as you wish."

"I must stay for our twilight ceremony," Pell said. "You should also stay; your mother is among the dead we sing for."

"My voice will only hinder you."

"But..." She seemed unsure what to say and pursued him silently to the front doors. It was Dav who spoke next, pausing as he was exiting.

"Will you ask Mrs. Vowery to sing for her?" he requested. "For my mother?" His voice broke, grief striking him unexpectedly. That poor woman. She had lived with so much faith. What had it brought her?

"Mrs. Vowery?" Pell asked.

"She has a voice that rivals the birds and plays guitar like she was born with the strings beneath her fingers," he said. "And tell her I'm sorry."

Without waiting for an answer, he marched directly to Druid, who he quickly untied before pulling himself into the saddle. He tipped his hat to the Iress before spurring the steed to action, riding towards the setting sun.

CHAPTER 22

A SONG

The Nameless Abbey

Crow's heart was still beating. Ameryn had confirmed this over and over, and she was finally growing less afraid it would diminish and stop.

She was alone in the chapel. Left to the wolves of her thoughts. Her mind kept replaying the events. The awful sound Crowan had made. The way he was flung back and fell to the floor. Now, he seemed to only be sleeping, though he couldn't be roused. Iress Em assured her the best thing to do was to wait and let him rest, two things Ameryn found very hard to do right now.

Why had she allowed Daverell to convince her to put her child, the last family she had in all the Midlands, in such peril? Why had the Goddess fooled and abandoned her? Why had she not listened to the warning voices in her head? What was she to do now?

All questions of the worst kind: those without answers.

Well, perhaps she could guess how she'd been tempted to come to this place and put herself and her child in this situation. In her grief and fear, she'd taken leave of her senses. Perceived meaning where there was none. She'd dared to hope the world was poised to finally make something of her. To give instead of take. She'd thought there was nothing more to take after Tamiron had been stolen from her. She was so wrong.

Tamiron. The image that had been pursuing her since his passing ambushed her again. His precious body, dragged away in pieces by coyotes and buzzards. There was no escaping it. Not when it was the truth of things. There was no destiny awaiting her, or anyone else, beyond that. Life was lived until it carried only fear. Fear that held the heart hostage for whatever moments remained. The lucky ones left behind a lonesome stone somewhere, bearing their name. At least until time and weather wore even that away. She'd been a fool to allow Daverell—even Tamiron—to convince her that joy was to be had from any source but ignorance.

When Crowan had first fallen and she cradled him in her arms, her heart bursting with terror and outrage, all these realizations struck her at once. The fire that had chased her all the way from the streets of Pyressa had consumed her again. It always did, in the end. The builders and planners, the faithful and patient had everything wrong. Those living lives of indulgence and stimulation saw the world for what it truly was, temporary and meaningless.

Even as she thought it, she knew that wasn't true either. Ameryn was left with the unfortunate, residual truth that no frame of mind made sense of life. People were made to be broken.

"Mrs. Vowery?" The Curial startled her with a small knock at the door.

Ameryn turned to her. "Yes?"

"Let's move him to the infirmary," she proposed. "He'll be more comfortable there."

"But..." Ameryn hesitated. "Dav's mother..."

"We carried her out to the courtyard with the others," Em said. "I've prepared another bed for your son."

"Thank you," Ameryn replied.

The two women gently carried the boy to the room that was, thankfully, not far from the chapel. *He's getting so big,* Ameryn thought as they heaved him into the bed. Once he was settled, however, she thought the opposite. *He's still so small.*

The healing woman brought her a chair to sit in while she waited by the bedside.

"The room's a bit stuffy," Ameryn remarked.

"I'll crack a window," Iress Em said. "Why don't you expose his chest a little, let the cool air at him."

Ameryn was unbuttoning his shirt when, behind her, the door opened and Iress Pell entered the room holding a guitar. She stopped in front of Ameryn, presenting it to her. Ameryn had never seen an instrument to equal it. It was a beautiful enough guitar on its own, but the elegant lidcrafting complimenting the design throughout made it unique and priceless, perhaps even holy. Ameryn realized her mouth was hanging open and quickly shut it, while shifting her view to the young woman who held it.

Pell, however, was not looking back at her, but at Crowan with a perplexed expression.

"Iress?" Ameryn asked.

"That charm the boy has around his neck—where did you find it?" Pell inquired.

"It was among the rubble in the exit chamber of Osgerath tower. It saved our lives against the demons within," Ameryn answered, hating to remember it. The miracle had gone sour and now seemed like nothing but a cruel trick.

"Truly?" Iress Pell's eyes widened in amazement. "I threw it into the tower when pursued by an evil creature, hoping to distract the devil without losing it. The door was locked, and I thought it gone from me forever. It is an ericle given to me by my grandmother."

"Then you'll have it back," Ameryn said, unclasping the copper charm and holding it out to her. "With my thanks."

"What of an exchange?" Pell suggested, motioning to the guitar she held. "It was Iress Gan's; twilight doesn't last long, and none of us left here are musically gifted. Will you accept this guitar and sing with us? The captain said you're a rare talent. He asked me to make this request for his mother. I make it for all of us here as well. Please, we need you."

Ameryn shook her head. "I don't sing anymore. Not like that."

"You clearly know the scriptures," Pell observed. "Do you know the hymns?"

"By heart," Ameryn said, "but I no longer have the voice for such songs. I'm sorry. Nor could I accept the guitar if it was as special to her as it appears. But please, take the ericle."

"She would not have minded." It was Iress Em who spoke. "I took lessons from her. I was a very poor student I'm afraid, but she would often say nothing was sadder to her than an instrument with no one to play it. I think she partly said it to keep us practicing, but I've no doubt she believed it. She would be thrilled to know it would be used and cherished beyond her mortal span."

"I'm sorry," Ameryn repeated. "If the victims outside died in the Light, they will find their way to the Embrace without me."

"They did not die in the Light," Pell said, "slain, as they were, by a demon. My friend, Iress Mai, surely died in the Dark..." She paused, waiting for emotions to pass. "She asked me once why it seems hell trespasses into our world more than heaven does. Why we share the Midlands with demons but not angels. I didn't have a good answer for her then. Now, however, I'm reminded of the passage from *The Song*, Book Four, Seventh Chapter, third verse."

"'The Goddess hath no angels but thee,'" Ameryn quoted.

"Precisely," Pell said. "Is there no way I might convince you? It's a ceremony that, the way we practice it now, is meant less to aid the dead than comfort those still living. But even to that end, we are in need of such comfort—of an angel—tonight."

"No." Ameryn was adamant. "I'm sorry. Besides, Mr. Kain exaggerates my ability. He was wrong about many things, it turns out."

"Very well." Pell laid the guitar against the wall. "Then you may take it up when you find the heart to. I cannot thank you enough for this." Pell took the ericle from Ameryn. "It's an obscure little thing but priceless to me."

Pell motioned at the Curial. Together, they walked to the exit.

"Iress Pell?" Ameryn called.

The young woman, nearly out the door, paused and faced Ameryn.

"Why would the Goddess lie to me?" Ameryn asked.

"You mean about your vision?"

Ameryn nodded.

"I don't think She did," Pell said. "Like Daverell before, the timing was wrong. I think your son will indeed be able to wield the Sword. Someday."

Ameryn turned to look at Crow and feared the young woman was right.

Iress Pell left. The door clicked shut, leaving behind a total and heavy silence. Ameryn could not remember ever feeling so alone.

Where were her angels? It was easy to identify them, but they had all been taken away. Her parents, sister, Tamiron, and now Crowan— for a time—had been stolen from her. She'd lost two homes to fire. Daverell, and even the Goddess, had abandoned her.

The young Iress saved you, Ameryn thought. *With her ericle, even if she didn't intend to; she's among your angels...and you just refused to help her.*

Ameryn pictured the small group outside. She even imagined herself joining them, singing in the ceremony. Just the thought spread the crawling sense of vulnerability over her. But strangely, it did not make her feel any worse. Perhaps it was an imperfect cure for her aching loneliness. She might even be able to do it, if she could only borrow

317

some strength from a friend. But there was no one, not a soul in the Midlands, whose company might comfort her now.

"Oh Tamiron," she whispered, and the oppressive quiet that answered back pierced her like a dagger.

Her fingers were handling the envelope in her pocket. Doing so had become a constant habit, yet now, it struck her like an answer. A cruel one. Reading his words would feel like losing him all over again. She pulled the letter out of her pocket and held it in her hands. She'd not considered opening it, even when her life had been in mortal danger. But now...now she desperately needed the words. Needed a friend.

Ignoring the screaming protests of her mind, she tore open the envelope and unfolded the paper within. She stared at the handwriting, studying it before really reading it. True to his way, it was short and written in a hurried hand. The words didn't even fill one full side of the delicate parchment.

Ameryn, my angel,

As I wrote in my last letter, I miss you. I'll more than like write you another one next week and say it again. That don't make it any less true, but I'm not sure what I really have to say beyond that, and I hope you and Crow are all right. Give Romy a good scratch for me.

I'm fine. Feeling down is about the worst of it, but there don't seem to be a way around that. As bad as things have got, I try, every day, to take a moment with the trees and birds. I hope you're doing the same. I hope you're singing. I'd give anything to hear a song from you again. It would do me and the boys here a real kindness. A little lifting of the spirits is like to be all we really need to win this thing.

Love you,

Tam

Ameryn stood, folded the letter and carefully placed it back in the envelope and into her pocket. She bent and kissed Crowan's cheek, with both her lips and the tears falling from her eyes. Looping the strap of the guitar over her shoulder, she walked out of the room.

Pell had asked Em, nearly begged her, to be the one who prayed over the bodies in the courtyard. Pell felt too responsible for their deaths. Things had been hard enough, wearing a mask of bravery for their mysterious visitors. Visitors that made her failure cut even deeper. Had they shown up one day before, just one, so much death might have been avoided. She hoped Daverell Kain would find Vulsipher soon, but she worried that even with the Illumed Blade, the demon would prove to be a daunting enemy.

I can help him, she assured herself, but worried it wasn't true. Could she even find him again? What if he chased Vulsipher to the armies below? Did she dare enter a battlefield? What if she were killed? Would it be worth it to clean up this mess she'd made? Redeem herself to some degree? Looking at the rows of bodies laid out before her, how could she answer with anything but yes?

After the Singing Ceremony, she would ask the Vowery woman if she could borrow her horse. She'd ridden only a few times before and had made a fool of herself and, somehow, even the animal. However, it was her only hope of catching Captain Kain.

She shook her head in an attempt to clear it. She had one job at the moment, and it was already one she had no confidence in, even without so many distractions.

"In twilight," she recited shakily, trying to recall the words. "Between night and day and under Thy star, we sing for these departed souls who also wander between Light and Darkness. As they can no longer be with us here, we pray You may accept them there. May our voices be as Your voice..." Pell was despairing at how unlikely that would be when she heard the door behind her open; she dared not turn around and break from the ceremonial prayer, but her heart leaped. Who could it be but the Vowery woman? Pell's voice gained some strength. "May they recognize Your call, and answer. Finding peace in Your arms forever."

Everyone in the small group to her sides whispered an "amen," and before the word was off their lips, the tender sound of strumming strings kissed their ears. Pell knew nothing about music, but even she could tell that Daverell Kain had *not* exaggerated when he had complimented Ameryn's skill. Indeed, he hadn't praised it highly enough. Pell didn't find fault with the man in this. Music, she had always thought, was the most elusive of all things to describe with words. Were she to describe what she was hearing now, she would say it was a rich sound that made her feel warm and safe. It reminded her of deep forests and open skies, of windblown pappus in the sunlight and secret corners of forgotten places. But none of that would help anyone imagine the melody.

Then the woman began to sing, and all thought left Pell for a while; she could only listen.

Of mortals old and mortals young,
Too oft are hymns of sorrow sung.
Upon this world their spirits roam,
Until our voices bear them home.
To leave all dust and blood behind,
And dwell with Mother, wise and kind.
To hear Her voice and see Her face,
To feel the peace in Her embrace.
And as we sing, we also pray,
'May others sing for us one day.'

The hymn was called "Mother, Wise and Kind" and was the choice for most Singing Ceremonies.

Ameryn effortlessly wove one melody into another and began another song, "To Live Again, in Her Arms." It had never been a favorite of Pell's, but under Mrs. Vowery's care it was transformed. She brought a grace to it that Pell had never detected before. It was a mark of any gifted performer, to find new appeal to an old song. To coax it out

320

while making it her own—often in ways unintended by the composer. If there ever was a voice to draw a soul to the Goddess, Ameryn's was it.

Pell was under a spell; it was as if she herself were being lifted to the stars when Ameryn shifted into a third hymn. This one was "Fear No More," about the trials of mortality that were lain aside by the dead. Pell's favorite lines were:

Fear not the pain of absent rain, on fields left bare and dry.
Fear not the pain of brothers slain, nor need to fathom why.

Ameryn replaced the word "brothers" with "sisters," and though Maiyen had never strayed far from Pell's thoughts since the events of the previous night, this brought her memory back sharply. A part of Pell was convinced that if she were to simply turn her head, or cast her mind, she would find Mai, still alive. She had been the most constant thing in Pell's life for years now, and her instincts and habits refused to believe her closest companion was gone. Lost in the most dreadful of all ways.

When the song ended and the vibrations of the strings slowly faded, giving the stage back to the world, quiet weeping replaced the sound. Pell was among those contributing to this new anthem, less melodic but still lovely in its own way. Though Iress Pell was robbed of Mai's body to say farewell to, she turned her ear to the Hollow, in which she feared her friend now roamed, whispering, "Goodbye."

She gasped. Not from what she heard but from what she didn't. Her inner ear, trained to that empty space, listened, and nothing returned. She was certain that even in the shrouded hours, even in the catacombs, she would find it appropriately empty. The awful feeling that had permeated this place so completely—only mildly lessened after Vulsipher's escape—was finally and completely gone. She could breathe, really breathe, for the first time in months. Even in the dying light of the day, the colors around her were more saturated and bright. Despite lacking her sensitivity to the hidden planes, Iress Em, Breek, and Master Halvett were blinking the tears from their eyes as they breathed anew, knowing *something* had changed but unable to define what it was.

Ameryn herself appeared mystified. "What was that?" she asked Pell. It was almost an accusation. "I…I *felt* people listening. Not just all of you but…others. So many others. What happened?"

Pell took her hand. Steadying and being steadied. "You healed this place."

Ameryn looked back at her, fear and wonder shining in her eyes. "What does that mean?"

"You have the gift of the Opravics; you're a Singer," Pell said. "Your voice reaches the Hollow—the lost spirits—and calls them home."

"But isn't that what we all do when we sing?" Ameryn asked.

"At best, our songs reach those who died in the Light. Those who die in Darkness and wander in the Below, however, cannot hear any of us. But they *can* hear you."

"I could almost hear them back," Ameryn remarked. "They were so lost. So sad."

"This old abbey has a long and tragic history. Every brick and beam was haunted. The catacombs nearby were such a howling mass of misery that I could sense the uproar from here. Not anymore, not after your song. Can you not feel the change in the air?"

"I can," Master Halvett said.

"Me too," Iress Em agreed.

"You can hear the world of the dead?" Ameryn asked Pell. "Can I?"

"I don't know," Pell said, smiling now. "But they can hear you. The Below is empty here for the first time in a very long time."

Iress Em gave Ameryn a hug, made awkward by the guitar she still had around her neck. Master Halvett took Ameryn's hand and kissed it as though she were a saint. Breek smiled for what was the first time Pell had ever seen.

An angry roar tore through the air, echoing through the canyon below. It was faint from their position but still chilling. Enough that it doused Pell's newborn hope, but only for a moment before it returned,

322

stronger.

"Vulsipher," Pell breathed. "Mrs. Vowery, that sound came from the Elder Demon, you've robbed it of its soul slaves. It fed off their misery, creating the feeling of despair around us."

"What?" Ameryn voiced her confusion.

Iress Pell could not portion out the information any slower, time was swiftly running away from them. "It is a remarkable thing you've done here," Pell explained, "but there is a field full of men down there that Vulsipher is eager to consign to the Darkness. It could collect as many souls in minutes as it did here over centuries, each one adding to its power while making those fighting it downcast and ineffective. Unless you, Ameryn, steal the departed spirits away. Send them home."

"You want me to go to the battlefield?" Ameryn balked at the prospect.

"I'm sure that's where it's heading."

"I can't leave my boy," Ameryn protested. "What if it comes back?"

"It will," Pell assured her. "And when it does, it will do so fueled by an army of victims. Unless we stop it. We have to find Daverell. He has the means to destroy the creature, but if the old stories are true, the demon will still prove a formidable foe. He'll need our help to defeat it."

"I'm sorry, I can't...I don't know how..." Ameryn stammered.

"It can only be killed by the Sword of Light and the one chosen to hold it. It will be desperate to kill Daverell. To kill any that can, or may one day, wield it."

"Crowan," Ameryn murmured.

"Mrs. Vowery," Pell said, "what you did, what you can do...if you can do it again, lifting those spirits may be all we really need to win."

These words brought Ameryn's head snapping up to meet the Iress's eyes. "What did you say?" she asked.

"Lifting those spirits may be all we really need to win," Pell repeated, confused.

Ameryn's expression hardened into one of resolve. "Yes," Ameryn said, "I will come with you." Mrs. Vowery then turned to Iress Em.

"Please, take care of Crowan. He's all I have left in this world."

"Move him to my room," Pell said. "It's safest."

Iress Em bowed her head. "You have my word. No harm shall befall him."

"Are you able to ride through the night?" Ameryn asked Pell.

"I am quite weary," Pell admitted, "but it seems we've no choice."

"I'll ready my mule," Ameryn said before walking over to the animal and making adjustments to the saddle.

Master Halvett approached Pell. "Breek and I will begin moving the bodies to the catacombs. I don't know if there's any reason to stay here, but I'll not leave until I fashion seals for each of those who died last night and see them well put to rest."

"Thank you, Master Halvett," Pell said. "May the Goddess guide your steps on whatever path life takes you."

Halvett nodded gratefully and retreated. Em approached her next. "What do I do if neither you nor Mrs. Vowery return? I'm so sorry to ask."

Pell was unsure. "I don't know. Keep the boy safe and trust all else to the Goddess. But don't lose hope. It may be that our mission may yet succeed."

"Oh, Goddess above, let it be so," Em pleaded.

Mrs. Vowery approached, holding the reins of her mount.

"The Star of Saeris is bright tonight," Ameryn said. "She will light our way."

With Ameryn's help, Pell got herself into the saddle behind the frontier woman. "Hold tight," Ameryn said over her shoulder.

CHAPTER 23

TANNIS FIELD

Tannis Field

Not long after he'd started out, a cry, from what could only have been the very thing he hunted, sounded through the canyon. Hoping to kill it before it could reach the armies in the field, Dav rode hard in the direction of the anguished sound. When he eventually spotted it, the monster was far ahead of him and moving quickly. Even Druid could not catch up, given the unfamiliar terrain.

Something about the Sword of Light helped him see exceptionally well, even at great distances and in the dim light of the moon and stars. That was not all; an old injury that had given him a limp in his left leg was now completely gone, as was the general stiffness he'd grown accustomed to as age had crept up on him. His heart and lungs were stronger; everything was more limber and resilient. He'd not been in such peak physical condition in...perhaps ever. He didn't even feel tired.

The creature was easy to track. It was near nine feet tall, with great horns upon its head and flames spouting from its feet with every step. From these fiery footsteps crawled unholy monstrosities, bestial demons that were similar to the cadaverous thing he'd seen outside Osgerath. Given what Vulsipher had accomplished while in the body of a young woman at the abbey, Daverell shuddered to think of the carnage the monster was capable of now that it had regained its true form. Even in this desolate canyon with very little to destroy, the demon cut a path of scorched ground. What little thorny vegetation there was here had withered and blackened as Vulsipher had passed beside it.

When Daverell first began tracking the creature, there had been only a handful of lesser demons surrounding it. Now, Vulsipher stood in the center of a vast, writhing mass of hell-fiends. Its profane silhouette occasionally reached out, petting them affectionately. If it was aware of Daverell and the Sword not far behind, it didn't appear to care, or perhaps it was simply distracted. He could almost see the roiling rage within the thing.

The morning sun broke over the horizon but struggled to light the world through the thick storm clouds that concealed the sky in every direction. A heavy boom of distant thunder swept through the air as Daverell rode over the summit of the foothills at the base of the Gray Mountains.

Laid out, like a stage before him, was Tannis Field and the two opposing armies on either side of it. His quarry, a third army itself, was now entering the scene. The new force was smaller in size than the other two but had a primal viciousness far beyond them both.

Even from here, Daverell could sense the tension in the empty space between the three parties. This new, ravenous addition would break the standoff, drawing all three into conflict. Daverell, his fury having abated very little during his nighttime ride, was determined that most of the blood would spill from the Uthiri and the demons they worshiped.

I wonder if their love for these monsters will diminish once they come face to face with them? Daverell wondered with satisfaction. Perhaps Vulsipher would direct its minions to only attack the Threyans, but he doubted the beasts were too discerning between one warm body or another. Every Uthiri ripped to pieces by the sharp teeth of these Beloworld devils might be the best justice seen on this battlefield today. Until he killed Vulsipher.

On the edge of the field now, Dav watched as the Uthiri soldiers, in armor meant to resemble these creatures, began staring in disbelief at what they were seeing. It appeared many hadn't believed in demons to the same degree their mad king did. Even if they had, it was one thing to believe something safely behind the veil of history and legend, another to actually face it. Here, before their very eyes, was a horde of Beloworld hellspawn led by their lost god.

Vulsipher had set the grass at its feet alight, and a fire was spreading. Many Uthiri didn't take notice; they were falling to their knees and praying as deep war drums pounded around them. Someone began cheering, and in moments, the whole camp joined in. Thousands of voices whooping and clapping, some singing. Others on the edge were torn apart as the creatures met up with them. The demons that had stayed in line looked to have only done so under extreme control by their master. Each quivered with anticipation and watched the men surrounding them with ravenous eyes.

The Threyan side was a distorted reflection of the Uthiri. Just as many soldiers stared in unbelief. There was even a fair amount of falling to knees and praying, but no cheering or songs of praise. Indeed, many looked ready to flee. Captains and generals, many of whom Dav knew well, called for their men to stand their ground, ready themselves for battle, take positions.

The collection of malformed beasts turned to face the Threyans now, salivating at the prospect of being set loose.

"Let's go, boy," Daverell spoke to Druid, rubbing his neck.

Dav wasn't certain if the effects of the Sword were passed to Druid, but he suspected they were. After a night of hard riding, he sensed no weariness in the animal as he rode him out to the center of the field at a gallop. Despite the flat lighting of the overcast morning, Druid's brilliant coat stood out against the dark forces serving as a backdrop to the watching Threyans.

Because of the heightened senses from the Sword, even at this distance and over the pounding of his steed's hooves, astonished whispers reached him.

"Is that Captain Kain?" one man asked.

"Daverell Kain? I thought he was dead," said another.

"I'd heard rumors he was still alive. What's brought him here? Now?" someone muttered.

"It must be his ghost!" assumed one.

"It's him. I'd know that brute he rides anywhere," came the voice of Norill, the man that had been with him when this whole thing had started. Other voices he knew and many he did not reached him, all astonished but growing in confidence.

The Threyans were forming ranks and drawing weapons.

Dav pulled Druid to a stop just at the head of the Threyan troops as another voice he—along with everyone in the Threyan army—recognized as General Entwest roared, "If we're to fight hell itself today, men, we do so knowing Captain Daverell Kain is on the field with us!"

Fight hell itself, Dav thought, his hand going to the sword. *That, I think I can do.*

A cheer erupted from the Threyans.

With that swelling chorus behind him, Daverell pulled the Sword of Light from its scabbard and held it over his head. A small window broke through the clouds, sending a shaft of light onto the already gleaming blade. Across the field, Vulsipher's hateful face sneered at it and Dav with such loathing it was hard to detect the hint of fear beneath it. But it was there. Dav met its eyes, leveling the point of the Sword in its direction before kicking Druid into motion. The charger took off like an arrow, directly at the opposing force. The Threyans behind him did the same.

The Uthiri line also broke, charging, except for the Elder Demon. The Lord of Long Shadows let the horde of men and demons swirl around and beyond it, as though it had an ocean wave at its immovable back.

The armies clashed, plunging Dav into the center of a thrashing tempest of striking swords, screaming men, and roaring beasts. Dav cut through the army, trying to get to Vulsipher. A few Uthiri fell to the holy Blade in Dav's hand. To them, the Sword seemed no different than any other. When a feral demon leaped at him, however, the bite of the Blade turned it into a burst of swirling cinders.

When he'd almost reached Vulsipher, the demon jumped far into the sky, coming down in a crash among the Threyan ranks. Those not crushed were sent flying in all directions as an explosive wall of fire rolled out from the impact. Men and horses were set ablaze and fled in wild terror.

Daverell pulled Druid's reins hard in Vulsipher's direction. The horse whinnied a complaint but turned immediately, racing towards it. The demon picked a screaming man up in both hands. Daverell recognized him, Tomaras from Rawk. Vulsipher bit the soldier's head off and launched his body at another man on a horse. The second man was sent tumbling off his mount, and before he could recover or even scream, his head was crushed by the immense creature's fist.

Other Threyans attempted to close around it, but with a stomp of its foot, they were sent sprawling in another spray of blood and flames. Daverell had to jerk Druid to the side so as not to be hit by a burning corpse falling from the sky. Not even a minute had passed since the fighting had started, yet the monster had killed dozens.

Vulsipher bounded into the air again before Dav could reach it. How had the ancient warriors ever managed to capture such a thing? The ground from which the creature had just sprung was an inferno that birthed several lesser demons.

An Uthiri to his right attempted to spear him in the side. Daverell cut through the hard wood of the spear as if it were made of paper before striking the man's neck. The spearman fell, and a twisted, snarling, boar-like demon took his place. It sunk low, atop the corpse, baring its teeth and tusks, trying to look like it wasn't cowering before the Sword. It dodged a swipe from Daverell before lunging. Druid spun away from the creature, and Daverell stabbed it in the flank as it sailed by. An agonized scream escaped its dripping maw as its body exploded into whirling ashes and embers that were soon lost among those already in the air.

The fire was a complication to the fight that affected all parties except the demons. Several men around him ran screaming while ablaze and were fully consumed in moments. Soon, Druid was tripping over as many charred bodies as slaughtered ones, and Dav was choking on the smell of burning flesh. He turned his mount to escape the fire, cutting through the enemies in his path while looking wildly in all directions, searching the maelstrom for the Elder Demon.

He couldn't kill it if he couldn't even get to it.

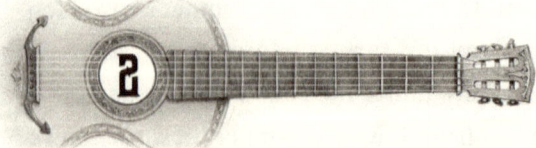

Ameryn had ridden Gooter hard over the unforgiving terrain of Ankr Pass all night, and the mule was losing its strength by the time she and Iress Pell reached the field. Gooter was a sturdy animal and Iress Pell was a tiny thing, but two was a struggle for him to carry. They walked the mule for the last leg of their journey, Ameryn patting his neck and apologizing for the exhausting night she'd subjected the creature to.

Iress Pell had spent much of their travel time informing Ameryn of the history of the Opravics, and her head was buzzing with the information.

All thought fled, however, when the awful sights and sounds of battle assaulted her senses. She and the Iress halted on a hill above and took in the scene below. It was so shocking, she hardly managed to breathe.

Fire. War. Death.

Through raging flames and plumes of smoke, she could see the fighting was fierce and desperate. Creeping, slithering, and darting through it all were the distorted shapes of monsters. Standing out among all the chaos was the shining form of Daverell Kain atop his white steed.

He and Druid were moving swiftly through the crowds, the white charger weaving around the throngs of men and beasts, plowing through anything it could not dodge. Every Uthiri soldier to either side of them perished with a whistling slice of Daverell's blade as they passed. Two demons, tearing mercilessly through the Threyan soldiers, and even a few Uthiri who got in their way, bolted when they saw Daverell. He cut them down with the glittering Sword and they perished in a shower of sparks and vapor. The Threyan forces cheered for him as he passed, and many followed in his wake, emboldened.

Further away, over the mayhem, surrounded by an unholy blaze, towered the Elder Demon. Looking at its blasphemous shape turned her heart to leaden ice. Unlike the other hellspawn, it moved with intelligence, authority, and deadly purpose. It danced and dodged and drove through the Threyan forces, a cyclone of death. Some faced it bravely, others fled, mad with terror. It made no difference. None were spared its savagery. Those not gutted by its claws or burned by its fire were sent flying through the air in pieces, raining blood on the brawling men below.

"Goddess above," Pell said, behind her. "I pray we're not too late. Can you get me to Captain Kain?"

"You want to ride...into that?" Ameryn pointed at the battle.

"Stay deep on the Threyan side; they'll not attack an Iress."

Ameryn nodded, forcing a breath—deep and steadying—into her chest. She and Pell mounted Gooter, who was somewhat rested now, though reluctant to ride toward the conflict. Maybe as much as Ameryn herself.

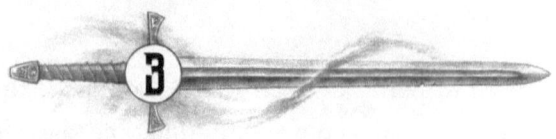

Daverell spotted Vulsipher, far into the Threyan ranks. He turned Druid and sped in its direction, watching as it lifted a screaming man, wrenching him in two over its head. It bellowed a roar as it threw the remains into the ranks of terrified men surrounding it. Others were running at its back with spears, searching for a vulnerable place to stab. The creature's body was already full of spearheads, swords, and arrows that were not bothering it in the least.

Dav steered Druid behind a supply cart; Vulsipher would run again if it saw him coming. Peering around the edge, he waited until its back was to him before kicking Druid into action. This time, it didn't see him until he was nearly on top of it. It rounded on him, as if sensing the Blade. The demon hissed, drawing back.

Daverell, for the first time, could really study the thing's naked, sinewy body. The pale gray hue of its skin made the crimson blood coating it stand out all the more. Its face was vaguely human, but also bestial and skull-like. It glared at Daverell as he jumped from Druid's back and attacked.

It was fast. Faster than Dav would have thought possible. Even with the speed granted him by the lightness of the Blade, he failed to land a hit. Every swing and thrust was dodged. The best he could manage was to keep the monster on the defensive, and that was surely only due to how wary it was of the Sword. Daverell tried multiple times to fool it into thinking he'd left himself open for an easy attack, but it never took the bait. Damned thing was smart.

"You think you can defeat me?" it spoke.

Daverell was so surprised that the demon nearly got away. As it turned to run, Dav struck and it spun away, sidestepping the Blade and keeping Daverell safely in its view. The soldiers around them had backed off, leaving the two of them in a circle.

"Yes," Daverell answered.

It laughed, its face cracking into a twisted rictus. Unexpectedly, it looked up, beyond him. Daverell was tempted to turn and follow its gaze but remained poised, with the Blade between them.

"Ah, the girl," it said, no longer speaking to him. "And you brought a friend. Have enough not already died because of you?"

Daverell risked a glance over his shoulder. It was Iress Pell from the abbey, and Ameryn was with her. Why was she here?

"It's feigning confidence, Captain," Iress Pell called. "It's very afraid of you and the Sword. It's—look out!"

Dav sprung back but wasn't fast enough. In a flash, Vulsipher struck out, raking its claws up Dav's torso. With the young woman's warning, however, he was able to also strike at the clawed hand as it did so. The demon pulled its hand back, shrieking and cradling its wounded fingers while Daverell was sent spinning backwards. He landed in a spray of gore, having just enough strength to gaze at the open, seeping mess of his body before his head collapsed, and he began choking on the blood filling his throat.

Ameryn watched Daverell's mortally wounded and twitching body before the chilling voice of the demon brought her attention snapping back to its hideous visage.

"Small, foolish girl," Vulsipher whispered in a mocking tone as it descended on Iress Pell. "You may know my mind, but I know yours better. I've killed your champion, and yet I can see you believe there is another who may one day wield the Blade and slay me, a sleeping brat at the abbey. Before you die, know that once I am finished here, I will return to that place and slaughter him."

With another swipe of its claws, it opened Pell's throat in a crimson geyser, and she fell with a gurgling, bubbling scream. Ameryn watched her fall and remain motionless on the ground before she realized the demon had stopped moving. It was watching *her* now, smiling.

"And you," it said. "The mother." It leaned close. So close she shut her eyes against its hot, sulfurous breath. Whispering in a voice that sounded like snakes slithering against each other, it rasped, "I will crunch your son's skull between my teeth. I will allow you to live long enough to watch, then keep your weeping souls close."

Moments passed. When she finally dared open her eyes, she was alone. Vulsipher had disappeared into the fray again.

CHAPTER 24

FLAMES

Tannis Field

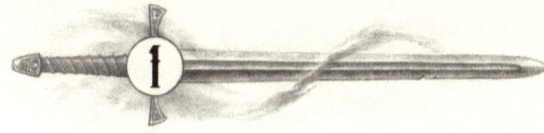

Daverell stared at the wafting smoke rising into the sky above him, waiting to die. He could breathe again, which he found odd. He tried one more time to move his sword arm and was shocked to find he wasn't entirely unsuccessful. It had been uselessly limp at his side after the demon's attack, but now his arm felt whole. He gripped the Sword tightly and held it up. The light from the sun through the break in the clouds had never left it. That light reflected onto his wounds like a Curial's Restorative. Under those beams, he watched the injuries reverse themselves. In minutes, he was on his feet.

Surrounding him were wide-eyed soldiers and Iress Pell, a crumpled heap on the ground. He ran to her side and turned her onto her back. She was pale, perhaps already dead. He didn't stop to check, only held the Sword up, reflecting the Light over her wounds and watched the same miraculous healing take place. Moments later, she twisted herself around, on her hands and knees, coughing up blood and catching her breath.

"Dav," Ameryn said from his side. "That demon said it was going to kill Crowan."

Dav wanted to assure her he would kill it first, to speak with confidence, but the words refused to come. It was too fast. Too powerful. Even with the Illumed Blade, he could not defeat it.

Iress Pell was on her feet again, standing to his side. "Thank you," he said, turning to her. "If not for your warning, I'd be dead."

"And I, if not for you and that Sword," Iress Pell replied.

"Can you read its mind again?" Dav asked. "Help me fight it?"

The young woman's expression was blank. "I don't know. I thought I could, but then it saw Mrs. Vowery's son in my thoughts." Iress Pell turned to Ameryn. "I'm so sorry. I was able to hide that it was you who stole its sustaining souls last night, otherwise I'm sure it would have attacked you too, but...when I thought the captain had died, my mind went to your son—our only other hope."

"Please," Dav pleaded, his mind racing, trying to make sense of his encounter with Vulsipher. The Blade had wounded but not killed it instantly as it did the lesser hellspawn. Did he have to wear it down? Strike it multiple times? Stab it in the right place? "Please try," he continued. "I don't think I can defeat it without you."

"No," Iress Pell said with a swallow. "You cannot defeat it without *us*." She nodded to Ameryn.

Daverell glanced between them, confused.

"She can steal the souls it's feeding on," the Iress said. "Send them to the Embrace, which will slow it down."

"I...I'll try," Ameryn said.

"Go," Iress Pell instructed Daverell. "We'll work on our part; I'll connect with your mind when it's been weakened, but for now, you've got a tool that can heal these dying men—use it!"

"Yes," Daverell responded, "of course." He searched the crowd around him for Druid.

A young man was holding the horse's reins. Daverell took them, thanking the boy before climbing into the saddle.

"You men," Dav addressed the soldiers around him, "these two women are vital to our success here today—protect them. No matter the cost, they must be allowed to finish what they begin."

"We'll see it done, Captain Kain," one of them answered, and the rest shouted their agreement.

Daverell nodded gratefully to them before taking in the state of battle. From his mount's back, he could see it well. It was not good. Despair was rising like a thick fog. He'd been in hopeless battles before, but this felt different, like a tangible force weighing on them all. The body count from the Elder Demon alone was massive. Dead and dying were everywhere. Each face not blank with death was numb with fear.

And then he thought he saw her. Watching him with eyes that were neither dead nor afraid. The legless girl. He dropped his gaze in shame; it settled on the Sword in his hand. The divine masterpiece he had warped into a tool of death.

It was not only that. *He* was not only that.

He rode through the crowd to where he had seen the ghost girl. When he came upon the spot, he found, instead, a young Uthiri soldier. To Dav's eyes, he was just a boy, sixteen at the most. His legs, while not completely severed, had been hacked to the bone. The boy was scooting himself away from Daverell, watching him with tear-streaked and wide-eyed terror. The boy had lost so much blood that his movements were beginning to look clumsy. He'd be dead in minutes. Daverell knew this all too well.

When Dav knelt over him, the young man cried in alarm and tried to crawl away faster. He said something in Uthiri, covering his eyes when Daverell lifted the Sword in his hand.

337

In moments, under the reflected Light, the boy's legs knit themselves back together. He peeked through his fingers at the wounds that were no longer there. The fear fell away, and a hesitant hope unfolded on the boy's dirty face. A face that looked at Dav in confused wonder.

Dav climbed back in his saddle. The Threyans surrounding him looked at one another and the Uthiri soldier, unsure what to do with the boy. "Don't kill him," was all Dav said before riding away.

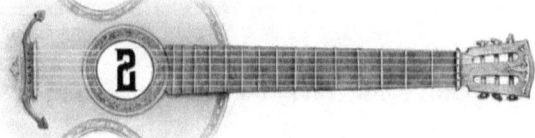

"Mrs. Vowery, you have to sing." Iress Pell retrieved the guitar from Gooter's pack.

Ameryn took the instrument in her hands. "Will I even be heard over this uproar?"

"You will," Iress Pell assured her. "In the Hollow. To the lost dead, your voice will travel across this entire field. The wandering souls who need to hear it *will* hear it."

Ameryn placed a hand on her chest, trying to settle her wildly beating heart. She thought of Crowan sleeping in the abbey infirmary bed and the threatening words of the demon. She would not lose him.

Ameryn knelt in place, throwing the strap over her shoulder and propping the instrument on one leg. She noted, briefly, how filthy her dress and hands had become. Her shaking fingertips hovered over the strings as she attempted to block out the cacophony of dying men and clashing metal around her. She began to play with clumsy fingers and sing with a quivering voice. She forced the hymn, *Mother, Wise and Kind* past her lips but didn't even finish. It was no use.

Ameryn felt a hand on her shoulder.

"Think of a place that might allow you to play the way you did at the abbey," Iress Pell suggested.

"What?" Ameryn asked.

"May I share your sight?"

"Of course, but..." Ameryn started when the holy woman's voice echoed in her head.

Close your eyes, Iress Pell directed her. *Imagine a place, as vividly as you can. Anywhere and with anyone. Open your eyes when you're ready.*

Ameryn didn't know what the Iress was attempting but followed her instructions. Shutting her eyes, she let her mind wander, and her heart pulled it immediately to home. To Crowan playing in the shadow of her old cottonwood. To her big sky, humble cabin, and loyal dog.

And Tamiron.

While it was her truest desire, she knew it was wrong for this moment. She was more than just her heart. She was her head as well, and her head knew, even against her wishes, that parts of the world she yearned for were gone forever. The constant land was there; all else was lost. She could ache for lost things with her whole soul, but it would do no good to anyone, least of all herself. She needed to sing to save her son, and she could not do that in a lie.

Ameryn conjured instead the image of Crowan as she'd left him, helpless and asleep in bed. The boy was peacefully locked in the steady rhythm of slumber. His familiar, boyish features were losing, day by day, the softness of youth, though he still bore a ruddiness upon his cheeks.

When she opened her eyes, she gasped. She was there. The abbey infirmary. But no, there was something shifting, thin, and dreamlike about it. This was some magic of the Iress. Ameryn's heart panged when she saw Crow. So safe. So vulnerable. She sat by his bedside, her hand on his. This would work; she could sing here.

"I'll not let that vile thing lay even its eyes upon you, Son," she whispered.

She pulled her hand back, and it automatically found the familiar frets on the instrument while her other hand went to begin plucking out a melody. She paused. She had been about to play a lullaby. It was right for Crowan—though he might object to that reckoning—and his situation, but it was not right for the men who had fallen in this battle.

Ameryn thought again, but not for long. She knew, perhaps she'd known from the beginning, what she actually needed for this moment.

"One more time," Ameryn said, closing her eyes.

In some ways, this was a harder scene to paint in her mind as it was one she'd never experienced. Tragically real as it had been, she wasn't sure it existed in the way she'd pictured it. And she *had* pictured it. Again and again, and because of that, in other ways, it was easier to imagine. She didn't know why her mind insisted on torturing her, but because it did, the images came, and, though she was afraid to, she opened her eyes on a dream for a second time.

She was in a wide meadow surrounded by an uneven edge of trees. It might have been a peaceful place were it not for the scene scattered on the ground around her, the aftermath of a horrible accident. She stood in the center of it. Though all was still now, the tangle of splintered wood and crushed bodies bore witness to the violence that had taken place moments before. Those who had survived the collapse of the watchtower had already been dragged away. Only the dead were left, and the war was raging too furiously to spend time on them. In this stolen and still moment, she searched among the bodies until she found the one she was looking for.

Ameryn didn't know if this was her husband's final resting place. Perhaps the army had returned to bury him or burn him on a pyre with the other victims while Iress sang over them all. However, as this was the worst possible scenario, it was the one she'd imagined. Tamiron, a mangled corpse under wreckage, forgotten and abandoned.

While she was sure her man had died in the Light and found his way to Her already, she wanted desperately to have sung for him there. Here. A desire that, graciously, the Goddess would allow her to experience, even if it wasn't entirely real.

As she prepared to play, the fire returned; the heat was at her back. It was there at the abbey as well, bringing with it the exposed helplessness she'd spent so long trying to outrun. She'd resisted it at the abbey but sensed, in her fallen audience of lost souls, a mirror. Loss and longing echoed back. The price of love understood. This time, she embraced the flames. In this sensory dreamworld of her mind, her skin was set alight. She only felt the blaze on the inside but doubted the pain would be much less if her skin were truly burning. For once, she just let it hurt. And oh, how it hurt.

Kneeling by Tam's body, she whispered with intimate affection, "Goodbye...for now." She brushed the hair out of his vacant eyes with fingers that afterwards, just as tenderly, began to play. Ameryn poured her pain into the music and was surprised to find the sound richer for it. Offering solace to even her.

She played for Tam but hoped that, in her voice, the fallen soldiers would hear their own wives and lovers—even the promise of one, if they had neither. It wasn't a hymn, nor one of the traditional Opravic tunes. It was a love song.

Who then owns the stars and to whom belongs the sky?
Who can claim the soil or the breeze's whispered sigh?
Who do songbirds sing to, and not just who, but why?
They sing for you and I, dear, all for you and I.

Who can trap the thunder or sight of mountains high?
Who might hold the sound of rain or coyote's lonesome cry?
Who can taste the sunlight? Oh, who might even try?
Only those who love it so, only you and I.

Who could catch the clouds and the rivers rushing by?
Who can hear the voices of the bee and butterfly?
Who dares love another, knowing they will die?
Sadly, you and I dear, sadly, you and I.

When she finished, she pressed her eyelids together again, sending welled tears tumbling down her cheeks. They disappeared with a hiss of steam, lost in the blaze. The scene around her faded, taking the fire with it until it burned only in her chest. She knew the pain would never leave, not completely, but she was no longer running from it, and maybe she could live with the hurt more than the fear.

The real world around her returned. Odors of blood and smoke. Sounds of battle. But above them all, a wail of anger much like the one she'd heard the last time she'd sung. Few other sounds could have brought a smile to her lips in that moment.

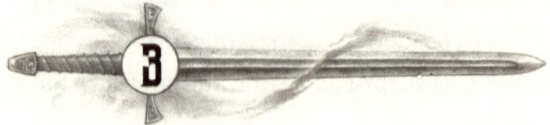

Daverell Kain leaned over a man who had been impaled on a ser-rated Uthiri blade. He was beyond even a Curial's aid, but Dav had yet to find an injury outside the healing ability of the Sword of Light. Re-flecting the sunlight over the wound, he watched as it sealed and the man's breathing eased. He stared at Daverell, his eyes wide.

"I thought I was bound for the Embrace," the man said.

"Not yet," Dav answered, before hurrying off to find others.

He came across several slaughtered men. Only Ameryn could help them now.

There was a groan at his feet. A soldier, bearing a long slice across his back, was unable to pull himself out of the mud. With the Blade's Light, Daverell helped him up in seconds.

A sudden skirmish broke out behind him. Daverell whirled to find an Uthiri soldier attempting to break through the line of men who had rallied around him. The furious enemy was thrown back and run through by more than one length of sharpened Threyan steel. It was as the man sunk to his knees, unable to do anything but bleed and fix Daverell with a hateful glare, that Daverell recognized him. Gyorick. The madman who had pursued him across the frontier.

Daverell approached the dying man, weighing the right and wrong of healing him or watching him expire, when a mad howl of rage echoed over the battlefield. Even this thunderous sound was over-whelmed a moment later by the voice of the Iress in his mind.

Captain Kain! she thought at him, *Can you hear me?*

"Yes," Daverell replied aloud, feeling foolish when a few sideways glances focused on him. Regardless, Pell understood the response.

Praise the Goddess, she said. *Ameryn has done it! Strike the demon now before it regains its strength.*

Where are you? Dav asked, internally this time, searching the area around him. *You must stay safely back.*

I'm able to connect with you from here, she explained. *With that Sword you shine like the sun through Embrell Sight. I could forge a bond from a mile away.*

Daverell whistled at Druid, who darted toward him at a canter. Dav spared one more glance at Gyorick. The man lay motionless in a puddle of red. Daverell supposed the Midlands would get along just fine without Gyorick's witless cruelty. The sword was needed elsewhere. When it came to Vulsipher, Dav had no question whether to use the Blade to restore or destroy. Druid reached him, and grasping the saddle rigging, Dav used the momentum of the steed to pull himself onto the animal's back. Together, they streaked like holy lightning towards the fire demon, leaping over and cutting through anything standing in their way.

There was a lightness in the air. Whatever the crushing weight had been, dragging down the hearts of the soldiers, was lifted. They fought with hope.

Before he reached it, the demon turned. Seeing Daverell bearing down upon it, an expression of unbelief burned upon its foul face. Daverell pointed the Sword at it, and the creature spun and crawled away into the swarms of men behind it. While it didn't move nearly as quickly as it had before, it was still swift enough to escape.

"Move!" Daverell commanded the Uthiri before him. They actually scattered. None wanted to face him, but it did no good. The crowd beyond was too thick. Daverell tore through them anyway.

I've lost it! Daverell thought.

I can help you, the Iress told him.

Pell searched the field. She had a half-formed idea, but she needed a ridge overlooking the battle. There were a few of them, but they were occupied with archers of both sides firing into the fighting below.

No, there was another. A rocky bluff jutting out among the foothills of the mountains. It was between the two sides, and no one—at least that she could see from here—was atop it. It was an ideal place to observe the conflict and track the elusive demon.

"Mrs. Vowery," Iress Pell turned to the woman. "Can you get me there?" Pell pointed behind her.

"That ridge?" Ameryn asked. "Yes, if we circle behind the Threyan army."

"Ride as fast as you can," Pell said.

They mounted Ameryn's mule and bolted across the field, giving the battling armies a wide berth.

When she'd first connected to the captain, even back at the abbey, Pell sensed the blinding Light of the Sword. Now, as she sustained that bond, the Light filled her too. Her fatigue was gone, her eyesight was sharper than ever, and she moved with an ease she never had before. How else might it enhance her abilities?

As they rode, Pell closed her own eyes, watching through Daverell's instead. With the aid of Threyan soldiers, he had chased the demon down again. The Uthiri had realized what Captain Kain and the Threyans were doing and were changing tactics from general combat to specifically protecting their god.

"We must protect Vulsipher!" one of the enemy generals shouted in Uthiri. Pell translated for Daverell, unsure if he understood the language.

The Uthiri attacked in force and pushed them back, allowing the demon to escape again.

Another complication, Captain Kain thought in frustration.

At least it hasn't killed anyone else, Pell returned.

"We're here," Ameryn announced.

Pell cut the connection to Daverell as the mule came to a halt. The delicious Light she'd borrowed from the Sword and the captain faded as she hopped down and ran to the edge of the ridge. The scene below made her feel like she was overlooking a tumultuous sea during a harrowing storm. A strong breeze lifted her cloak, making it flow and flap behind her.

Pell pulled the ericle over her head and handed it to Ameryn. "If one of the lesser demons comes at us, which I think is likely if Vulsipher realizes what we're doing, distract it with this and kill it. You have a weapon?"

Ameryn answered by pulling her sword from a scabbard strapped to the mule's saddle.

"Pray you don't have to use it," Pell said before turning back towards the battle. She could see Captain Kain on his white charger, an imposing figure even at this distance. *Captain,* she directed her inner voice to him, feeling the Light pour into her again, *look to the ridge at the far edge of the field to your right, do you see me?*

The Iress waved her arm, and in a moment, he waved back.

From here I can see the whole field, Iress Pell commented. *I'll guide you to Vulsipher; it's easy to track with my Sight from this vantage point.*

Where is it? Dav asked.

Straight ahead. Behind that group of mounted Uthiri with the flag.

Daverell kicked his horse forward and charged toward the host she'd indicated in a crooked line, dodging arrows as he was fired upon. Pell gasped when one struck him in the shoulder, and she felt the pain just as acutely. He pulled it out almost casually, tossing it to the side as he lifted the Sword, letting it reflect the light of the sun back at him.

With the immense amount of Light energy filling her to bursting, she had no trouble connecting with Vulsipher at this range either.

It knows you're almost upon it and is fleeing again, Pell informed Daverell. *It saw the Light from the Sword when you lifted it. It is moving towards me, to your right!*

She watched Dav shift direction and was about to intercept the demon when rows of Uthiri soldiers rushed to stand between him and it. The captain broke through them, and more than a few lost their lives in that process, but their blockade had slowed him down enough that he was lagging behind Vulsipher again.

It's still coming towards me! Pell shouted internally. *To the east!*

Daverell went to follow her instructions but was further impeded by more enemy soldiers. Vulsipher was getting away again.

Two Uthiri soldiers at the base of the cliff pointed at her, shouting. She'd been spotted. It was only a matter of time now until an arrow found her. The Light from her bond with Dav was so powerful, she decided to attempt connecting to both the Uthiri below without breaking her current connection. Incredibly, it worked. She added a connection to the demon as well. She was now bonded to four minds and with little effort. She projected an illusion upon their senses. There was one thing she knew the Uthiri would not fire upon. To their eyes, in a cyclone of dancing embers, she transformed into an Elder Demon, even larger and more impressive than Vulsipher itself.

The men cowered, fearful and reverent. They shouted to the men beside them, pointing.

Pell cursed her foolishness; what did she expect to happen? Surprisingly, however, she was able to add the new observers to her connections. Emboldened, she pulled the entire horde of onlooking men into her influence and fed them all the same illusion. There was so much Light! She could manage it, as long as she held tight to her connection with Dav and the Sword.

What in hellfire below happened to you? Captain Kain asked her.

Her mind scrambled. She was fairly sure anything Daverell communicated to her could only be heard by her, but any clear thought back would be heard by the growing number of soldiers she was connecting with. She pounced on a preposterous idea.

Breaking her connection to the great demon, she spoke. "I am Vulsipher, the Lord of Long Shadows." Her voice thundered over the field—or so it seemed to all ears she had command of.

What? the captain questioned, bewildered.

Deeply and vaguely, so as not to be overheard by her hundreds of eavesdroppers, she prayed the man would understand what she was doing.

"That way," she ordered, and everyone watching her saw the great counterfeit creature sweep a clawed hand to the north and heard its voice as a chilling rumble.

Thankfully, understanding dawned in Daverell's mind, and he spurred his horse in the direction she indicated.

"Hold, attack the Threyans from your position at the wagon," the cliff-top devil purred.

Captain Kain, approaching a wagon, changed directions, and the real Elder Demon howled as it jumped upon the empty space Dav and his men would have occupied but for Pell's warning. It screamed and beat the ground with its fists but fled again as the captain turned to pursue it.

"To the west," Pell, as Vulsipher, commanded. She risked connecting with Vulsipher's mind to read its intentions. She only did so in short bursts so it wouldn't also see what she was doing, but there may have not been a need. Dav's pursuit was all it was focusing on at the moment.

Pell was garnering a bigger audience. Even with the stream of energy from the Sword of Light, mentally juggling so many tasks at once was difficult and exhausting.

She realized, connected as she was to the Uthiri below her, most of them were convinced. They viewed her, or her illusion at least, as the real Vulsipher and the demon being pursued across the field by Daverell as another, lesser demon. Impressive, yes. A general of the dark forces summoned that day, certainly. But not the Elder Demon itself. The thing on the ridge above them, more magnificent and with the ability to order the other demon about, was their real demon-god.

"All hail the true Lord of Long Shadows!" someone praised in the Uthiri language and others joined in. Despite everything going on around them, Uthiri were falling to their knees, worshiping her.

347

Thankfully, the Threyans had picked up on the fact that so many Uthiri were distracted and were attacking from behind, stealing her audience away. She had selectively excluded the soldiers in blue, and even from here, she could see their puzzlement at the Uthiri gazing with such awe at a simple Iress atop the ridge.

In a flash, she remembered another element to destroying Vulsipher. One they had been neglecting.

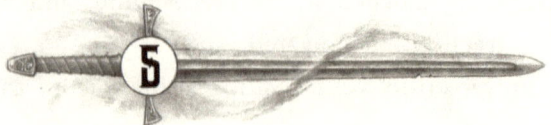

The Uthiri were abandoning Vulsipher.

It didn't help that Vulsipher had begun killing men in its own ranks. Several Uthiri trying to protect it had been slaughtered. Even now, as Daverell approached it, an exhausted soldier ambling too close to the creature was grabbed and beheaded.

That unfortunate man was not the only one walking in a daze. The battle had entered its dying stage. Daverell had come to know it well. The survivors, too exhausted, injured, or shocked to continue the fight, wandered aimlessly around with weapons limp at their sides. Daverell watched several men like that now, blank looks on their faces. Some, though still alive, bore injuries that would eventually kill them, maybe even months from now. Hot embers fell on them all like snow, some flinched and brushed them away. Others did not. A horse covered in the blood of its absent rider cantered in a panic across the smoking field.

With the way cleared between himself and his quarry, Daverell Kain pulled Druid to a stop, dismounting onto the blackened ground, and approached the monster.

"Insignificant," Vulsipher bellowed, dropping a corpse at its side.

"Avoid the Light of the Blade!" roared the amplified voice of Pell, the impostor demon, over the field.

Vulsipher didn't react. Could it not hear the Iress? Daverell glanced at the Sword in his hand. What would the healing Light of the Sword do to it?

The creature took advantage of his distraction. It swung a clawed hand at him. The Elder Demon was still fast, but not nearly as fast as it had been before.

I can beat it, Dav thought as he parried the thing's attack. *Goddess bless you forever, Ameryn and Iress Pell.*

It still cut him across the shoulder, but he scored a hit himself. Vulsipher pulled back as if stung. Dav had put a small, sizzling slice in its forearm.

Daverell was about to heal the minor injury to his shoulder, but the demon didn't give him time.

"Fire!" echoed the altered voice of the Iress across the field as Vulsipher struck again.

It stamped its foot, sending an inferno at him. Daverell held the Blade before himself, cutting through the blaze. Flames shot past either side of him, doing little more than singeing his hair and the edges of his duster.

"From behind," the Iress shouted.

Spinning, Dav caught Vulsipher advancing on him. He lunged, blade first, to meet it. The point bit into flesh, and Dav's ears were filled with agonized screeching.

He swung the Sword. The demon dodged to the side and attempted to grab Dav's arm but succeeded in only scraping it with its claws. Daverell howled in pain this time. His grip on the holy weapon went slack. This injury would have to be healed in order to effectively fight the thing.

"Strike again!" shrieked Pell.

Dav could do little else but stagger back in reaction to her warning. It saved him from another injury, but he fell to the ground. Remembering her words from moments before, he turned the Sword, reflecting its Light at the demon. It wailed and backed away, covering its smoking face.

Daverell then turned the Light to himself, restoring his sword arm, before darting to the side just as Vulsipher's foot came down again, nearly crushing him.

"More fire! More beasts," the voice of the Iress called as fire engulfed him, intense heat burning every exposed surface. He ran, praying he was not on fire when an intense pain in his leg halted his progress. Instinctively, he swung the Blade at whatever it was, slicing through a snake-like lesser demon. It burst into ashes.

It was not the only one, however; as the Iress had warned him, he was now surrounded by snarling creatures of various shapes and sizes, ready to strike when his attention turned from any one of them. He was backing up, aware that he'd lost track of Vulsipher when claws like daggers raked across his back. He was sent sprawling forward but managed to turn the movement into a somersault that bit like needles as he rolled away.

When he regained his feet, he was set upon. The feral demons drove him back even as he cut through them, one after another, and through the resulting shower of ashes came Vulsipher, leaping.

Daverell bolted to his left, turning the Blade to reflect Light on the demon again. It howled and shrank from the slivers of brightness. Dav moved closer, keeping the Light trained on it. It lashed out again, a desperate move but enough to send Dav flailing with deep lacerations across his chest. He landed on his side and watched blood pour out of mangled strips of flesh. Every breath was agony. Vulsipher leaped atop him, rolling him to his back and sneering so closely he could feel its hot breath.

Daverell's sword arm was pinned under the creature's hand. He pulled, trying to free himself but the demon responded by shifting its weight and breaking the bones. Dav screamed in pain as its free claws descended on him. Dodging the blow, Dav rolled to his right side and gripped the hilt of the Sword in his left hand. Rolling back, quick as lightning, Daverell slashed the Sword across the demon's neck. The bright Blade separated Vulsipher's head from its body and doused Dav in hot blood.

Daverell expected this to kill the creature. It did not.

Amid the fountain erupting from the things severed neck, its hand grabbed the shocked warrior by the throat and lifted him. So sharp and tight was its hand that blood was pouring from his own neck now. He couldn't speak, couldn't breathe.

Daverell hacked at the arm strangling him but was at a poor angle and weak enough that he only succeeded in causing its grip to slacken. He couldn't even do that when the thing's free hand grasped and held his only effective arm out of the way. He could still angle the Light, however, and he did, right into the open wound where its head had been moments before.

If shining the Light upon its skin held it at bay, then doing so on a gaping injury was pure torment. It jerked away, dropping Daverell. Without taking time to catch his breath, Dav cut into the legs of its headless body and watched it fall. He bent over it as flailing arms blindly slashed at him. He was unused to fighting with his left hand but managed to sever the thing's arms. He watched with horror as the disembodied limbs continued to reach for him.

His heart was thudding in his ears as it pumped blood out of the slashes in his back, chest, and neck. He was losing strength fast but dared not take the time to heal himself. Even now, groping tendrils had emerged from the severed ends of the arms, inching towards its torso to knit itself back together. With his left hand, he clumsily cut deeply into the chest, leaning on the Blade, pushing it deeper. He didn't pull the weapon back until the brighter, redder blood of its heart bubbled up around it. He shined the Light of the Sword into the gash. The body began convulsing and smoking, shuddering in anguish before bursting into white, otherworldly flames. Dav jumped back, watching as the body was consumed.

Moments later, it was nothing but embers in the air. It took much of Dav's waning energy to direct the Light into the stumps of the thing's arms. They too were set alight and incinerated.

Vulsipher's head, the only piece left of it, was in the mud before him as he collapsed to his knees. It was trying to escape, small tentacles had sprouted from the base of its skull and out its mouth, pulling it along. As he crawled towards it, barely fast enough to catch up, it turned to look at him. The panicked fear he saw in those eyes gave him the motivation he needed to keep moving.

Barely able to lift the Sword by then, he shone the Light on the gore at the base of its neck. After setting the head ablaze, his arm dropped limply to his side, and he could only watch as the head burned away, leaving a small, pulsing mass of gray tissue behind, no bigger than a man's fist. Even this writhed and slithered away from him.

His vision was darkening, and his body was barely following his commands. He had seconds left. There was only enough life in him to make a final stab at the thing or heal himself, and stopping to mend his wounds might let it escape. He didn't even consider it.

A downward plunge impaled the twitching thing with the legendary Sword. In a blinding flash, Vulsipher the Elder Demon was vanquished for good, and Daverell Kain fell on his back where he was granted a glimpse of the gray sky before closing his eyes.

He had time for a single thought. It was of the boy and his mother.

CHAPTER 25

UNDER RAIN

Tannis Field

The stream of Light flowing into Iress Pell was cut off, and given how many minds she was connected to at once, it began fading from her fast. Two of those connections were lost forever. In a flash for Vulsipher and in a dissolve for Captain Kain—both had perished. Pell let out a sigh, sorry for the captain, but after so much time and effort, so many lives spent in the quest to end the demon's life, she considered it as valorous an end as any man could ever hope for. It had finally been done.

Before the Light faded from her completely, Pell, in the guise of the demon, called over the battlefield. It was still an active one. Those not watching the battle between Dav and Vulsipher were brawling and dying, though the heart had gone out of the fight.

"Cease this conflict!" she cried in what, to their ears, was a demonic growl. "I am freed, the Threyans have lost their champion and have suffered for their deceptions. Let us return to Uthir in triumph."

Pell was thankful to hear the uproar of clashing swords and furious shouting die down. The Uthiri generals were calling retreat, and the Threyans were doing the same, each side eager for the fighting to cease. With the last of her energy, she fed the watching eyes the illusion that her form was changing, until it matched, in size and appearance, what it truly was. Once the reflected Light of the Sword was spent, the fatigue of the travel and sleepless nights returned, in addition to all the effort her part in the battle had taken from her. She was barely able to remain on her feet and walk from the cliff edge to Ameryn.

"You must reclaim the Sword before anyone else," Pell insisted, removing her outer cloak. "Wrap it in this, be careful not to touch it directly."

"Yes, Iress," Ameryn said, handing the ericle back as she took the cloak.

"It's to the west of here, in a burned, empty part of the field with white rocks around it. Hurry."

Ameryn climbed onto Gooter and rode away.

Now they will kill me, Pell mused. *Not that it matters.* She was friendless and without family, hardly anyone in the world knew her name. At least the Elder Demon was dead. If that was the Path the Goddess had sent her on, then she had traveled it. Costly, even deadly, mistakes had been made, but after hundreds of years of failure by the considerable resources of the Church, she wasn't in the mood to be too hard on herself. Perhaps she was simply too tired for that.

Around the hill walked a group of Uthiri soldiers in their twisted, thorny, black and red armor. Among them, she recognized the two men who had first seen her before she had changed her appearance. She reached out and shared one of the men's sight. She felt so weak and constricted now, being only able to make a single bond.

"I tell you," said the man in Uthiri. "I saw the demon in this form before it became its true self. This *is* Vulsipher. Oreb saw it too."

"I did," agreed the man named Oreb. "General Farrek speaks the truth."

Well, she thought to herself, *some of them believe, and one a general! That's good.*

As they drew closer, she stood as straight as she could manage. Who better to impersonate the demon than one who had closely studied its mind?

The man in command, perhaps of the entire Uthir army, stood at the fore of them. He bowed to her, and the men behind him all did likewise. Even if he wasn't convinced, he was at the very least treating her as though she were indeed Vulsipher. For now.

"Fierce Lord," the general said, "why did you call an end to the bloodshed?"

Though he was trying to hide it, the man had one hand on the grip of his sword, and he was not the only one. Pell held her life in her hands, one wrong word...but she knew Vulsipher better than any of them.

"You think me one of the sniveling lesser demons?" Pell asked in perfect Uthiri. "Unable to control my bloodlust?"

"I..." the man started, and Pell was happy to hear uncertainty in his voice. "No, Lord."

"You think me a primitive beast ruled by my instincts?" Pell shared the man's sight and, when he dared a glance at her face, provided a hint of glowing fire behind her eyes to the general. She kept it subtle and hoped that later, when the general swore he saw it, his men would agree they had, too. "In the battle of Settek when the invading Haysians had been driven from our shores and General Tiega wanted to pursue them to their islands and exact a higher price for their treachery, did I not also call an end to the battle?"

"Y...yes, fierce Lord," the general conceded. Pell didn't need the Sight to know that the man had no clue if this was true. She was happy

355

to notice, however, two sorcerers near the back of the group share a look. The battle was real, as was the general, and while history didn't record if Vulsipher had actually called an end to the fighting, it seemed plausible, given the accounts. Pell was relieved her mind, tired as it was, was still able to put all her study to good use.

"Understand this," Pell continued, "I prize ruthless efficiency over mere bloodletting, especially when it no longer grants me my desires. What was the point of this battle? Of this war?"

"To...to find and free you."

"Am I not free?" Pell opened her arms wide.

"Yes," the man replied, "but...but the Threyans, do you not want revenge on them?"

"Revenge?" Pell asked, an edge to her voice. "I am an eternal being. A few hundred years of captivity for me is as nothing. The Threyans share less blame for my imprisonment than the Uthiri. Your incompetence in letting it happen, then abandoning me for so long, has earned you a greater portion of my fury than they. Beyond that, did you not topple their most well-loved sacred structure? Did I not subject them to the rage of my hell-spawned slaves? Were not hundreds of them ripped to bloody ribbons? Did we not leave children across this accursed land fatherless this day? The Threyans will speak in trembling fear of this battle for generations; if that is satisfying enough for an immortal god, then it should be for such a dismal creature as you."

Pell could discern, from inside the man's mind, that he was convinced. In fact, he was nearly shaking with fear.

One of the sorcerers spoke, "Why have you chosen this form, Lord?"

"I'll choose any form that pleases me. Do you expect me to walk to Uthir? I must fit within one of your coaches for the journey back. Bring one to me now; I'll not be gawked at."

"Of course," the general said, rising finally. "I'll ready my own." Turning to the man named Oreb, he whispered, "Fetch it for me, will you? There are two women in there, have them removed and be sure it's clean."

"Leave the women," Pell commanded.

The general turned, astonished she had heard him.

Pell smiled. "Something to play with." In truth, she needed a reason to have food brought to the coach; demons didn't require such sustenance. If it gave the women a break from this man's unpleasant company, all the better. Finding her way to food was only the first in a sudden flood of challenges that overwhelmed her. She seemed to have sold the lie for now, but it would continue to demand all her cleverness to perpetuate doing so in the weeks and months—years?—that followed.

"Whatever you wish for, my Lord," the general submitted. "We must get you back to Uthir in haste. This whole effort was started by our king, Orugos; he will be very eager to see you."

The wheels of Pell's calculating mind came to an abrupt stop and were replaced by images of her exiled family, her betrayed grandmother, all slaughtered at the hands of assassins. She remembered sleepless nights as a little girl spent planning any number of impossible punishments for an untouchable madman. A smile spread on her face.

"Yes," she crooned. "I, too, am eager for that meeting."

A gentle rain had begun falling by the time Ameryn found Daverell's body and the Sword. A circle of men had gathered around the scene. The glowing Blade stood straight up, its point embedded in the dirt. Plunged there by the man who now lay dead beside it.

She gasped when she saw him, broken and bloodied. Druid was there, too, though the horse was only interested in the fallen man, not the Sword.

No one spoke, no one moved. If they were breathing, Ameryn couldn't tell. They simply stood and took it in. Ameryn imagined one or two of the men might have the presence of mind to know they were looking on a scene that they would one day be describing to their grandchildren. Children who, though they would already know the story well, would listen to the tale with chins on their fists and brag to their disbelieving schoolmates the next day that their grandfather had been there. He had seen the very Blade.

Some of them would even remember the man. What had made him special was harder to see and thus was, tragically, less memorable.

But Ameryn knew. She would remember.

Breaking through the circle, she walked slowly towards the Sword. She was afraid someone might stop her, but no one did. They assumed she knew what she was doing, and she wished she shared that assumption.

Throwing the Iress's cloak over it broke the spell, at least a little, and as she was carefully wrapping the Blade, a man with a dark beard asked her, "What shall we do with him, miss?" He nodded to Daverell.

"Get him out of this mud, before anything else," she responded. "After that, bear him away with as much honor as you can. He deserves it all."

She retrieved the scabbard before no less than ten men surrounded Daverell's body and reverently lifted it. They carried him in the direction of the Threyan camp as Ameryn, taking Druid's reins, began walking away herself. The men moved aside to let her through except for one man, who appeared far too old for war. She remembered Dav first arriving at their homestead, claiming *he* was too old for the conflict.

"What do we do, miss?" he asked. "What if we need him, or that—" he motioned at the bundle tucked under her arm, "again?"

She thought of her boy, Crowan, sleeping peacefully somewhere in the mountains.

"Another will be ready," she answered confidently. "If it is needed... when the time is right. Another will take up the Sword."

The man nodded as she walked past him and strapped the priceless treasure to her humble mule. She mounted the animal and watched as Daverell's limp form, held aloft by his fellow soldiers, was carried to the warm fires and dry tents of the war camp. His fight was finally done, and she hoped he was granted the peaceful rest of a hero.

As she was riding her mule and leading Druid off the field, a rider approached her from the Uthiri side. At the sight of that spiky uniform, she readied herself to flee. The man, sensing her reaction, lifted one open hand from his mount's reins in a clear sign he meant no harm.

"Please," he said in accented Threyan, "please, I come with a request only."

"What request of yours do you think I'm likely to grant?" Ameryn eyed him suspiciously.

"It is not my request," he corrected. "It is that of our lord, the Elder Demon, Vulsipher. It is asking me to watch for the woman leaving with two horses and request a meeting."

"The...demon wants to meet with me?" Ameryn asked, confused.

"Yes," the man confirmed. "Our fierce lord is telling me you knew it under the form and name Pell."

Ameryn tried to keep the shock from showing too plainly on her face. "Yes, of course," she said.

"Follow me." The man turned his horse and led her back to the Uthiri camp. She followed him to a stagecoach that was the focus of a great many staring eyes and nearly as many averted ones. He swung off his horse and knocked timidly on the door, saying something in Uthiri.

Iress Pell's voice gave an answer, and the man opened the door. Pell spoke to the man again in Uthiri. He nodded and turned away, looking unsettled. Ameryn pulled the wrapped Sword of Light from her mule's back. She loathed to touch the thing but also feared parting from it. She was about to enter the stagecoach when two women, dressed in silky robes, exited, wearing a look of barely controlled panic.

"Watch my horses carefully, please," Ameryn said to the Uthiri man.

"Of course," he complied. "Lord Vulsipher has also asked that I fill your saddlebags with supplies while the two of you converse."

She nodded before ducking through the door.

"What did you do to those women?" Ameryn asked Iress Pell, once the door was shut and they were alone. "They looked like they were about to jump out of their own skin."

"They're simply scared to be in the presence of an Elder Demon," the Iress explained. "I thought we needed a few words between us, before parting."

"Yes," Ameryn agreed. "Thank you for the provisions."

"I also ordered them to load your bags with as much gold as your mule can carry."

"Thank you," Ameryn said in shock. "But how..."

Ameryn couldn't finish the question. Thankfully, Pell understood and provided the full story behind her current change of fortune, along with a recounting of all the worries she had about maintaining the charade going forward. Ameryn shared her fears but also, despite only having just met her, trusted Iress Pell was an inventive and clever young woman.

"Can you find your way back to the abbey?" Pell inquired.

"I think so," Ameryn said without confidence. "I watched the way carefully as I rode here. Any help you can offer me?"

"Other than seeing that you leave here well provisioned, I'm afraid not," she replied apologetically. "I first traveled there blindfolded, and even had I not been, I've never had much of a sense of place or direction."

"I'm sure I'll find my way," Ameryn said.

"It appears you got to the Sword in time," Pell observed. "You must remain its caretaker for a while."

"What am I to do with it?"

"Keep it safe for now. We must find a new home for it. The mountaintop abbey won't do."

"But the demon is dead."

"Vulsipher was one of five demons in the prophecy. There may be others out there. Crowan, or another, may need to take up the Blade again one day."

Ameryn thought of Crowan. "Where might it be secure?"

"I don't know," Pell said. "We'll think of something. It must be hidden somewhere secret and sacred. Only you and your boy should know where. I will think of something. Wait for word from me."

"I will," Ameryn promised.

"What happened to Captain Kain's body?" asked Pell.

"The army took it. I expect he'll get an honorific military service. I will sing for him before leaving."

"There are surely people who need your voice after the battle, but Captain Kain is not one of them."

"But he died at the hands of that demon."

"Whether by his sacrifice, the sword, or Vulsipher's death—he died in the Light; I can say that with confidence." Pell's expression grew distant. "I was connected to him when it happened and caught a glimpse, fleeting as a flash of lightning, of what greeted him as he passed from our world. It was a small assemblage; Iress Lee was there, among others. A little girl with long, dark hair was smiling and running to him. When he saw her, I sensed the most wonderful sensation, as if the thing he most longed for, maybe what we all most long for in the end, was well met."

Ameryn nodded but remained silent. The story with the girl was not hers to share.

"It was a good death," Pell continued. "It was the opposite for my dear friend, Maiyen. I'm already forced to endure her absence, but I have you to thank for sparing me the greater agony of knowing she's lost, forever in the Dark. Wherever you go, I hope you sing for poor lost souls like her. The Church may not have Opravics anymore, but the world certainly still needs them. Needs you."

Ameryn was silent, unsure of what this new responsibility meant for her life, but certain she wouldn't find answers in this coach.

"It's time I leave," she said. "I wish you every good fortune. May the Goddess guide your steps."

"And yours as well," Pell replied. "May you be ever bathed in Light, embraced by Truth."

They hugged, and moments later, Ameryn was on her way back to her son and the hidden castle in the mountains. She didn't know when Crowan would wake up, nor what path she would take to get home, but she *would* go home. She wanted a life there too much, impermanent and ever shifting as it might be, to let anything stop her for long. The trees, the birds, every scurrying creature, and the very dirt itself was calling her back. She and the frontier belonged to each other.

Later, on the mountainside, she paused on her journey to sing over the battlefield and to watch the sun drop below the horizon. The rain had stopped by then, the clouds breaking up, providing an abundant canvas for the dying light to paint upon. She'd always found the sun's risings and settings after a storm to be the most stunning, and this view only reinforced that reckoning.

The sunset, like music and like people, didn't last. As Ameryn rode on, she thought that perhaps it was that very thing that made them so lovely.

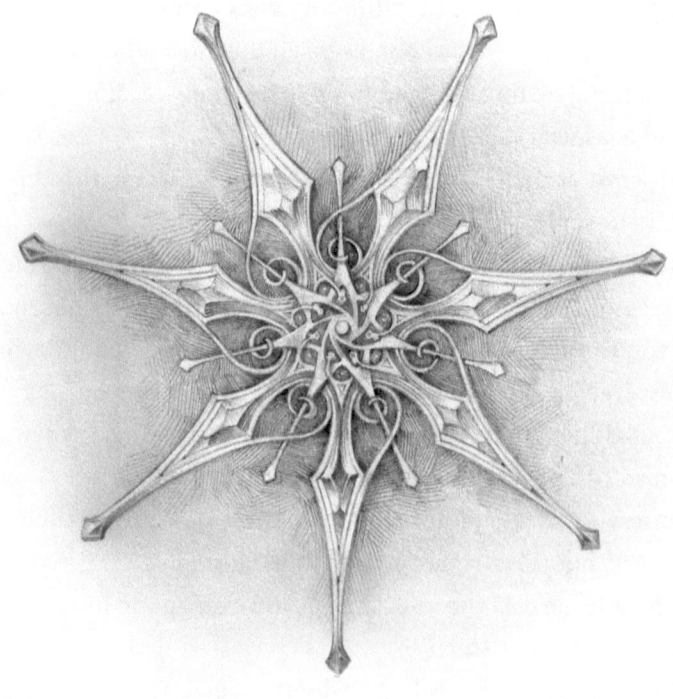

EPILOGUE

BEHIND THE WALL

Threya, Red Chapel, the year 624
Nearly two years after the end of the war.

A letter arrived. Ashal wasn't allowed to read it until it had been checked over by one of the guards. The man searched the words briefly before saying something Ashal did not understand. His Threyan was getting better, but he still required daily help from the woman he paid to stay on site as an interpreter.

"He wants to know what this part about you going to Lockwood is all about," she relayed.

The guard was pointing to a section of the letter. Ashal recognized the careful handwriting of his wife, still in Uthir. Words she'd been forced to write. This was the letter he'd been dreading.

363

"Yes," he said, hoping his words didn't sound as rehearsed as they were. "My wife has an acquaintance on a homestead there. She sent me with some small gifts and is reminding me to deliver them."

The guard read the rest of the letter and said something more before handing the paper to the interpreter, who then handed it to Ashal. "He says you'll have to get the master builder's permission and go under guard," she told him.

"Of course," Ashal said with a small bow to both the armored guard and bilingual woman. "Will you help me explain the situation to the master?"

"It's what you pay me for," she said, following him.

Ashal explained everything to Cavam, the man in charge of the effort to rebuild the Red Chapel Cathedral. At first, he misunderstood the situation.

"He asks, are you leaving the project?" the woman interpreted.

"No," Ashal assured. "I will remain here until the work is finished. I need only four days to make this short trip to Lockwood and back." Ashal was pleased to see relief pass across Cavam's face as he spoke again.

"He says you may take the time," the woman translated.

"Thank you." Ashal bowed and turned to leave.

"One moment," the woman said.

Cavam paused and took a deep breath. When he spoke again, he did so without meeting Ashal's eyes.

"He says he wants to apologize for the way he treated you and your men in the months after you first arrived," conveyed the interpreter. "He has come to believe that, since the king of Threya is unwilling to devote any resources to this project, your gold and workers are the only things making it possible."

"Tell him his reaction was completely understandable. I do not blame him in the least."

Cavam looked at him now, repentant and grateful. He said more and the interpreter passed on the words. "He says that since the demon, or whatever rules your people now, has not stopped the aid

364

you're providing and has imprisoned the previous Uthiri king, he has reason to hope the future of our two nations may be a bright one."

"I share that hope. Ask him if I might send for my wife and daughter to join me."

She did and smiled while relaying the master builder's response. "He says he will even help make the arrangements."

After another bow and expression of gratitude, Ashal left to prepare for his journey.

He set out the next morning. The few days he spent on the road were lonely ones. He suspected that, even had they shared a language, his two Threyan guards would not have conversed with him much anyway.

Lockwood was rebuilding, but evidence of the war remained easy to see. As a well-guarded Uthiri man, he garnered more attention than he'd have liked. It mainly manifested in hateful glares. Ashal was grateful for the men at his sides.

An old man recognized him and knew only enough Uthiri to introduce himself as a craftsman named Halvett. It was the very name Ashal had been listening for. He followed the craftsman along the river to a framed farmhouse, newly built. They were all greeted at the door by the mother and son who lived there. The woman fed him, his guards, and the old man an excellent Threyan dinner, and after eating, she performed music. It was remarkable. Ashal could not understand the words she sang, nor did he share the cultural connection the others had with the melodies, but his eyes filled with as many tears as any of them.

They spent the night beneath a swaying cottonwood by the river and left the next day. The old craftsman traveled beside Ashal and his guards, leading a mule laden with tools and, of all things, a door covered in cloth.

Ashal hired the craftsman immediately upon their return to Red Chapel. Cavam objected at first. After seeing the door, he was sure the man was some sort of thief. Anyone capable of creating something half as stunning must surely be a celebrated figure in Threya. However,

Halvett had all the papers and licenses he needed to convince the master builder. In the end, Cavam said it would be an honor to have Halvett's help and assured him his door would find a home somewhere within the rebuilt cathedral.

Ashal spent his first day back working on the wall at the end of the second wing. He lay stone beneath what would eventually be a shimmering window of stained glass. The day wore on until, under a setting sun, his team called for him to join them in a drink.

"Ashal, enough," one said. "You've been at that wall all day, and after only just returning. Come with us."

"In a moment," Ashal answered, noticing the Threyan guards had already left as well. They'd grown casual in the time the Uthiri had been helping them, and why not? There had never been anything to concern them. After tonight, Ashal guessed, there never would be.

His friends shook their heads as they walked away, laughing, and Ashal was left alone on the site, but not for long. Halvett, who'd obviously been watching for this opportunity, walked to him. He carried a box wrapped in canvas, just over four feet tall and less than a foot wide. Ashal stood back as Halvett slid the oblong box into the cavity Ashal had intentionally left within the wall.

Halvett stood back, and Ashal returned to his work, moving quickly but carefully. The Threyans would be inspecting this wall tomorrow and must not find anything amiss. His very life depended upon it. He laid the last few stones that would hide the object from the world, perhaps forever.

With each brick he laid, he wondered what it was. Might it be some sleeping weapon that could be activated and destroy this church all over again? Perhaps a wicked artifact meant to secretly defile the beauty of this place or disrupt its spiritual flow? He was not a religious man and knew little about such things, only that the longer he thought about it, the more he was devoured by guilt.

But then he thought of the singing woman and young man. They seemed to be good and honest people. So did this craftsman, Halvett. Additionally, beyond this effort, his orders were to remain on site building this cathedral until it was finished. Why do that if the demon, or whomever had hired him, was concerned with nothing but hiding this object within its walls? The sorceress who had sent him here had insisted that she, and even the demon itself, be ignorant of the box's exact location. Ashal was only to reveal it to the mother and son from Lockwood when they visited this place some weeks later. Then he was to keep the secret until the day he died. The little sorceress would know if he did not. She had seen into his mind. Perhaps there was some darkness there, but in terms of this task, beyond its source—of which he was dubious—he could detect no wickedness. Secrecy, yes, but that was not the same thing. Even Cavam had said that Uthir appeared be taking more honorable directions.

Was it possible, did he dare believe, that this act was not an evil one?

Once the cut stones were in place, Ashal covered all evidence of the encased cavity by coating the tops of the interior bricks with the same mixture of mortar and gravel they used for filler between all outer and inner walls. He checked his work, ensuring both that the object was completely hidden and the masonry was straight and true. It was, and, standing back, he knew no one would ever suspect a thing.

It was good work. Even Halvett, a master, nodded at him approvingly.

And why could that not be enough? He'd done nothing knowingly wicked. If he was a cog in some sinister machine, it was the designer's wrongs, not his. All he could do was the right thing in whatever situation he found himself. He thought he had risen to that ideal. No man, woman, demon, or god could say otherwise.

Ashal picked up his tools and walked away. The worst of this dangerous and secretive business was over. Soon, he could focus on building and on forgetting there was anything hidden beneath the window at the end of the cathedral's second wing.

Acknowledgements

I've got a veritable mountain of gratitude to impart, and the first chunk goes to my parents. Both my mother and father cultivated a deep love of story in me and showed tremendous support throughout this project. I can never thank them enough, but sometimes I try.

An equally generous portion goes to my wonderful wife, Heather. She is tirelessly supportive of all my creative endeavors.

Big thanks to my siblings especially Kristal, Josh, and Jake. They're always willing to let me throw ideas at them and equally willing to let me know if they landed or not.

There's a very good chance this book would not exist without the help of Andrew Hayes and Ashley Higbee, members of my excellent writing group. When writing something, it's immensely helpful to have other people care about it (even before it's any good). For that and all the valuable feedback along the way, thank you!

I'm very indebted to my editors as well. My developmental editor, copy/line editor, and proofreaders: you know who you are, and you know how rough this was before you helped me fix it. A massive thanks to you, too!

I want to further mention the legendary fantasy cartographer (and my friend), Isaac Stewart. Thanks a bunch for helping me with my map.

Lastly, to my alpha and beta readers (at least the ones I haven't already mentioned) goes tons of gratitude. Faralee Pozo, Melissa Bastow, and Greg Swensen. You're the best!

Kevin Keele has worked as a book illustrator and video game artist for over twenty years. He's created images for the works of Nicholas Eames, Christopher Ruocchio, Rick Riordan, and Brandon Sanderson, among others. As a game developer, he's worked on the Disney Infinity and Hogwarts Legacy franchises. When he's not drawing or writing, he's spending time with his family or stuck in traffic. Kevin lives in Utah with his wife. They have three great boys, one tuxedo cat, and thousands of Italian honeybees.

The Deathless Dark is Kevin's debut novel.

www.ingramcontent.com/pod-product-compliance
Lightning Source LLC
Chambersburg PA
CBHW030228120726
47903CB00005B/1404

* 9 7 9 8 9 9 3 4 5 3 3 0 9 *